THE
CHANGE
ROOM

ALSO BY KAREN CONNELLY

THE CHANGE ROOM

KAREN CONNELLY

RANDOM HOUSE CANADA

www.penguinrandomhouse.ca

Random House Canada and colophon are registered trademarks.

Library and Archives Canada Cataloguing in Publication

Connelly, Karen, 1969–, author
The change room / Karen Connelly.

Issued in print and electronic formats.

ISBN 978-0-345-81426-5
eBook ISBN 978-0-345-81428-9

I. Title.

PS8555.O546C43 2017   c813'.54   C2016-904987-6

Text design by Rachel Cooper

Cover design by Jennifer Griffiths

Cover image © Felix Clinton / Stone / Getty Images

Printed and bound in the United States of America

2 4 6 8 9 7 5 3 1

Penguin
Random House
RANDOM HOUSE CANADA

For women who love
reading

For the woman who left Marseilles

In memoriam, for the women
and children of Shahr-e-No, Tehran

Ourself, behind ourself, concealed,
Should startle most.
EMILY DICKINSON

⤮

Virtue is an excellent thing, and we should all strive after it,
but it can sometimes be a little depressing.
BARBARA PYM, *Excellent Women*

⤮

Look at me
How I run fearless

To the borders
Of the old stories.
GOOGOOSH, from her song "Fasle Tazeh" ("New Season")

THE
CHANGE
ROOM

Stars

SOMETIMES SHE FELT DESPERATE FOR IT.

After she dropped the boys off, she hurried along the icy street, afraid of slipping. A few other parents, late getting their kids to school, waved in her direction. They were also in a rush, no one could stop and chat. Thank god. I have forty-five minutes, she thought, and picked up her pace.

The intensity of her own need was unfamiliar. Not need. She didn't *need* anything. That was for children. And Andrew. She *wanted*. It's desire, she thought. One foot skated forward unexpectedly on the ice; her arm shot out as she caught herself. Resettling her heavy bag on her shoulder, she felt a twinge there, the old ache. Torn ligaments, years ago in Greece. One serious surgery when she returned. The sidewalks were treacherous, the roads worse. Accidents were already happening today, across the city, on the highways. She'd asked Andrew to leave the car at home, but he said, Don't worry, I'll be fine.

She had not thought of that word for a thousand years. *Desire.* Who had the time for it? *De sideris.* She'd taken two years of Latin at university, four of ancient Greek, the brilliant, useless languages. Dead, like the stars. "Desire" came from the Latin root *de sideris.* Meaning *of the stars.*

She had started to swim a year ago, when the boys were five and six, and she was in the floral studio again every day, working long hours. Her work was complicated, busy, mostly satisfying. She would never tire of flowers, though the people who bought them sometimes drove her crazy. Clients came to the studio as though to a therapist's office, upset about their daughter's choice of husband, worried about aging, or anxious about money, and good style. Human weirdness was part of the boutique flower gig. Her business partner, Kiki, often said that because flowers came from the natural world, they brought out the animal in people. Eliza loved the flowers first and foremost, but she also loved the crazed tap-dance of running a business that sold something as ephemeral and as unnecessary as *flowers*. Beauty, that's what she sold, beauty's ancient promises, too—*this is true, this will be good*—especially from May to October, when she and various wedding planners worked together to create lovely, personal, idyllic, glorious, increasingly lavish weddings. Approaching the city's three top wedding planners had been her idea, and an excellent one. The clients who came through them were the wealthiest people she had ever met in her life. They could afford truth and beauty.

Eliza worked hard to give it to them, every day. Though she relished hard work, the pace had grown relentless since she'd had kids. The list of things to do constantly replenished itself. One after the other, she shot down the tasks, yet still they rose up and came at her (like zombies, naturally; her boys loved zombies). If it wasn't the main sink clogging at the studio, it was the flooding basement at home, or a sick child, or a bossy client. In the past couple of months, it had been Kiki, in a romantic funk, whining about her loneliness and threatening, vaguely, to return to Montreal to find a real man. Wanting to be one of the "good" mothers, Eliza had even volunteered for school council. Now some disorganized flake of a woman called her every week, begging her to do yet another school-related task. Andrew never seemed to work himself into the same frenzied pitch. Was it because he was attached to an institution? Was it because he was a man, and didn't know how to wash the floor?

She felt alone in her exhaustion, but she knew that she was not alone. She was one of millions of women working their brains out and their asses off. She had no right to complain, sitting as she was at the top of the pyramid: white skin, warm house, healthy kids, a loving husband. Some days, usually on the weekends when she read the newspapers, she felt her luck swell and stick in her throat. She swallowed it down with clean water, queasy, stomach churning, her eyes open, eating up the articles, the reports, the photographs in the world section. People stood at the flooded, burning heart of the world, howling kids in their arms, or dead on the ground. Bombs fell, the plague spread, the refugees fled, and fled, and fled. And always, always, there were women trapped somewhere, in rape camps, raped lives.

Eliza was *free*. She said it out loud sometimes, in the midst of whining about all she had to do. This is *freedom*! Two times a year, she got melodramatically sick; her body knew that only illness would bring real rest. Last year, sitting on the examining table, she'd said to the doctor, "It's just my cold, finally breaking up." The doctor had lifted her eyes from her cool stethoscope on Eliza's hot chest, and responded, "Actually, it's just your pneumonia, settling in."

Even while the kids were babies and toddlers, she had worked; maternity leave did not exist for the self-employed. Years passed, as they do, with at least one breast and half her mind attached to her babies. Now Marcus and Jake were big boys going to school. She still felt the elastic delight of being out of the house full-time.

Thumping their hips, her friends would say, *The baby weight is disappearing. My body's coming back.* A lie. It never came back, the body before children, the old life. She knew the truth: love cleaves you right through the middle. She would never be closed again. Never again, singular. She was divided in three by husband and sons. No, she was divided in four, because of the house, an old Victorian four-storey, always clamouring for attention. They had renovated it slowly, room by money-sucking room. The house belonged to both of them, but she was the one who took care of it like the housekeeper out of an old English novel, right down to the keys, the platters, the good cutlery, the power tools, pliers and paint cans. To say nothing about keeping the place clean.

Which reminded her of that shelf in the fridge, covered in some sticky, gelatinous substance. She shook her head and stepped over a gleaming artery of ice. This was it, this gift of an hour on Tuesday and Thursday mornings, she must not think about the fridge. The water whispered: *you are not as divided as you feel.* Her skin was still complete, despite the cuts, broken glassware at work, a slip of a new pruning knife, her heel punctured by that nail during the flood cleanup in the basement last spring, even the way she tore—twice—with the births. The wounds closed. She floated.

Someone was out on the sidewalk breaking up the terrible ice in front of St. Anne's Community Centre, referred to by those in the know as Annie's. She liked the name; St. Anne was the patron saint of families. It was a solid place, built in the sixties, nothing fancy, no big glass window or state-of-the-art equipment, just a squat two-storey building at the edge of the park, operated by well-organized people who took good care of children. When the boys had been little, the daycare had saved her life.

She pushed through the first door, then the next. Tina at the front desk stamped her pass with a wink—she was busy on the phone. Eliza hardly slackened her pace down the hallway as she detoured around the mother who was down on her knees in front of her crying two-year-old. The change room door was yellow; she went through it into the warm, chlorinated air, and immediately felt better. Echoing voices drifted in from the pool, the lifeguards talking loudly across the water. And water falling: someone was taking a shower. Maybe it was Sheila, her neighbour. Just as she looked toward the shower area, her good friend Janet came out from behind the tiled wall, and said, "Hi there! I was wondering if you were going to make it today." Janet had a towel around her voluptuous body—she claimed that her breasts simply never stopped growing—and another wrapping up her curly dark-brown hair.

Eliza hung her coat and bag on a hook. "It's always a panic in the morning, but I will not give up my swimming! How are you?"

"Sophie is driving me bonkers, otherwise I'm fine."

Eliza made sympathetic noises as she pulled her sweater over her head. Sophie was Janet's increasingly argumentative teen-age daughter. Another regular swimmer came from the showers into the change room, smiling nearsightedly. Annoying woman, with a perpetually sore neck. She always talked about her son in Vancouver, how much money he was making, tearing down old houses, ripping around the city in his fancy car. *Who cares,* Janet would say after the woman had left. *Who cares about a damn Porsche?*

Eliza was in her bathing suit already, keen to get in the water; it was only a half an hour before the toddler swim classes would arrive from the daycare. Sheila *was* in the shower room, a petite woman with what Eliza's mother would call "a lovely figure"—and the only mother who swam in her bikini, which added to the impression that she was about twenty-five. But she was older than Eliza. The women greeted each other; Eliza glanced surrepti-tiously at the hourglass curve of Sheila's waist. The deep brown skin was almost unlined. Sheila said, "Watch out, the showers are cold again today."

Eliza stepped into the cool spray. "Brr!" She showered quickly and called out her goodbyes, then slipped through the last door.

Beyond the pool, the long eastern wall was painted in cartoon style with bright tropical fish, a diver, a red-haired mermaid peeking through seaweed. Above the mural, graffiti letters bulged: *St. Anne's Is a Good Place to Be*. Only one other swimmer was in the water, finishing a length at a fast clip. Eliza was pleased that she wouldn't have to vie for a clear lane.

She sat down and licked the insides of her goggles, embarrassed by her tongue sliding over the plastic lenses; saliva kept them from fogging up. The bored young lifeguards seemed always to catch her doing this; today was no exception. She waved at the one sitting across the pool in his raised chair and fit the goggles over her eyes. Blue lenses made the water bluer. She lifted her whole weight up with her arms and dropped herself straight off the edge of the pool.

If Only the Sea

DOWN SHE WENT, DOWN, DOWN. IF ONLY IT WERE DEEPER; if only, the sea. When her toes touched the rough paint on the bottom of the pool, she pushed off, stretched out, dolphin-kicked half of her first length underwater. The undulations made her think of an otter. Then a snake. She was animal again, returned to her element.

She loved the pool. It was in no way noteworthy, and only twenty metres long. The high-ceilinged room smelled of chlorine and wet cement. For most of the day it reverberated with the voices of small children. Now it was quiet with rhythmic splash and echo. She kept her head under the water as much as possible so she heard nothing but the water-insulated, held-breath, blood-in-her-head world. It counted, this half-hour of stretched-out amphibious memory. In a few spots underwater, the blue paint was worn through to other paint from years before, and years before that, blue, white, aquamarine.

The other swimmer was two lanes away. A woman. Once Eliza had done a few lengths to warm up, she tried to keep pace, but the other woman in her sleek black suit was too fast. Taller. Longer arms. That was all she could see underwater, or when she paused to get her breath at one end of the pool.

She returned to her own rhythm. Competition was not what she was here for. The dripping weight of her elbow lifted out of the water; her hand flicked forward, pointing down like an arrow. Her legs, silent, powerful propellers of the body, barely breached the surface.

She was on the east side of the pool, the far lane, for a reason. Here it came. The sun. It had been an overcast morning but now the sun shone through the narrow windows. Light fell in a band here, only here, refracted in rippling white and rainbow lines over the blue-green bottom, through the water itself. The sun illuminated the air bubbles, minuscule, shining globes; it was like swimming through glitter. The lines of light wavered forward, undulated back, the blue bluer, the white whiter. She stopped her front crawl and floated in the sun. The memory was bodily: floating in the sea, the Aegean, the sun warming her. The only salt water now was inside her; it stung her eyes. The joy and sadness came together. Water did that, blurred the lines. Keep swimming, she thought, and dove under, came up in breaststroke. But with each frog kick, she felt the memory pull at her, that place, its sun; she had fallen in love, once, on a Greek island. A lifetime ago.

The rippling net of light drew her down. She stayed underwater for the whole length of the pool, kicking hard, then returned to the front crawl, her best stroke even after the shoulder injury. For three lengths, she swam as fast as the tall woman. The other woman, sensing a race, picked up her pace. Eliza smiled as she flipped, pushed off, did the length stroke for stroke. But in her next flip-turn, only one foot fully connected with the wall; in those lost seconds, the Amazon leapt ahead. When Eliza finished the length, the woman was waiting in the water, goggles up on her forehead. It was over. The children were coming in, their towels over their shoulders.

The Amazon pulled herself out of the water in one motion, long and lithe and gleaming, water sluicing down her legs. Eliza watched her walk through the change room door. The lifeguard, down from his perch, gave her an inquiring look, eyebrows raised. Last week, he had to ask her, loudly, to get out of the water; she'd forgotten the time. "I know, don't worry," she called to him. It was like this every Tuesday and Thursday. She was always the last one out of the pool.

The woman was naked under the shower. It was impossible not to look at a naked body framed by the white tiles. Gorgeous breasts. Full but lifting also, lifting up into dark pink nipples. Such beautiful breasts were rare. She was shaved, too; the line of pubic hair that rose up from the slit was slightly wider than a finger. Eliza put her goggles around a tap across from the Amazon, then went to get her shampoo and conditioner.

Children were still getting changed; she wasn't going to take off her bathing suit until all of them had left for their class. Two naked women might be overwhelming. They were three- and four-year-olds, the age of perfection. She felt a quick, light stab in her lower belly. No wonder she felt so in love with the water today: she was about to ovulate. Or maybe that was it, just then, the egg had dropped off the ledge into the Fallopian tube like a swimmer into her lane. Is that where the word *desire* had come from? Here they were, the children, every one of them pulled out of a woman who had ovulated nine months before they were born. The beauty of small children was a covert plot to make her get pregnant again. But she would resist. Not another one, *no no no*. They were rosy and talkative, bubbling with news and questions. Even the less-beautiful were beautiful, their large eyes vulnerable and open and (she always made a hasty prayer) not yet ruined by anything, by anyone. Two daycare workers herded the kids toward the showers. The women turned the taps on and jumped out of the way; the children rushed in. Their voices filled the white-tiled room like birds, squawking, cooing, complaining, *But it's cold!* One of the workers replied, *Don't worry, the pool will be warm.* Which was true. It was the warmest pool in the city—they kept it that way for the kids. A dark-eyed, olive-skinned little girl turned to Eliza and said gravely, "I can put my head under the water." To which Eliza replied, equally grave, "Maybe you were a mermaid once, in another life." The child's eyes sparked; she ran with the story. "It's true," she admitted. "I *was* a mermaid once. In the ocean." And she stuck her head into the shower. Coughed. The tall woman did not look at the children; she stood magnificently naked, her hair lathered with shampoo, eyes closed. She had a small loofah sponge, twice the size of a square of Shredded Wheat and the exact same colour. She was rubbing her thighs with it, then her flat, light-brown stomach.

"All right, everybody, turn off the taps. Let's go!" The children did as they were told, and the small bodies, the swimming suits in red and pink and green—one boy was wearing the same bathing trunks that Jake had, bright yellow with green frogs—began to file out. The Amazon began to scour her prize-winning tits with the loofah.

The children disappeared. As they would disappear, soon enough. Children never lasted for long. They would return as young adults in their twenties, and Eliza would still be here, a naked old woman, rubbing shampoo over her back and under her arms because she couldn't be bothered to bring soap.

She was forty-two. Not old yet. Though older, she thought, than *her*, the naked woman across the room, bent over now and shaving her legs. Amazing what women did in public places these days. The Amazon seemed to have no shame. None of the regular women ever shaved their legs here. It reminded Eliza to at least take off her swimsuit and soap up her chlorine-smelling skin. One shoulder, the other—the polyester was thinning already. She pushed the suit down over her breasts, her hips, legs, stepped out, hung the dark blue skin of herself on the shower faucet.

At least the woman had turned her ass to the wall to bend over. What, Eliza wondered, did the wall see? The flower of the vulva, intricate folds and layers. Thin or thick labia? Slender and folded in and in, like her own, or fleshy and succulent, folding out, like a red canna or a calla lily. The comparison was right, she thought, defending herself to an invisible judge. It used to be Andrew's fond joke: my wife peddles genitalia. Though it was never completely a joke. It was true. Flowers are the sexual organs of plants.

It was hard *not* to look at a naked body, bending like that. The nipples gathered water, turned into two small waterfalls. The length of the planes of bone invited the eye to glide down the healthy flesh. Creamy skin, black hair. Like the heroine out of which novel? The muscles in Eliza's legs and arms flexed as the Amazon sent the razor down her ankle. Maybe she was a fitness instructor. Ashtanga teacher. Personal trainer. Did anyone do aerobics anymore? It was spin classes and hot yoga now. Even Pilates had become passé. Every time the woman drew the razor up her shin, a series of muscles in her torso actually rippled.

Eliza closed her eyes, glad no one else was around to see her staring. They all looked at each other's bodies, covertly, shyly, it was natural. There were so many bodies, long and lush like this woman's, or voluptuous and plump, like Janet, or straight-hipped and small-breasted. The woman with the sore neck and rich son still had a slender waist and a nice ass, despite stretch marks and more than sixty years of life behind her. Another older woman came sometimes, too, and she was hilarious, always crooning in the change room about how wonderful it was to see the other women naked, how different everyone was. People didn't talk to her too much; her enthusiasm frightened them. She was large and jiggly, great-breasted. Hers was the shape of that ancient goddess dug up in Turkey, and it became mightily apparent how much she liked that fact when she announced it one day, to the embarrassed silence of the other swimmers. Eliza had smiled and said, "Well, it's always good to have a goddess in the change room." A few others laughed politely while the big woman guffawed with delight. That's why she was frightening; it wasn't just her enthusiasm. People were not accustomed to blatant happiness; it made them as nervous as naked flesh.

Eliza's own was a fairly fit, fairly shapely body, the round, stretched belly of a woman with kids. Muscular thighs from years of cycling, though now, with the kids, she hadn't made any overnight rides in years. She rode her bike around the city, through the ravines, sometimes down to the lake. She loved bringing the boys with her—they were getting more and more confident on their own bikes. But having the boys along meant that cycling wasn't exercise. She guarded the swimming as her own. It made her body smoother, stretched away some of the extra fat.

She glanced at her again, then away. Lovely to look, not nice to stare. The Amazon straightened up and thrust her long-bladed shins into the spray. She was finished. But she stayed on, under the hot water, rubbing the last of the soap off herself. Their eyes met briefly; briefly they smiled. Eliza felt a tug at the root of her clitoris. She felt wet. Down there. That's what happened with ovulation: it was biological.

She squeezed some conditioner into her hand and massaged it into her hair. Other people had sex once a week. She had the pool. Twice!

She couldn't remember the last time she had had sex with her husband. More than a month ago? More like six weeks. Surely the current dry spell couldn't have been more than two months? Please god. That was life with two small children, night-wakers both. It was nothing to be ashamed about, sexlessness.

And I'm not ashamed, she thought. I'm just horny. She realized she wanted to be fucked upside down and sideways. *Obviously* she was ovulating. The survival of the race had once depended upon fucking. No longer, of course. The opposite was true now. The last thing the planet needed was more fucking humans. And Andrew did not want to have another one; the last of her eggs were falling through her body. Soon there would be no more. She had never felt so lustful in her life.

The Amazon spoke in a surprisingly loud voice. "That was fun."

"Sorry?" Eliza tried to decipher the echoey words, but she had water in one of her ears. She felt her face turning red. Knowing she was blushing made her blush more.

"It was fun to race you."

"You beat me."

"Mmm," mm-ed the tall woman. She grinned. "I *did* beat you. Soundly. I like winning." She grinned more.

Eliza found she couldn't respond to the come-on of the woman's tone. Who talked like that? No one she knew. She smiled back politely and brushed water away from her face. "I would love to swim more. Get in shape."

"You're in *beautiful* shape."

Okay, so maybe some people did talk like that. Eliza closed her eyes and put her head back into the spray. Her neck felt too exposed. She said, "Thank you. Likewise." She knew the Amazon was looking at her, for she had invited the other woman's eyes by closing her own. She felt the live current running through the air between them. That much electricity in a shower room had to be dangerous.

Her heart thumped in her throat and her water-drum ears. It has come to this, she thought. Flirting with a hot young woman at the pool. Andrew and I *must* have sex. But had Eliza flirted? Or had she been flirted *with*? She was too busy for sexual innuendo, or too tired. She flipped through her mental Rolodex of fellow school moms and dads. In eight years, in the school playground, at the park, dropping off and picking up for playdates, she had not flirted with a single one of them. They were sexless zombies with toddlers and full-time jobs. Just like her.

She put her hand on the tiled wall beside her to keep her balance. That was the solution, she had found, to many of the problems of middle-aged, middle-class life: Keep the eyes closed. Maintain balance. She listened to the water splashing. When she turned her head sideways, to get water out of the one ear, she peeked at the tiled floor. Someone's tangle of long brown hair. You'd think women, at least, would clean up their own messes. A pink hair elastic, too, curled like a little neon worm on the white squares. Her other ear filled up with spray.

When she opened her eyes, the Amazon was gone. Eliza stayed exactly where she was, her heart still pounding. She did not want to be reminded of the past. But that's why she came here, partly, to be reminded of those two long hot seasons in Greece at the beginning of her adult life. On the island of Lesvos, as a matter of fact. She would not admit to anyone how often she remembered the island and all that happened there. Not daring to go out into the change room, she put a second round of conditioner on her head and stood swaying under the spray, deconstructing their brief exchange. She rinsed her hair, again, hoping that, as the label said, the rosemary oil would stimulate her scalp and the horsetail would nourish her follicles. (She read the label five times.) Skin ruddy in the heat of the spray, she stood there, frozen, wasting the precious water of Lake Ontario.

When she entered the change room, it was empty. As she had hoped. But now she was disappointed. She stood there naked, dripping, and imagined herself fully dressed, pushing out the swing door and catching up with her to say . . . what? What could she say?

She put her towel on one of the benches and sat down. Unbidden, the voices of the children in the pool came to her. She pushed them away. All children sounded like her own children now; it was infuriating. She would have thoughtlessly thrown her body in front of a speeding car to save any one of them. Little bloodsuckers. She didn't want to hear them, nor the lifeguards calling commands across the water.

She took up the towel between her legs and dried her thighs, her belly. Then she stretched it higher, to dry off her breasts, and opened her legs slightly, pushing against the taut fabric. There wasn't enough pressure. So she held the towel loosely in her left hand, covering herself, and with her right hand she burrowed under, and slid her middle finger between her labia. She was shocked by how swollen her lips were, and her clitoris, how wet she was. At least the electricity still *works*, she thought. She had to stop herself from doing more, though the pornographic narrative came to her with surprising ease: *She sprawled back on the wide bench and spread her legs wide. She slipped her middle finger into . . . At that moment, the tall dark . . .* Et cetera.

She shook her head. Pathetic! There were tears in her eyes. She was crying for it! Which made her laugh; a plaintive squawk leapt up and collapsed in the air of the change room. Could it actually be longer than two months? Was that possible? There wasn't a rule in the standard marriage contract about conjugal rights. No legislation stated, You must have sex with your wife/husband at least once every fortnight. Now that the kids were older, she was ready to go back to the original agreement, at least once or twice a week. More in the summer.

But the last time they had managed an intense, fast session of fucking was . . . before Christmas. Before Christmas shopping. Usually she did her Christmas shopping in November, to avoid the crowds. And it was before that last teacher professional development day, because she was in a bad mood about it then, too. Would that have been . . . early November? Forget lovemaking, though she liked that, if it happened. Lovemaking required planning, time and a total absence of children from the house. The hurried sex suited her; it was to the point. They were usually both so pent-up that it was excellent, like desperate teenage sex, though with a better sense of humour and finer mechanics.

Anyway, without sex, she was becoming a menace to society. She stood up, dried off brusquely, like she was drying off—what? she wondered, surprised at her own roughness. A wet dog. No! A wet pussy. Good grief. Hurry up and get some clothes on, you slut.

~ 3 ~

Ice

SLUT. THAT WAS ANOTHER WORD SHE HADN'T THOUGHT of in ages. She was out in the cold morning air, walking quickly, a hat on her head. But she was warm from swimming; she could walk all the way to work without feeling the chill.

Slut was a word she liked, now that she was safe from it. In high school, it had been the dreaded insult: *you slut!* She had been called that, a few times, by mean girls. That horrible year, Grade 10. Why? She couldn't remember the details anymore. Alas, she had never been overtly slutty. *Alas?* Did she regret it? No. Had the woman at the pool been slutty? Was that slutty behaviour? Or just sexual?

For a teenager, being slutty made life complicated. She had never dressed like a slut. She always had one nice boyfriend at a time; she didn't lose her virginity until she was in Grade 12, at seventeen, like many of her friends. How they had wanted to get rid of it, the albatross of virginity. When she had sex for the first time, with a boyfriend of many months, she was so happy. Not because the sex was good. It was non-orgasmic, perfunctory and painful. It hurt more than she had expected it to. But when she walked out of his parents' house (they were away for the weekend) into the wind and red leaves of a bright October morning, she thought, Here I am, now I *know*.

She knew almost nothing, but every girl has to begin somewhere. She was thrilled by that invisible slip of broken skin, ever
grateful to the boyfriend for doing his best. *He* came in about
twenty strokes, and he'd come three times before that, while they
were driving each other crazy with kissing and touching and licking. It was his first time, too. *There*, said the condom, and the sex
smell, and her blood on the towel underneath them, *there*. Con-
gratulations! You are now part of the glorious human mess.

When she had her first son, she felt the same sense of joining,
becoming the rightful holder of a passport into the human world,
this (he was screaming, ten days old, colicky, while she held him,
feeling as helpless as he was, tears running down her face more
slowly than the milk springing from her macerated nipples), *this*
is what it means to be here. Sex and the squalling infant. They
were as basic as food, as mundane. And as laced with the same
mystery as that other big event, death.

What had happened there, in the change room? Would she
really have followed the Amazon out into the street?

Slutty essentially meant horny, didn't it? Or *showing* you were
horny. Showing that you liked sex. But weren't most healthy girls
(and women) horny, at least sometimes? She certainly had been,
in school, and a lot of her friends were, too, though they masked
it as longing for certain boys. *Horny* wasn't a word for girls in the
mid-1980s. Boys were horny. Girls were *pretty*. Or not so pretty.
Or really smart. Or sluts. *Stupid slut.*

A terrifying yet perfect word, with that slippery *s* and the gaping
u and the *t* sharp as a slap. *Slut*. Satisfying to say. Like *fuck*. The
sounds contained the meanings. How about *cunt*? She recoiled
inwardly. Awful. *Cunt* was such a bad word. Once, an aggressive
driver had pulled into her lane so quickly that he almost slammed
into the vehicle ahead of him. Incensed by his own mistake, he
stuck his whole shaggy head out the window and furiously screamed

at her, *You fucking cunt!* From the back seat, five-year-old Marcus piped up, "What's a cunt, Mommy?" She managed to say, "Oh, the man was just unhappy, dear." In a joking voice, she called out, "There's no need to yell!" And Marcus called back, in their usual game, "Because my ears are *very good*!" and they laughed, though she was still gripping the steering wheel too hard, shaken by the man's ferocity.

She shook her head, to fling the words away. *You fucking cunt.* She was passing the kids' school now; the sidewalks had been salted. But once she crossed the street, the ice was positively glassy again. Yesterday, the city was a giant slush pile demarcated by puddles. Overnight the temperature had plummeted. The morning news had listed the accident locations across the city, with a seven-car pile-up on Highway 401; amazingly, no one had been killed, though three people were hospitalized in serious condition. She'd listened to the report while putting the cereal bowls on the table, getting out the milk, a bowl of raisins. After Andrew had ushered the boys downstairs, she had told him about the accident and said, "Take the subway. Don't drive today. I'll walk the kids to school." But he reminded her that it was the last day of a sale at a local sporting goods store; he wanted to get the boys new skates. "Be careful, then, okay? Please?"

Something, someone drew her eyes up and over a passing car. Speaking of the word *slut*. Sophie was on the other side of the street, coming toward her. Janet's daughter. Lovely Sophie, who had recently undergone a transformation so profound that her mother was still reeling. Before the girl had left for Victoria to visit her (recently absconded) father in August, she'd been a sweet fifteen-year-old wearing pedal-pushers and rubber boots, helping her mother dig up irises in their front yard. When Eliza saw her again in the fall, she was on her way to school in high-heeled boots, black tights, and a tight shirt opened to reveal something hot pink and bustier-like: an item of clothing that would have been at home in a stripper's closet.

The mid-winter Sophie wasn't showing cleavage, but even in the cold she managed to project the promise of naked flesh. She wore wedge-heeled army boots this time, with grey tights as the base, layered with black thigh-highs that didn't quite reach the hem of her private-school-girl skirt. Sophie was not in a private school; her clothing dialect was stripper-ese, with the thigh-highs clearly enunciating *garter belt*. She wore a close-fitting wool jacket, also army green, that emphasized her waist. Bright brass buttons. A fat slash of China-red lipstick on her full lips. Her whole face had a plump suppleness to it. She looked *juicy*. Eliza's gaze summoned her, for Sophie suddenly lifted her kohl-ringed eyes, searched for a split second before a big smile wiped the sullen intensity off her face. Eliza waved.

Janet still mourned the loss of her sweet girl to this secretive, angry teenager who smoked on the sly. She said they fought almost every day. Janet couldn't help blaming it on her ex-husband—what the hell had happened in Victoria? Nothing, he maintained. Sailing. Gulf Islands. Yoga. (The yoga had incensed Janet: his new lover was a thirty-year-old yoga instructor.) But Sophie was always relaxed with Eliza. She pulled one of the buds out of her ears and waved back, calling out in her usual sweet way, "Hi there!"

Eliza grinned conspiratorially. "Aren't you walking *away* from your school?"

The young woman stage-whispered, "You do *not* see me, okay? I'm just skipping English." The whisper became matter-of-fact. "I'm *good* at English."

Eliza winked; she used to skip high-school classes all the time. "Are we still on for this Saturday?" Sophie was her most reliable babysitter.

"Of course! Six o'clock, right?"

"Until about midnight. So where are you off to?" As if Sophie would tell her.

"Coffee with a friend. At that new café."

"With all the old painted trays on the walls?"

"Yeah! Amazing coffee." She did a curious little hop, straight up in the air, and Eliza had a flash of the pretty little pre-Raphaelite child she'd been. "This meeting is our little secret, right?"

Eliza squinted at her. "Who is that beautiful young woman? She looks like someone I used to know." Sophie walked backwards for a few steps, waved again, then popped the music back in her ear and spun around, her school-girl-fantasy skirt swinging in a worrisomely tantalizing way.

Thank god I have sons, Eliza thought. Did Sophie look slutty or horny? Both, poor thing. Yet she also looked innocent. Sexed-up and innocent. It was precisely that knot of contradiction that made teenage girls so attractive and vulnerable. There she went, sashaying into a world of online stalkers, Facebook bullies, revealing photos gone viral. Janet was always worried about pictures, and videos, and how much time Sophie spent on the Internet; apparently she loved taking pictures of herself and her friends.

What *kind* of pictures, Eliza wondered, as she walked on. See? The children always tug at us, even when they aren't ours. They *need* us to think about them. Is it a crime to think about myself for five minutes? She tried to conjure up the flirtatious Amazon again, but her mind looped back to Sophie—her cold red cheeks, her clandestine mission at the beginning of the day. Coffee with a friend. Right.

She walked through her own breath as it hung white in the air. The cold was so wet that it set her teeth on edge, yet she craved its sharpness. If only it would snow. Today was the twelfth of January; Christmas had barely been white. She missed the snow, loved how it concealed the dirt but revealed the shape of the city. Roads, sidewalks, the parks—all became land, again, to be traversed. You had to wear boots, lift your feet, move through, fly down. She loved tobogganing. Her sons loved it, too. But they'd only been tobogganing once this winter, two days after Christmas. Then the snow was gone.

She started down the next block, old houses on either side, mostly renovated, with manicured gardens and slate pavers. Stout, well-crafted retaining walls. Always a lawyer or doctor or corporate person in the couple. This was not a block of massage therapists and graphic designers; only one person in the pair could make under $60,000, she thought, doing her own calculations. Suddenly her legs whisked out from under her. She crashed down on her back; her skull cracked against the ice. The pain dazzled right through her head and poked through her eyes. Tears burned and blurred her vision for the third time in an hour. She lay there. Waiting. Had she re-injured her shoulder? She blinked down the tears and stared up at the cross-hatching of black branches above her, up and up, blinking, from the lower limbs of the little ash tree into a tall Norway maple. The tire of a parked car was a couple of steps away from her head. No one had seen her. Not that she cared. She was not going to do what she usually did when she fell or slipped: jump up, grab for balance and pretend everything was fine.

She could feel a goose egg already forming at the back of her head. Marcus, her older boy, would be impressed. He was fascinated by wounds and abrasions of all sorts. He wanted to be a doctor, as well as a fireman.

Then, as she lay gazing upward, she saw the snow. Perhaps it had begun to fall the moment she did. Some of the big cottony flakes landed on her face; she felt them melt. Her eyes followed the flakes up through the lattice of branches, trying to find the beginning of them. Snow caught in the woollen threads of her lime-green hat.

She blinked and felt the cold of the melted flakes on her eyelids. When she blinked again, tears slid down either side of her head. She turned on her side, bent her knees, rolled. Lifted the weak shoulder: no serious damage. This realization brought a surge of gratitude. Nothing broken. Or re-broken. That was the forties; that would be the rest of her life. At twenty-two, she had torn her shoulder from its socket in a riding accident (she had always called it an accident) but the searing pain hadn't prevented her from getting back on the horse for another hour, worsening the damage. Not now. She stood up and carefully swung her arm forward. Back. Down the street, more patches of ice gleamed dully on the sidewalk; her eye went again to the dry winter gardens in front of the houses. She saw a butterfly bush, rosehips, lavender. Marcus had given her a handful of dry lavender the other day from their own front yard.

She felt giddy, mildly drunk. "It's snowing!" she said aloud. No one was in the street to hear her announcement. It was blowing every which way now. She started walking again, slowly.

The snow thickened as she approached College Street. When the wind whipped around her head, she had to shield her eyes. The street and its red brick houses drained of colour; the air whirled white and beneath the white, the buildings turned grey. It hadn't snowed like this for so long that the entire streetscape seemed unrecognizable. Could she be concussed? The wild squall was invigorating, but it disoriented her. She put her hands in her pockets. No gloves. Her fingers scrabbled, blind, among the dry, pokey bits, until she realized what they were, desiccated lavender. Flowers! That's why she loved them. They were the earth in fancy dress, dirt and light turned into lace and colour. She rubbed the crumbling blossoms between her fingers and breathed in the familiar perfume. Marcus's face rose into her mind, hazel eyes more green than brown; he raised his cold hands, offered her the pale blue confetti.

The scent cleared her head. She squeezed the lavender, loving him, that boy, her boys. Her life. Sometimes love was like this, inchoate, rising out of nowhere and suddenly everywhere, thick, blinding. It knocked you in the head, tossed you into the storm. And smelled sweet. Flecks of white and silver-white blew into her sideways, wind-propelled, caught in her eyelashes and hair and mouth. Love. It was exactly like this.

Walk, she thought. Here is the first blizzard of the year. Go into it.

In she went, letting the blue flowers drop from her hand.

4

Fleur

ELIZA WALKED PAST THE BRICK STOREFRONTS AND HIP cafés, greeting various sidewalk shovellers, including the gruff landlord with the handlebar moustache (clotted with snow) and the tall, skinny woman who ran the laundromat with military precision. Both of them smiled at Eliza with uncharacteristic enthusiasm. The gallery owner a few shops away from the floral studio had only a broom to face the storm. "Thank you," she said, crossing the stretch of sidewalk he had just cleared. His trouser legs were dusted white to the knee, but he, too, grinned happily.

Her place, Fleur, was not so different from the other two- and three-storey shops on her block, though she had chosen the corner-lot building because it was slightly larger than most on the street. It also had big west-side windows and a finished basement for storing all manner of accumulated event gear: glassware, standing vases, pedestals, baskets, the cloth-and-wire tree, the papier-mâché unicorn, hundreds of wedding candles and holders.

As Eliza pushed open the glass front door, the cape of cold around her met the almost tropical heat and scent of green stuff. "Bianca! Thank you for shovelling the walkway."

"No problem," Bianca murmured. She smiled up, calm and beatific, Madonna as receptionist and worker of organizational miracles. "It's gorgeous outside."

"I know. Everyone seems thrilled by the storm." But when Eliza banged off her boots, her head throbbed. She slid her fingers through her hair, searching gingerly for the lump. The skin felt as though it had broken; she felt for the scabby blood, but there wasn't any. "It's like a skating rink out there, though. *So* slippery!" She put on her shoes and went past the front desk and the flower fridge, to the workbenches at the back of the studio. One was piled high with delivery boxes. Kiki was trimming and dipping new hydrangeas, stem by stem, into conditioning fluid. "Bonjour," she said, eyes flicking up to Eliza and down again to the cutter in her hand. "You smell like snow." Kiki looked sharp, as usual, in a little green knit dress with brown tights and ankle boots; perfect colours for a redhead. Eliza glanced at the new boxes of orchids, roses, alstroemeria, aspidistra leaves, eucalyptus. Kiki anticipated her question. "Jack Armelle was 'ere; all de orchids are from 'im. Good stuff. Even these amazing purple alstroemeria. No one else knows 'ow to find these flowers."

And no one else knew how to make such beautiful designs out of them. A sculptor, Kiki was adept at handling wire, glass, foam, cloth, clay, even ice; she could make any space look extraordinary—ballet-infused, Gothy, romantic-cottage, old European, whatever adjective the clients laid down with their credit cards, and wherever: a warehouse with the pipes showing, a cavernous tent, the icy rotunda foyer at the Royal Ontario Museum. She was a genius.

Eliza opened another box of hydrangeas. "The Mandarin's standing order is today, right?"

"It is. Can you 'elp me with it?"

"Absolutely." Sometimes, if they hadn't hired freelancers, Kiki got grumpy about doing the standing orders by herself. Because she was the better designer, it was natural that she would do most of the arranging; Eliza was the business person. But the weekly and biweekly standing orders bored Kiki, especially if they involved a lot of small, cookie-cutter arrangements.

She usually wanted either Eliza's or Bianca's help to finish the order quickly. The Mandarin, a fancy three-storey dim-sum place, was that kind of job.

On her way to the shelf to get a clean stem cutter, Eliza walked through a band of light. "Look! The sun's already coming out! And it's still snowing!" Two large industrial sinks and counters lined the western wall; above the sinks, long windows let in snowy beams of winter sun. The room was narrow but deep, lined with shelves that rose to the ceiling and were packed with vases in various shapes, sizes and colours. She went back to the workbench and started cutting the ends of the hydrangea stems. She did a lot of the prep, and followed along behind Kiki. Eliza was a competent designer now, but she was slower than Kiki, who barely needed to look at her hands. She rarely hesitated; she simply knew what would work.

The phone rang; Bianca picked up. "Three arrangements? Oh . . . but those are out of season right now. Even if you were willing to pay a premium, we wouldn't be able to get peonies in time. . . ." Bianca listened without rolling her eyes, which was more than Kiki and Eliza could do. She refrained from looking in their direction, though, because they often made lighthearted jokes about phone clients with impossible orders. With the patience of a good kindergarten teacher, Bianca said, "I'm so sorry, but the good news is we have the *most* beautiful orchids. They just came in this morning from our favourite supplier. . . . White, yellow and deep orange with a dappled throat. Absolutely. I promise that we'll make something beautiful for her. What would you like for me to write on the card?"

Eliza lifted her eyes to the ceiling and whispered, "Peonies in January! Where do people think they live, the Garden of Eden?"

Bianca put down the phone and called, "Kiki, you were so right to get all those orchids from Jack Armelle today! This guy is throwing a lavish party for his wife at Sunfish, in the back room."

"A fancy place to throw a private party. I took them their new arrangements on Friday."

Bianca said, "That's why he called. The manager recommended us. Isn't that sweet?"

Kiki shook her head. "Amazing dat da 'usband leaves it until one day before the big occasion."

"Not really," Eliza said. She lifted a tall bucket of water up onto the workbench; they started putting the new round of conditioned hydrangeas into it. Ten tall stems to a bucket, that was the rule, to prevent cross-contamination if one of the stems had a fungus. "Most husbands leave flowers to the last second." Or forget them altogether.

Kiki smiled, without irony. "But *Andrew* would remember flowers!" It was not dangerous that she had a crush on Eliza's husband; she was an honourable woman and he rarely visited the studio. Tall, lanky, good-looking in an unkempt, professorial way—he was, in fact, a professor of mathematics—Andrew was charming *and* reliable. No doubt Kiki wished he were younger, and not married to Eliza. Kiki was thirty-five. The tick of her biological clock was like the time-bomb in a Hollywood movie. Everyone could hear it.

"But Andrew *does* forget the flowers. On a regular basis." Eliza felt an unpleasant wish to criticize her husband. If she could enumerate his faults, she would have *cause*. Cause for what? Thinking lustful thoughts about a beautiful swimmer, of course. "When I met him, he'd almost killed not one but two gardens. In the front of his house and behind it. The only reason he remembers flowers now is because of me. I'm always the one who reminds him to stop and pick up something nice before we drive out to see his parents." Even Eliza found the Chinese grocer's flowers cheaper than her own shop's. She smiled fondly, falsely, while a sharp flare of anger shot up into her mouth. She was not going to say anything, though. Her parents-in-law had serious money troubles. Last week, she noticed that Andrew had once again paid his mother's Visa bill. But she would never talk about that at work.

Kiki hauled a freshly washed bucket up onto the workbench. "De only reason you complain is because you know Andrew is the perfect 'usband!"

Eliza laughed. "You're such a romantic. There are no perfect husbands. Or wives. Do you want me to stay tonight and do the Sunfish arrangements? You've been working a lot of evenings lately. It's my turn. I just need to get hold of Andrew and make sure he can pick up the kids."

She snipped another stem, trying to cut away her irritation, pluck it off with the blemished hydrangea leaves. Part of her was gone, slipped away into another world. With a lover. Who had breasts. Yet here she was, up to the elbows in the water buckets of her life.

She put down the cutters, dried her hands, and tapped out a quick text to Andrew.

This is *real. This* is reality. Andrew, the kids, our schedule. She pressed Send and put her phone on a shelf away from the water, then picked up two buckets of conditioned flowers and went into the fridge. It was good to stand in the cold. She tidied up the greens shelf, pinching off dried fern fronds and tossing out three whole stems of asparagus greens. The cocculus and coffee leaves were fine; they lasted for a long time. It was important to get rid of anything that could start decaying; she kept the fridge as clean as possible, to avoid passing any mould or fungus among the plants. She took stock: ten different kinds of roses, snowberries, bells of

Ireland, lilies, lots of cedar and holly left over from Christmas. Her teeth started chattering. She would freeze the heat of the pool right out of her flesh.

How quickly you could cross from one world into another . . . if you did actually cross. She walked out of the chilled air carrying a bucket of dark orange roses. A moment of lust meant nothing. She was here again, this side of the border, with a thousand things to do.

5

Snow Angels

THE SNOW KEPT FALLING. ALL DAY IT CAME DOWN, covering the cars, the dirty leaves, filling in window ledges, drifting in waves across the sidewalks. The keen morning shovellers surrendered; they would wait until it stopped. It did not stop. It caught in people's eyelashes and hid the wickedly slippery streets. Cardboard coffee cups, cigarette butts, black stains of gum on the pavement disappeared.

All day long, Eliza tried to get in touch with Andrew. He didn't answer his phone or text messages. He rarely used his office phone at the university, but she left a message there, too, and heard nothing back from him. If she couldn't get in touch with him, she couldn't stay late to do the Sunfish arrangements. Late in the afternoon, she had to go downstairs to the bathroom, close the door, sit on the toilet and take deep breaths. Was he dead in a car accident? Or just being the absent-minded professor? Should she weep for Andrew or swear at him? She peed, flushed the toilet and ran back upstairs.

Kiki said she didn't mind staying late. Again. Bianca slowly lifted her head up from her laptop—her gaze like melted chocolate—and said, "Eliza, don't worry. I'll stay tonight and keep Kiki company. I'll trim and wrap." Their policy was to make sure that all morning deliveries were finished the night before. "And I'll pop out at six and get us some Thai food."

Eliza pulled on her boots. "Bianca, you are an angel."

"Oh, please," she said modestly, smiling from one woman to the other. Then Eliza rushed away to fetch the kids from their after-school program at Annie's.

The snow had transformed the old grey city into a newly painted door. She and the boys walked through it, laughing. At the house, she found mittens for herself and went to the shed to get shovels. The boys refused to put on their snow pants. They set to heaving snow into the street, onto the garden, until the shovels rasped against ice and concrete. Still the snow floated down, so light in the air and heavy on the ground, accumulating quickly.

"I give up!" Marcus cried dramatically and fell over backwards. Jake copied him. They made snow angels, *swish-swish swish-swish*, mouths wide open, tongues skyward. Then Jake asked, "Do angels eat snow?"

"Yes. They eat it before it falls out of the clouds. And they put it in too-hot hot chocolate."

They begged her to make an angel herself; she fell over and flapped her arms, the boys sprawling beside her. Snow dropped down their necks, jumped into their boots. The only way she could get them inside was to promise tobogganing at the park on Saturday morning. There was just one more day of school.

"Maaaaaawm!" That was Jake. Marcus was hammering away on the piano, his fifteen-minute turn long over, but still he pounded out *Old MacDonald had a farm, E-I-E-I-O*.

Jake shrieked, "Marcus! It's my piano, too."

"It's Mom's piano, stupid."

"I'm not stupid."

"Marcus!" she yelled as she put the colander in the sink. "Don't be rude to your brother. Come down and help me set the table."

"But I'm still practising."

"It's Jake's turn. Would you please come down here right now?"
She hated her cop-voice. She cut the broccoli and stirred the hamburger. The boys were fighting openly now. Jake started crying.

"Marcus! One of your chores is to set the table."

He screamed, "No! I will *not* set the table." He boomed away on
the bottom keys. He was the defiant son, even as a baby. His first
utterance was not "Da," not "Ma," and definitely not "Mama." It
was "No." *Don't put that dirty cookie in your mouth, sweetie*, she'd
said. He was holding the sandbox Oreo tight in his fist. The sugary
filling was pitted and grey. He said, "No," and bit the cookie in
half, chewing through his smile. How she and Andrew had
laughed, delighted that he had said his first word.

If only they'd known how often they were going to hear it. She
already worried about his adolescence. He was a popular, bossy
child, striding cockily into a world of violent video games, Internet
porn, alcohol, drugs, cars, crazy parties, knives. . . . She made herself stop thinking about it. He was seven.

She could hear the TV. Which one of them had turned it on?
Probably Jake, in pure frustration. The piano stopped; the boys
went silent before the cable glow. She dumped the broccoli, steam-
ing, into a bowl, and lifted the sizzling hamburger from the stove.
Poured in the tomato sauce, stirred dutifully. The slow-bubbling
domestic cauldron often made her think of the past.

Kids' spaghetti had brought her low. And breast milk. She had
been mighty, once, in the kingdom of food. Thalassa. That had
been the name of her restaurant. The Greek word for "sea." Her
late father's best friend was her silent, generous partner. Her timing
had been perfect. She'd opened at the crest of the wave of good,
expensive, but accessible food in the city. No precious towers of
vegetables or over-extravagant deglazings. Nothing stuffy. Even
though she was the chef, she sometimes served the dishes herself.

The kitchen was in plain view of the dining room, making food an act of community theatre, with Eliza as the attractive leading lady. She wanted the high-end lunch crowd, the high-end dinner crowd, the weekend moneyed hip. She got them all, with Greek and northern Italian dishes, brightened up and degreased, accompanied by a solid, reasonably priced wine list.

Ah, Thalassa, she thought, swaying nostalgically in the spaghetti sauce vapour. She wasn't the only one. She still had women friends in the food world, though none of them were chefs anymore, because they had had kids. It was just short of impossible to run a restaurant kitchen and a home kitchen at the same time. Eliza had not even tried. After Zoë, who had been her right-hand woman at Thalassa, had twins, she had opened a pastry shop on Bloor Street; after Kelly had her first baby, she opened a successful fresh tortilla business.

Eliza smiled down into the boiling vat of water, fondly remembering the adrenalin rush of restaurant work. She forked out a strand of spaghetti—it needed two more minutes—and turned away to set the table. Though she often complained, and regretted, and wondered what it would have been like if she'd stuck it out with Thalassa, she wasn't complaining at this moment. She was thinking. Considering. That was another starry Latin word, *con sideris*: "to be with the stars." It must be a consolation of age, that she could sift through her forty years of life, pull out one section or another, like the different drawers in a jewellery box, and consider the treasures inside. Single earrings were plentiful, and rings without their stones. But you couldn't get rid of that stuff. Every experience became valuable loot, including the sleep deprivation, the children fighting, and routine problems at work.

Treasure, she repeated to herself. That's all there was. *This is mine, my own life.* She turned off the taps and watched the water swirl down the sink. When she blinked, two tears dropped straight into the basin. What was wrong with her? He would be home soon. Or he would call. She wiped her eyes. Something had happened, but nothing terrible, not an accident. Not a disaster. But why didn't he call?

"Marcus! Jake! Dinner's almost ready. I know you're watching TV. You're going to have to turn it off! In five minutes!"

One more minute, one more kiddie dinner on the table. Cooking at Thalassa had never been so monotonous. She tasted the sauce—fine—and frowned. She went to the front of the house, the sitting room, and stared glumly out the large window. She wouldn't shut the blinds until Andrew was home. The wind gusted snow off the rooftops across the street.

Back in the dining room, she checked her phone.

Finally! His name blinked in her list of messages. Relieved, she read:

Picked up skis for boys. Martin in town!!! For
lay-over. Going to airport, dinner w him. Home
by 9.

She read the lines again, nodding. Then shaking her head, anger clotting behind her eyes like a headache. Just like Martin to have a layover that wasn't long enough for him to visit his nephews. Too busy saving the world, the fucker. No doubt they were having a lavish dinner at that new restaurant in the fancy airport hotel. She unclenched her grip on the phone; no need to crack the screen. Andrew, she noted, had sent the text at six. While she was with the boys in the front garden. She tossed the phone back into her bag and swore under her breath. Then yelled, "Oh, shit!" and rushed across the dining room.

Too late. The spaghetti was overcooked.

6

Lost to the World

SHE WORKED THROUGH THE EVENING ROUTINE DOGGEDLY, wondering how single mothers did it. Night after night, day after day, they managed the weight of total responsibility. Her own mother had done it.

Eliza was sitting beside Marcus, trying to help him read, but she was so tired her eyes were crossing. He wasn't reading at grade level yet, so practice was part of his homework. His difficulty with reading made her impatient, which was the worst thing; he was already self-conscious about how slowly the words came out of his mouth. Tonight, unable to sit still, he played with an elastic band, then an eraser, then a piece of Lego. She snapped, "Stop fooling around, right now! I'm sick of this!" She instantly regretted the meanness in her tone. Marcus responded by pounding his pencil, sharp end down, into the kitchen table. "Marcus!" But instead of remonstrating further, she sagged back against her chair. He scowled at her, preparing to do battle. She met his glittering eye.

Why bother? she wondered. What battle? She murmured, "I'm so tired," and kissed the side of his head. His hair smelled doggish with sweat and dirt. The charismatic, good-looking son was also the one who didn't like to bathe. She eyed the shallow hole and pulled away in surprise. "Our poor table! It's bleeding!"

"Is it?" he said, leaning forward to look. "Mommy! It is *not* bleeding."

She whispered, "I think it's bedtime."

He snuggled up against her. "Thank god it's bedtime!" he said, and she laughed.

It was ridiculous for six- and seven-year-olds to have homework every night. Andrew was supposed to help Marcus with reading but the job usually fell to her. Like cleaning out the dishwasher, doing the laundry, wiping down the counters and the fridge, washing the floor. Rinsing out the compost bucket. Dusting the windowsills. The baseboards. The thousand slats of the window blinds. Vacuuming the crap out from under the stove. Filling in school forms, renewing the healthcare cards, calling the babysitter, fundraising for the school.

Her mother—she *adored* Andrew—told her that the way to ruin a good marriage was to keep score of who did what. So Eliza did many tasks herself, resentfully, or in a state of resigned oblivion, often late at night after the kids had gone to bed. When Andrew told her to hire a cleaner, she asked him, "Why don't *you* hire a cleaner?" He did. After a couple of duds and one klutz—the woman knocked their wedding portrait off the wall: the broken glass, scratched photo, reprint and repair bill came to $400—she went back to doing it herself. Even now, while she shepherded the boys into the bathroom to start teeth-brushing and washing up, she critically eyed the mess. The toilet was like a Jackson Pollock painting, artful sprays everywhere.

Dirty clothes in the hamper, pyjamas on, storybook chosen, another day of helping them to be clean, kind, healthy humans. As opposed to the wild animals they would naturally be. She loved the little beasts, too, curled up against her, one on either side, in Marcus's double bed. Jake would hop over to his own after the reading was finished. She was a page away from the end of the storybook when they heard the back door open. Jake threw back the covers, ready to leap out of the bed and rush downstairs, but she put out her arm as a barrier. "Daddy will come up *here* to kiss you good night. Let's finish the story."

"Why the hell didn't you answer your phone?"

"I was teaching all day! I forgot to turn my phone back on until I got to the airport. When I finally read your text messages, I texted you back right away."

She stared at him, a spatula in her white-knuckled hand. Then she spun on her heel and stomped off to the kitchen island. She filled the spaghetti pot with tap water, poured out half and scrubbed the metal unnecessarily hard. "You could have called me at some point. I've been worried about this snow all day long."

"What am I, a mind reader?"

"No, it's fucking clear you're not a mind reader because if you were, you'd know that all I want right now is an apology." She dumped the rest of the water out of the pot; it tidal-waved out of the sink, flooding half the island countertop. "Have you forgotten that my father was killed in a *car accident* in a *snowstorm*?" She was yelling. "My mother waited and waited for him to call, but he never did, did he?" She stalked off.

"Where are you going?"

"To pee!" She pounded upstairs and slammed the bathroom door as hard as she could. Then stood still, hoping she hadn't woken up the kids.

She didn't have to pee. She just had to get away from her husband, now that he was home. She sat down on the toilet seat and let the wave of the past rise up and crash through her—it had been there all evening, waiting to break—and just like that, she was crying. She cried silently, not wanting Andrew to hear, but hard, two streams pouring down her face. She cried like a child,

unsurprisingly, remembering the child she had been, whose father
had died. She wished the impossible, that she could somehow
embrace that girl now, send her love backwards through time.

Her childhood ended at ten, with her father's passing and her
sudden transformation into her mother's best friend and help-
mate, the adult girl who put the adult woman to bed those nights
when she'd sat up too long, one hand propping up her head as she
blinked uncomprehendingly at the bills, the bank statements,
the business letters. Genevieve Keenan did not have her own bank
account; it was joined to her husband's in holy matrimony. She
would sip at her small glass of rye and Coke until it was gone, then
pour another and sit a while longer, to write the numbers down
again, more carefully. She did the addition in pencil over and over,
until Eliza went after school one day and bought a calculator with
her babysitting money. Even then, the sums always added up to
not-enough and *there-are-still-outstanding-debts-Mrs.-Keenan*.

During those nighttime sessions with her mother, little Eliza
saw many things blurrily, through her own tears, but she saw one
thing clearly: the power of money. She was so sad, the first year
after his death, because she missed him—his mild humour, the
dark blue eyes magnified behind his glasses, his funny little stories—but she was also angry because his death marooned them
on an island of poverty. Genevieve lost the heavily mortgaged
house; she had never known about her husband's other debts.
The family moved to the poorest neighbourhood in Calgary and
rented a duplex with holes in the walls. Eliza made a solemn vow
in her diary (a small notebook she would later burn, ashamed that
she had been so judgmental toward her mother): *When I grow up,
I will have my own bank account, my own business, and my own
kitchen table without any bills on it, or stupid crying.*

The early loss gave her an eerie intimacy with death. Anyone,
she knew, could disappear. At any time. You could be average. You

could be great. And you could still die in a snowstorm. She became practical and organized yet secretly wild—stormful—knowing that despite carefully saving her money and cleaning the house for her mother and taking care of Rachel and tolerating her bossy brother, any disastrous thing could happen. If the world was wild, she would match it. But carefully.

She believed that her older brother and younger sister came out of it more wounded than she was. Fourteen-year-old Dean dropped into a gang of troublemaking kids, dropped out of school, then lost years to alcohol and drugs before going to a technical college. Now he was a crane operator in oil-booming Calgary, making scads of money. He owned a house, but his smart, pretty wife had recently left him, taking their daughter with her. Eliza suspected that a lot of his boom money was still going up his nose.

Her sister, Rachel, never complained about the past, though the present was a source of constant fury. Only six when their father died, she had lost two parents, one forever, the other to grief, fear and minimum wage. Genevieve worked long hours as a waitress, a chambermaid, a clerk at the mall. In her absence, her youngest child withdrew. Rachel barely spoke. She had trouble learning to read, just like Marcus. Eliza read to her, played with her, took her to the park. She remembered boiling the water, day after day, to make Kraft Dinner. Kraft Dinner and her mother on the phone, her voice tight, arranging another visit for Rachel with a useless school social worker, trying to find out the results for her learning disabilities test.

During that time, Genevieve took solace in God. A handsome man named Garry came to the door one Saturday morning with *The Watchtower* in hand, and, in short order, Genevieve saw the light. She began to go to meetings on Monday, Wednesday and Sunday at the Kingdom Hall, where Elder Garry and his fellow elders often gave beautiful, stern Bible talks about wickedness, goodness, paradise, Armageddon. Eliza and Rachel sat beside their mother, doodling on notepads, sucking on candies, and trying not to fidget. Dean categorically refused to visit the Kingdom Hall; he was already "lost to the world," as Elder Garry said of those who were offered The Truth but turned it down.

Lost to the world. She secretly loved the phrase. How to choose between being Lost to the World and The Truth? The truth was depressing. It made her mother cry. Eliza received Genevieve's confidences late at night, when no one else could hear. "Oh, Eliza, I'm so glad to be in The Truth now. Because I've met him. And he is a very . . . He's so . . . persuasive. I can't help myself," Genevieve said. Eliza wasn't entirely sure if her mother meant God or Garry. "But it's *wrong*." And her tears would begin.

If it was wrong, it couldn't be God. But why was having dinner with Garry so wrong? What was he feeding her mother anyway?

Dean often said, sneeringly, "Elder Garry is just after one thing." Eliza was too embarrassed to ask: What thing? It couldn't be money because they never had any. Her mom's pancakes? When Garry came for breakfast, he always said Genevieve was the best pancake-maker in the world.

One night, Genevieve whispered her good news to Eliza: Garry loved her. He had said the words. "He loves you, too, Eliza. And Rachel. And even Dean." By that time, Dean was sixteen, Eliza was almost twelve. She'd lied about her age and started working at McDonald's to get out of going to the Kingdom Hall. Poor eight-year-old Rachel didn't want to go, either, but Garry loved having her there. Genevieve confided, "He feels like he could really be a father to her." On meeting nights, he usually drove them home and tucked Rachel into bed.

Soon after Garry's declaration of love, Genevieve took a shift off from the hotel one Saturday morning to make the family a big breakfast. To the delight of her children, Garry was not invited.

As she set the pancakes and bacon on the table, she told them she had an announcement to make. Uncharacteristically, they did not begin to fight over the food or compete for the syrup bottle. They just stared at her. She smiled bravely. "Garry has asked me to marry him. And I have said yes." Rachel folded in on herself and started crying. Eliza shook her head, mouth open.

Only Dean could find words. He stood up from the table. "If you marry that fucker, I'll kill him with my bare hands." He raised his future murder weapons, showing her how large and calloused they were. He'd been doing the grunt work on construction sites for a whole year; he was extremely strong. "I'm not kidding, Mom. That guy is a creep. I'll kill him. I'm only sixteen. I won't be in jail for that long. It would be worth it." Then he left the house, calmly, like an adult. He didn't even slam the door.

So. Their mother left The Truth and became lost to the world again. It was a relief. Rachel started reading. Two years of night school and computer courses later, Genevieve was offered an excellent position with the Calgary Police Department as a 911 operator. The shift work was exhausting but she was good at her job; she had a knack for dealing with tragedy. Eliza flipped burgers, finished high school, became a line cook, started university (wondering: Was it the Jehovah's Witnesses who gave her an interest in dead languages, metaphor and literature in general?) and graduated to sous-chef. Dean continued to work at both legal and illegal trades and ingested a copious amount of drugs. After high school, Rachel did a criminology degree, trained for the RCMP and became a forensic investigator, mostly of sexual crimes against children. She was the funniest person Eliza knew, and the most outraged.

Eliza blew her nose and flushed the toilet. Enough! The past had served its purpose and diluted her anger at her husband. He was still downstairs, reasonable, alive. She washed her hands, splashed her face and leaned critically toward the mirror. Every day a new wrinkle appeared under her eyes or across her forehead. But she was red-cheeked and bright-eyed from crying.

7

Family Stuff

WHEN SHE CAME BACK INTO THE KITCHEN, ANDREW asked, "What were you doing up there? Masturbating?"

"Ha-ha," she said, and turned away to hide her smile. She wasn't ready to let go of the argument just yet. "I thought you might remember that relevant bit of my family history during the biggest snowstorm of the winter. On a day that I didn't want you to drive to work."

Andrew shook his head. He could never win. He knew she'd been crying upstairs and was now in a better mood—the air was soft from a sudden release of tension—but she was a woman who liked to turn the screws when she was pissed off. She kept mucking about at the sink. Housecleaning was another form of torture, obsessively performed by her, relentlessly inflicted upon him. Perpetually the loser (and the victor, because he knew how their arguments usually ended), he stood there, silently looking—really looking—at the profile of a tired, angry woman.

She was so beautiful. And not only that. He *knew* her beauty, had seen it grow and change over time. He knew how the shape of her body and her intractable mind fit together. He loved them both. He loved her as he had never loved anyone else in his life. He knew her inside out. Yet he did not understand her. His

acceptance of this extraordinary fact—she confounded him—
was the key to his happiness.

"Eliza."

She continued scrubbing a pot that no longer appeared to be
dirty. Because Martin came through Toronto so rarely, his unexpected arrival had wiped several things out of Andrew's mind.
He'd forgotten about Eliza's anxieties around driving in bad
weather. When the boys were babies, he hadn't driven at all during
heavy snowfalls or storms. She couldn't stand it; she couldn't control her fear, her conviction, even, that her husband was as vulnerable to death as her father had been. Which, of course, he was.

"Eliza, I'm sorry," he said. "I knew that if I spoke to you in person
you wouldn't want me to drive out there to see him."

"Because it was snowing."

"Maybe. But for the usual reasons, too."

Eliza disliked his famous brother, the anthropologist who wrote
bestselling books about communication across cultures, languages,
even species. Within five minutes of seeing Martin in her restaurant arguing with her front-of-house staff (he was demanding a
table without a reservation) she had nicknamed him I'm-So-Big-
and-Hungry. She claimed that she didn't resent his accomplish-
ments as a scientist, a writer, a spokesman for the U.N., even his
extensive knowledge of food and wine. "How could I resent any
of that? Okay, maybe I resent his food snobbery *a little*. But I get
it—he spends a lot of time in New York. What I *do* resent is that
everyone is supposed to be so impressed with him. Everyone
should accommodate Martin because he's such a *genius*."

After meeting him a few times, she'd asked Andrew if Martin
was lying about something. He'd stared at her, wide-eyed, and
said, "Not again. Please don't ask me if he's a spy. Why do women
always think my brother is a spy?"

She had made an impatient huffing sound. "I don't think he's a spy. I think he's a jerk. He's so mean to you. Disrespectful. Half the time, he talks to you like you're a kid."

Andrew laughed it off. "Ah, he doesn't mean it. He's just the older brother. He's jealous that I'm so close to our parents. He went out into the world much earlier than I did. I stayed behind, the careful son. I've always known that someone would have to take care of them and it would not be him." He kissed her. One of the things he'd found attractive about Eliza was her complete allergy to Martin, his charismatic woman-magnet brother. It attracted him still.

She wiped the water spilled on the island countertop back into the sink. "I wish I liked him, for your sake."

"That's kind of you."

"I try to like him, but he makes it impossible."

To this, Andrew had nothing to say.

"I hope you weren't drinking on top of driving in the snow."

"I had two glasses of wine. Small glasses. Martin drank most of the bottle."

"Typical."

"Eliza, he was flying to Brazil. He wanted to sleep on the flight."

"So why didn't he take a proper layover and come and have dinner with us? His *family*. Why didn't he come and see his nephews, who adore him? I wouldn't have minded that."

"He probably has to be in São Paulo at a certain time. He promised he would take a day or two next time. We'll take the boys and go visit Mom and Dad in Uxbridge."

"It would be nice if he could think about you, too. *Your* life." She hung the rag over the long neck of the faucet and carefully placed her hands on either side of the double sink. Gripped the granite edges. "And your mother's Visa bills. Did you guys talk about that?"

"I had two hours to see him, and months to catch up on. Come on."

"Come on, what? We cannot keep paying their bills. Your parents lost a ton of money. Your dad seems to get it, sort of, but your mother is living in a dream world. You *and* Martin have to deal with that. We cannot afford to foot three-thousand-dollar Visa bills for the rest of your mom's life. You seem to forget that we're trying to pay off the line of credit for the basement reno. And the flood cleanup. The weeping tiles installation, remember? We have a debt of eighty-seven thousand dollars. Sure, it's *my* line of credit, but it's money *we* owe to the bank. Instead of paying your mother's Visa bill, I wish you would help me pay down that fucking debt."

He exhaled, trying to keep calm. Was this a problem most women had, or was it just his wife? With her, one complaint led to another until he felt like he was drowning in a sea of discontent. If he told her not to be a nag, she'd be annoyed, but wasn't this nagging? He said, "Eliza. Please. I don't want to talk about this now."

"You never want to talk about it."

"Martin *has* given them money. He gives them money sometimes. He helps out."

"How much money? Five hundred here and there. Does he even know how much they lost when the U.S. housing market tanked? Does he know that almost all of your dad's investments were stuck in fucking *Florida*, foreclosure heaven?"

He laughed, cautiously. "Fucking this, fucking that. Language, cowgirl."

"Don't try to change the subject by shaming me for my western origins. It won't work. We have our own credit card bills to pay. Martin doesn't have kids. When he's in Europe, he rents out his little flat in New York for god knows how much money. He works for the U.N. Plus all those speaker fees. Let *him* take care of your parents for a while."

"You're going to have to let me deal with this family stuff in my own way."

"Okay. No problem. The family stuff I'd like you to deal with in your own way, then, is paying off the basement reno. That is *your* family stuff. You take it over."

"But I've been paying for the roof repair and the new washer and dryer!"

"You should have paid those off already. The new roof was three *years* ago, Andrew." She licked her lips, repeatedly, having nothing else in the immediate vicinity to clean.

Andrew glanced at the stove-top clock. Just after nine. He took a tiny step backwards, away from the island. "You know, I'm just gonna go upstairs—"

"And watch the news?"

"Well . . ."

"Paying their bills is not fair to *us. This* family." She suddenly craved an enormous blowout. Screaming and yelling. Or at least— because Andrew almost never yelled, it was one of the best and most aggravating things about him, his essential unflappability— she wanted to keep at it until they were both spent from squabbling. It was so hard to draw him into an argument. He preferred being passive-aggressive and forgetting to call and shrugging problems away. She reined in her voice and asked, almost nicely, "Where was Martin, anyway?"

"Borneo. He must have flown in from Jakarta."

"Borneo!" She groaned. "I wish I had just flown in from Borneo! No, I wish I was just flying *out* to Borneo."

A smile threw itself up on Andrew's face—a crow-foot-eyed, lopsided grin that he knew she liked. See? He would even flirt with her, not to get her into bed, sadly, but to extricate himself from an argument.

"Go!" she said, waving her hand toward the staircase. "Go watch the news. I'm packing my bags and catching the first flight to Asia."

Andrew allowed his smile to deepen, better crow's feet and more eye-twinkle. Passing a hand through his thick mess of dirty blond hair, he turned around. "Bon voyage," he said, and waved bye-bye.

She got the box of chocolate ice cream out of the freezer. She envied Martin his lack of responsibilities. He travelled all the time, often in high style. She even liked his books, goddammit. He'd been one of the earliest linguistic anthropologists to identify and research the link between the extinction of indigenous languages and cultures and the degradation of the habitats where they evolved. It had been a fascinating theory that was now a proven fact with far-reaching implications: the state of a human language could be an indicator of environmental health. Because of his books—adventure combined with high purpose—and his charm, he was an internationally popular speaker.

Though he'd never been popular with her.

Mr. I'm-So-Big-and-Hungry believed that the world owed him for loving it. Women especially were in his debt, because he was so sensitive to Mother Earth's deep power and terrible fragility. Puke. A couple of years ago, at a black-tie fundraiser, Eliza had watched him use that script to seduce the only single woman at their table, a pretty biology student from York University, there because she had won a science competition. Unlucky girl. He seemed to have everything he could possibly want and still wanted more. As he satisfied his appetites, they expanded. She was sure that, in bed, if he came first, he would do nothing to help his lover have an orgasm. A no-fingers, no-tongue kind of man. She laughed, quietly, and ate the last of her ice cream. Quietly, because if Andrew heard her, he would ask what she was laughing about.

Should she lick the bowl? Listening to the broadcaster's familiar voice from the second floor—it was that intrepid woman reporter they both liked—she applied her tongue to the convex glass. Licking chocolate out of a bowl reminded her of how horny she was. Instead of having an argument with her husband over his mother's Visa bill, she had intended to tell him about the pool Amazon and seduce him with a naughty bedtime story.

Damn Martin. She was glad he hadn't had a proper layover. He talked so much that he used up all the oxygen. She stood up abruptly and got herself one more scoop of ice cream.

When Andrew heard his wife snicker in the kitchen, he turned up the volume on the TV. The journalist Adele Tabrizi was reporting from the Iraqi border with Syria. The news segment was long and depressing. What Bashar al-Assad had not managed to destroy in his country was now being destroyed by increasingly violent groups of "rebels" and ISIS battalions. Andrew shook his head at the images of ancient cities ravaged by a fresh war. It could fall apart so easily, he thought, a country. A civilization.

He stared bleakly at the screen: women, men and children coughed and hacked, if they were lucky; if they were not, they lay motionless on the ground. Al-Assad had attacked his own people with chemical weapons. Many of the smaller bodies were already shrouded by thin blankets. The next report was about a homegrown war, local, historical, mostly ignored: the murdered and disappeared indigenous women of Canada, two thousand and counting.

Andrew listened to the end of that report, horrified and baffled. What to do with the world? He changed the channel. The remote control was a handy invention, and cable still a reliable opiate, despite the rise of the Internet, Netflix and smartphones. He landed on a popular family sitcom and watched in mild disgust as the TV parents engaged in a stupid argument in front of their mortified children. The laugh track aggravated him so much that

he muted the sound and listened longingly for Eliza. The water
was running again. He hoped she wasn't going to wash the floor.

She did not understand his family. Fair enough. Who could
untangle that knot of attraction and repulsion, love and duty, griev-
ance and debt? He was bound to them; that was all. And enough.
Each of them was flawed, as he was flawed; not one of them was
monstrous. He acknowledged that Martin was difficult. Despite
his charisma, he was adversarial with those closest to him, and still
angry at his mother for various things that had happened when
they were kids. But they *were* family. Andrew didn't like to think
of his brother changing planes in Toronto and not seeing anyone
he was related to in the city. Andrew had made him promise to
have a meal with their parents the next time he was in town. "They
miss you," Andrew said.

"Oh, please." Martin made a sour face.

"Mom is your greatest fan. She tells *everyone* about her son,
the famous anthropologist. She learned how to use Facebook and
Twitter just to follow you."

His brother laughed. "I know. She sends me private messages
all the time."

"Do you answer her?"

"Someone in the office does. I don't post that stuff myself, you
know."

"Martin! She's your mother."

"Yes, but if we didn't have the same last name, my receptionist
would think she was a stalker."

Andrew heard the light, crystalline chime of wineglasses from
the dining room below and looked expectantly to the stairs, ready
to get up and meet her. Then reconsidered; Eliza liked it better
when he played hard to get. She liked to draw him out of something else, toward her. He switched the channel back to the news.

8

Bodies

WHEN SHE FINALLY APPEARED WITH AN OPEN BOTTLE of wine in one hand and two glasses in the other, he was half-asleep on the sofa. "I'm here to salvage the evening," she said, and sat on the floor near him. Poured. She'd undone the top two buttons of her blouse.

"Salvage?" he replied, opening one eye wide and grinning. "Why 'salvage'? I had a great visit with Martin."

She handed him his glass. "Don't say another word about it. I've almost forgiven you."

He turned off the TV. They clinked glasses and drank. She settled back, cross-legged. "A young woman was flirting with me at the pool this morning."

"Uh-oh," he said.

"Beautiful woman. Black hair, big dark eyes. And tall. Tall and long. All long bones and muscles and the most gorgeous tits."

"Eliza!" He didn't like the word *tits*. It was a teenager's word. Reminded him of *teats*. "Besides, that's impossible. *You* have the most gorgeous breasts in the world."

She undid another button and popped both breasts out of her bra; the cups and underwire pushed them plumply together. She looked down.

"Mmm, see what I mean? Look at those!"

"I am looking. Hers were different, though. Not voluptuous like this. The dewdrop kind. Big nipples."

"You were really looking."

"She was right in front of me! She almost had a six-pack. And a scrumptious round ass. She's probably a personal trainer."

Andrew shook his head; Eliza could tell that he thought she was making it up for his benefit. She took another sip of wine, then walked on her knees to the sofa. Slipped her finger into the pool of wine in the bottom of her mouth. Lifted a drop to her nipple. "Who should lick it off?" She arched her back toward Andrew.

He leaned toward her and said, "The woman from the pool." He bent his head to lick. Eliza undid her trousers. He murmured, "Whoa, wild one. Let's go upstairs." He didn't like fooling around on the second floor; the boys' room was just a few steps away.

On the narrow flight up, he had his free hand on her hip, then the inside of her thigh. He shut their door; she put down the bottle and her glass and lit a candle. They undressed quickly. Two more swallows of wine, and they lay down, goose-fleshed, on the sheets, the duvet pulled away. It was pure delight for her, to be naked with sexual intent. She bit his shoulder. "Why don't we do this more often?" she asked. "We *have* to do this more often!"

Andrew didn't answer. He was above her, tonguing her nipple. He took the hard nub of it in his mouth, bit gently, licked again, bit harder, trying to get the reaction he wanted. A moan or a whimper. Instead she whispered, "It's not just a story. She really was there. I think she was flirting with me."

He squeezed her breasts, one after the other, and rubbed his penis between her legs, nudging. "Did she do this to you?"

"Well, she didn't have a hard-on. But she had a shaved pussy."

He misunderstood. "She shaved her pussy? Right in front of you?"

"Wow, that made you hard immediately. Maybe I should shave *my* pussy."

"She shaved her pubic hair right there? In the shower? What's going on at St. Anne's these days?"

She giggled and took his cock in her hand, gave it a squeeze. Hurrah! she thought. And said out loud, "I'm so happy!" They kissed like teenagers, lots of wet mouth and tongue. "It was already shaved. She showed up that way. Smooth! But she *did* shave her legs, right across from me. Which was kind of shocking. Well, I was shocked. I was the only other person there. Just me and a beautiful naked woman bending down, sticking her butt in the air. As I said, a beautiful butt. Nice and round. I wish my ass were rounder."

"Eliza, you have a lovely ass, what are you talking about? Turn over so I can look at it."

"She had her back to the wall much of the time, but still. One imagines."

"What does one imagine?"

She turned over and arched her back to lift her own ass up to him. "Her pussy, of course. Shaved. So tidy, like a new bud. Mmm." He started to massage her. "Closed flower."

"Isn't the pussy always like a closed flower? I mean, if the woman is just, you know, standing there."

Her voice was thoughtful. "Sometimes they're more open. Oystery. A little . . . frill. Every woman's different. I wanted to see it. And her ass. Bent right over like that in a public shower room." She gave a quiet mock howl.

"You really are horny." Eliza's legs were still closed, though as he massaged, he pulled apart the cheeks every once in a while and pushed his cock in between them, teasing, up and down, from one hole to the other, until the head was wet; she was already slippery. And swollen. She started moaning. Which meant soon she wouldn't really be able to talk. Sadly. She was a great talker, up to a point. Then she went pre-verbal. He leaned down and gave her neck a chomp; she squealed.

They often used to have sex this way, before the kids. The two of them would undress and conjure other people into bed with them: friends, sometimes strangers, that checkout girl from the Shoppers Drug Mart who was so proud of her piercing—who could ever forget her, sticking out her tongue to show it to them?— the handsome Japanese chef from their favourite sushi bar.

It was Eliza's doing; she'd shown him how to find sex everywhere, anywhere, and bring it home to play with. That's exactly what it required, playfulness, and these days most of their play went to their children. Eliza complained that it was unfair, how the latter (healthy offspring) cancelled out the former (the amorous activity that had created them). But Andrew didn't mind. With the boys, he had entered the expansive country of fatherhood. He adored his sons in a way that he did not adore his wife. That was healthy, he thought. Until his forties, he was sure he wouldn't have children. Then, unexpectedly, they had arrived. The having and the raising of them was the best thing he had ever done. It was true that he often preferred wrestling and looking at the stars with them to lying down naked with his wife.

This year he would turn fifty-four. He just wasn't as horny as he used to be, especially after herniating that disc two years ago. His physiotherapist's verdict: too much improper bending to lift up toddlers. It gave him a reprieve; he had a medical reason to stop thrusting. Eliza invested in some sex toys. Once or twice a month was enough for him, and he didn't notice if it was just once a month. Or once every two months. They'd seemed to reach an understanding. At least, she'd stopped complaining. When she started rubbing up against him and demanding some attention, he would tease her by asking, "Honey, who's counting?" To which she always replied, "Me. I'm counting."

He kept rubbing his penis up and down, hoping she would say what she usually said after that particular bit of foreplay. And she did say it. "Let me suck your cock." He loved his wife. She turned over easily between his long legs and wriggled down between them and opened her mouth, took him in, swirled her tongue around the head of his penis, mouth full, moaning; he felt her hand in the dark go down to touch herself. Greedy. She would come once, quickly, out of pure and seemingly mechanical lust, then again, with more intent, after he pushed inside her. He loved it when she came first on her own like that, partly because he could watch her, partly because she was so tight after an orgasm. He knew this about her; it felt like an extraordinary secret. Or was it just . . . anatomy? It didn't matter; he had never known a woman's body so well.

He loved entering her just after she came, and, sometimes, if it had been a long time and if he rubbed up close, right on top of her with his thrusts, she could come again without touching herself with her fingers. Occasionally, while all this was going on, she would manage to keep talking about their invisible third lover, though usually she became the invisible one, and emerged on the other side, known, unknown, this hungry, lust-drunk woman he had married. Who was she? It shocked him when she said, "Fuck my mouth," because it had been months since they had had sex like this and somehow he had forgotten it, he had forgotten that this busy woman with her silver laptop and her smartphone and her slightly obsessive housecleaning could also turn into this naked animal. Were other women like this? He couldn't remember; it didn't matter. He obliged his horny wife, dropped down on his hands, braced his knees against the sheet and started to thrust his cock into her wet open mouth as though it were her pussy.

Against the underside of his leg, he felt the muscles of her shoulder working as she rubbed her clitoris, back and forth, back and forth, he knew the rhythm though he never got as good as she was at playing it with his own hand. He kept thrusting; her sounds turned into vibrations along his penis before they emerged as moans. She had once told him that sometimes it was better to have his cock in her mouth than in her pussy because it became more a part of her body. She liked the force of it that close, on her face, in her face, against the back of her throat, while knowing that she was also driving him on, eating him up, just like her vagina took him in, pulled him in, the mouth of her cervix open, hungry. Sex was always about consumption, in one way or another, tender or violent consumption, eating, merging one part into another. He stared down at her face as his cock went into and out of her mouth. Then he had to shut his eyes, to make sure he didn't come.

He knew she was close herself: her breath was faster, louder. It made him want to come, too, but he held on as her orgasm began. He knew she would be annoyed if he followed her lead and came himself. He loved the sound coming out of her, over him, on him; the moans and cries pouring rough and loud over his penis. He could feel her hips bucking on the bed, knew that her muscles were tightening so hard around her fingers that for a moment she wouldn't be able to pull them out, she was locked in. She slid her fingers out as he drew his cock out of her mouth and moved down the bed until his face was floating over her face and he felt her heat and wetness. Her legs rose and opened like a wishbone on either side of him and he pushed against her, trying to get in, pushing the head of his cock against the wet softness, that slippery, pillowed tightness; suddenly she gasped, rammed her heels into the bed and propelled herself away from him.

"Fuck! I'm so horny I forgot I'm ovulating. Or have ovulated. Or will soon. Dammit. I wonder if any sperm got in there just now. I'll get a condom for you, you *have* to fuck me. Penetration is the priority here. Don't go anywhere."

"I can get one. Just give me a second."

He jumped up and disappeared into the bathroom. Listening to him rummage through the first drawer, she groaned. He seemed programmed to forget where things were located in the house. He needed a domestic GPS. "Andrew, they're in the bottom drawer. On the right side. You know, that purple box." Another drawer drew open, slid shut, hard. Like my libido, she thought, closing her legs and pulling the duvet up over her slowly chilling body. She sighed. A neural ghost of anger floated through her brain. That he hadn't called about missing dinner. Had gone out with Martin.

From the bathroom, Andrew called, "Sweetheart, I'm sorry but I can't find them."

It was a good thing that she'd had an orgasm already. "It's all right." She hopped out of bed and walked blinking into the starkness of the bathroom. He stood there naked, the bottom drawer open in front of his ankles. She cupped his balls and kissed him, hoping to encourage the slowly departing erection to return. "Come back to me, darling," she whispered. "Don't leave me like this." Andrew did not laugh or smile. She kneeled down to rummage around in the bottom drawer. "I looked," Andrew said. "They're not in there." She shuffled a tube of first-aid cream, looked under a box of Band-Aids. She held up the box. "Here they are, darling. Come. Watch me in the mirror for a bit. That will get our friend to return." She closed the drawer and walked on her knees to his thighs, then leaned against them, making him walk backwards until he was in front of the mirror. She already had a condom in her hand, the little square silver package torn open.

"Put your hands on my head," she instructed. He obliged, and pulled her head, her open mouth, toward him. "Now think of the shower room." She licked. "Bright light like this, and two women taking a shower together." She put her lips against his penis and talked. "Kissing and touching each other. Tonguing." She demonstrated. He started to get hard. "And you walk into the women's change room by mistake. It could have happened this morning, really, there was nobody but us at the pool. And we wouldn't have minded if you'd been there. The tall woman waves you in and gets down on her knees and starts sucking your cock. Just like this."

She knew his penis so well. It could be timid, worried, preoccupied, but some tongue and storytelling restored it to its assertive self. She knew he was looking down her back to her ass, which she stuck out for his benefit. She pulled her mouth away to say, "She has the most beautiful ass. And I say, 'Go behind her and push your cock into her pussy. I want to watch you fuck her. Fuck her for me."

Andrew was so into it that he was going to do exactly as he was told but Eliza jumped up, grabbed his hand and said, "Let's save our knees and go back to the bed." She was so pleased with her success at restoring his hard-on that she skipped back to the bedroom and threw herself spread-eagled on the mattress. The condom was in her hand; she slid it onto him. And there he was, above her, finding home; his cock pushed in slowly, impressively. He had the discipline to tease her. She moaned, and grabbed his ass, and pushed herself farther up. Right now she didn't want any teasing. The last two months had been one long tease.

She was wet from her orgasm. She whispered, "Andrew, please don't make me wait any more." She felt him pull out a little and brace himself to thrust, which is what she wanted. Needed. It was need, to have his cock push in there and open her, reach into the centre of her body, to her heart way up there, past her clit, through her pussy; she knew he could go all the way in, through her cervix, her uterus, in and in and in, to penetrate the tiny egg floating down, waiting for the teardrop of sperm that might escape from the edge of the condom. The thought of getting pregnant again made her suddenly hornier. "Please just fuck me. I want you to fuck me."

He paused. "Shh. Sorry. Do you hear that?"

She didn't care; she didn't want to listen. If it was a burglar, he could take the silverware, the computer on the table, the Cuisinart, her wallet on the sideboard. . . . She knew it was not a burglar, but Andrew had stopped; he lifted himself off her like a man in mid-push-up, his head held in the tense aspect of listening. She sighed, loudly. That was just like him, to hear a sound at this moment when much of the time she wondered how soon he was going to need a hearing aid. "What is it?" she asked, though she could hear it now, too. "He's just down in the kitchen getting something to eat. You didn't have to stop. It's like you stopped on purpose!"

"I did stop on purpose, to try and figure out who might be in the kitchen at eleven thirty at night." He moved off her body and folded up into a sitting position.

"You know it's our son. He's getting a midnight snack." She sighed again. Andrew didn't like to have sex when the boys were awake.

In a voice of genuine perplexity, he asked, "Why is he doing that?"

"He's going through a growth spurt or something."

"Do you want me to go down?"

"On me," she said, grabbing her crotch. "On me!" He didn't laugh. Good thing. She wasn't really joking.

"Eliza, please don't be upset. I'll just go see what he's up to."

She gasped. It was that bad: she was at the gasping level of indignation. "I'm sick of this."

"What?" Though he knew. But he also knew that she needed to say it. At the moment, it was the only satisfaction he could offer.

"It has been *months*. Since before Christmas. Since before Christmas *shopping*. Which I did *early* this year."

He heaved his own sigh. Which reminded her, precisely, of Marcus. Also given to the dramatic sigh of disappointment, her oldest son was in the kitchen two floors below, eating chocolate ice cream or (she hoped) Cheerios. She heard the spoon clank against the bowl. And, now, because she had begun to listen carefully to keep herself from saying anything else, she could hear that he was humming a little accompaniment. It was that Korean YouTube hit: "Gangnam Style." *Ooo, sexy lady*, sang his little counter-tenor voice. God help me, she thought. Though she had not believed in God for a long time.

She said, "Don't you find me desirable anymore?" There it was again. That troublesome old word. *De sideris*.

"I do. I do find you desirable. But I'm tired. I'm older than you by more than a decade."

"Don't start with the age thing. Please. You're fifty-four. So what. Men in their fifties can still have sex once a week. Once a month!"

He shrugged. "I just . . ." Guilty resignation suddenly flipped inside out. "Couldn't you be more relaxed instead of keeping an orgasm chart and demanding another star? The pressure makes the whole idea of sex so *stressful*."

"I never even complain about it anymore. We rarely even *mention* sex, let alone talk about it."

"But you always act like you're . . . starving. It's *not* starvation, you know. Sex is not as important as food."

"Sex is *more* important than food because we already *have* food!" She realized, belatedly, that she was almost yelling.

From the second floor came the call, "Mommy!" Jake. He was crying.

"Great," said Andrew. "They're both up now. Just like old times. I'll go."

"Never mind. I'll do it," she snapped, wanting him to feel guilty. And unhelpful. He *expected* her to do night duty. "They go to sleep faster with me."

Jake's crying intensified. He howled, "Mommy! I had a bad dream! Where's Marcus? I had a dream of a big crash!"

Eliza was already off the bed, pulling on a T-shirt and sweats, muttering under her breath. That child. He was connected to her by some as-yet-undiscovered genetic telepathy. Earlier that evening, while snow-shovelling and secretly worrying about Andrew, she had thought about her dad's death, wondered about the car accident; she'd never asked her mother about the details. And Jake had suddenly lifted his head out of the snow, looked right at her, and said, "Mommy, don't be sad about Daddy. I'm an angel!" How long would this thought transference continue to work? She knew what he would tell her through his breathless sleepy sobs. It wouldn't be a train or a plane or a building. It would be a car crash—the spectre that had haunted her all evening.

The feeding and calming took forty minutes. She timed it; the boys had a digital clock on their dresser. Once again, and metaphorically for the rest of her life, she lay sandwiched between her two children. She looked at one, Master Marcus of the mysteriously Asian eyes, long dark eyebrows pointing toward his temples, his dark, thick hair already sticking up here and there where the horns were poking through. He slept curled up, his back pushing hot against her, like an athlete crouched and frozen before the starting gun goes off. And Jake, the milder child, brown hair with blond sifted in, like hers, every part of him rounder and softer than Marcus. The toddler reappeared in slumber, his hands together in prayer position, tucked under his pillow-side cheek. From the time he was born, he had slept that way; he must have rested like that in the womb. His blue eyes were not quite closed; she could see a grey-blue sickle of iris. Then, as she watched, they swivelled back and forth under their blue-white lids. Her sons were dreaming a million miles away from her, and yet were right here, pushing against her flesh.

She would lose them. She knew she would. That was the whole

outrageous point of parenthood. You taught them to walk so they could walk away from you. You raised them well so they could move far away for university and forget your birthday and love other people and want to go to Barbados instead of suffering through Christmas with their parents.

She carefully dislodged herself. Then she lifted Jake and managed not to drop his little wrestler's body onto his bed. What toddler? He weighed almost fifty pounds. She pulled his dolphin quilt over his torso and looked back and forth, from one boy to the other. How had either of them ever been so small as to fit inside her body? More improbable, she had *grown them* in there, with her blood—it was science fiction, the basis of *Aliens*—then pushed them out into the light and air. Birth was ridiculous. And banal. It happened every day, over and over. Yet each time was always the first, like falling passionately in love.

She turned off their little lamp, thoroughly awake. It was after midnight now. She heard Andrew snoring. Should she clean the boys' filthy bathroom or go upstairs, get the Wave and masturbate down the hall in the TV room? Since she'd walked up the stairs, wine in hand, penetration had been the goal. It was still stubbornly there, the physical longing. But the sharpness had dulled. That's married sex, she thought; the sharpness dulls. The Wave—the model's actual name—was a large, marine-blue dildo. Lately, she and the Wave had developed a deep bond. A very deep bond. It was consistently dependable. Always available. Happy to do the job. Housework or the Wave? Orgasm or sleep? She shook her head. There was no *door* on the damn TV room. And the office, which had a door, was a mess of her and Andrew's paperwork. It was also a guest room, with a single bed lining one wall, but the bed was covered with a hundred student papers and at least two dozen textbooks. Never mind. There was always the morning. Not for sex, anymore, but for masturbation. At least Andrew got up first with the boys. That was why she did middle-of-the-night duty, she thought, more generously: Andrew let her sleep for another hour in the mornings.

She went up to the third floor and lay down beside him. Breathe deeply, she said to herself. Don't just *sigh*. She went through the yoga thing, relaxing her shoulders, her jaw, her forehead. It was helpful to do nothing but breathe. Difficult to breathe and not think. To think of nothing but breathing. She sank straight down, weighted with the fullness of the day, the fullness of her life, into a dreamful sleep.

9

Firefly

ANDREW PUT HIS HAND ON ELIZA'S THIGH, NOT TO encourage her, but to try and keep her quiet. They were at Maliq and Heather's place, sitting side by side in the glittery, mirror-filled dining room with three other couples. The first course, almond soup, had been a little watery, it was true, but why did Eliza have to offer *three* different suggestions to thicken it? He squeezed her thigh. She concluded, "Adding a third of a cup of ground almonds would be enough." Heather made tight bobble-head nods, her blonde hair bouncing on her shoulders. Andrew moved in to do a quick repair, smiling into his hostess's eyes. "I loved it this way, Heather. It's so light!"

The woman was in an obvious rivalry with the chef Eliza *used* to be. This had happened before; Heather had made dishes that used to be on Thalassa's menu. Did she realize that she was competing with a woman who no longer existed? Jealousy was probably the most ungovernable emotion, Andrew thought, mopping up the last of his soup with a chunk of bread, because it's rooted in the imagination. Heather *imagines* that Eliza's cooking is excellent, superior to her own. He longed to tell her about the overcooked leftover spaghetti he'd packed for lunch.

Dinner parties were easier at their house, not so uptight. Heather liked her table to be over-the-top lavish, with real china and silverware, candles, an embroidered tablecloth. It was beautiful, but for what? He'd come thinking that this time it was just a casual get-together. The wives worked together on the school council's spring fundraiser, which was a big kiddie fair with a silent auction. Eliza contributed organizational advice and a couple of Fleur gift cards. He glanced at Maliq's nicely detailed jacket and felt underdressed in his old sweater. Maliq was a corporate lawyer who always looked like he'd just walked out of a *GQ* ad featuring Distinguished Older Gentlemen. Big deal, Andrew thought. As a mathematician, I'm in touch with the sublime no matter what I wear. He smiled magnanimously around the table.

Seated across from him were John and his wife, Zi Lan, a stocky, scrubbed-looking woman wearing fire-engine red on her beautiful lips. (What chemicals must be in lipstick, he wondered; she was eating energetically, but the blazing colour did not fade.) He knew Zi Lan from the boys' school; she dropped off her seven-year-old every morning with the rest of her brood in tow. What did John do again? An engineer of some kind? Of bridges? Highways? He had close-shaven tawny hair; a tensile, straining look flicked over his face, into and out of his eyes. When Andrew glimpsed John, now and again, through the flowers, it was like catching sight of a chained coyote. Obviously the flowers weren't from Fleur; the arrangement was too tall and English-garden blowsy. Eliza's dinner party flowers were compact yet voluptuous little sculptures, in one or two colours; they sat low on the table so guests could see over them. He knew she would mention this to him after they left.

"Andrew? Don't you think so?"

"Sorry? I was busy admiring these lovely flowers."

Heather blinked an eyeful of gratitude in his direction. In a flash of useless insight, he realized how unhappy she was. But why?

Eliza repeated, loudly, "I was just talking about how great it would be if we could find some *fathers* to participate in the fund-raiser this year."

She had that disturbing glitter in her eyes. What was up with his wife these days? She swung her head rakishly to the left, the right. "So, gentlemen, any takers? At our last meeting, we decided that our husbands should join us in our efforts." Laughter gurgled weakly round the table. "Who's prepared to do some good for their kids' cash-strapped school?"

Heather smiled. "Eliza, that's *not* what we were saying at the last meeting. At least, we weren't *all* saying that."

Zi Lan jumped in. "Don't you remember, Heather? We were complaining about the hours of labour we give to the school while our husbands are busy at work. Or playing on their iPads." She poked her tawny-headed husband in the side; he yelped in surprise and rushed without hesitation to the defence of manhood itself: "Women have a gift for school fundraising. Men have other gifts, like . . . rewiring the doorbell. And war. And understanding the stock market. We can't organize a bake sale to save our lives."

As Eliza put down her glass of wine, Andrew braced himself for whatever she was going to say. "You get war and the stock market and we get the school fundraising! Thanks so much. Does that come before or after nursing and teaching?"

"That's not what I meant—"

"That's how it sounded. And I understand the stock market, too, thank you very much." Smiling, she indicated her empty glass to Maliq, who was pouring wine on her right, at the head of the table. Andrew touched her thigh again; she swatted his hand away. "Come on, John, you've got a house full of children. A bake sale would be . . . well, a cakewalk! Contribute a few hours to the cause!"

"But that's *why* Zi Lan volunteers at the school, so she can get away from me and the kids. Especially now."

Everyone at the table knew that John and Zi Lan, a couple in their mid-forties, had an eight-month-old baby daughter. Andrew knew more, though, because Zi Lan was also a swimmer. Eliza had told him how the petite woman had stood weeping in the change room, two weeks overdue, her towel popped out like a tent over her legs. "Unexpected" did not begin to describe her pregnancy, she told Eliza. She'd been on the pill because their third child had somehow slipped in under the rim of a condom. With three small children, her career on hold, she and John already worn out, they decided almost as soon as they learned she was pregnant to abort. But on the morning of the procedure, they just couldn't go through with it. Women and fertility, Andrew thought, equalled a veritable minefield. He smiled at John. "How is your new baby girl?"

John beamed, despite all the talk of being tired. "She is *gorgeous*. We adore her. But we've stopped sleeping. Sleep is for wimps. We don't need sleep."

Zi Lan piped up, "Oh, stop being so macho!" She looked around at her friends. "Four kids under seven, my friends, and two still in diapers. Tonight is the first time we've been out together in *over a year*. John asked me whether we should go to a hotel room or to the dinner party." Everyone laughed.

John said, "We decided we needed adult conversation more than we needed sex."

"Really?" Eliza asked.

Zi Lan said, "*You* forget what it's like, to be surrounded by children and Cheerios all day long."

"No, I don't," Eliza replied. "My brain atrophied, even though I worked part-time with both of them."

"It's the breastfeeding!" Miriam cried out. She was a doctor and medical researcher who studied the effects of various drugs on aging bones. "I lost whole chunks of my memory with each kid. I should be studying memory loss, not arthritis!"

"Amazing, isn't it?" Eliza said.

"What's that?" Heather asked brightly. Andrew heard in her nervous voice how much Heather wanted to change the topic.

But Eliza was just getting started. "It's amazing that we keep having kids. What the fuck is the human race thinking? The planet doesn't want any more of us!" Heather frowned at her—the word *fuck* did not match her china, admittedly—as Eliza forged on. "Really. Don't you ever ask yourselves if it was the right decision?"

Miriam's husband, Simon, the fashionably bespectacled architect, said, "We only allow ourselves to ask that question about our cat. The little bastard has started peeing on the sofa." Frowning at Simon's language, too, Heather said, "But children are not pets."

Eliza clapped her hands. "Exactly my point! So much more is at stake. Parenthood is a monumental undertaking. Why don't we talk about it more honestly?"

John said, "You mean, how much we regret having sex that one time, the shag that produced yet another baby?" Zi Lan hit him, not so lightly.

Miriam said, "No one wants to talk about regrets when it comes to their kids. Regret sounds like the opposite of love. And someone might call the Children's Aid Society on you."

"Tell me about it!" Zi Lan said. "Last week, I left Xander in the wagon for about twenty seconds by himself at the bottom of our porch steps—I just had to run up the stairs and grab something I'd forgotten by the door—and some older lady walking by told me that if she ever saw the child unattended again, she would tell my employer! She thought I was the nanny. When I told her I was Xander's mom, thank you very much, she said, fine, if there was a next time, she'd call the police!"

"What? What a racist bitch!" Eliza was incensed, as were the other guests. Righteous indignation flared around the table like a brush fire. Andrew sat back. No matter how right righteous indignation was, its blindsiding power almost always made him uncomfortable.

Eliza wasn't letting it go. "That's what everyone fears, right, even a total stranger—your child is in constant danger of being snatched away by a monstrous sexual predator!"

Zi Lan said, "Yeah, I should've asked that lady what *she* was doing, hanging around my unattended child. . . ."

Missing Zi Lan's ironic tone, Heather asked, seriously, "But women aren't sexual predators, are they?"

Eliza immediately responded, "Not the way men are . . ."

Andrew squeezed her leg.

"What?" Eliza snapped, turning sharply toward him. "It's true, men are—"

Andrew interrupted her in a surprisingly stern voice. "What's true is that predators rarely look the way we'd expect them to look, male *or* female." Everyone stopped talking and stared at him, expecting him to hold forth, but he did the opposite, and deftly steered the conversation away from predation of any kind. "Miriam, didn't you say something just now about regrets?" He grinned at her. "I can't believe *you* have any regrets." Through a common friend at the university, Andrew knew what the other guests did not—that Miriam had just accepted a prestigious endowed chair in the Faculty of Medicine.

Miriam tilted her head thoughtfully. "Regret is natural. I like to think of regret as a measure of wealth. Not necessarily material wealth, though a wealth of choices usually goes along with money. I could have chosen to live a different life. But I did not. I chose this one." She looked around the table. "We all have lives we didn't lead. Don't we? Sometimes it's a pleasure to think of those lives. And a luxury, I know. I could have gone to Boston for work. I was offered an excellent job right out of med school. Big pharma."

"Big bucks!" chimed in Simon. "We would have been rich!"

Miriam raised a finely plucked eyebrow. "Uh—no, dear. *I* would have been rich. And most likely, I would have married somebody else. An American."

He waggled his head back and forth. "All rightee then. I don't think this unlived-lives conversation is such a good idea. If my wife leaves for Boston next month, Andrew, you'll be hearing from me."

Miriam gave Simon a withering look. "It won't be Andrew's fault." Again she sought the eyes of her friends around the table. "Don't we all wonder, *what if*? What if I had chosen another life? We all have moments of doubt about the choices we make. Don't we?"

Eliza exclaimed, "Yes! What a great toast!" She raised her glass and waited for the others to do the same. "Here's to our doubts, not our certainties!" She tossed back her wine in one go.

Andrew removed his hand from her leg, turning her loose. He could only sit back and hope for the best. She leapt into the conversation, asking point-blank, "But Miriam, why *didn't* you take that job?" He hoped that she wouldn't ask poor Zi Lan if she regretted cancelling the abortion. His social life was full of episodes of not knowing what Eliza would say, or ask, or how people would respond to her directness. Sometimes it was awful. But it was also thrilling, and occasionally hilarious. He did not know where her curiosity and brashness would lead them. Which is why he followed.

At the end of dinner, Andrew announced, "That was delicious, Heather. Another wonderful dinner." Murmurs of assent rounded the table.

Eliza winked at Zi Lan. "And it's probably not too late to get a room. You know, fit it all in."

"So to speak," said John, guffawing. "But where could we go?"

In his lordly baritone, Maliq announced, "Upstairs. To my study. But you'll have to move all the guests' coats off the sofa." Surprised that Maliq had taken up the joke, his guests took a moment to laugh, but laugh they did. It was as though a window opened in the room.

"That's what used to happen at the *best* parties!" said Simon. "Sneaking off to the spare room."

"Yeah, when you were eighteen," said Miriam, drily.

"Eighteen?" John echoed. "I never saw the inside of a spare room until I was at least twenty-three." He tipped his glass to Miriam. "Late bloomer."

Maliq opened another bottle of wine. An erotic firefly flitted through the air, lighting upon each guest; they turned to each other, laughter erupting at a more private joke, or at nothing, just for the pleasure of it; they smiled into each other's eyes and wine-flushed faces. Why, Eliza wondered, don't we talk to each other like this more often? Why can't we just *relax*? She reached under the table to squeeze Andrew's thigh. To encourage him, not to keep him quiet.

Just before the party broke up, the women discussed their next fundraising meeting. Miriam quietly asked Simon if he would be able to come home early that night, to take care of the kids. He looked at her blankly. Eliza blared in a union-organizer's voice, "What about it, husbands? *Can* we count on your support? Can you look after *your own offspring* while your wives *tirelessly* contribute to the richness of the children's education?"

"Tirelessly and without complaint," Andrew added facetiously.

Simon mock-saluted both Miriam and Eliza. "Yes! Yes! I'll be home early that night. God, it's like having two wives."

"In your dreams," said Miriam.

Simon shot back, "Are you kidding? *Two* of you telling me

what to do all the time? In my worst fucking nightmares!" Everyone laughed.

Still making jokes, the guests all trooped up to the salacious second-floor study to fetch their coats. Heather touched Eliza's arm before she went back down the stairs. Eliza stopped, turned to her, smiling, pleasantly drunk. Heather murmured, "You know, I've been thinking about the conversation we had at the beginning of the meal."

Eliza smiled broadly. "Which one?"

"When you were talking about feeling so ambivalent toward your kids."

"Wh-what?" She had no idea what Heather meant.

"I wouldn't say this to just anyone, but . . . it really helped me. You might want to see a therapist."

"Pardon me?" It came back to her now, something about children and regret. Had Eliza used the word *ambivalence*? Then she got it: it was a *joke*. Heather was teasing her. Eliza grinned.

Heather's expression faltered into an awkward smile, then grew more serious still. "Because it could be wounding them."

It took another moment to sink in: Heather was serious. The realization made Eliza start laughing. Shoulders seismically shaking, stomach muscles clenched, she managed to say, "Sorry. I don't know why I find that so funny. But." She took a big breath and wiped a tear from her eye. "Come on, Heather. It was an *adult* conversation. I love my kids. They're fine. *I'm* fine." And again. "We're *all* fine." She thought of Shakespeare—*doth she protest too much?*—and another bolt of giggles hit her. She apologized again. Andrew called out, "What's so funny?"

In the car on the way home, however, she was not amused. Andrew, having consumed his usual two small glasses of wine over three hours, drove confidently and legally through the snow-filled streets, a bemused expression on his face as he listened to his wife, who mocked in a singsong cadence, "I think you need to see a therapist!" She made a strangled, desperate sound. "I can't breathe!" Her voice abruptly became that of a TV broadcaster: "Woman chokes to death at dinner party on wad of political correctness!" Then she returned to her rant. "Doesn't she know that you shouldn't pair a white soup with chicken breast? That was all just too fucking white!"

"Eliza, that's not very gracious."

"Gracious! She just told me I need *therapy*. Heather's going to call Children's Aid and get a social worker to check up on me. Make sure my maternal ambivalence isn't causing rickets."

"Come on, you're taking it too seriously. Heather's just—"

"A control freak! Do you know that she sent me an email *and* a text this afternoon asking me not to bring up the aftermath of the Arab Spring because it would be too upsetting for Maliq? She must have sent *all* of us that note. She meant that it would be too upsetting for *her*. He's *Egyptian*, for god's sake, and he's not supposed to talk about what's going on in his own country. She wants to micro-manage everything. Including this damned fundraiser."

"Last year, you said you weren't going to do it again."

"Oh, I know. But Miriam begged me. And Zi Lan. What John said is the absolute truth. The only time Zi Lan gets to visit a few girlfriends is when she does slave labour for the school. Or goes grocery shopping. I hardly ever see her at the pool anymore but I always run into her at the supermarket. Kids and food in the wagon, baby in the pouch on her chest, babbling a mile a minute. The poor woman is desperate for adult conversation."

When she stepped into the house, it was so quiet that she thought Sophie must be asleep upstairs in the TV room. Andrew was still in the car, waiting to drive the babysitter home. When she heard a sudden shuffle and thump overhead, she understood viscerally that someone *else* was in the house, too, apart from Sophie and the boys. Fear folded quickly over her shoulders, slid around her neck. "Sophie? Are you up there?"

On the second floor, one voice murmured low and throaty, as another rose up to call, "Hi, Eliza! We just finished watching a movie."

Eliza exhaled. Right; she remembered now. Sophie had told her that a friend might drop in. She felt so relieved she sat down on the bench in the entranceway, her coat still on. Maybe it was her boyfriend? But no. Two girls came down the unlit staircase, Sophie in front of her friend, who remained in the shadows. No, not in the shadows. The girl was black.

Eliza had expected another white kid, Sophie's height, with purple or green highlights in her hair. This young woman was tall, model-tall, and had a mass of braids caught up in one thick twisted rope. And pretty. Eliza flicked on the hall light. No, not pretty. She was beautiful.

"Hey, Eliza, this is my friend Binta."

Binta smiled brilliantly and extended a long hand to shake Eliza's, with an almost formal grace. "Hello, Eliza," she said, thoroughly self-possessed. "Nice to meet you. Your boys are *so* sweet." Binta's fingers were warm.

Eliza let them go. "Thank you. I hope they were well-behaved. Marcus can be a Tasmanian devil sometimes. How did it go, Sophie?"

"They're always good for me. Neither of them wanted to go to bed—"

"So of course you let them stay up for an extra half an hour."

"That's why they love me! Breakin' the rules! They started watching the penguin movie again. Then we had them do some serious teeth brushing."

The girls put on their boots and coats; Sophie was wearing her little khaki jacket with the brass buttons, and Binta pulled a long copper-coloured coat out of the front hall closet. "Andrew has your money, Sophie, okay?"

"Thanks, Eliza. Do you think he'll mind driving us a little farther north? Actually, north*west*. Little Jamaica. I'm sleeping over at Binta's tonight."

"Does your mom know?"

"Yeah." The two girls exchanged a glance. "Yeah, she knows."

Eliza levelled her most serious gaze at Sophie. "You're *sure* she knows where you'll be?"

"Of course! Andrew will see Binta's house, too. Don't worry, I swear to god we're not going to some huge house party up the hill."

She looked from Sophie to Binta. "Girls, you know that parents are annoying only because we want to make sure you're safe. Right?"

Binta said, "Don't worry. I have a brown belt in tae kwon do. And I'm six foot one." She put her arm around Sophie's shoulders. "I watch out for this one, too, believe me. Little people need protection."

Sophie pushed her away with a laugh. "Get outta here! I can take care of myself. Jeez." She grinned at Eliza. "Don't worry!"

Binta added, "Seriously. My mom is waiting up for us. She's probably playing solitaire on her iPad right now. She and my dad can't fall asleep until I'm home."

"All right, go on." Eliza held up her hands: no more explanation necessary. "Thank you for taking care of the boys." A brown belt in tae kwon do?

The front door opened, closed. Through the sidelight, she watched the girls go down the steps and turn to wave, the blonde foot soldier and the warrior princess. Eliza waited until the car turned the corner, then locked the door and went to look at her boys.

10

Eggs

ON SUNDAY MORNING, WHEN SHE OPENED HER EYES,
she realized what was wrong with her. Therapy wouldn't be necessary. It was a mid-life crisis. She'd thought she was immune.
How could she have a mid-life crisis when the middle of her life
was so good?

But in eight years, she would be *fifty*. The juice would dry up,
along with the last of the rotten eggs. It was another brutal irony
of nature. She had spent twenty-five years trying not to get pregnant. (Both her pregnancies, though celebrated, were accidental.
When she had a screaming-with-colic newborn and a sick toddler
of sixteen months, she used to think: this is all a *mistake*!) In her
teens, through every month of her twenties, through the first half
of her hard-working, hard-partying thirties, she had been desperate not to get pregnant. Fretful and sleepless in the early morning,
she had peed on those damn sticks, bought condoms, tried different birth control pills (they all gave her migraines or made her
fat *and* moody), submitted to the diaphragm, spermicides, jellies,
even cramp-inducing cervical caps and IUDs, and suddenly—so
suddenly—here she was, on Sunday morning in mid-January,
flipping pancakes. She turned from the hot stove to consider the
inhabitants of her small kingdom. The boys were upstairs watching cartoons and chatting during the commercials. Andrew was

sitting at the kitchen table in front of a freshly opened newspaper. She knew, suddenly, what was missing. In a voice of undisguised yearning, she asked, "Darling, do you think we should have another baby?"

Andrew choked on his orange juice, spraying a mouthful of it onto the editorial pages of the *Toronto Star*.

After blowing his nose in the bathroom, he came back to the kitchen and put his arm around her from behind as she hovered over the frying pan with the flipper in her hand. "Eliza." He kissed her neck. "Eliza, my love. Yesterday morning we had a long conversation about me getting a vasectomy. You know that I'm seriously thinking about it. Is that why you suddenly want to have another baby?" He squeezed her. She shrugged him off and carefully turned the pancakes. It was her mother's recipe. The best pancakes in the world.

He returned to the kitchen table and sat down. "All the reasons that I should get a vasectomy—reasons we have enumerated often—are the same reasons we should not have another baby."

"I just—I—oh, never mind," she said. He blotted orange juice off the newspaper. They went through some variation of this drama almost every time she ovulated. After which she had PMS. He had come to think of PMS as grief for the lost egg. A few more years, he thought, will bring the peace of menopause. What was a year or two of hot flashes in comparison with these monthly hormonal surges and radical bouts of baby longing? The descent of the viable egg was an event of such moment in the house that Marcus knew what *ovulation* meant. Even Jake had a vague idea.

He watched her back. She was wearing a bright blue T-shirt and a tight pair of yoga pants, half-dressed in mid-winter to his elbow-patch old-man sweater and plaid slippers. Her light brown hair was tucked up on top of her head, a sexy little bird nest with bobby pins; it wasn't long enough for a proper chignon. From the back she looked twenty. From the front, to him, she also looked twenty, not that he had ever seen her at twenty, except in photographs. She was more beautiful than those old photos, that was certain. She was a curious mix—she had *gravitas* and confidence mixed with a propensity for the zany. There were old spirits and young spirits and she was the latter. Andrew had met her when she was thirty-three, a hyper-successful, frighteningly organized, cleavage-revealing dynamo. People in the restaurant business, he learned, have great stamina. To bed at two or three and up at eight or nine, six or seven days a week, because her place was downtown on Queen Street, close to the financial district.

It was the sort of über-cool restaurant that he rarely bothered with. Martin had taken him there while he was on a promotional tour for one of his books. His older brother had flirted with Eliza, to no avail; Andrew loved how she had rebuffed him with frosty humour. A week later, after Martin left town, he went back. Then returned a week later. He didn't always see her. He never quite figured out her schedule; sometimes she was acting as head chef, sometimes she moved around as a kind of queenly hostess, sometimes she seemed to do both. He went on Thursday and Sunday nights; she was always happy to see him if she was out in the restaurant. Then, occasionally, he could tell that she was waiting for him. He was seeing someone at the time, an attractive lawyer in her late thirties, who, on their fourth date, was suggesting baby names and speculating the worth of their shared real estate. He broke up with the lawyer a week after Eliza invited him to share a glass of wine. A month later, he asked her if she wanted to spend a few days with him in Istanbul. It was a quick, modern courtship, or an extremely old-fashioned one, depending on one's point of view. She went with him to Turkey for ten days. It was the longest and most exotic vacation she had taken since she was twenty-one and had cooked and slept her way around Italy and the Greek islands for a year and a half.

Mixing food and sex at her restaurant seemed to happen a lot. Not with the patrons. With her front-of-house staff, usually dark, whip-like young men. She told him about these brief, offhand relationships in a brief, offhand way, making two things clear: that she had enjoyed them and that they were finished. He permitted himself a feeling he had never indulged in before: sexual pride. Yes, he took her away from all those raunchy *boys*. He swept her off her feet in a great, exotic city and returned her sex-dazed and in love with him. After Istanbul, he strode into the restaurant conscious of how tall he was, how good-looking, how well-cut his jacket, compared to those pipsqueaks in their torn jeans. The hipsters would either scatter like cockroaches or smile obsequiously and ask him what he wanted to drink.

Andrew, with his university degrees and his international conferences, hailed from another world. He knew that, for Eliza, this was one of his best attributes. But he had others. He was trustworthy. While she was still learning how and when to say the reasonable thing, Andrew was naturally diplomatic. He had learned to accommodate his difficult mother, his bossy father and his complicated, flamboyant brother. In the small, competitive world of academia, Andrew was popular in a way that impressed Eliza, once she knew about the megalomaniacs, the territory-obsessed, the various fighters of the internecine battles in the department. He was charming, but also a good listener, a quality that she had rarely encountered in her lovers. Listening generously was a *womanly* art. But Andrew was extremely good at it. He enjoyed drawing people out.

One late Sunday morning at his place on Olive Street, almost a year after that first glass of wine, she made him a strong cup of Greek coffee and talked at length about how bored she was with the restaurant business. She had no time to do anything else but work. "I can't read! Never mind, you know, literary shit. Even magazine articles are too long. My brain is fried. I can't even go to a movie. The restaurant is like a prison."

From the beginning of the relationship she had hinted that she was trying to figure out how to reinvent herself. She wasn't afraid of reinventing; that was the thing. He admired her lack of fear. "Is there anything else you'd like to do, anything that attracts you the way restaurant work used to?"

She'd stared out the window into a twiggy tangle of forsythia. "Flowers. I love flowers. You should have pruned that after it bloomed *last year*. It would be full of blossoms now if you had." She was bossy. Most of the time, he didn't mind.

"What are you grinning at?" she asked. "If I hadn't started cooking, I would have gone into plants. But I put myself through university by working in food. When school was over, food was still paying the bills. I'm not going back to school now, though. I have a mortgage to pay." She owned a nice condo in a fancily renovated candy factory. "The restaurant business isn't exactly retail the way the flower business is, but there's enough crossing over. Both food and flowers are primal. That's the psychological draw. Did you know that Toronto gets most of its roses from Ecuador?"

"It sounds like you've been doing some research."

"I'm trying to figure out the numbers. Building a business is like doing a multi-layered moving jigsaw puzzle. Maybe that's the problem. With Thalassa, I know exactly what to do. It's starting to bore me."

"Why don't you sell it?"

"Because it's the perfect time to sell! It's popular, the economy's good, people are spending money. But like everybody in the restaurant business, I'm a masochist. I'll just burn out and sell at a loss during the next recession."

"If you really think that's what could happen, then sell now." He leaned across the table and kissed her. "Masochism doesn't suit you."

She raised an eyebrow over their breakfast leftovers. "Is an innocent spanking considered masochistic?"

"After two decades of being a well-behaved academic, you have turned me into a pervert in less than a year. What am I going to do with you?"

"I'll show you *exactly* what you can do with me," she said. And she did. Soon after that talk about the primal nature of food and flowers, Eliza got pregnant.

They married three months later. Two friends acted as witnesses at City Hall. That night she threw a huge private party at the restaurant. The next week, to the bewilderment of all but her closest colleagues, she announced that she had found a buyer for Thalassa.

At five months pregnant, she started a summer job in a flower shop as an apprentice, helping out during the wedding season. She met Kiki there, and shared her ideas about opening a shop of her own, mostly to do high-end events and weddings. They had just got Fleur up and running when she got pregnant again. Marcus was only seven months old. She had cried to Andrew, "But I'm *old*! I'm one of those mothers who can't *get* pregnant!" Yet she never mentioned an abortion; Marcus had too recently been in the womb himself. "The baby has to come, no matter what." Those were the words of his beloved pro-choice feminist. He had always thought that she was as rational as he was. He needed a practical person; he was a mathematician. But when it came to babies, Eliza was like a shaman whose totem animal was an alpha wolf bitch. The puppies were everything.

All the rationality in the world couldn't dissolve the mystery of making and carrying another life. The essential unknowability fascinated him during both her pregnancies, but lately, her passionate baby cravings just wore him out. The thought of sleepless nights filled him with existential weariness. He decided right there, sitting in front of his juice-soaked newspaper, that he would call Dr. Richmond on Monday and ask her to recommend someone to do the vasectomy. But he wouldn't say anything to Eliza about that just yet.

It was, after all, Sunday morning. The cream was whipped; he had done it with the whisk under her appraising blue-grey eye. A whole plateful of her delicious pancakes was warming in the oven and the Mexican organic blueberries sat in a green ceramic bowl on the table. The boys' cartoon was almost over; in five minutes, they were going to charge down the stairs, howling for breakfast.

In a nutshell: domestic bliss.

She glanced over her shoulder, a peace-making smirk on her face. "I feel you looking. I hope you're not thinking that my ass is getting saggy."

He shook his head. "Your ass is not getting saggy. You look like a twenty-year-old girl."

"Flattery will get you everywhere, but I will not stand for outright lies."

"That's truly what I was thinking. That somehow I married a youthful woman. A young soul."

"I'm Dorian Gray. You just haven't found the nasty painting."

"No, you're my Eliza. Eliza Keenan, lady of flowers."

She spun around and pointed the pancake flipper at him. "I think I should take advantage of this touching moment and remind you to move all those cans of paint on the third floor to the basement. Sometime *today*. And we should vacuum this weekend."

"How unromantic of you. I'm trying to woo you and you're being a taskmaster."

"Someone has to be a taskmaster around here or we'd be living in a pigsty. You said you would do it last month." He wished that they'd had proper sex the other night. Then she wouldn't be complaining about what he did or didn't do around the house.

"Mom! Maaaaawm! Are the pancakes ready yet?" Marcus's voice. The commotion began. Andrew rose to gather the newspapers from the table; a small cavalry came charging down the stairs. The room filled with the boys. After Eliza put the hot plate of pancakes on the dining-room table, she stood back and adored her children, the blur of boy flesh, shiny hair, Jake's missing front teeth, Marcus gathering knives and forks into his hand. Jake began to describe the underwater monster from the cartoon, half-boy, half-fish.

Feeling the intensity of her gaze on the boys, Andrew suspected her of conjuring the third child right then, who could soon be crawling somewhere on the floor, heading for the basement stairs, no doubt. Dr. Richmond, he thought. Head it off at the pass, the invisible third baby.

But he was wrong. The baby had dispersed like a drop of blood in water. Eliza had stepped back into the present. She shook the oven mitt off her hand and picked up the bowl of whipped cream; the smell of it rose into her nose as she carried it to the table and the boys' eyes grew round, gluttonous. They were fine beasts, her boys. She watched them indulgently as they each swiped a finger into the bowl of cream. This afternoon, she would take them tobogganing, up and down in the snow for an hour at least, under a sky that was blue, blue, blue, sun-struck, glittering. The sudden descent would be like flying. Or diving.

11

Spray

SHE AND JANET STOOD BESIDE EACH OTHER IN THE showers, pulling off their bathing suits. Janet was talking, but Eliza heard nothing. She was waiting for the Amazon, who had done her lengths in the far lane, faster than everyone else.

"Well?" Janet said, wringing out her bathing suit. "Don't you think so?"

Eliza dropped her head forward, shook it sideways, as though trying to get the ketchup out of a bottle. The water didn't dislodge. "What? I have so much water in my ears."

"Isn't sleeping over at a girlfriend's house every second weekend too much? She's only fifteen. I have no idea what they get up to over there."

"Oh, she seemed like a good kid. And a gorgeous girl. Like a model—"

"*You* met Binta?"

"She was at our house on Saturday night when Sophie was babysitting."

Janet said nothing, but scrubbed her shampooed head too hard.

"Uh-oh," Eliza said. "I hope it was all right that she went to Binta's place that night? She told me that you knew where she was going."

"Yeah, she told me. I just didn't know they were spending the whole evening together, too. Binta hardly ever comes over to *our* house. Do you think she was there for a long time?"

"Long enough to watch a movie. But, you know, she mentioned that her mom would be waiting for them at home, and I didn't get the sense that either of them were lying. If you think they're going out partying or something, you should just talk to her parents."

Janet closed her eyes and rinsed her hair, then resurfaced to say, "Sophie doesn't want me to. She says she doesn't want me to make a big deal of it every time she has a sleepover. She's an adult, she says."

Eliza laughed. "We were all the same at that age. I remember wondering if getting my driver's licence would make me a grown-up. Now I wonder if getting Botox will make me a bad feminist." They laughed, while Eliza thought that maybe Sophie was using Binta as a cover for a boyfriend. To go over to a boy's house, most likely. Sneaky! She didn't want to mention this to Janet, who had enough problems dealing with her ex-husband and her anti-social son, who was getting into trouble at school and wanted to go live with his cool father on the West Coast. Usually Janet griped about her son, or her ex-husband. Despite Sophie's fuchsia bustiers and tight tights, she was the responsible child.

"So you think I should call the girl's parents?"

"Sure. Sophie *is* only fifteen. You need to know she's safe. And why don't you just invite Binta to come and sleep over at *your* house?"

Janet made a face and sighed. "Children! My son will live in my basement forever and my daughter will move out before high school ends!" She turned off the taps of her shower. "Are you done?"

"Oh, it's just so nice to take a long hot shower. It's something I never have a chance to do at home. And I . . . I want to put more conditioner on my hair. It's getting dried out from the chlorine. No need to wait if you're in a rush."

Eliza became invested in the fiction of moisturizing her hair. It was all a joke, this Amazon thing, an electrical distraction.

When the Amazon came to shower, it would just be the two of them, like last Thursday. Except that it was Tuesday; the daycare swim class didn't arrive until later.

Where was she anyway? Chatting with the lifeguards? *Why do you care?* I don't care. I'm just curious. *Then why don't you go out there and see where she is?* If I went out there, it would be to ask when the spring swimming lessons are going to start. For the boys. That would be the legitimate question.

Eliza put a generous dollop of conditioner on her hair, roiled it around. She felt dangerously awake. Or high on hash—did anyone smoke hash anymore? Streams of water ran off the ends of her nipples, down her butt and her thighs. Yes, this feeling reminded her of good drugs. Or her first intense sexual experience. Which happened, coincidentally, at a public pool.

She was eleven. She already knew masturbation was wrong and bad, according to all the old guys who represented Jehovah. Not only did Eliza have to endure Garry the elder hanging around their house, she also had to attend a Monday night Bible study for teenagers. In fact, it was at a Bible study meeting that she had first heard and seen the word *masturbation*. It was in a pamphlet about sexuality. There was no definition of the word, except that it was *unclean*.

Her curiosity was piqued. According to the pamphlet, many exciting, attractive activities were *unclean*. An illustration showed menacing handprints smearing a clean white towel: that's what happened when girls let boys touch their bodies. Kissing was also unclean, because it could lead to more dirty handprints.

Worried that Jehovah would see her inside her own house, she went to the public library—surely He wouldn't notice her among the crowd—and looked *masturbation* up in the dictionary. Which led to another word she'd never seen before. *Orgasm.*

Her mother had explained, once, about the actual mechanics of sex, and how easily a boy could make a girl pregnant, and *what a disaster that is, Eliza.* Meaning, she supposed now, more dirty towel. But she'd never mentioned any of this obscure vocabulary, like *clitoris* and *climax.* The library turned out to be a wellspring of seditious, delicious, adult knowledge. After a brief search, the Dewey Decimal system sent her directly to *Our Bodies, Ourselves,* first and radical feminist edition. She spent two hours sitting on the floor in a quiet corner, poring over the book. The mysteries were unveiled in beautiful line drawings and explicit photographs. The clitoris! Masturbation! Orgasm! Men fucking women, women fucking men, women fucking *each other*—so that a woman was always on top, unless they were doing that side-by-side thing. And her mother had *never* mentioned that people lick each other *between the legs!*

That particular line drawing mesmerized her. It was so *unlikely.* She had a keen, wordless recognition of the doubleness of human sexuality, its wackiness and perfect logic—*everything fits together!*— the desperate seriousness of this behaviour and its wonderful comedy. Look, she thought, at their *bums*, and started laughing. Then quickly glanced around, to make sure no one could see what she was looking at. Shifting position, she felt how wet she was between the legs, which frightened her. Was she sick? Was that normal? Fifteen minutes later, from the pages of the book on her hot lap, she discovered that it *was* normal. The book could read her mind; it had anticipated the secret slippery work-ings of her body. She liked reading the Bible, most of the time, but any dunce could see that *Our Bodies, Ourselves* was an equally important book to have in the house. And there were no unclean towels in it.

She learned that one way to *masturbate* was by using the water spray in a bathtub or shower. Like looking the word up in the dictionary at home, this was something she wouldn't be able to do in her own shower, for fear that her mother, brother or Jehovah would catch her at it.

The public pool, like the library, was full of godless people, the neighbourhood kids she went to school with, the tough-talking brats from the military barracks, packs of loud teenagers who were always laughing at jokes she couldn't understand. God wouldn't notice her misbehaving; he would mistake her for someone else. He couldn't really keep his eye on every sparrow that fell to the earth, nor on every curious girl. That verse in the Bible was what her English teacher called hyperbole.

She started swimming more often. In the showers, when the coast was clear, she began by sitting on the floor with the slack, off-white curtain closed behind her. Then she pulled the crotch of her one-piece aside and opened her legs into the institutional-strength spray, wiggling around until other girls or women came too close, or until it started to feel too weird.

Eventually, she went beyond the weird feeling. The memory woke her like a slap, a disconcerting, pleasurable shock of sensation. She had almost forgotten; or not thought about it for many years. The first time she had ever had an orgasm was there, in the Mount Royal Public Pool shower rooms, behind the slack off-white curtain, with tile-squares imprinted on her bum cheeks. She didn't know what was happening to her, except that it was glorious and frightening, too, because uncontrollable. She staggered up onto her feet—her thighs were trembling—and leaned against the wall. Drenched inside and out, dizzy, she wondered if someone at the Kingdom Hall had made a big mistake. Did Jehovah *really* disapprove of something that felt so crazily good? She wanted, more than anything else, to do it again.

Suddenly, the Amazon appeared and yanked Eliza across thirty years, from one shower room to another. As she sauntered in, she pulled down one of the shoulder straps of her bathing suit and a breast popped into the air. The breast remained exposed, nipple erect, as she stood and fiddled with the shower taps on the opposite side of the room. Eliza was taken aback by the woman's brashness. Who let a breast bob around like that while they tried to adjust the hot water? You either keep the suit on or you strip the suit off. This was a come-on. And not subtle. It worked.

"Sometimes that shower doesn't get hot," Eliza said. "We don't know why. It's the slowest one to warm up."

"Ah, thanks. I'll use another one then." The Amazon turned off the taps and walked across the tile floor, just three, four steps, to the shower next to hers. It was a border crossing. Turning toward Eliza, the woman turned on the taps, the handful of breast looking around for a hand. The water poured down cold, forcing her to step back.

When it was warm enough, she stepped back into it. "That's better." Then she turned again to Eliza, the breast still out, round, gorgeous, not as heavy as Eliza's, and looked her full and directly in the eyes, without smiling. She said, "Sometimes it happens."

Eliza had no idea what she was talking about. "What? What happens?"

The woman raised her eyebrows and stepped closer. "Chemistry." She lifted her shoulders and hands in that classic "who knows?" gesture, then pulled down the other side of her bathing suit. Still looking at Eliza, she peeled the whole of it down her torso, her hips, her legs. She only looked down to step out of the suit and hang it on the taps. Eliza glanced at that finger-wide line of dark pubic hair that stopped at the cleft. On either side of the line, the woman's pussy was freshly shaved, spotted here and there with a few ingrown hairs.

As she stood up naked to her full height, she said, "My name's Shar. Rhymes with star. What's your name?"

"Eliza." Her tongue felt thick. It was too real, too fast. And she was married. And she was in the shower room at Annie's. She was a mother of two small children. And thoroughly married. To a man. Janet was probably still out in the change room.

"Nice to meet you, Eliza. Would you mind giving me a little of your shampoo? I forgot to bring mine."

"Sure. Here." She bent down and handed Shar the bottle. It was a neighbourly gesture—she had often shared with or borrowed from other women at the pool—but the long, slender bottle, passing hands, contained more than soap. Eliza was aware that recasting a shampoo bottle as an emblem of lust was completely goofy. But it didn't feel that way.

Shar said, "Thank you," and poured out some of the creamy white liquid, passed the bottle back. From the corner of her eye, Eliza watched her rub the shampoo into her hair, then gather up some suds and rub them over her chest and shoulders. She cupped her breasts in her hands, squeezed them together, let water pool there, in the cleft. Eliza felt lust gather in her mouth, her throat, her stomach, then funnel straight down into her clit. The craving was like a needle; it hurt, but she was already getting used to it. Her breasts ached; she felt like a teenager at a high school dance. What she had wanted to do to the other woman, she now wanted to do to herself, hold her own breasts, squeeze her own nipples to make the electrical lines connect, clitoris to nipples, nipples to fingers. She opened her mouth; water poured in. She swallowed it. Then she cocked her head back, let the water spray over her face so she had to close her eyes.

Now what? she wondered, unwilling to accept what was happening. The fantasy had walked into the shower room and was rinsing the horsetail shampoo out of her hair. Shar? What kind of name was that?

Shar turned off the water and left the shower room.

Eliza followed her. There was nowhere else to go.

"I thought you'd turned into a fish!" Janet crowed. She was in front of the mirror, dressed, hair half-dried. Shar walked to the far corner of the room, where her bag and clothes hung on pegs. Eliza grabbed her towel and watched in a daze as Janet finished putting on her makeup.

Eliza dried her body, rubbing the towel between her breasts, aware of how swollen she had become just from standing beside the Amazon. Janet was talking. Shar was silent, her face giving nothing away, though Eliza felt her attention. Eliza made perfunctory conversational noises in Janet's direction. She felt separated from her friend by an invisible glass wall. Janet's mouth was still moving; she tossed her face cream in her bag, hoisted the bag to her shoulder and looked Eliza hard in the face. "Okay?"

"Sorry?"

"Let's have a drink next week. Okay?"

"Sure, that's a good idea."

Janet said goodbye in a singsong voice and walked out the door.

The two naked women stood looking at each other from opposite sides of the change room. The Amazon was smiling, to herself, it seemed, not showing her teeth. Was it a challenge, that smile? Or an invitation?

Eliza did not ask. She walked over to her, lifted her hand and touched Shar's collarbone.

"Mmm," Shar assented, and Eliza felt the woman's voice in her own mouth. She traced the bone outward, to the muscular shoulder, her fingers skidding on the damp skin, continued down the biceps and paused a few inches above the elbow. The breast was beside her hand. She remembered this, from years ago, in Greece, the urgency but also the languidness of touching Thalia, how sex with a woman was not defined by the penis and its insistent path, searching for the way *in*, and then, once inside, pushing for orgasm. With a woman, the sex could go on and on, and on. This was sex, standing beside a woman she didn't know with her hand on her arm. Orgasm could subside and more touching could begin, not the old highway of penetration but another road, barely defined, meandering off into the forest, dipping into the riverbed, re-emerging into another geography.

The surprise. That's what she had forgotten. How surprising a body like her own could be. How intimately she could know that body before touching it. And not know it.

Shar made a quarter turn. Her breast grazed Eliza's hand, and that hand opened, did what it had wanted to do and closed on the warm globe of flesh, fingered the nipple. Shar breathed, "Oh, fuck," as Eliza took the nipple between her thumb and index finger. Squeezed, rolled the nub of it harder while feeling her own clitoris respond in kind. Shar dropped her towel on the bench and lifted her hands to Eliza's breasts.

Many thoughts rose, knocked, insisted; Eliza refused them all, floating instead in the sensation of being touched. The only admonition she paid any attention to was *Don't get caught*. She was attuned to the door, to both doors, the one leading out into the hallway of Annie's and the other that opened to the pool. There was no one there; she would hear the daycare workers because of the children, she was always aware of children but now she didn't hear any of them. The lifeguards had no reason to come into the change room. *Don't get caught, don't get caught.*

Shar lowered her mouth to Eliza's lips. The Amazon had a small but full mouth. Her chin was narrow, her jaw narrow, she was so different, and so familiar. Requesting tongue, Eliza opened her own mouth wider. Shar didn't comply. Eliza licked her lips, asking again. *No.* When she licked them a third time, she felt the Amazon's hand slide, sideways, between her legs. Shar leaned down and took Eliza's lower lip in her teeth, bit down, close to hard, and in that way, by the teeth, delicately held her entire body in position. Eliza gasped and opened her legs wider, hoping Shar's hand would do more than it was doing. Eliza began to make small, shy hip-thrusts, hoping to encourage those fingers up, inside. *No.* Shar bit Eliza's lip a little harder, then let it go, pushed her tongue into Eliza's mouth.

Was it possible to come just by kissing? Eliza stood perfectly still, hoping that Shar would finger her clitoris, that she would bring her to orgasm; it would happen so easily.

But she didn't. She just grazed the tip of her clit, back and forth, back and forth. Eliza wanted to cry. The top of Shar's thumb and index finger lightly grazed the outer lips, too. Eliza had to stop herself from grabbing Shar's hand, pushing her fingers inside. She knew that wasn't allowed. Shar had stopped kissing her; she slowly drew her face away. Her eyes were enormous. They stared into each other's eyes: that, too, was sex, a penetration so intense that Eliza dropped her eyes, unable to tolerate the intimacy of this stranger's gaze, a stranger who had pinned her, trapped her precisely as she had wanted to be trapped. Her eyes slid down the woman's long arm, landed in the flash of palm there, the hand held sideways, rubbing between her thighs, oh excruciating slide, the sharp saw missing its mark. The incompleteness of the pleasure hurt her. The sound was small, a trapped animal whine; she was making it. Her head dropped down, heavy, her mouth hung open, empty, as she watched Shar's hand sliding her open, saw the long thumb, the side of her index finger pull back, away, glistening and slick, then slide forward again. The smell of sex was stronger than that of chlorine.

Shar's hand suddenly went still. Eliza went rigid with protest: *Why did you stop?* The Amazon leaned back slightly. In the separation between them Eliza heard herself: she was panting. Shar lifted her glistening hand to her nose, inhaled the smell, then drew her tongue slowly up from the base of her thumb to the top of her index finger. Eliza felt a spasm radiate from her clit through the flushed swollen skin: the first rise of orgasm. As Shar licked the side of her hand again, slowly, like a large animal licking salt, Eliza felt that same tongue licking her pussy.

She stepped backwards, almost stumbled across the tiles. This was her side of the change room, where her things were. She sat, heavily, mouth still open, legs akimbo. The sides of her thighs were slick; she shut them and immediately wanted to open them up, lie back, spread, pull Shar's face into her.

Shar smiled a happy wolf grin. "Waaoow! That was hot!"

Together they heard the sound of the children coming down the hallway. Eliza grabbed her towel, wrapped it around her body. Shar stepped into her thong: three black elastic bands holding a small triangle of blue leopard skin over her pubis. Looking at her ridiculous underwear made Eliza remember how young Shar was. Eliza had never worn a thong, nor wanted to. But watching Shar pull up tight jeans over moist skin, wriggling her round buttocks out of sight, Eliza saw for the first time the appeal of this impractical item of clothing. It was like Sophie's pink bustier: stripper clothing trafficked into daily life, made *underwear*. On cue and straight out of a striptease, Shar peered over her bra-strap shoulder, campily bit her fat lower lip, and winked. Eliza's whole body responded to these gestures. She felt vanquished. Shar had slain her with sexual *clichés*.

Again, she wanted to cry. To sob out her frustration. Instead she said, "The kids are coming in." The sound of her own voice brought her back to herself, the self she normally was, not a horny teenager but *businesswoman mother wife upstanding community member*. The sexual blush became the reddened face of guilt. What *on earth* was she doing? She reached for her blouse. The door opened. A chattering stream of children poured in between the two half-naked women.

12

Tu Es Libre

IT WAS A LAW OF NATURE, LIKE GRAVITY: SOMEONE HAD to walk away first. They had already said goodbye. Shar grinned, turned on her heel and left Eliza standing on the snowy sidewalk with her face undone, the stormy weather right there in the blue-grey eyes. How beautiful it is, she thought, when a woman conceals nothing.

Shar was so happy that she was almost dancing. The planets were aligning, here it was again, confirmation that the universe wanted her *right here*. There was a public pool close to her apartment, but the water was freezing—not only in the pool but in the shower room, too. Last week, she'd heard from another swimmer that the warmest pool in Toronto was at St. Anne's. Indeed.

She walked quickly out of the neighbourhood and turned onto Bathurst Street, the wide, traffic-filled thoroughfare to the east. She was headed to a nail jockey place on Bloor Street. She hated nail polish—her fingertips felt suffocated—but Benoît loved it, the brighter red or deeper purple the better.

She took extra-long strides, swinging her arms. Toronto, baby! I had no idea! If Shar hadn't had a date at one o'clock, she would have invited the flower-seller home and eaten her for lunch. Then again for dessert. As it was, they'd chatted for a few minutes, then exchanged numbers and email addresses.

Eliza was married. Which perhaps explained why she was so horny. Shar jumped over a small hill of slushy snow. It was good, this level of loopy euphoria. Her broken heart was clearly on the mend. She and Giselle had split up—after a lot of ripping and tearing—just before she left Ottawa. This had happened in August, so the wound wasn't fresh. It wasn't only her work that led to the breakup. During their two-year relationship, Giselle's life trajectory had slowly clarified: after passing her bar exams, she would find a good job and have a baby. Or two. Perhaps three. Shar had always been clear that she did not want to have kids, but Giselle believed she would come around; eventually she would be happy to fill her house with spawn. Yes, Shar's little bungalow in Westboro would be a perfect starter home for the family. It became clear why Giselle had been so thrilled to discover that Shar owned her own home. She wasn't thrilled to find out where the money came from for the down payment, but she was a pragmatist. Shar was ready to finish her first career and start her second one, was she not? That's why she was doing her master's in psychology. The beautiful children (of their impossible future) would have a lawyer mommy and a therapist mama. Not.

Shar swung her arms extravagantly, letting the past slide away, pulling the present closer as one bare hand carried on up to her nose: she inhaled. Under the sea-creature saltiness, the woman's pussy smelled as smoky as lapsang souchong, her favourite tea. When she licked the back of her thumb, her mouth flooded with saliva.

She pulled off her hat and shook out her hair; the edges that had been poking out were stiff with cold. The sun shone brilliantly on the snow-lined street; she wanted it on her face. As she turned onto College Street, she wondered what the husband looked like.

Eliza was beautiful, small but round and luscious-looking. And those eyes! Dark blue-purplish-grey eyes, almost slanty. She was as white as a yogurt container, but something about her face made

Shar think that her DNA had been strained, a long time ago, through a gorgeous Mongolian. She had an aquiline nose in a broad face; she was both chiselled and soft. Often the features of striking people were contradictory; that's what set them apart. Eliza's husband could not possibly be as good-looking as she was; it would be unreasonable.

Usually Shar wondered what the wives looked like, though she liked both husbands and wives, especially when they came to see her together. One of her favourite professional activities was turning a woman in front of her man, even if the lesbian awakening only lasted for the date. Often these women were in bed with her as a favour to their boyfriends or husbands, a birthday present, or the fulfillment of some long-nurtured fantasy, and they were shocked by the intensity of sex with another woman. But Shar knew how to manage that surprise. Since adolescence, she had loved the transgressive act of kinking up straight girls. Women. They were *so* much more challenging and complicated than men. Men were simpler, in a good way: anatomically, orgasmically, conversationally, emotionally. She'd paid her bills by having sex with them since she was twenty, in her second year of undergrad at UBC.

When she reached her nail place, Pretty Luvlies, she stood at the plate-glass window admiring the jelly-bean-like display of nail polish bottles, gleaming in the sun. She didn't have time to kick the snow off her boots; Mrs. Shinx, upon seeing Shar, stuck her small head and large bouffant hairdo out the door, mouth open. "It too cold! Come insigh!" It was not a question. "You freese out here!"

"Mrs. Shinx, I like the fresh air."

"But you freese to death! Come insigh! I gi' you hot tea!"

Shar nodded; it was impossible to ignore her commands. Mrs. Shinx would have made a great dominatrix. Shar kicked the brick wall to dislodge the snow from her boots. Mrs. Shinx ushered her in and began to fuss over her, along with a pale young woman who didn't speak a word of English. A couple of other clients were in the shop, sitting on the big raised manicure chairs, reading women's magazines. Their toenails were drying, shiny black and matte blue, respectively. Ladies from the neighbourhood, she supposed. From Eliza's neighbourhood. Shar had a wicked impulse to start chatting, to see if they knew her. But she subdued her wickedness, slid her feet into the basin of hot water and closed her eyes.

Sex work was not the part-time job her hyper-educated immigrant parents had encouraged her to seek out. They had suggested she wait tables at a good French restaurant where she could make decent tips, which is exactly what she had been doing when one of her regular customers asked her out. She had smiled, kindly. He was a polite guy, generous. And, surprisingly, French. He always defaulted to French with her. It was their little bond. Her co-workers knew that he liked to be seated in her section. But to go on a date with him? Not only was he a *man*, but he was ancient, certainly in his late forties. Almost ugly. She lowered her voice. "*En général, je préfère les filles.*" He nodded, held her gaze. He did have that broken-nose handsomeness, a hybrid of Bill Murray, Gerard Depardieu and Harvey Keitel. He quietly responded, "I would be happy to pay you for your time." His tone was neither sleazy nor pushy, just matter-of-fact. "Only one date. In public, for a meal or a movie. If we enjoy ourselves, we can try it again. Several times. Then you can think about whether or not you would like . . . *more*." He smiled. "For more money. Of course."

Still smiling, she shook her head but slipped his card into her pocket. She was surprised, but not horrified, or insulted, or disgusted. She was intrigued. It was an opportunity to try to be unafraid. To not hate them. Men. Those fuckers. And to make some money. In her tiny apartment in Kitsilano, she flipped open her computer and looked up his name (Benoît Martel), his company (Essler Systems, computer security) and his contact information. The North American headquarters were located in Quebec, but the company was French. She found a picture of him at a hospital fundraising event in Montreal.

How much would a wealthy man pay for a date? Just a date. She would have to negotiate the money over the phone; in person, she would just accept whatever he offered. But what was reasonable? In the late 1990s, escort agencies in Vancouver were online, but it wasn't so easy to find independents with websites to check out.

Not that she was going to have sex with the guy! She was just considering dinner. She turned to the yellow pages. Page after page of ads for escort agencies! Could there really be that many men in Vancouver who wanted to have sex enough to pay for it? She called a couple of the numbers; blushing hotly, she told them about the date proposal. Both receptionists asked for her height, her weight and her age, then they told her to come in for an interview as soon as possible. They also told her the going hourly rate for various jobs. But, she explained with an earnestness they must have found touching, this wasn't going to be a massage or a blowjob. Really! It was going to be dinner and a literal walk in the park.

She decided to overcharge him. That way, he would say no, rescind his offer, and hopefully keep tipping her well at the restaurant. At $100 per hour, she reasoned that an average dinner would stretch over two or three hours; it would be more and easier money than she made waitressing. She wrote it all out first, exactly what she was going to say, and practised aloud, in French and in English. If he decided to switch languages to flummox her, she'd be prepared. Ten days after he'd given her his card, she called him and calmly named her terms. When she heard him smiling through his agreement, she almost changed her mind. What was so funny?

Instead, she wrote the number one down on the notepad beside the phone.

1 1 1 1 1 1 !!! 1 1 1 1 1 1 1 1

She would go out with Benoît *one time*. If there was anything off about it, any scent of danger or coercion or even of him laughing at her, the first time would be the last.

After the phone call, she sat at her desk, tapping the pen so hard that it made holes in the pad of paper. She was not afraid of Benoît Martel. But maybe she was missing some instinct, the protective gene for fear, because she hadn't been afraid of that other man either, two years earlier, in Marseilles, a man with a nice accent and a big yacht in the beautiful old port. *Right at the far end, a view to the open sea. Some friends are coming by for drinks. Join us!* He, too, had seemed decent.

The shock. Even as it began—so quickly, he was waiting for her, hoping she would come—she could not believe it was happening. Inside the well-lit, glittering boat, the music thumped under her head. There had been no other friends but a knife. And rape, repeatedly, each entrance forced, quickly or slowly, sometimes the knife on the teak bench beside them, sometimes the knife held close to her neck, the blade slicing her skin open, lines like long paper cuts as he swore at her and rammed away. The circulatory systems exam flashed across her mind—92 percent was her mark, she was such a smart girl. There were two major vessels in the neck, the carotid artery, the jugular vein, serious damage to either could result in death. She thought about that until finally he ejaculated inside her and took the blade off her throat, smacked it down like a hammer on the teak bench above her head. Still he didn't get up; he pushed his weight down on top of her, squeezing the air out of her lungs. *Hard to breathe, baby? Wait until you go swimming.* After a few minutes of taunting her, he stood up, promised *I'll fuck you all night and when I'm done with you I'll take your body out there*

and dump it in the sea. No one will ever know what happened to you.
He turned away to pour himself a glass of wine. Then the knife
was in her hand. She moved quickly, out of pure instinct. She
stabbed him twice, in the neck, hoping for either the vein or the
artery. It was beginner's luck, and chance, because he turned his
head at the precise moment, shocked, in search of her eyes. That
twist of his neck made the carotid artery vulnerable to the second,
deeper thrust of the knife. His eyes met hers but just as quickly
their gaze was bisected by a dark line, flying, that she did not
immediately recognize as blood though her body did. Her body
knew; she stumbled out of the way, and did not look at him again.
She found and pulled on her clothes with her back to his death.

He had been right about one thing only: no one ever knew. She
did not run from the port; she tried to walk upright, without limp-
ing. A block away, she caught a cab, the knife at the bottom of her
knapsack. She went back to her grandmother's house, showered,
slept, and woke to drink a bowl of café au lait. Her grandmother
always said the police of the city were incompetent and corrupt.
They fulfilled their reputation. No one found her because no one
came looking. She did not deviate from her plan, the high school
girl's plan to spend time in Europe the summer before university.
Her grandmother put her on a ferry to Italy; she travelled onward
into her life, her one life, which she herself had saved. There she
was, two years later, poking holes in her notepad, setting herself
another task to make sure she was over it, forcing herself to remain
open, unafraid. And if not unafraid, then daring.

Her instinct about Benoît was sound, though. They had dinners,
lunches, runs in the Endowment Lands near UBC, trips to Lighthouse Park, runs along the seawall all the way to the *Girl in a
Wetsuit* sculpture. Benoît remained the same person he had been at
the restaurant, polite and generous. He was also kind, witty, interested in her life, open about his own, and obsessed—sometimes to

the point that he bored her—by books about World War Two.
And spy stories. He was forty-eight, married to a woman he still
loved but had not had sex with for several years. She and their
two children were still in Paris; she was willing to vacation in
North America, but she refused to live there. He believed that
was because she had a lover, and did not want to leave him behind.
Though Benoît travelled back and forth a lot, and tried to spend
a week at home every second month, he missed his family terribly.
He would live in Vancouver only long enough to establish his
business on the Canadian and American west coasts, then he
would move back to Paris.

To say hello and goodbye, he kissed Shar on the cheeks. Once,
after a great film, they hugged for a long time, feeling each other's
bodies through their jackets. But that was the extent of their physical contact. At the beginning of every date, he gave her $300 in
an envelope. Except for the time they went to *Turandot*, Puccini's
opera, the Persian fairy tale of the murderous, beautiful princess
who refuses to give herself to the man who adores her. That night,
after they sat down, he told her there was extra money in the envelope. She counted the hundred-dollar bills in the restroom during
the intermission: a thousand dollars. Two hours later, over a glass
of wine at the Wedgewood Hotel, he asked her if she would spend
the night with him.

She'd been flirting with him all evening, leaning against him
while they watched the opera, letting her foot rest against his under
the table. "Do I have to?"

"No. Of course not. You do not have to do anything. But I
would be happy if you did."

"Do you think I'm like Turandot, the cold princess who will
give in to love in the end?"

"*Mais non!* Please don't. I don't want your love. I just want affection, which is much less stressful. And good sex. A few hours with

you every week or two, because we amuse each other. A continuation of what we already have, but more. We're friends, don't you think?"

"Yes, we're friends," she said, hedgingly.

"But it's a professional arrangement, too."

"Yes, absolutely." Those words calmed her. If it was professional, she could keep her distance.

"I will continue to pay you for your time. Which would be about the same number of hours that we see each other now. You are free to do whatever you like. With other people, sexually, or . . . ending it altogether with me. It might not suit you. But I'd love to take you on a short trip this winter. Maybe to Martinique. Just for a week. Anyway, I would give you two thousand a month. In cash. Just to start."

She was dumbfounded by the amount, and immediately suspicious. "You would give me all that money just for sex?"

He shook his head. "But Shar, it is not just for sex. You are charming. You are funny. You are very beautiful. But, *most of all*, it would be a token of my appreciation for your excellent French grammar." She laughed. He lifted up her long-boned hand and kissed it. "Sex can be had easily. And cheaply—but then it also *feels* cheap. I am fortunate to be able to afford fine things in my life. Not just sex, but *Turandot* and conversation and food. And, yes, a beautiful young woman like you. I respect all of these for what they are. I am a fortunate man."

Like the opera, the evening had a happy ending for him. Shar had no interest in fairy tales, but he was a good man. She used his goodness to learn again about the goodness of men. After Marseilles, she had found it difficult not to hate them, all, evenly, uniformly, for what they could do to her; for what had been done to her.

For the first few weeks, she could not believe what she was doing. She felt outside her own life. She had an on-again, off-again girlfriend, Leanne; she couldn't tell her what she was doing, because

Leanne was beginning to believe in separatism, not the Quebecois kind, but the feminist kind: daily life as separated from men as possible. And there was Shar, secretly sleeping *with a man*, listening to his stories and eating dinner with him and chatting with him on the phone at night, fondly. For money. She was sucking his cock—it wasn't that bad, once you got the hang of it—for money. Yet, within two months, the situation had so normalized that she ached to tell Leanne what she was up to.

To test the waters, she pretended she'd *read* about a young woman doing what she was doing in a magazine article at the dentist's (Benoît paid for the cleaning and checkup). Leanne was disgusted. "What crap magazine was it in? *Cosmo*? The most important things have been left out! The hidden truth always needs deconstruction. Where is the coercion, the degradation? That woman had probably been sexually abused as a child!"

"But the relationship didn't sound abusive. It was just . . . sort of . . . an intimate business arrangement."

"How can you be so naïve? Prostitution is violence against women; the money *legitimizes* the violence. It's economic as well as physical rape. Prostitution was invented by the patriarchy to keep women in the lowest sex class, even lower than marriage!"

"But the woman in the article didn't think of herself as a prostitute. Or abused in any way. She was only having sex with that one man."

Leanne's voice rose. "If she is having sex with someone for money, she is not only a prostitute, she is *being* prostituted by the patriarchy. As soon as money is exchanged, the woman loses even more of her agency. And all protection, too; everyone despises a whore, the police most of all. A whore is a slave, no matter what she herself thinks. Haven't you read Andrea Dworkin?" Shar had not. She was studying applied psychology, still doing the requisite biology courses and coaxing mice through mazes with the promise of different rewards. Yes, she was a feminist and a card-carrying member of the campus QueersRHere Club. But she had neither the vocabulary nor the temperament to argue with Leanne: the notion that Benoît was raping her was stupid. And wrong.

She knew, early on, that Benoît *adored* her. Occasionally, shyly, he would tell her that. *Je t'adore.* Pourquoi? *Parce que tu es adorable.* He seemed to know, somehow, beyond language, outside or possibly inside the borders they maintained, that he was helping to dissolve some poison in her body. Usually they had traditional, reasonably passionate sex, intimate without being overbearing. But once, when they hadn't seen each other for a few weeks, their lovemaking tumbled, fell, crashed into aggressive, hungry fucking. Even before it was done, she turned away from him, her body flooded with memories from that night in Marseilles. She began to cry; the crying quickly became uncontrollable. Until Benoît put his hand on her naked back and said her name. Then slid his hand up higher, touched her neck. She shuddered. "Shar." Benoît touched the precise spots where the blade had entered, once, twice. She let go the scream that she could not release that night in Marseilles. Benoît did not flinch. He did not raise his voice. He said, "Shar, you're here. With me." He didn't take his hand away. He drew the knife out of her; she felt it go. Relief rushed into her body. She cried for a long time, curling back into his arms. After a while, he said her name again; she stared at him. He knew without knowing. "If you ever need to, you can tell me what happened."

"I think . . . No. I needed . . ." What? "I needed someone to see me."

"*Et voilà.* I see you." He pronounced in a triumphant voice: "*Ma belle amie, je te vois. Et tu es libre.*" He spread his palm over her heart. Then he said lightly, "Now, let's eat something. You must be starving." She was.

ꙮ

Clackclackclackclack! Clack-clack! Her eyes were still closed but the clatter could only be Mrs. Shinx. Shar on her pedicure throne slivered open an eye and grinned: Mrs. Shinx had donned a pair of fluff-banded ruby-red mules. Kitten heels. The young woman drew away from Shar's scrubbed and rubbed feet as Mrs. Shinx clattered toward them, a plastic box full of Shar's preferred nail polish carried in her arms like a baby. "What colour you want today? You like this? Vely lucky colour!" She held up a scarlet bottle.

Shar nodded just to make her happy. Then she wrinkled her nose at the fumes. The other two women's toes were done; they were getting their fingernails painted right beside her. Giselle, her recent lawyer ex, had *hated* nail polish, partly as a manifestation of the capitalist beauty industry, but mostly because it meant that Shar was going on a date. With Benoît. He had always loved nail polish. *Lacquer*, he called it, in English. Fourteen years and several cities later—he had also lived in New York, and in Montreal—they still saw each other regularly. Giselle had never met him, but she had always disliked him; he predated her. Near the end of their relationship, she'd asked Shar, "Why did you tell me how *long* you've been having sex with him? You didn't have to. You could have . . ."

"Lied?"

Shar shook her head at the memory of it. That was the problem with sex work and its complexities. People *said* they wanted the truth, but they preferred the lies.

This morning Benoît had flown in from Paris for business, but also for the pleasure of seeing Shar. He was her oldest, most generous client and one of her dearest friends. After all this time, it was fair to say that, yes, finally, she loved him. The very least she could do for him was her nails.

13

Orchids

THE CRUCIAL THING, ELIZA THOUGHT, WAS TO LIE. BUT she was a terrible liar, always had been. How could she lie to *every-one*? Andrew, Kiki, Bianca, her girlfriends, her kids, the school moms she worked with on the fundraiser. She could not do it. She could not lie to Andrew. It was wrong. Impossible.

She sat at her desk and attended to the morning's emails while her body buzzed. Kiki had left an Ivory Mammoth orchid near her computer. Eliza gazed at the bloom closest to her face. She wanted to lick it. No. She wanted to eat it, the whole thing. Swallow it down. To no one in particular, she said, "This orchid is extraordinary." An echo seemed to distort her voice. But only she could hear it.

The white bloom was as big as her fist. *Fist* made her think of Shar's hand, a hologram of fingers that still slid exquisitely back and forth between her legs. She was wet again. Or, still. Was that normal?

The orchid was gorgeous. *Orkhis*: ancient Greek for "testicle." Eliza licked her dry lips. *Orkhis* referred not to the flower itself, but to certain varieties' bulbous, ball-shaped root tubers. While Shar and Eliza were in the change room, Jack Armelle had parked his refrigerated garden outside Fleur. Kiki had purchased ten Ivory Mammoths, some Azafran and Bibi roses (peach and orange tones) and a bunch of purple and mauve alstroemeria, haughtily referred to by Kiki as *fake orchids*. The true ones stood in various spots around the studio—the fridge was too cold for orchids— each one meticulously staked and covered in blooms.

Eliza gazed into the velvet throat, where both the female and male sex organs of the orchid were located. "It's tougher than it looks."

Kiki, walking toward her from the workbench, raised one finely tweezed eyebrow. "What?"

"The orchid. Such a hardy flower. And prolific. There are 25,000 different species of orchids on six continents . . . Probably it's the kinky sex that makes them so successful."

"Orchids are kinky?"

"Some of them are mimics. They often look like their pollina- tors or produce scents that smell like *female* pollinators—bees— so male bees are tricked into having sex with them."

"Why do you know about this? Bee sex?" Those eyebrows drew tightly together, deepening the wrinkle at the top of Kiki's nose.

"Orchid sex—the bees just get frustrated. I read about it last night, on an industry website, natural versus mechanical means of pollinating domesticated orchids. Male bees confuse the orchids for female bees, so the bees try to mate with the flower. Of course it doesn't work. But while they're busy trying to screw the flower, they get covered in the pollen. When they get totally frustrated, they fly as far away as possible, so the pollen gets widely distrib- uted. Taa-daa! Kinky orchid sex."

Gazing down into the sexual parts of the plant, Kiki asked mournfully, "Why is it so 'ard to find a 'usband?"

Eliza laughed. "Bad date last night?" Her colleague's round face was pale, which made the dappling of freckles across her nose stand out. She had telltale dark circles under her eyes.

Kiki flicked a chunk of her red, high-gloss hair over her shoul- der. "You know I'm on dese websites. After working all day, I go to work at 'ome, scroll trough, read profiles. Basically, you try to figure out one ting: who is da psychopath." She paused. "And you do *not* choose him even if 'e is de only good-looking one. It's like online shopping. But more difficult."

"But what about that guy you really like? Aren't you still seeing him?"

Her expression grew complicated. "Jonatan. 'E told me 'e can't have kids. Infertile. Some genetic condition. Extra chromosome. And you know what 'appened?"

"What?"

"When he told me dat, I lost interest. I never want to kiss 'im again. Isn't dat sad? But why didn't 'e tell me right away? I'm so glad that we didn't go to bed yet. Then it would be even *worse*, I would be *more* attached." Her voice dropped to an anxious whisper. "But also it's *awful*, that we didn't 'ave sex. I 'aven't 'ad sex for . . . Oh, god, since dat last guy. You know . . ."

"The one who was living with his mother?"

"It's not that 'e was living with his mother! It's that 'e lied and told me she was *'is roommate*!"

Eliza nodded sympathetically. "It does seem like slim pickings out there, in the world of the single, heterosexual woman. The available men go down fast." Like a wildebeest attacked by lionesses, she thought, as the images thrust into her mind; a couple of days before, she and the boys had watched a documentary on lions in Africa.

"A *desert*! Da men are creepy or they cannot put down de iPhone long enough to remember your name. Or on the first date, they ask you, Do you do anal?" She shrieked, "Who would 'ave a baby with any of dese idiots?" She marched back to her workbench. "Do you do *anal*? How can you ask a complete stranger such a question? In a Starbucks?" And picked up her cutters. "I'll trim da stems. I need to relieve my frustration."

Eliza also stood. "I'll strip the roses." Her mind tripped over the word *strip*. She yanked it back to the task at hand by reading the standing order list for the Regent Hotel out loud. "Three for the big lobby, two restaurant arrangements. Fifty-six small ones for the elevator lobbies and public washrooms. Good. We can do this in a couple of hours. And Bianca will be back by then. She can drive you around to do the deliveries." Kiki hated driving. Whenever she drove anywhere, Eliza worried about both her and the van.

Eliza put the first of the stems into the stripper pipe and pulled, slicing away the thorns in one smooth go. *Yes!* Strip off those thorns, baby. She did twenty white roses and twenty pale pinks without so much as pricking her finger. Then she pinched away bruised leaves, pulled off the tired outer petals and answered the phone several times. Kiki was almost finished the second large arrangement when Eliza had an idea. "Why don't I get some of those red pincushions from the fridge?"

With a rose between her teeth, Kiki turned her head from one side to the other. Removed the rose. "Yeah. Dat's a good idea. You 'ave not lost it!" She cast a full smile at Eliza. "You're quick today. A sign dat you're in da mood."

The expression boomed in Eliza's head like the refrain of a bad song. She *was* in the mood. She was intensely focused on the flowers, the arrangements, keen-eyed, but she was also driven by nervous hunger. She wanted to get on to the next thing; she wanted time to pass. She wanted to hear from Shar.

They finished the hotel arrangements in record time. Bianca and Kiki began loading the van while Eliza went to the cramped washroom downstairs. After peeing, she leaned over the small sink and put her forehead and her palms against the cold mirror. As soon as she closed her eyes, Shar was there, behind her, pushing her up against the sink, pulling down her trousers, reaching around, down, between. Every preposition was pornographic. She opened her eyes, stared at the heat-flush that had risen from her chest right up into her face. "What have I done?" she whispered. Maybe it wasn't just lust. Maybe it was a perimenopausal hot flash, induced by the sudden influx of hormones into her bloodstream.

Should I send her an email right now? Should I call her? Text? Where does she live?

Calm down. *Shar* had to get in touch with *her*. Eliza would control herself. Important to have the illusion of control anyway. If Shar didn't get in touch, that would be that. She was too old to be desperate. No, not too old. Too much of an *adult*. In the mirror, she saw the naked Amazon, breast, hand, black stripe of hair on a narrow triangle of pale flesh. She wanted to get *in*to her. She wanted to have a cock. What? Yes, that was dissonance. She had had crushes on women before, and, in university, a few brief flings. They were try-it-on affairs that never fit well enough to become relationships.

Thalia had been different, of course. Why *not* think of her, especially now? It wasn't like Thalia was a deep, dark secret. Andrew knew. Her close friends knew. But that was on a Greek island, twenty years ago. It was the only time she had been comparably dazzled by a woman. It didn't end well, but the ending was not what she remembered. That spring and summer on Lesvos were the most beautiful seasons of her life. The superlatives had held as she aged, giving them more power. She had never encountered any other place like that rich island world—flowers, fruit, olive trees, almonds, and light, so much clear light pouring down—nor any other human being like the woman who led her through it. And it was also there, in the village of Eresos, that she learned right down to the soles of her aching feet how to run a restaurant. But before she started working, she and Thalia spent a month together, days sliding into nights into new days when they barely walked out of the stone house in the olive grove except to watch the sunset, or to go down to the sea, usually on horseback, for a late swim. All they did was make love and eat and sleep and fuck and drink wine and ride around the maze of donkey tracks and tip ouzo down their throats and eat grilled sardines and salads and swim and swim, mouths open, full of salt, full of each other. They often swam in the Aegean at night. When there was moonlight, the silver water was so clear that they could see twenty feet down to the rippled metallic sand.

"Eliza? Are you in dere?" Kiki's loud voice made Eliza jump straight into the air. "Are you all right?"

"I'm fine! Just looking for that earring I lost last week. I think it's on the floor somewhere." Eliza's eyes dropped to the floor to scan the painted cement. She tilted the garbage container, peered behind it. Lifted up the bucket full of toilet rolls. Then she straightened and faced the mirror again. Her face was her own face, unchanged. Yet she had just told a lie so well that she'd believed it herself.

14

Rhymes With

THE AMAZON DID NOT CALL, TEXT OR EMAIL HER. NO
smoke signals either, or surprise visits to the studio. Eliza waited
for that, from hour to hour, day to day, illogically, because she
hadn't told Shar where the studio was. At any moment, she expected
her to walk through the door or directly out of a brick wall. But
she did not. Tuesday came again; Shar was not at the pool. She did
not come to swim on Thursday either.

To the implicit rejection, Eliza responded by refusing to even
think her name. She allowed herself only the descriptive phrase
rhymes with star, then envisaged the small but full mouth, the length
of her, limbs, hands, legs, the accordion of muscle bracing her ribs.

Half of the heavy snow melted. From the playground, in an
unexpected role reversal with his older brother, darling Jake
brought home a new word, *bitch*, which he gleefully shared with
Marcus, so that both boys swung the swear around like a hammer
for several days, despite their parents' patient and not-so-patient
remonstrations. A new event rose on the horizon, possibly a great
leap forward for Fleur: someone from Ayeda, the cosmetics and
haircare company, called Kiki to schedule a meeting about their
three-day international sales conference. She and Kiki promised
each other that if Fleur got the contract, they would bring Veuve
Clicquot and oysters to the studio and throw a party.

She whose-name-rhymes-with-star receded whence she came, into myth. Yet the long naked minutes remained vivid in Eliza's mind, and ached elsewhere. She did not think of them, could not stop thinking of them. She regularly swept the feelings and memories away with a brush of her arm, saying inwardly, or out loud if she was alone, "It's a stupid crush!"

She surveyed the mess of the breakfast table. Everyone was upstairs getting ready to begin the day. She was still wrapped in her robe. It *was* a crush, and she was being crushed by it. Andrew was taking the boys to school because she felt ill. PMS, she said at breakfast, to which she added the word *melancholic*. Andrew started to laugh—until he realized she was serious. "I'll walk the boys," he told her. It was another Tuesday morning. Swim day. She felt keen regret, gazing into her mug of tea. It was cold now, a skin of milk on it and her toast untouched, when usually she liked to eat with the boys, who always woke like hungry cubs. Nothing interested them in the morning but food and milk and making a mess of the kitchen, spilling something.

What did *Eliza* rhyme with? Fucking idiot. It wasn't only the marital betrayal, but that the purity of the pool was ruined. And I have ruined it, she thought. The pool was the only thing in her life that had been all hers, her pleasure, her escape, the bars of sunlight sometimes falling in that one place, sun undulating through blue water. That time had been her only freedom. But she wouldn't swim today; if who-rhymes-with-star wasn't there, Eliza would be disappointed. If she was there and uninterested, Eliza would be mortified. And furious. She had spent two weeks in a welter of longing, lust and indecision. Like a teenage girl. Or boy. Or a dopey middle-aged woman making a fool out of herself.

She could hear the rumble of feet upstairs, the boys in the bathroom now. She went into the front room and waited for her men.

Andrew came down first. "Have you seen that old sweater I like, the beige one?"

"It's in the same place in the closet that it always is."

"I couldn't find it. Why are so many things invisible until *you* look for them?"

"Because you are wilfully blind in order to make me think that you would be helpless without me." She reached up to pull the frayed shirt collar out of a different sweater.

He kissed her quickly. "I *would* be helpless without you."

"That shirt's getting old. I'm going to cull it soon."

"But it's just getting comfortable!" He loved worn-out, holey pieces of clothing. "Don't you think swimming would make you feel better?"

"No. No, not today." Insufficient explanation. She patted his chest and turned away to ready the boys' boots. "The pool was so crowded last week." It was two weeks since she'd kissed the Amazon. This morning was both a debauched anniversary and a mocking salute to her frustration. "I think I'll just take a hot bath." Andrew went into the kitchen; she heard him gathering up a few bowls. She put the boys' winter coats out.

She would heat up her tea. Drink it in a hot bath and feel sorry for herself. Despite all she had to do at work. She would spread her legs wide open on the edge of the bathtub as if she were still on the bench at the pool and rhymes-with-star held the Wave, that tube of blue silicon, and she would slide it in, stir it around her cervix, play with her clit and come so hard that she would howl before sliding back into the tub, spent, cowed by the intensity of her own fantasy, how much she wanted it to be real. Her tea would be cold again.

Andrew returned and shouted up the stairs. "Come on, you two! It's time to go." He turned to her. "Feel better then." He came over and kissed her on the top of the head. "Do you think you'll be well enough to come to the faculty gathering late this afternoon?"

"Oh, shit, I forgot about that."

"I wrote it on the fridge calendar."

"I never remember unless it makes it into my work calendar. We have to sort out our various calendars before one of us forgets something important. Do you really need me to be there?"

"No. I *want* you to be there. Come on, it won't be onerous, I promise."

She made a face.

"Honey, it's a social gathering for the doctoral students, not a lecture. There'll be wine. And Kajali would love to see you. We can still pick up the kids at Annie's by six thirty."

Though it hadn't been announced officially yet, he was going to be the assistant dean next year, so these social events would become duties for him soon enough. Not that he minded. He enjoyed most of the faculty gatherings, even the dreaded meetings, which mystified Eliza. She put it down to mathematicians being geeky together. And brilliant. Some of them were famous, in their number-filled fields, but she could never remember the geniuses' names.

"I'll do my best to get there by five thirty. And I'll have to work on the weekend for a few hours."

The boys thundered down the stairs; they were thrilled when Andrew took them to school. He raised his hands. "Whoa, you maniacs! Order, order in the court!" He directed the opera of boots and coats and school bags while Eliza went to heat her tea in the microwave; from the kitchen, she listened to the accusations about stolen mittens and pilfered cookies, then coats went on and she returned to kiss them goodbye. They shouldered the bulk of their backpacks, Andrew opened the door and out they stepped onto the front porch, then the street, waving at her from the sidewalk. Andrew left last, angling his wool cap jauntily. It made him look like an early nineteenth-century farmer, a Yorkshireman maybe. He tipped the cap to her. "Good day, my lady," he said, hamming it up, yet genuinely gallant, handsome, too, his eyes cat-green and glimmering in the cold morning air, his hair more gold than grey in the sun. She loved him, utterly. He was insepa-rable from her life, the boys' lives, the house, this good solid world they had built. She shut the door on the cold with a strange reluc-tance, not wanting to lose sight of her sons, her husband.

They are *everything*, she thought.

What more, monstrous woman, could you possibly want?

After work, she rushed over to the university in a cab. The recep-tion was in one of the old stone houses on campus, its ivy winter-dried and brown. Inside, an immense fireplace crackled with burning wood. How had she forgotten about the fireplace?

Within fifteen minutes, she stood near it, alone, with a glass of wine in her hand. As usual, she was mildly awed and fully bored by the company. After the initial greetings, she could never under-stand what the hell any of them were talking about, because they actually did stand around and talk about math. It was like another language, another country. What fascinated her was that Andrew lived there—he knew the lingua franca as well as several dia-lects—in a place where she was, at most, a dumb, attractive tourist. Occasionally, one of his more generous, socially adept colleagues—usually Kajali—would notice that Eliza's eyes were glazing over, and would try to interpret, but it wasn't like other languages; there was no direct translation. No matter. Eliza stood happily mesmerized by the fire. A chunk of wood, fallen below the iron grate, twisted with red-coal worms; orange flames licked at the blackened stones of the hearth. No wonder humans worshipped fire; it was ferociously alive.

The wine was excellent. She took another sip and looked around the large room. Kajali spoke with quiet intensity to one of her PhD students, a young blonde woman Eliza had met once before. Andrew talked about her often, too. A new genius, apparently, with a name that sounded oddly mathematical. What was it again? Eliza admired her slender grace; she was wearing a long, high-waisted skirt and a nifty little Chanel jacket knock-off. Unexpectedly stylish for a math prodigy. Eliza tried to remember what area her brilliance illuminated. Algebra? Something called a theory of lies? Could that be it, or was guilt driving her crazy?

No, she remembered now—that's really what it was called. Lie theory. Andrew had tried to explain it to her. Something about a unifying principle for equations, based on symmetry, geometry. She was getting too hot, and stepped away from the hearth. The fire was eating up the oxygen. A moment later, the prodigy put down her glass of wine to slip off her jacket. The young woman's arms were painfully thin, with popped veins and knobby elbows.

Andrew crossed her field of vision, tall, smooth-moving, stopping here and there to chat with people. She felt an unexpected shiver of pride. He exuded male authority in the most non-threatening way. Was it the smile? Good looks? Or his slightly scruffy approach to fashion? The women drifted toward him. Soon Kajali and her student fell into the current and eddied around the wine table, where he handed his colleague a new glass of red and cajoled the student to have a splash more white, which she declined, accepting a glass of bubbly water instead. Cheryl, that was her name. Cheryl Link. The genius. Who did not like to eat. She lifted her blonde head toward Andrew and pushed a tendril of wavy hair behind her little ear. She spoke shyly, her eyes beaming. His height called the child out of people. Eliza had experienced that herself, early in their relationship, some deep comfort in his tall, solid trustworthiness.

A sliver of nausea pushed toward her throat—guilt, eating away at her guts. What was her own theory of lies? How could she rationalize her fraction of betrayal? She watched the little scene unfold across the room. Women were so attracted to Andrew. She sighed. A long-married wife wasn't a new lover either. She suddenly felt pathetically unglamorous and stupid. These math nerds understood the secret language of the universe, which she would never, ever learn.

Andrew threw his head back, laughing benevolently upon (count them) two, three, four women. She felt a jab of suspicion, watching this attractive man surrounded by the female sex: maybe he was jumping into the sack with Cheryl Link! No—he was the most honourable man she had ever met. That was why she'd married him. Honour was an old, neglected word; no one took it seriously anymore. But when she'd got to know him, she said to herself, and to her mother: he is honourable. (Her mother had replied, in her now-practical way, "That's nice, dear, but does he have tenure?") Something restless and changeable in Eliza—something inconstant, she feared—had risen to meet his steadfast goodness. He was still that honourable man; she had not been wrong. Whenever he heard about some professor, male or female, getting romantically entangled with a student, then publicly outed, often after the student cried foul, he shook his head and allowed himself to say something mildly cutting, such as, "It's hard to believe that idiot has a PhD."

If not a student, though, what about a younger colleague? The university was filling up with young assistant profs in their thirties. Eliza smiled, remembering her own lustful, baby-craving years. A childless woman in her mid-thirties could tear down an office wall with her bare hands if a viable sperm donor was on the other side of it.

And look at them! The math genius harem seemed to get younger around him. Even Kajali, in her sixties, stood there tilting her head coquettishly. Granted, Kajali had a beautiful head; her long black hair was streaked with a single glimmering ribbon of silver-white. She seemed ageless. Cheryl continued to gaze up at him, too, one thin arm wrapped around her waist, hooked under the bottom rung of her rib cage.

When she'd married Andrew, Eliza had been sure that he had nothing in common with his brother, save his looks. But she soon came to understand that he was as much a handsome charmer as Martin. The difference was that he charmed to no end, or at least not to the end of self-aggrandizement. He charmed quietly, often by attentive listening, which seemed to set him apart from other men. Was it really that rare, still, for a man to listen to a woman?

He didn't always listen to Eliza, of course. Sometimes he tuned her out completely. But it was different when you were married. Domestic life demanded relentless and dedicated intimacy, whereas charm was predicated on not knowing too much, not being too close. To lean forward and listen meant that you didn't know what the speaker was going to say. Listening was a way of pulling a stranger toward you without touching.

But the honour remained. And he could still make her laugh.

As though on cue, Kajali exclaimed in her musical Indian English, "Oh, Andrew! You *can't* be serious!" and she clasped her hands together under her chin like a girl of fourteen. Her debonair husband and half a dozen women couldn't be talking about *math*. Eliza took her wineglass off the mantelpiece and went over to find out what was so funny.

15

Bone Picking

ANDREW'S PARENTS CAME FOR DINNER ON SUNDAY afternoon. His father, Bruce, drank too much wine and held forth as usual about politics and the economy. Eliza was always amazed by the way everyone listened to him so attentively, despite their boredom. She and Andrew disagreed once in a while, mildly, even as a tension slowly grew in the room. Eliza cleaned one little lamb rib after another, then gnawed on the bone to keep from speaking. Bruce blathered on about how the government needed to get its act together and attack the deficit or "our grandchildren will be paying the price."

Eliza sighed, and chewed on another bone. Just two days ago, she had noticed yet another chunk of money sucked out of the joint bank account. Surely for Andrew's parents.

Bruce reached over his plate for the wine bottle. Corinne, his delicate wife with tendons of steel, still pretty and vain at seventy-four, said, "My dear, you know how much I hate driving on the highway. Please don't have too much." Bruce smiled at her condescendingly and began to pour. He winked at Eliza. "I'm fine!" he said, raising a glass to his lovely daughter-in-law, the chef. Everyone toasted, the boys keen to clink their cups with their grandma's crystal wineglass. Corinne repeated her complaint. "Bruce. I do not want to have to drive." She took a tiny bite from her minuscule portion of rack of lamb. Then she cut another one of her roasted potatoes into dice-sized cubes.

Maybe that's how she stays so thin, Eliza thought, reaching over to manoeuvre a forkful of food into Jake's mouth. He was old enough to feed himself, but it took forever. For the next five minutes she worked diligently at making sure the meat, at least, went into him. He was the slowest eater she had ever met, born into this family of hyenas. Except for Corinne: maybe he inherited his slow, careful style from his slender grandmother. But weren't you supposed to have a little extra weight on you in your seventies? In case you got sick?

Eliza said, "Marcus, please pull your chair in closer to the table. Your food is falling on the floor."

Corinne smiled coldly at the boy. Eliza couldn't understand her coldness toward the children; when Genevieve came from Calgary for one of her rare visits, she was always loving and fun with them, even overindulgent, in classic grandmother fashion. Corinne said, "Come on, Marcus, your mother is right. You don't want people to think you're a messy slob, do you?" Eliza glanced at Andrew; he was pouring himself more wine, too, ignoring the way his mother insulted his child, and, by extension, his family.

The two of them, fine old blade and rebel boy, stared at each other for a moment, while Eliza wondered if he would swear at her. After eyeing her for a few more seconds, he shrugged. "Oh, all right, Grandma." He stood, pushed his chair in and sat down again. He even put his napkin on his lap.

Corinne said, "There you go. I know you want to be a *gentleman*. Just like your uncle Martin. And your daddy, of course."

Here we go, Eliza thought. She'd been waiting for Uncle Martin to enter the conversation. Martin's greatest fan, in his universe of fans, was his mother. Which was sweet, but still. She was blind to his faults. The old lady gazed at Marcus, then at Jake, the cold smile warmer now. "You both look *so* much like your uncle," she murmured. Marcus chewed his meat, ignoring her, but Jake smiled. Eliza refrained from mentioning the obvious; Martin and Andrew were sometimes mistaken for twins. The boys, therefore, looked like their *father.*

Oh, Eliza, you're so petty, she said to herself, just before Corinne shook her head. "It's such a mystery, why he hasn't met the right woman."

No, it's not, Eliza thought.

"Any woman would be crazy not to want to marry him." The monologue would proceed in one of various directions now. Corinne might become genuinely fretful about Martin's geographical distance and his health: Was he okay? Would he ever come back and live in Toronto again? It would not be the first time that Eliza had watched her tough mother-in-law get anxious for her son. On the other hand, she might start talking about his latest international triumph. She kept up with everything he did through his Twitter feed and website. Or she might continue talking about the dearth of suitable women for her famous offspring.

"It must be difficult for him to be single." Bingo.

Bruce grunted. "If he'd had the guts to propose to that last one, the English lady, she woulda married him."

Corinne's eyes popped open. Perhaps she hadn't had the English lady in mind. "Oh, I don't think that was so serious. And she was in the same field. She was such a competitive woman, always talking about her *projects*. It would be hard to be an anthropologist and compete with Martin."

"Yes," Eliza said crisply, "it certainly would be." Andrew poked her with a glance. She fork-lifted some kale to her mouth and chewed.

Corinne took a sip of wine. "He's a genius," she said, setting the glass down. "*That* is the problem. He cannot find his equal in a woman. And women don't want to be helpmates to men anymore. So it's been hard for him to find a partner."

Eliza met Jake's concerned eyes, smiled. Her little human thermometer registered the rising tension; his eyes travelled from face to face, trying to figure out what was going on. His mother put some beets into her mouth and chewed; it was the best way to keep from talking.

Andrew said, "Mom, Martin will find a wife if he wants one. And I don't think it's proper," he said carefully, using the P word, which he used only with Corinne, who had an innate respect for it, "to talk about him like this. You two could discuss this stuff together on the phone."

Corinne pursed her lips. When she spoke, her voice was high, strained with emotion. "Andrew, you know your brother never talks to me about private things."

Bruce cleared his throat noisily. "He probably doesn't talk to anyone about that stuff. It's *private*. Remember? He's an adult now. There's no need to interfere."

Corinne cried, "I'm not interfering!" Eliza lifted her head, glanced from Corinne to Andrew, trying to figure out what had just happened. She had missed something. But what? The boys stared at Corinne, too, on alert, worried it was their fault. Their eyes widened as their grandmother spoke again, angrily. "I'm just wondering about him. Can't I even do that anymore, wonder how he's doing?"

In a deep, gentle tone, Andrew answered, "Of course you can, Mom. We all do. We all miss him."

Not me, Eliza thought, peeved once more. Even when Martin was on a different continent, he could monopolize a conversation.

Bruce immediately undid the effect of his son's conciliatory words. "For Christ's sake, Corinne! Martin's a successful, grown man now. He's perfectly *fine*. Stop worrying about him all the time."

Corinne's face crumpled. The anger was gone, usurped by a sadness Eliza had never before seen in her mother-in-law. "I just want him to be happy! And I want to *know* that he's happy!" Her eyes filled with tears. "Is that a crime?"

The table was still and silent. The food and tablecloth and napkins absorbed Corinne's words as readily as the humans did. Eliza looked from Bruce to her mother-in-law, once more to her husband. None of them would meet her eye.

Unable to stand the tension anymore, Jake piped up, "Is Uncle Martin in trouble, Grandma?"

Corinne made a strangled noise deep in her throat but smiled bravely at Jake, her eyes shining with tears. "No, Jake, Uncle Martin isn't in trouble. I just miss him."

Jake tilted his head to the side. "I miss him, too, Grandma." He reached over and patted her hand. "He'll come and see you in the spring."

Andrew laughed. They all started laughing at Jake's quiet assurance, his adult little-boyness. Eliza asked, "Anyone for some more wine?" Too late, she realized that this was not an invitation that Corinne would appreciate. "Or water?"

Bruce boomed, "I'll have some more wine."

Corinne only looked on disapprovingly, sadly.

Bruce smiled at his wife and said, "Just a little splash, Eliza." He raised his glass and Eliza poured in a small amount. A round of water, wine and juice pouring commenced, loosening up the taut atmosphere, rehydrating throats old and young. Jake smacked loudly after he drank a gulp of apple juice. Eliza smiled at him, thinking how sad it was that Corinne obsessed about her eldest son's well-being. Her life wasn't full enough. No wonder she went shopping so much.

Andrew asked, "So, Dad, tell me. What did you do with the boat this winter? Did you store it at the old marina or drive it out to your friend's place?"

Eliza sat up straighter. The boat? They still had that *boat*? She thought that they'd sold it in the fall. She glanced from Andrew to Bruce to Corinne. None of them seemed to think it was odd to own a boat when you couldn't pay your bills. She wanted to scream: *You still have the fucking boat?* Instead, she reached for her wineglass.

Corinne was now instructing Jake on how to hold his fork properly. Eliza tried not to listen, focusing instead on the lack of resemblance between the woman and Andrew. Petite, WASPily reserved, narrow-minded—how on earth had she raised the boy who became Andrew, relaxed, squeamish about nothing, naturally magnanimous. He had his mother's blue eyes, Eliza thought, and her attention to detail, at least when it came to math. But no one, seeing them together in a room, would think they were mother and son.

That's a blessing, she acknowledged, eyes flitting back and forth from mother-in-law to husband. Corinne and Bruce must have done something right. The saving grace of copulation had mixed up the genes. She watched Corinne demonstrating for Jake with her own knife. *Just let him do it the way he wants to do it. Let them be who they are.* Why was that so difficult? She was guilty, too. Sometimes she heard herself say, "Oh, you're so good at drawing," or whatever, and even the praise sounded bossy and instructive. She didn't know how to let the boys be more free, though until her father died she herself had been free as a child, bicycling and skating and tobogganing through a landscape of almost endless parkland and sky and long afternoons with friends. Free of their parents, free of adults. Free. Would her sons remember *any* freedom? She feared not.

The boys got up to take their plates to the island. Marcus snapped, "Jake, stop pushing me. I'm trying to put my plate up here." Jake elbowed him. That was that. After abiding his grandmother politely throughout dinner, Marcus had reached the end of his patience. He pushed his plate onto the counter with a clatter, turned, and swiped a handful of lamb bones off Jake's plate; they landed on the floor. Somehow Jake managed to hold onto the plate itself.

"Marcus!" There it was again, a voice like a machine gun, her very own. "Pick those up right now!"

"But Jake was pushing me! He kept sticking his elbow into me. I was just trying to find a space on—"

"Please pick the bones up right now."

Jake was staring down at the floor, his lower lip pushed out. "Mom, I didn't do it!"

"I know you didn't, dear, it's all right," she said. "Marcus. The bones please."

"No! He was pushing me and he *never* gets into trouble." He looked at his brother with narrowed, hateful eyes. "You stupid little kid!"

"Marcus! Apologize to your brother!"

Andrew just sat there, saying nothing. Chewing his cud! When the kids misbehaved in front of his parents, he often pretended it wasn't happening. Eliza *had* to handle it. Didn't she?

Sneering at Jake, Marcus sauntered past his father, his grandparents and his mother. He was aimed for the staircase near the front of the house. She knew he wanted to go upstairs and watch TV.

At least Bruce had stopped talking about the uselessness of the current mayor of Toronto. That was a blessing. Eliza said, "We don't throw food on the floor. No TV without picking up the bones and apologizing to your brother."

She heard him take a sharp right, away from the stairs and into the front vestibule. Everyone heard a susurrus of coats, the thunk of boots. "Andrew?" Eliza said.

"Marcus," Andrew said through a mouthful of food, "could you please come back here and just do what your mom asked you to do?" He wielded a half-cleaned bone in his own hand; a moment later, he bit into the remaining meat with gusto. Marcus yelled, "Only if Jake says sorry to me, too!" Then he muttered loudly, as if to himself, "Where's my other boot?"

Jake cried, "I didn't even *do* anything!" Corinne sat up straighter and put her hands in her lap, prissily, back to her old self. Both she and Bruce believed their grandchildren were overindulged. That was rich, considering how undisciplined they were about spending Andrew's money. Eliza tried to find her husband's eye, but he was busy with the kale salad. He served himself a dark green scoop of it and said to his father, "Have you tried this, Dad? Eliza marinates it with lemon overnight, so it softens up. Delicious."

Fine, if that was *his* contribution to disciplining their child. There wasn't going to be a big scene. No screaming, no yelling. She ignored the son who was running away from home and turned to the one standing by the island. "Jake, don't worry about it."

"I don't have to pick the bones up?"

"Only if you want to. As a favour to me."

Though he obliged her and tossed the bones into the sink, one by one, he said in a constricted voice, "I didn't throw anything on the floor. Marcus did it. On *purpose*." It was an expression he had just learned.

"I know. Thank you for being helpful. I appreciate it. Do you want dessert now or later?"

The offended expression transformed into a big smile. "Now!"

From the front vestibule, Marcus yelled, "I'm running away from home." It was one of his favourite threats.

Bruce glanced toward the front of the house; Corinne gazed at Eliza. They did not look at Andrew, who put another forkful of kale in his mouth; his big lantern jaws pumped obliviously. I am married to a cow, Eliza thought. To Jake, she said, "Come and sit down, honey, I'll get your dessert." She rose from the table. "Marcus, if you run away from home, you will not get to have apple pie and ice cream. But if you come in here and say thank you to your brother for picking up the bones, you can have your dessert. You decide."

He yelled, "Apple pie is *disgusting*. I'm never eating it again. I'm leaving. For *real*."

"Okay. Goodbye, honey." She smiled at Bruce. "May I take your plate? You don't have to eat the kale." He blustered about how good it was, then let her lift the plate and uneaten salad away from him. Eliza glared at Andrew before taking a few other plates to the kitchen island to add to the expansive array of cooking implements, bowls of sauce, pots, cutting boards and leftover appetizers. Eliza looked over the mess. In magazines, the kitchen island was always spotless, pristine. It must have been invented by a man, for it bore the mark of male delusion: a clear surface in a family kitchen. She said aloud, "No man is an island cleaner."

The front door opened. Slammed shut.

Sometimes Marcus faked his own exit and hung around to hear what his parents were saying about him. But no sounds filtered back into the dining room; he was gone. She glanced out the large kitchen window into the backyard; it was dark out there. Eliza served Jake his apple pie and ice cream. "Corinne, Bruce, would you like some, too?" Bruce, she knew, would eat a big piece; Corinne would have nothing.

Andrew stood up to fetch his father's and his own dessert and sat down again. Corinne asked Eliza, "Don't you think it's a little late for him to be out on his own?"

Busy scraping leftovers off a plate, Eliza asked her own question without looking up. "Corinne, I *do* think it's too late. What do *you* think, Andrew?"

She knew this would piss him off. He snapped at his mother, though the bite was meant for Eliza. "Just relax. He's not going anywhere. He'll be back in five minutes. No wonder he's stir-crazy, all this pick-pick-picking. No wonder he wants to run away from home." Andrew plunged his fork into the piece of pie that Eliza had set down beside his dinner plate.

Eliza and Corinne exchanged a comradely glance. *Men.* Eliza shrugged. "Andrew thinks I'm too controlling."

"Eliza, that's not what I think. But the kid has a big personality. He needs space, instead of adults always pushing back at him so hard. So he threw something on the floor. It's no big deal. It doesn't have to become a huge—"

The high screech of brakes shot through the front window of the house. It seemed to go on and on, sounding in Eliza's inner ear long after she dropped the plate in her hand, raced to the front door and out of it in her stocking feet. She leapt down the steps. Andrew and Bruce and Corinne were still rising from their chairs as she was high-stepping over the bank of ice and slush, leaping into the street from behind the tall parked van. She was dazzled by the glare of headlights. Like her son, she didn't look; she just ran out from behind the big vehicle that had been sitting there for days, blocking their view. It hid a child completely, especially a petulant child who was looking back at the house he'd left, not at the road in front of him.

Marcus was in a crumpled pile in front of the car, his arm and his head underneath the front bumper. She saw his blue and red Spiderman boots. The driver's door was already open, a person rising out of the car like a ghost, floating toward her, but she couldn't see into the headlights and she didn't care. She had already dropped down and said his name into the freezing air, afraid to touch him.

Icy slush soaked through her socks, her jeans, soaking her knees and shins. Everything she had ever done in her life had led to this moment, and it was wrong. Everything had been wrong and here was its issue: the child in the road, headlights shining above him.

He was curled away from her. She had to turn him over. But maybe she shouldn't move him. She found her voice but was afraid to look at his face. "Marcus, Marcus!"

The small body rolled of its own volition; she jumped. His face was unmarked; his eyes opened and fastened onto and into Eliza's like the day he was born, when the nurse had laughed and said a newborn can't focus; but she knew he saw her. And now he saw her and only then started crying in a way she had never heard before, low-toned, short cries, as though he was trying to say something but couldn't. He's been hit, she thought again, his head, he can't speak. The young man from the car knelt down beside Eliza and raised his voice over Marcus's weird keening. "I didn't hit him. I'm sure I didn't hit him. I stopped in time. The car didn't touch him, I would have felt it."

As though to confirm these words, Marcus cried, "Mommy!" Then Andrew was there, too, bending down, asking him to move. "Does it hurt? Did the car hit you?"

"I don't know," Marcus said, and began to sit up. Andrew lifted him off the road then, and Eliza stood up, too, her hand still on his head. The young man had stopped talking but he was there, waiting. It wasn't dark out at all, with the headlights, the streetlights. She saw him so clearly, clean-shaven, dark-haired, his soft, youthful face altered, marred by fear. With an odd formality he shook her hand. Eliza thanked him, which seemed paltry, *Thank you for not running over my son*, so she stepped forward and hugged him, briefly, a small woman's bear hug. She felt it go through her, his tremor; his shoulders and back were shaking, his teeth chattered above her ear. Another car came up behind his now. The driver, unaware of the nature of the gathering in the middle of the road, laid on the horn. The young man hurried back to his car and drove away with his excellent twenty-four-year-old reflexes, his 20/20 vision, his tendency, irritating to his friends, to drive conservatively, a habit that would never leave him now.

Eliza pulled Marcus out of Andrew's arms and carried him into the house herself; she needed to hold his intact body, to keep him in her arms even as she scolded him for leaving the house, for not looking, for not being careful.

He stopped crying soon enough, snuggled up with her on the sofa, almost too big for her lap. "Mommy," he said, timorously. Andrew, Bruce and Corinne were there, too, and Jake, who had stood at the door with his grandparents and still didn't fully understand what had happened. "Mommy," Marcus said, "I'm sorry I threw the bones." Then he remembered who he was supposed to apologize to. "Jake, I'm sorry. Mommy, can I still have my dessert? Please."

16

Domination

AN HOUR AND A HALF LATER, CORINNE WAS MERGING, nervously, onto Highway 401, the boys were asleep, and Eliza stood at the sink with a sponge in her hand. She'd turned up the volume on the radio to hear the news above her dishwashing. Hundreds of thousands of people across the Middle East and North Africa were in the streets, demanding political reform.

Eliza frowned at the burnt-on potatoes as the report moved from the reporter's excited voice—*Here in the square, tens of thousands of ordinary people from all walks of life have come together*—to the people shouting slogans in Arabic. The oldest, most entrenched regimes in the Arab world were changing, hopefully for the better. Could anything be worse than the dictators? Yet the sound of this good news frightened her. Eliza's only phobia was large crowds, getting crushed by a throng of people. That's why she did her Christmas shopping in November; even a busy mall put her in a cold sweat. She didn't know how the diminutive reporter, Adele Tabrizi, did her job.

The voices surged into the dining room. Tabrizi was recorded, somehow, speaking over them. She was the foreign correspondent for the public broadcaster's TV channel; the sister radio station often borrowed voice footage for important international news. Andrew was probably watching her right now upstairs on the TV.

Eliza could see her pale face, the dark, curly hair pulled back. Eliza had been following her for years, and especially in the last few months, as she bounced from North Africa to Oman to Egypt to Syria, back to Egypt, describing the relentless engine of change that had turned over with a fruit cart in Tunisia and was still roaring through the Middle East.

Eliza scraped rib bones into the compost bucket as snapshots of Marcus flipped through her mind: in the bathtub, perfect in his nakedness. Fighting with his brother at dinner. His body prone on the road, head under the car's bumper. His ribs were thicker, now, than these lamb bones. She snatched one of them out of the compost and felt its texture, tested its strength under her thumbs, as though trying to snap a thick twig. But she didn't want to break it. It reminded her of their wedding feast—whole roast kid. Turned on a spit in Thalassa's courtyard. One of her Greek suppliers and his brother had pried up a few flagstones, dug a trench and sat there all morning, turning the *souvla* by hand.

This evening, too, she had eaten from the body of a young animal, torn the flesh off its bones. She liked eating meat, always had. She had learned how to cut up freshly slaughtered lamb and goat at Aphrodite's, the restaurant on the island. *Aphrodite*. It was a common name for women there, without silly overtones. It was Aphrodite, the woman who ran the eponymous restaurant, who showed her how to feed two hundred people a night with unfailingly delicious food.

The bone snapped under her thumbs. She saw Marcus sitting in the tub, sucking in his belly, each rib visible. The air whisked cleanly out of her lungs for a few seconds and she gasped to bring it back.

If the driver had been going too fast. More ice. Bald tires. Even here, a peaceful city, with a hospital straight down Bathurst Street, she could not have saved her son from the force of impact. Her stomach churned; she literally felt sick with relief. With luck, blind, unknowable luck, so good, so harsh. Parents the world over had just lost a child.

If Marcus had been hit. Her thought braked there, over and over. Instead of crying, she became furious at Andrew. Though it wasn't his fault. But he was so *passive*. After turning off the water, Eliza dried her hands quickly and aimed the remote control at the radio, silencing the world.

The next moment her phone buzzed. She glanced around. There: her leather bag slumped on the writing desk. She crossed the room and dug out the phone.

> Hello swimmer. Was unexpectedly out of town this wk.
> Home again! You free tonight, quick drink?

Though it was the message she'd been waiting for, it did not please her. This woman expects me to drop everything, just like that, and rush out to see her? *Oh, sure, baby, whatever you want.* She threw the phone back into her bag and returned to the sink. She wasn't going to leave those last pots; she was going to *clean* them. Fucking things. Those burnt-on potatoes; that lamb grease. Cleaning, in the end, was domination. A brief, unsatisfying domination. They should make deposed dictators do it: life sentences of washing floors, toilets, the constant dirt of human life. For a few minutes, the only sound in the kitchen was the *cratch-cratch-cratch* of the metallic sponge. She rinsed out the last pot and flipped it over on the counter.

Why was *she* doing the dishes? To go upstairs to fight with Andrew, she had to pass the small desk, their bill and junk table. With her bag still on it, with her work iPad, makeup bag, bulging wallet and phone. A woman was hiding in her handbag. *Sure, a word from you and I will come running like a dog.*

Disgusted, she dropped the steel wool in the sink and took her first step away from the island. It was a gauntlet, to move along the table, walk past the chairs, the desk, away from the Amazon. But she triumphed, placing her foot on the bottom step of the staircase. She rose up the stairs, almost floating, the way heroines do. It was easy.

17

The Silk Route

SHE LOST HER NERVE AT THE STREET WHERE SHE USUALLY turned right to go to the studio. Pulled over and sat blinking in the icy air. She had told Andrew the truth: the revision of that wedding proposal *was* driving her crazy. And she often slipped out at night, when the studio was backlogged, and put in a few hours. She was on her third try, flowers, candles, table configuration, the whole scheme. Mrs. Minta, mother of the bride, just kept saying no. Her money gave her veto power. The official wedding planner was equally exasperated; she had called Eliza twice, mostly to vent. "How can the woman be against twenty different varieties of roses? Who is *against* roses?" Eliza answered, "It's not the flowers. It's the wedding. She doesn't want her daughter to marry the guy." That was also true. Meaning that Eliza might reconfigure the proposal and lay it all out again—different flowers, different tableware, taller candles, which were a fire-code nightmare—and Mrs. Minta could still reject it.

Thinking of all that work, gone to waste again, made her put the car in gear and drive straight south, to Queen Street.

It was as dark as a movie theatre. She had forgotten bars, except for the pub up the street from their house, where they sometimes took the kids for french fries and hamburgers. This was not that kind of place. You would never bring a kid in here.

The Silk Route. Deep plush divans were tucked into the corners. The Amazon was not sitting on any of them. I'll get used to
the dark, Eliza thought, trying to keep her breathing steady. My
eyes will adjust. She began to notice the carpets on the walls, a
couple of pieces of elaborate jewellery hung in shadow boxes.

She twisted between the first jumble of crowded tables, chairs
draped with women's coats and bags, thirty or forty faces floating
in the air, animated, talking above glowing candle holders of red
and green mosaic glass, the light flickering a kaleidoscope across
those faces, men and women who were all soft-looking, anony-
mously young. A jazzy, drunken buzz animated the air. She sat
down on the edge of one of the divans. A couple of tables away, a
blonde woman was raising her glass to make a toast when one of
her friends threw in a joke, derailing the whole group with laughter; several people almost tumbled from their ottomans. Eliza
watched surreptitiously at first, then openly, admiring the heads
tipped back, the glossy lips, smooth throats, every top low-cut or
revealingly open.

Drink, she thought. No thinking. Yes, like the responsible adult
you are. You're driving, Eliza. She looked around for a waiter or
waitress, feeling self-conscious. Embarrassed. What if Shar didn't
come? What were all these people doing out on a Sunday night
in early February? Didn't they have to work in the morning? She
shrugged off her coat and stood up, swaying in the too-loud
music. Back she went, through the tables, toward the bar, feeling
disoriented in this old world of young people. The black-haired
bartender approached her with a grin on his foxlike face; tattoos
encircled both his arms. Eliza thought he might be, at the outside,
twenty-three. Twenty-five? She couldn't tell their ages anymore,
except *younger than me*. She ordered the most expensive wine they
had on their chalkboard wine list, a Shiraz. A moment later, he
winked as he put an almost full glass down in front of her. "Good

choice," he said. Not wanting to gulp it down out of nervousness, she turned to survey the avid faces again. Half of them were busy on their phones, suspended in digital bubbles beside their friends. Did they know they were there, at the crest of the hill? Their twenty-five or twenty-nine or thirty-two years would click over soon into thirty-five, thirty-six. The dazzling rush down the other side of life would begin. They couldn't see it coming. The joy was in not knowing how everything would change, and change again.

Catchy French pop boomed over the sound system; she listened to the refrain, a name called over and over. *Aisha, Aisha, écoute-moi. Aisha Aisha, t'en vas pas.* Arabic rhythms threaded through the usual thumping. Right. That's where she was. The Silk Route. Where was the silk route again?

She turned around again, steadied herself against the bar and lifted her glass. Put her lips to the edge. But did not drink. Someone had come up behind her. He was too close. He felt as tall as Andrew. She half-turned, slowly, the wineglass still in her hand.

"Bonjour, ma belle amie," Shar said. "Madame Fleur, comment ça va?"

Eliza slid around, her back against the bar. Shar didn't step away; they stood face to face, or, more accurately, face to shoulder, for Shar *was* taller, though not as tall as Andrew. Eliza kissed her on the cheek, a hello peck to the *Bonjour.* When she drew back to kiss her on the other side, Shar moved forward and caught Eliza on the lips. The women kissed, to the surprise and delight of the bartender and a few people who happened to be ordering drinks. Four full lips. What else could they do, but invite tongues to join in? At such close quarters, what could the bartender and customers do but watch? Then glance away. When the customers moved off, the bartender continued to stare with frank appreciation.

Eliza thought: I have to stop kissing this woman in public. She drew her head back and answered with a decent accent, "Ça va très bien. Et toi?"

"Waa-ooow," Shar said, *en français*, which turned the retro wow into a word of sensual pleasure. She took a big theatrical step backwards to look Eliza up and down—her black knit dress, her thigh-high boots, surreptitiously put on in the car—and said in a French accent, "Yeah, I see you are well. Nice boots." Then, taking a step closer, whispered, "And you are *so* horny."

Eliza fell up into the large, deep-lidded eyes. She had been wet since she left her house. No, it had started when she replied to Shar's text. Ridiculous. It was like bad erotica, the old Penthouse Forum: *Eliza's pussy was dripping wet.* She put her hand on her forehead. Did she have a fever?

At home, this would be just another quiet Sunday night.

"I feel like I've been lured to this bar against my will."

Shar laughed. "It took so much persuasion to get you here! Let me lure you a little further, to my apartment. It's not far."

"Oh, really? I was hoping you lived on the east side. Or in Mississauga. That way I'd never be able to see you again. If it can't happen in my own neighbourhood, it takes too much time. Forget the suburbs."

"Sorry, ma chère. I live two blocks away."

"Oh, no. That's terrible."

"Should I move? Leave town?"

"Peut-être." They grinned at each other.

"Do you want a drink?"

"I'll have what you're having."

Eliza waved to the bartender, who jumped, almost stumbling, toward them. A moment later, setting down Shar's glass, he said, "This Shiraz really is good, isn't it?"

"The elixir of gods," Eliza responded. "No! Of goddesses." The women cracked up. The bartender licked his lips.

Shar winked at him. "You should have some yourself."

Eliza pointed to the corner where she'd left her coat. "Let's sit, shall we?"

They sat, facing each other; Eliza snuggled into the corner of the sofa. Shar lifted her glass; black liquid slid into her mouth. "Shiraz," she said. "A city in Persia. Close to Persepolis. The oldest wine-making region in the world. The Persians made wine thousands of years before the French."

Eliza couldn't think about wine. She must not think about anything. Rational thought would force her to leave the bar and return to her children, the house, her husband, even that wedding proposal, printed out, sitting on her desk.

The collar of Shar's white blouse opened to reveal a surprisingly wide expanse of chest in a body so narrow. Eliza could spread both her hands on that flesh, press down, not touch the white fabric at all. She could see Shar's black bra straps. But no cleavage. It was tailored like a man's shirt. Was it a man's shirt? Like the jeans, loose, frayed at the hem—don't think it, she thought, too late—exactly like a pair of her husband's jeans. Shar had not dressed up. The black belt had a plain large buckle at the centre. The sleeves were rolled up to her elbows; she wore no rings, no bracelets, no adornment, though Eliza's eyes glittered on her, slid down the long neck, back up to her face, her mouth, dropped to the slender forearms. Shar raised her glass, drank, stretched to put it down. She laid her left hand palm-up on the velvet sofa like an offering.

If they had spoken. If they had prodded each other with words, those old, blunt tools. If they had never seen each other naked. If they had not already breached mouth and skin. If she had never entered the water. It might have stopped there. A show-off kiss at the bar, a drink. Nothing more. Just the mistake of a woman in her forties (the skin around her eyes grown thin, lined) as she squinted back toward the abandoned part of her life, what she had left behind.

Shar raised her glass and they toasted to nothing, tangled up as they were in each other's eyes. This is exactly how it had been with Thalia. Desire so powerful she could not control it. Refused to control it.

It no longer seemed dark in the bar; Shar's wrist and inner arm glowed pearlescent. The long hand spread open, with its knobby opposable thumb, always separate from the other fingers. Working with flowers, cutters and glass made Eliza conscious of the extra-ordinary machines she used every day, two hands, ten fingers, hundreds of interlinked bones, woven tendons, the skein of fascia overcoating and connecting all, that net under the skin. Her hands were hard, calloused.

As she stared down at Shar's fingers, her mouth filled with saliva. She wanted to suck them. Make them wet enough. She wouldn't think. Nor organize, plan, sort, do the accounting on the back of a napkin, in her head, on her phone, she would not add or subtract or fill in another spreadsheet.

The expression slid across her mind, fell over backwards. Spread out, on a sheet. She smiled at Shar, who smiled back, not a wolf grin this time but a plum over-ripe, split. Shar hooked her lower lip with her teeth in a campy, blue-movie gesture that nevertheless looked sincere, and so sexy that Eliza felt again her own slipperiness. Sitting there, looking at the Amazon, her clitoris was already a hard nub, a wish: for it to be the small stone inside the fruit of Shar's mouth.

She didn't care if she had chosen wrongly *then*. The past was gone, the path lost even as it had opened before her, the pale, plain way of a woman's arm, extended. *Now* was the only time left.

18

Press Here

EVERY HAND SHOULD COME WITH A LABEL AND A manual. Miraculous hand, treacherous hand. Press here. Go on, do it. You know you want to.

Go ahead. Blow up your life.

Who is thinking this? Both of them. Eliza touches the tip of her middle finger to the centre of Shar's palm. Life, work, love lines, the web of days recorded in a handprint. Shar's long strong fingers close over Eliza's. Fingers slide in between other fingers. One palm presses greedily against the other palm, pushes, insists the hand is the body in miniature. Their hands writhe naked on the sofa, over and under, as their bodies hover above their hands, and their minds flicker through and around their bodies. At different moments the thought floats from one mind into the other until they are both thinking, like a Greek chorus: I will have to lie about this.

Press here. You know you want to.

Kaboom.

Has Eliza ever felt so much? Surely she has. She has worn this skin every day for the past forty-two years. It is the largest, most diffuse organ of the body, each bit of it connected to every other bit. That's why, she thinks, the Amazon's long fingers between my fingers are actually between my legs. The ring of muscle at her centre tightens up, though all it wants to do is spread wide.

Her mouth opens and Shar closes it with her own mouth, leans up against her and pushes her down at the same time, almost on top of her, while Eliza's hands are on Shar's hips, pulling her in. Shar braces herself against the high back of the sofa. Two mouths open, close, open, tongues everywhere. If a snake tries to slide down your throat, swallow it. Tongues, too, need instruction manuals. Stretch it out, put it in. Don't let it lie in the mouth. Can you lie to yourself, really? The two of them think, again, one right after the other, *I shouldn't be doing this in public.* Eliza yanks her sweater dress higher up her thighs. One of Shar's knees angles between them. Eliza pushes against it.

Both of them ask: Who is this woman?

Shar stops up her laughter. Not because it's funny but because it's not. Her own excitement unsettles her. This is not how it goes. Usually she manages both the pace and the intensity of the lust, her own, others'. She pulls back, glances around. The bar has never seen two women going at it like this. Nor the bartender. Shar feels his eyes the entire time, hot on them like the red tip of a laser. So much better than porn, isn't it, *mon petit chou*? Hopefully he doesn't start taking pictures with his phone.

But she can't keep her distance by thinking about him, worrying about what they're doing. She disappears into Eliza's mouth. They both disappear into an avalanche of breast and thigh and hip, falling down the divan, rising up, falling down, oh. Which way is up? White shirt, black bra, tights, dear god. Dess. Aphrodite, Athena, Beyoncé, Eliza, Shar.

"Eliza! Easy, girl!" Shar finds her way out, pulls away. Clear the way, I'm coming up for air! She does up her undone buttons, businesslike. They cannot take off each other's clothes in the bar. Eliza's eyes already have that glassy stoned-with-sex look. Shar gathers up her tumbled-sideways hair and tosses it off her face. "Would you like another glass of wine?" Without waiting for

Eliza's answer, she stands up and stalks over to the bar in her almost-cowboy boots.

It's an escape. Bar first, then the bathroom? Anything to slow this down. Drink more. Is that wise? Not telling, is that wise? Lying by omission. She's done it her entire adult life, for various reasons. But almost never, anymore, with lovers. She is not ashamed of what she has done, and still does, for a living. So why isn't she telling Eliza? Talking about sex work certainly would be a way to slow things down. Or stop them altogether. She puts her hands, palms down, on the bar.

The ogling bartender was not so ogley now. He shuffled shame-facedly, sideways, toward Shar. That's sweet, she thought, he has an erection. His embarrassment won her over. And his politeness. Without a trace of a leer in his face or in his voice, he asked, "What would you like?"

Shar blew her hair out of her eyes. "A cold shower."

It took him a moment to think of something to say. "I can give you a glass of ice water."

"That's something. I'll have two more glasses of the same wine, too. It's lovely."

"When I recommended that Shiraz, I had no idea it was *that* good. I think I'll have to, you know, take home a bottle. Or two."

Shar raised her eyebrows. "You mean you'll have what we're having?"

He put the glass of ice water on the bar. "In my dreams."

She tilted her head back and downed the glass of water. Set the tumbler back on the bar. "Sweet dreams, then. We'll try to keep it under control."

"No worries. I'm happy to see you enjoying yourself."

"I bet you are."

She dropped the two glasses of wine off at their table, excused herself and went downstairs to the washroom, that last bastion of solitude in the postmodern world. She really hoped that Eliza wouldn't follow her for the classic lesbian stall maul. After peeing, she pulled her jeans back up and sat down again.

Usually, strangers getting to know her *talked*. Her clients talked. They often talked a lot; they asked questions and waited patiently while she answered them. They also asked questions she could not answer (which was the point). They told her their fantasies, sometimes, but they also told her their worries, their fears, their actual struggles in the world. She already *was* a therapist. Even the thought of sex cracked certain people open and impelled them to talk. She had a long session with a man who spent the first half-hour of it crashing into her body so hard that she had to ask, several times, that he ease off; he was hurting her. Each time, he apologized, and became more gentle, but then slowly worked back up to the same furious pounding. He came, apologized again, and started talking. His wife had terminal ovarian cancer. They had three young kids. He said he had never been so angry in his life, at everything. Then he wept in her arms for almost an hour. That, too, was sex work, though not the kind that "society" wished to acknowledge or understand. Once she'd flipped through the childhood photo album of a woman who had been confined for the last seven years to a wheelchair, paraplegic. Shar listened to stories about the little girl, then the young teenager who ran and grew and danced through the yellowed pages. That was the foreplay.

Shar talked, too, but a central part of her job was to listen. People did not typically think of whores as skilled listeners, but for her, it was as important an attribute as giving good head and faking a wonderful orgasm. The activities were not that different. Mouth open or shut, genuine ecstasy or acted, it all required a similar kind of attention, a presence. She attended her clients, tended to them. Which was why becoming a sex therapist was a logical next step. The step out of bed, true. But she would still be doing *it*; still working with sex, in some capacity. The thought made her calm.

Luckily, her lovers talked. Women *loved* talking, about everything, not just sex. They talked and talked and talked. They let Shar see who they were by talking. Often it wasn't *what* they said; it was just that they were saying, and she was listening. Talking was also foreplay. Just like eating was. Food and drink was often the beginning of sex.

But Eliza had jumped straight into Shar's body, into her veins, like a dangerously high dose of a recreational drug. Ecstasy. Was it like this? She had never tried it; manufactured ecstasy would be wasted on her. And chemicals were not good for the body.

The wild woman Eliza in the bar, on the red-plush divan, working her dress up her thighs: ecstasy would come from that. Absolutely. But Shar was used to protocol, either established—the rules on her website were explicit—or carefully discussed. Eliza had wanted Shar to put her hands down her tights, reach through the neckline of her dress to touch her breasts. She had undone three buttons on Shar's blouse. There, in front of the patrons of the bar, it seemed that Eliza would have allowed anything.

Shar stood up. She flushed. The toilet, that is.

There was only one thing to do with a woman like that.

Returned from the washroom, she didn't sit but leaned over the back of the sofa and whispered in Eliza's ear, "Let's get out of here. I'm going to take you home and fuck you."

19

Open-Mouthed into the Sea

THE KEY ENTERED THE LOCK; SHAR TURNED IT AND stood back to let Eliza in. They were both breathing hard from rushing up the stairs. The bedroom was just a few steps down the hallway; a green light spilled out of the doorway onto the floor. "That's the bedroom, isn't it?" Eliza asked, grinning. "How convenient!"

Shar pointed down the hallway in the opposite direction. "Let's go to the sitting room. Don't worry about your boots. I'll take them off for you."

Eliza looked inquiringly at the bedroom. Shar smiled. "No need to rush."

"But I do have to rush."

She tucked a loose strand of hair behind Eliza's ear. "There is only one first time."

Eliza said nothing, but shrugged out of her coat and hung it up on a hook beside the door.

"I'll get us something to drink. Hydration is crucial." Shar disappeared into the kitchen, which was past the bedroom at the far end of the hallway.

Expecting to find a student's space filled with rickety furniture, Eliza was pleasantly surprised by the simple elegance of the sitting room. A thick Persian carpet covered almost the entire floor, a soft pile in blues and greys. The sand-coloured sofa along one wall was obviously expensive. Likewise the matching wing chair in front of the window and the sleek glass and wood desk with a computer and a neat pile of books on it. Eliza immediately deduced generous parents—or a huge student debt. A wall of bookshelves in dark wood had two tiers dedicated to small mementoes and framed photographs. Stepping toward them, she quickly realized the photographs were of Shar's family, and turned away; she didn't want to be reminded of families. Instead she gazed out the large window at the snowy expanse of park. She could see herself running across it. The longer she was in the room, the more Eliza's boldness ebbed away. The apartment made everything too real. Surrounded by objects, photographs, books, the smell of her, her style, Shar resolved into what she was, neither memory nor fantasy, but an actual woman.

What am I doing here, Eliza wondered. This was wrong. And stupid. She turned to look at the entrance to the hallway—she could just walk out, couldn't she?—and saw instead an old painting, tall and narrow, beside the doorway. With little perspective, a walled garden filled the canvas from top to bottom. She had to step closer to see what kind of trees were in the background. The paint was faded, but she made out pomegranates, both ripe fruit and bright red blossoms. The only place Eliza had ever seen those trees was on Lesvos, but their fruit was still green when she left the island. And the painting wasn't Greek; the writing on the upper left-hand side of the canvas flicked down, licks of ink in a language like Arabic.

Narrow canals divided the rectangles of red flowers. Men in turbans tended not only the flowers but the water also, leaning over little streams, peering into them, diverting one of them with a spade. The canals formed a blue maze around and between the men and the flowers. It was a painting with the sound of water in it. She looked up; the Amazon was coming down the hallway.

"Here I am," Shar said lightly. She came into the room holding a tray laden with wine and water glasses, one for each of them, and a bowl of almonds and raisins.

"This room is lovely," Eliza said. "It feels like another country. Old European or something." She sat down on the well-appointed sofa and closed her legs.

"That's what my mother says. She's French, from Marseilles originally, but when I was little, we lived in a Parisian suburb, just this sort of place, a long hallway with a series of rooms, one big window in the sitting room. That's why I took this apartment. It felt like home. There's a great view to the west. Every room is bright." She kneeled down in front of the small table, handed Eliza a glass of water.

She popped an almond in her mouth, stood and crossed the room, flicked on her computer. Music rose through the air, not only in front of Eliza but behind her from two small wall speakers, complex rhythms on an oud or mandolin, tied up with a horn's high silver ribbon. A woman began to sing in a Middle Eastern language. Shar sat down on a pillow in front of the sofa. "You can relax. I promise I won't bite."

"That's too bad."

"Okay, I promise I *will* bite, but not hard enough to leave any marks." Eliza shook her head, a drop of smile on her lips. Shar drew an X over her chest. "Cross my heart. I said I would take off your boots for you, but first I want to look at them. *Very* nice boots." She popped another almond in her mouth. Still chewing, she rose up on her knees and used her hand and elbow as a wedge to spread Eliza's closed legs just that much, elbow to fist. Eliza did not re-close her legs. She just sat there, frozen. Shar sat back and took a swallow of wine. "Now pull your dress up to your thighs."

Eliza was almost offended by the command. But it worked. She slowly pulled up the thick sweater. Lap level. "Keep going," Shar said. Eliza lifted her ass and hips, stopped when the folds of the skirt were resting on the tops of her thighs. The air came in; she felt the wet gusset of her tights and underwear.

Shar turned her head sideways to get a better view between her legs. "Mmmm. Waaow. Gorgeous boots." She ate a few raisins. "Sorry I don't have grapes. They're sexier." She held out the bowl; Eliza shook her head.

"So, tell me," Shar continued, "have you ever had an affair before?"

It was like being hit by an elastic band. Eliza snapped her legs closed. "No."

"You haven't slept with anyone but your husband in . . ."

"Ten years. Since we got together."

"Wow." Shar lifted her eyes above Eliza's messy hair. At the painting, maybe, those men in the garden. "I don't know how anybody does it. Monogamy, I mean. It's like . . . being a nun."

Eliza opened her mouth, set to defend the marriage contract, then clamped it shut. It was absurd to defend monogamy on the eve of her first infidelity. Instead, she drily asked, "Why do you ask?"

"I'm wondering if I can go down on you without a piece of plastic." Shar was serious. "I'm all about safe play. I'm clean, I was tested recently. And I'm extremely careful."

Piece of plastic, safe play, tested. These words intimidated Eliza so much that she had to ignore them. The apartment *was* another country; she could only pretend to be comfortable here. "If I have an STD, it was immaculate infection."

Shar laughed. "Or from the pool."

"You can't get an STD at the pool."

"Well, *you* could, the way you behave in the change room."

Eliza pulled her sweater dress down to her knees. "That's not how I usually behave at the pool."

"Hey, I'm joking. Sorry." Shar raked both her hands through her thick hair. "I love the way you behaved."

"You know what, I think I might have made a mistake. This is . . . I . . . I should go."

"If you wanna go, go. I get it." Shar held her gaze while languidly unfolding her legs. She stretched them out in front of her and leaned back on her hands like a kid watching TV. Eliza did not move a muscle. Shar smiled, generously, considering that she had just called Eliza's bluff. Then she said, "Now pull your sweater up again. And pull down your tights."

"What are *you* going to take off?"

"Me?" Shar took in a big swallow of wine; Eliza heard the gulp. "I'm going to take off your boots. At the right moment." She eyed them, and the rest of Eliza's legs. "Those tights are great. Thick. Is your pussy still nice and wet?"

Eliza made a sound between laugh and cry.

"I guess that means yes." Shar smiled differently now. Her face had narrowed, somehow, with sly intention. "Spread your legs." Eliza spread her legs. "Up on your toes a little. Lift your ass. Imagine taking in a nice big cock." That shocked Eliza; it showed on her face. Shar whispered, "Oh, yes, I have a *very* big cock. A strapon. You'll love it. I will fuck you better than any man ever has."

Eliza swallowed. Lust and fear and distress brought sweat out under her arms. She didn't want Shar to fuck her better than a man. She did not want to think about men; one man in particular needed to be shut firmly, impossibly, out of her mind. This was simply a . . . ladies' night out, a drink with a friend, they got a little tipsy, and here they were. It wasn't meant to have the same force as sex with a man; it was supposed to be *just fooling around*. She knew this rationalization was specious, yet she clung to it.

Besides, it *was* different. For one thing, if Shar were a man, Eliza would already be naked; they would be fucking by now. She would be a fallen woman instead of one perched, legs awkwardly spread, at the precipice. Her whole lower body was thumping, as though her heart had liquefied and poured into her genitals. She said, "If I put my legs together, I think I could come. I'm basically vibrating down there."

"*Down there*! Name the parts, baby. Do you mean your *cunt*?"

"You know what part I mean. Throbbing."

"Do you come easily?"

"No. I almost never come without touching myself."

"You don't like to give it up, huh?"

"It's not a matter of giving it up or not. I just . . . It takes a while."

"Keep your legs spread." Eliza complied, writhing slightly. Shar said in a low voice, "It's hard for me not to lean over and pull those tights off you. I love seeing the pussy for the first time. All wet and ready . . . How you doing?"

Eliza just shook her head.

"Touch yourself. Give yourself a little pat so she knows I'm coming." Eliza gingerly placed her whole hand between her legs, and squeezed.

This time Shar smiled differently. Playfully. Oddly innocent, considering the circumstances. But it was infectious. Eliza grinned, bobbed her eyebrows up and down. "So. Now what happens?"

"*Ma belle amie, il y a deux méthodes.* The slow method and the fast method. As you can tell, I love the slow method. Why should those foodies have all the fun? I've started the slow sex movement. If you wait for an hour or two for an orgasm, the orgasm is really delicious."

Eliza let her head fall back against the sofa. "Shar, I do not have two hours."

"Another time. Tonight we'll just have a snack. Speaking of which, you're going to have to close your legs to pull your tights down to your knees."

"Say please."

"Please." Shar undid the buttons of her white blouse and pulled the shirt off one shoulder. Eliza inhaled a deep breath and hooked her thumbs into the tightly woven material of her tights. She wriggled her hips and ass out of them, unconcerned about the rolls of fat on her belly. With a woman, even the first time, you didn't have to wish you were thinner or pretend you were perfect. Most healthy women had flesh on them; it was natural, unremarkable except that her whole body felt remarkable right now, open, soft, tense, agitated for touch. She left her purple underwear on.

In front of her, just like that, Shar's shirt was off. Her bra dropped to the floor. Those lovely breasts! Eliza involuntarily gasped.

"Keep pulling down your tights. And keep your legs open. I need to be able to see you."

By the time Eliza had worked the tights down to her knees, she realized why Shar had made her keep her boots on. Because she couldn't *take off* the tights. She was stuck.

Sitting directly in front of her, Shar licked her hands like a cat and rubbed them up and down her nipples. "Don't be shy," she said. "Pull the panties down, too. I've never seen your pussy. Remember that day at the pool? I touched you, but I didn't get to look." Eliza pulled her underwear to her knees. "Keep your legs open at the same time."

Eliza spread her thighs against the elasticity of the tights; it was like doing an absurdly erotic resistance exercise.

Shar's voice dropped lower. "You're going to have to work harder if you want me to get my fingers in there. Isn't that what you'd like right now? Hold your knees open as wide as you can." Eliza literally felt weak in the knees, but she performed her task.

When Shar was satisfied, she crawled over, eye-level with Eliza's quivering thighs. She slid her hands slowly along them, then slid the right one further, until the fingers came to her lips and pushed in between them. With her other hand, she spread Eliza's labia.

"Ooo-la-la. Look at that. So swollen!" She began to rub the dark red nub with her thumb. Eliza didn't know where to send her eyes, to that expert thumb, to Shar's face, or her gorgeous tits, the big hard nipples, or back to her own body. Shar slid two fingers across the whole glistening mound, found a good rhythm for rubbing and caressing and pressing every wet contour. Eliza couldn't keep the quiver out of her thighs. Each exhalation of breath became a small cry. She stared down, mesmerized; one finger slid inside her slowly. She gripped it and whined to feel it pull out. Two fingers entered again and she pulled Shar's hand against her and bucked against it. When a third finger slid in, she cried out. "Shhh," said Shar. "Don't scream." She kept her fingers inside and massaged Eliza's cervix while still flicking her thumb over her clitoris.

How long did Eliza writhe around on Shar's hand? A minute? Three? Ten? She had no idea. No thoughts; she was all body. She closed her eyes. Rising up, Shar came close to her face and whispered, "Don't close your eyes. Watch me." Eliza ignored her, and kept her eyes closed; she wanted to come. She lifted her hips up higher, pushed down. Shar's voice was so sexy, so deep and pushy and soft, so unabashedly *slutty*, that each phrase was like another set of fingers, or a cock, or a tongue; each expression pulled the orgasm closer. When Shar said, "That's it, nice and deep. *Fuck* my hand," a ring of energy bloomed open inside Eliza and just as quickly began to close. She kept thrusting; she heard her breath become whimpering and was surprised to be coming so fast.

Then Shar relaxed her arm. Stopped moving her thumb.

Eliza cried out. Shar slid her fingers away and stroked her again, more slowly. For Eliza, the momentum was lost. For Shar, it was beginning in earnest. She caught Eliza's angry eye, flashing wide and open, bluer than she had ever noticed, and grinned.

"Don't be grumpy, Madame Fleur. I think it's time to take off your boots."

As soon as they were naked and sprawled on the bed, Shar said, "Lift up." Eliza raised her hips, the pillow slid under her. She would not have liked it if a man had positioned her this way. Strange. She was not herself. Shar was naked, too, acres of skin and muscle, her hair electric, a short mane tossing around her head as she leaned over Eliza, man-handled her. Woman-handled. She caught her ankles, spread her legs just so, lifted her knee. "So I can get in there," she said. Eliza was pure attention. Shar murmured, "You look gorgeous right now. And your eyes! Your eyes are turquoise. Are you stoned?"

"Utterly."

"On what?"

"Lust. And confusion. Why do women ever have sex with men?"

Shar laughed. "Because they're men. I like men. They have a certain attraction. I mean, beyond their cocks." She smiled wickedly. "But I have a lovely cock, too."

"So you said. I thought you were kidding."

"It's always hard! Would you like to see my strap-on?"

Eliza squawked, "No!"

"Nothing to fear but fear itself," Shar whispered, still grinning. "But I agree." She sent her eyes wandering over Eliza's body. "No need to be gluttonous. This is already a . . . feast."

It was like falling into the sea with an open mouth. Live-wired and snapping through Eliza's flesh and mind was a single, happy certainty: *She's going to lick my pussy!* She did not allow herself to calculate how long it had been since Andrew's tongue had touched her there.

She fell down the deep ravine of Shar's spine, fell up, onto her big round ass curving in the air. Then she gasped (diving open-mouthed slowly into the sea) because Shar didn't lick her. Shar took her own breast in her hand, arched her back and applied her erect nipple to Eliza's clit. Rubbed, flicked, slid, pushed. Eliza doubled up the other pillow under her head to see better. She wanted to cry from the pleasure of it but she also wanted to *watch*, to remember it. No one had ever done this to her before.

Shar switched sides, rubbed until both her breasts were wet. Her whole chest was slick and red. Then she slid her fingers inside and began to lick. For a long time (What is long? What is time?), she licked Eliza's pussy teasingly. Then she began to kiss her, lips to lips, tentatively, gentle little kisses that ranged outward, to her thighs, where they turned to easy bites, not too hard, but sharp, before going inward again, back up and over her clitoris. Eliza was amazed. She could not remember the last time anyone had spent so much delicious, decadent time with her body. Well, actually, she could. Thalia had been like this, sometimes; different, but generous like this, languid, the flesh and its combinations unravelling and unravelling and unravelling, the maze inescapable. Eliza gave up trying to rush. After all, it might never happen again. She swivelled her hips, following the movement of Shar's mouth, trying to get that roving tongue where she needed it to be. Still kissing her, Shar slowly slipped her fingers out of Eliza's pussy and let her hands range, too, over the expansive flesh, following the curves, reaching up to her breasts, her nipples. Eliza opened her mouth, inviting those fingers. Shar teased her there, too, sliding her middle finger in time with her tongue around and around the lips of the two openings, entering both only slightly. Eliza went still, trying to absorb the exquisite doubleness of pleasure. She let her head fall back. The room disappeared. She had never been so naked in her life. She spread her legs wider and moaned.

Shar's fingers left her mouth and slid down again. She rested her head and neck for a moment on Eliza's thigh while her fingers kept the momentum going, flicking back and forth, inside, back and forth, inside, pressing deeper. Her tongue took over again, and flicked more quickly now. Her tongue knew how to keep time and find time and ignore time. Tongue out, rigid, Shar slipped fingers in Eliza's pussy again, then in her ass (Which one? How many fingers did she have?) and began to shake her head, slowly at first, *no no no*. Eliza mouthed, then whispered, then cried, *oh yes yes yes*. Covering her own mouth was not a possibility. The cries of her children had long ago ended her own sexual cries. With her thighs clamped around Shar's head and hands, she howled in time to the bucking of her hips. She hoped Shar could breathe.

Shar hoped that her new neighbours wore earplugs. Or slept deeply. When Eliza's legs fell open, she lifted her head, grinning again. "So. Did you come?"

"What did you do to me?"

Shar lightly bit the inside of her thigh. "*Ma belle amie!*" she said. "That's *just* the beginning." She put her head down again, tongue out, and began to lazy-circle around Eliza's clitoris. At first Eliza was going to protest, but then—she didn't. She just lay there, slowly moving her hips in time to Shar's mouth and tongue. Within a few minutes, Eliza came again, more easily and not as noisily. Shar let her rest for a few minutes then lowered herself again.

Six orgasms later—she counted each one carefully, on her clenching and unclenching fingers—Eliza said, "You're just showing off now."

Shar's eyes swivelled up from her ministrations. "I love doing this."

"I'm dizzy. My body is not used to experiencing so much pleasure."

"Tantra, baby. The spiral. Up and up. Just take a few slow, deep breaths. Pull some of that energy into the rest of your body."

"I want to do it to you. It's been so long since I've . . . done that."

"Done what? Just say the words!"

"Gone down on a woman."

"You mean it's been so long since you've licked a woman's clit and made her come in your mouth? So it won't be your first time, then?"

"No." Eliza smiled, almost demure.

"Ah! So you have a tantalizing story to tell me about your past!"

"Maybe later." Eliza sat up and grabbed Shar's ass, trying to haul her up. "I can't talk with my mouth full."

"Oh, yes, please," said Shar. She crawled panther-like over Eliza's body, already spreading her legs.

20

What Ecstasy?

THE NEXT MORNING, ELIZA LOCKED THE BATHROOM door and stood naked in front of the mirror. She was disappointed. Bang your shin, you get a bruise; make a mistake with a razor, you bleed for an hour. But ecstasy just *vanishes*.

Desire was all-consuming, all-encompassing, a ravenous god. And invisible. Was it invisible? She stepped closer to the mirror and examined her hips and her breasts for bruises. Reflected around her naked flesh was the glass-filled room, turquoise towels, opaque white glass tiles. She saw nothing but Shar's hands on her. She had remained in bed, eyes closed, until Andrew had got up and gone downstairs.

Well, adulterous lesbian sex looked good on her. Despite three hours of sleep, she was glowing. Seeing herself naked made her feel how swollen and chafed and hungry she still was. She wanted to lie down on the cold marble floor and masturbate. Not that it would be the same as last night. Nothing could be the same as last night. Last night had gone on for too long. If she hadn't had to leave, she would still be there: a terrible fact. The guilt lay down in her alongside the lust.

Naked, breasts covered in fingerprints, she cleaned furiously. Andrew had left the entire contents of his electric razor in the porcelain sink. She did not curse him. She poured out Mother

Hubbard's Organic Cleanser (no harsh chemicals for her family, nothing toxic in her hallowed home) and swished away his gold and copper and grey stubble. To the tears that pricked her eyes, she muttered, "Oh, fuck right off."

She let the shower run hot, then stepped into the glass cubicle. Just as she was washing the DNA evidence away, Jake stuck his head through the door. Under the noise of the water, she saw his mouth form the word that she could not hear him say: *Mommy?*

She opened the glass shower door. "What is it?" She tried to keep the impatience out of her voice.

"Daddy says my hair smells like dead dog. He says to take a bath with *you*." Jake stepped into the room and pushed down his pyjamas pants.

She sighed. Jake asked, "Are you mad at me?"

Why did Andrew do that? "No. It's okay. I'm just in a rush. And I'm not taking a bath, as you can see." He stepped into the shower. Self-conscious, she folded her forearms over her breasts before leaning over to sniff his dog-head. He's only six, she thought. There was nothing for him to see or smell. But she always wondered what Jake could feel. "Honey, I disagree with your dad. It's not dead dog, not yet."

"So I *don't* have to wash my hair?" He pressed up close against her body, then turned and elbowed her belly as he angled for a greater portion of spray.

"You *do* have to wash your hair, now that you're in here hogging the water."

They washed together. After he rinsed the shampoo from his hair, he stood away from the hot water and eyed Eliza. Critically, she noticed, waiting for whatever was rising in his mind to lift out of his mouth. And there it came, less like a speech bubble in a cartoon than a bubble clotting inside a vein, disrupting the rhythm of her heart.

"Mommy, you don't have to scrub so hard. You're not *that* dirty."

By the time they went downstairs, blow-dried and dressed, it was already after eight. She braced herself before entering the kitchen; Andrew would be there. She exhaled a long controlled breath, then gasped, going in.

But he wasn't at the table; he wasn't by the island. "Where's Dad?"

Marcus's eyes remained glued to the iPad screen. "Second floor. Office." She'd glanced at the office door at the end of the hallway on the second floor, but the light was off.

"Have you had breakfast, Jake?" They needed to be out the door by eight thirty to get to school on time.

Marcus piped up, "He wouldn't eat the quinoa crunch. Dad got mad at him." He held the edges of the iPad as if it were the yoke of a small plane; he was shooting enemy targets.

"Marcus, I wasn't talking to you. Jake, what do you want for breakfast?"

"Cereal."

"Cornflakes?"

"Anything except for that healthy stuff."

"Yeah, we'll have to feed the quinoa crunch to the birds." She poured Monsanto-engineered cornflakes into a bowl and splashed in some milk.

Still swerving in his seat, not looking up from his mission, Marcus said, "Dad already tried that. Even the birds won't eat it."

"Have you brushed your teeth, honey?" He launched a missile at an enemy target. It was a hit; the explosion was too loud for a seven-year-old on a Monday morning. "Can you please turn that thing off and go and brush your teeth? How long have you been on there anyway?"

Through a mouthful of cornflakes, Jake said, "Since he got up. And he won't let me have a turn."

"I did *so* let you have a turn, you liar!" The boys started arguing. The word *liar* reverberated in Eliza's head. She marooned herself at the far end of the island and chewed on a piece of cold toast, sipped at a glass of water. It's all I deserve, she thought. Bread and water. She glanced toward the staircase. What was Andrew doing in his office? Online, sending his mother most of his salary, probably. Good, it would keep him occupied. She might be able to leave without seeing him.

The fight was escalating.

"Enough, you two! Jake, eat your breakfast." She stalked over to Marcus. "You have three seconds to give the iPad to me. Turn it off." He swore under his breath. "What did you say?"

"Flowers." He smiled at her mockingly.

Jake crowed, "He said *fuck*!"

For the first time since Eliza had come down the stairs, Marcus looked up from the iPad long enough to shoot his sibling a look of disgust. "Stop being such a tattletale!"

"One . . ."

"Jake said a swear word, too!"

"Two . . ." Jake took his bowl to the counter and walked by Eliza, sticking his tongue out at Marcus, who turned the iPad sideways and blasted out another shot.

"Three! Right now, Marcus. Otherwise there will be no screen time tonight."

Marcus sneered in protest but snapped the cover shut and shoved the iPad toward her.

From the third floor—he must have left the office and gone up to their bedroom again—Andrew yelled, "Do you know where my blue shirt is? That nice Italian one?" She swore under her breath more quietly than her son had.

"Hurry up, boys," she said. "We have to go."

She went to the base of the stairs and called, "I took it to the dry cleaner's, remember?" He did not remember; he never did. The boys filed into the downstairs bathroom and began brushing their teeth. An essential act of wifedom, she thought: shouting from a distance about other people's clothes. "Okay, guys, boots, coats. Jake, where are your mittens?" She remained at the base of the stairs, pure-hearted, deceitful, and desperate to get out the door heard but unseen. "Darling, we're off! I'm taking the boys to school!" To the boys, "Say goodbye to Daddy."

"Bye, Dad," shouted Marcus, gruffly, and left the house. Jake trundled past her, boots on, and called, "Daddy, I love you *so much*!"

"I love you, too, Jacob! Have a great day!"

"I'll be careful, Daddy!"

"I know, Jacob! Don't you worry! You'll have a great day!"

Eliza wondered what he'd been worried about, but forgot to ask him in the final push to get out the door. All the way to school, the boys fought verbally, sparred physically, swore covertly when they raced ahead of her, complained when they trailed behind, and kicked slush at each other. One dirty plume missed Jake and caught her silk-and-wool trouser-leg instead. She hissed at them, flapped her arms. She couldn't get them to school soon enough.

Which turned out to be literally true. They were late. Mother and sons stood at the locked playground doors, peering in the windows. "This is what happens when you're distracted in the morning. You have to go to the office." She pulled on the door again, uselessly. "No one's going to open for us. Come on, we have to go all the way around to the front."

Jake said, "Mommy, it's *good* the school is locked. Because if it was open, the bad man could walk in and shoot us."

"What? What are you talking about?" She glared at the back of Marcus's head. "Were you watching some horrible zombie video this morning?"

Marcus glanced over his shoulder at his brother. "You weren't supposed to tell her."

"Tell me what? Jake, don't walk through that puddle!" He sloshed directly through it. "Tell me what?"

"Daddy was listening to the news this morning."

"And?"

"There was a big shooting."

"In the U.S.?" Or had the gun virus migrated? Was it here now, too? She gazed at the windows of the school, dark with reflection; it was impossible to see the children inside.

"He got the gun," Marcus began in an eerily adult voice, but Jake broke in boisterously, "From Walmart!" Marcus continued, still formal, "It just happened a couple hours ago. A man shot fourteen children. They were at school early for a volleyball prac- tice. Daddy said 'fuck' and turned off the radio."

The hair on the back of Eliza's neck stood up; her stomach flipped. She could not know what destabilized her more in that moment: the tragedy of the news itself or the cool, oddly mature voice of her seven-year-old relaying it to her. Some noise escaped her; she stopped walking. Didn't you have to stop? How could you keep walking? She forgot about the silk-and-wool-blend slacks and dropped down, braced a knee on the sidewalk, opened her arms. "Come here. Let me give you each a hug. That's such hor- rible news." Hugging them, she teared up. She often told Andrew not to listen to the news at breakfast time; this was exactly the sort of thing she didn't want the boys to hear. Yet they would hear about it at recess, or after school. The terrible world pressed up against their lives; they lived in the terrible world. She squeezed them to her, harder, until she could feel their shoulder blades through their coats. Marcus said, "Okay, Mom." She let him go. He said, "Don't cry." She wiped the tears off her face and stood up. They kept walking along the sidewalk; Jake sloshed through the next slush puddle.

Marcus remained serious. "Dad said that it could have been worse. The man was going to hide in the school to kill more kids. He had lots and lots of bullets. Hundreds of them. He didn't know about the volleyball practice. But a janitor caught him. He shot the janitor first, then he went to the gym."

"Sweetie, we can talk about it later. Maybe we can talk about it at home, because it's not a happy way to begin the day." If she told them not to talk about it at school, it was the first thing they would bring up. They stood at the front doors now, which were also locked. Jake pushed the buzzer. With uncharacteristic patience, both boys stood there, waiting to be let inside. Locked doors and a goddamn buzzer! Her stomach twisted. As if some rampaging nutcase couldn't just shoot his murderous way through in fifteen seconds. And the Americans, ah, the endlessly innovative, powerful Americans, and their fine gun lobby. A moment later, a different buzzer sounded, from inside; Marcus stepped forward to pull open the door. Normally Eliza would leave them as soon as the door opened, but this time she went to the office with them, signed her name, made sure they got their late slips, stamped with a turtle. The dark-haired secretary was chatty, smiling; she hadn't heard the news yet. Eliza did not tell her.

The moment she stepped out of the school again, her phone rang. Work, Kiki. "Da main sink is blocked." Again. A month ago, they spent $300 on an emergency plumber to unclog the sink. It didn't have commercial-size pipes. "And I poured flower-ass water in dere dis morning, so it really stinks." In crisis, her accent and her gift for hyperbole kicked into overdrive. "It stinks like dead bodies rotting in da cupboards."

Eliza let go a dry sob, turned it into a cough. "Open all the doors and windows. Mrs. Minta is coming in this afternoon, and you know how difficult she is."

"Dat woman! Bianca's trying to air da place out already, so we are freezing in 'ere. We need da plumber!"

Eliza rushed down the street, hoping that the ice under the slush had melted. She couldn't afford another fall. Think of those parents right now—*no, don't think of them*—the pipes for that sink were non-commercial—the landlord had lied about that and still refused to change them—and Mrs. Minta was coming in. Stupid woman. Who, in the midst of so much ugliness, did not love flowers simply because they existed? *Every day, I leave the kids at school, trusting they'll be all right.* She hurried across the street, undone, the trail of pleasure through her body lost. She had begun the day thinking, unbelievably, of ecstasy.

What ecstasy?

21

Day of Liberation

AFTER THE NEWS, ANDREW DECLARED THAT HE WAS peckish. "We should celebrate all these liberation protests in the Middle East. Come down and have a glass of wine with me."

"Wine, at ten o'clock at night? That's romantic," she said, and gave him a come-hither smile. "But it will make me fat."

As she stood up, he slapped her butt. "Good. You're looking way too fit lately. All that swimming. Eat something!" He wanted to tell Eliza about his visit to the urologist; to do that, he needed to fortify her with food.

In the kitchen, while his wife put out cheese and crackers and sliced up an apple, Andrew opened a bottle of reasonably good red. They sat down on stools along the island, clinked glasses. "To liberation," he said. She echoed his words with a smile. He added, "I'm not just talking about the Arab world."

"Good. It *should* be an aspiration for the whole planet."

"Actually, I'm toasting something closer to home. *Much* closer to home."

"What do you mean?"

"I had an appointment with the urologist today."

She stared at him blankly.

Then fear, of cancer or some other illness, rose into her eyes. He quickly said, "Nothing disastrous. I went to discuss getting snipped."

Her mouth opened; no word came out.

"We've been talking about a vasectomy since Jake was born. So I finally went and met the urologist. Just a preliminary appointment." He decided not to reveal that he'd already booked a date for the procedure. It couldn't happen until May. She would have plenty of time to adjust.

Eliza took a larger sip of wine and held it in her mouth for a few seconds. Swallowed. Then she said, "How could you *do* that to me?"

He laughed. Judging from the expression on her face, this was a mistake. "Come on. It makes sense. And nothing is going to happen to *you*."

"It *doesn't* make sense. What if . . . ?"

Andrew reached across the cool stone counter and took her hand. "What if *you* wanted to have another baby? You have to face the facts, Eliza. I'm done having kids. And if I have a vasectomy, we would be free. We wouldn't have to worry about an accidental pregnancy anymore. Sex would be a lot less stressful. In case you haven't noticed, condoms are not working all that well for me these days."

"It's not 'what if I wanted another baby.' I don't want another one. I am managing the longings. No more babies." He looked unconvinced. "Really. But what if you have the same pain that Sheila's husband developed after *his* vasectomy?" She slid her hand away from his.

"Sheila's husband had a vasectomy?" Andrew frowned. "Really?" Sheila's husband Karl was a tall, athletic man—Andrew often saw him out running; *running*, not jogging—who wrote historical novels about his Norwegian ancestors. They were Andrew and Eliza's neighbours to the south. Sheila was an English professor, and an author, too. "What pain? Karl didn't mention anything to me."

"How often do you see him?" Eliza asked in a withering tone. "At the neighbourhood barbecue once a year."

Andrew ignored the jab. "At Janet's, for Christmas drinks, remember?"

"Okay. Twice a year."

"We always chat if we run into each other at Loblaw's."

Eliza shook her head. "He's not going to tell you about the excruciating pain in his genitals at Loblaw's. He was in agony. He had to get it reversed. And their sex life *still* isn't back to normal."

"When do *you* see Sheila?" Andrew asked, baffled by this surfeit of personal information about neighbours who were friendly but not close. When did women talk about all this stuff, anyway?

"At the pool. She swims too."

"Why did *he* get a vasectomy?"

"Andrew! Don't you remember the summer I was pregnant with Marcus?" He squinted. No. He did not remember. "I can't believe that you could forget. She was pregnant with twins. And miscarried in month five. The babies died."

"Oh, god, yes. Oh, yes. I remember now."

"*That's* why Karl got a vasectomy. Sheila never wanted to experience anything like it again. Don't you remember how freaked out I was? We were in the middle of renovations and my ankles were swollen up like gourds. I was just past five months myself. How could you forget that?"

He was losing his way in the conversation. This was supposed to be about the *opposite* of babies and miscarriages and pregnancy. This was supposed to be about *freedom*. "I do remember now. I do. But you know . . . the urologist said the pain usually resolves within a week or two."

"Naturally the urologist would say that. I don't care about *him*."

"It's a woman."

"Oh! Well, she doesn't have sex with you."

At the sound of his laughter, Eliza jumped off her stool. He shook his head. Here it was, spreading before him, the swamp of emotions his wife experienced when it came to fertility. Quicksand everywhere.

"I don't want you to do it. When a man gets a vasectomy, he barely produces any semen." She went to the sink, turned on the tap, squeezed out a rag. "What comes out is just a little trickle."

"How do you know that? I didn't know that until I went to see the urologist."

"Oh, I read it somewhere. In a woman's magazine, probably. And I don't *want* you not to have any semen. I *like* it." She wiped down the island.

"But it doesn't affect sexual performance."

"Unless you experience pain that doesn't go away. That won't help our sex life, will it?"

"But the pain complication must be very rare. It's a procedure that's done all over the world."

"You don't *need* to have a vasectomy. We're already free enough. I'm practically menopausal, okay?"

"Stop exaggerating."

"Don't worry, we're not having another baby." He could hear her voice rising from an E-minor unreasonable into F-flat whine. "I just don't want anything bad to happen. Any kind of surgery can go wrong." An unusual stillness blossomed in the room. It billowed out and out; he felt like it was filling the entire house.

He pulled his hand over his nine o'clock shadow; the wiry red and blonde hairs of his beard scraped his palm. The doctor had made it all sound so simple.

Eliza had finished wiping down the island and had taken up the broom. She swept the floor slowly, diligently, collecting the detritus of the day. Then she suddenly stopped and fixed him with those blue laser-beam eyes. "I know this sounds weird, but I have a superstitious belief in your come."

"Eliza!" He felt embarrassed for being so flattered. In a baritone Wizard-of-Oz voice, he said, "Ah, yes, the great potency of my magical jiz!"

"Not so much in its potency. Obviously the sperm does the job; we have two kids. But more I just . . . I just love it. You know, when you come on me. The mess of it. It *is* magical—there are a bjillion human seeds in that stuff!"

He narrowed one eye at her, making a show of his doubt. She was being nostalgic; he hadn't done that in a long time. But it was true. Before Eliza, he had never come on a woman's breasts—but she'd asked him to do that. To say no to such a request would have been uncharitable. She even wanted him to come on her face. Again, he obliged, but it wasn't his thing. It felt impolite to ejaculate on a woman's face. Once he had got her right in the eye; hours later, it still looked as though she had conjunctivitis. He'd had no idea that semen could be such an irritant.

One of his earlier girlfriends had found semen disgusting (the slimy texture, the smell), so Eliza's delight in the substance came as a thrilling surprise. He remembered what a turn-on it had been to be with a woman who wasn't repulsed by the physical evidence of male orgasm. "It's true that the urologist didn't spend much time talking about shutting down the flow. I have the pamphlets and everything. I'll read them."

"Don't turn off that tap! What if you leave me in five years and marry a thirty-three-year-old who wants a baby? It happens all the time."

He threw back his head and laughed. "How generous of you to think of your future rival's biological clock." He chomped on a piece of apple. "I will not be leaving you in five years. And definitely not for a younger woman. Are you insane? Do you think

I want to go through this all over again? I'm holding out for the peace after menopause. The nice old crone."

Eliza swept her way closer to him. "If you ever say the words *old crone* again, in reference to me, you'll never get another blowjob. Got that? It will be mac-and-cheese and the missionary position for the rest of your life."

"That doesn't sound so bad." She punched his shoulder. He caught her fist, turned it over and kissed the inside of her wrist. "I had no idea you were so attached to my penis in its pristine state."

"Of course I'm attached," she said. "Do *not* get a vasectomy. Ask Karl."

But Andrew didn't want to talk to Karl about his dick. Eliza was right: he barely knew the guy. I'll look it up on the Internet, he thought. His lovely wife was probably exaggerating, subconsciously angling to get what she subconsciously wanted. He could almost feel their third child hovering in the still, full air of the room, wanting to enter their bodies and become flesh.

22

Escape

ONCE, WHEN JAKE WAS STILL A BABY—DURING THE early days of motherhood, with two small creatures constantly tugging on her, crying for her, drinking her—Eliza had tried to explain her anxiety to Andrew. No matter how much she loved her babies, and loved their love, and sought to fulfil their needs, she also found so much love and need oppressive. No doubt about it: she was trapped among diapers, little shoes, little socks, squirming little bodies. At times, she could barely move, and when she did, her (newly enormous) breasts leaked constantly. For two and a half years straight, the cries of *any* baby or toddler caused her milk to let down.

Andrew had nodded, wearing his let-me-help-you-understand expression. "Honey, it's all passing so quickly. They're babies for just a blip in time." She bit her lower lip; trust Andrew to think of eternity. If she were a fellow math geek, he would spout some algorithm of infinity, but because she was just a normal person, he said, "*I* don't feel oppressed by fatherhood."

"Yeah, that's because it's always been easy for men to become fathers. How many sperm in one shot?"

He gave her a dirty look. "I want to *be* a good father, too."

"You are a good father." He was. "But fatherhood has made you . . . grander. The patriarchy is slapping you on the back. You have *sons*. There's still lots of cachet in that."

"Oh, come on, there is not," he protested, though his small, self-satisfied grin suggested otherwise. Jake, the newer baby, woke up and started to cry. They both jumped up to check on him. Eliza let Andrew go, and collapsed back onto the sofa. Motherhood weighed her down. And piles of baby gear.

Though the kids were older now, and the physical burdens lighter, Eliza still thought of motherhood as a heavy cloak, a mantle similar to the ones worn by shamans and witches, except that this one was decorated with frayed shoelaces, bacteria-laden pacifiers, greasy birthday candles, and another lost permission slip for a field trip that required, inevitably, $23.75 (*please enclose exact change*).

Who wouldn't want to shrug all that off for an afternoon or two? Or for three weeks? She had been seeing Shar for that long, plus two days. Time had slowed down (*Only three weeks? It feels like months*) and sped up (*Is that clock right? Jesus, I have to leave right now*).

Escape was wrong, yes. Yes, it was. She put the car into third gear and glanced at herself in the mirror. Smoky grey eyes today, encouraged by lots of eyeliner. Deep red lipstick; new. But escape was also *fabulous*. And *real*. It didn't feel like escape. She had just left Marcus and Jake at a birthday party—a reptile-themed cele-bration that had cost the birthday boy's parents at least $400. She knew because she looked it up on the LizardArt! website. The parents had invited her to stay but she could not flee the throng of hyper children fast enough.

Which was wrong, she knew. Escaping demonstrated an inabil-ity to accept life as it was. What did a mother and a wife have to be? She had to be right *there*, helping her kids make cake into lizard art. Or art into snake cake.

She parked a ten-minute walk north of Shar's apartment. Never too close. Fleur was only a dozen blocks to the northwest. She also had three regular clients on Queen Street. She kept herself from walking too fast. She didn't want to be panting *before* she got there. At the building entrance, she stood and breathed in and out five times.

It wasn't escape. It was return. When she crossed Shar's threshold, she came back to herself. *That's* why she felt so guilty. And it wasn't only the sex. Though the sex was ridiculous. She had never experienced anything like it. The sex was drug-like and occasionally terrifying, but the kind of terrifying that snatched the idea of terror away from serial killers and suicide bombers and gave it back to a girl-child with huge eyes screaming her head off on a roller coaster. She remembered how much she loved the fairgrounds as a kid—the good old Calgary Stampede—being thrown through the air and caught hard, howling with pure joy, pure fear.

But it really wasn't only the sex. Shar fed her. She loved P.D. James and Proust, as well as Irvin Yalom and a bunch of French feminist writers Eliza had never heard of. She loved to lie in bed and read out loud. She wrote almost daily in a journal and called it her *diary*, a word that Eliza had not considered in any serious way since she was fourteen, when she'd burned her own diaries in a back alley in southwest Calgary, banishing childhood from her life forever. Shar was a rare individual in that she seemed to have enough time for life. Eliza tried to figure out how she managed it; partly, she just did not do, or want to do, too much.

It wasn't that Shar had no ambition. She often talked about finishing her never-ending education, and hanging out her shingle as a therapist specializing in sexuality. Early on, when Shar had told Eliza that she was training to be a sex therapist, Eliza had laughed out loud at the joke—then quickly discovered that Shar was serious. She had come to Toronto to attend the Klippert Institute for Sexual Therapy and Research—a prestigious facility that trained only a small number of grad students and established therapists every year. Eliza had never heard of it, but a quick online search showed how well-considered the Institute was. Shar had received a generous grant that covered the tuition and living expenses for her training year; it came with an almost guaranteed therapy practicum once she was finished her studies. So, yes, she was dedicated to her professional goals, but she was equally ambitious about enjoying her life.

Midday, in a cascade of sunlight from the west-facing window, the two women sat cross-legged in silk kimonos on the sitting-room floor. The carpet was dotted with plates of Camembert and baguette slices, rice *dolmades*, a bowl of pomegranate seeds that Shar had firked out of their honeycombed husk with the dexterity of a monkey. Pomegranates were her favourite fruit. Eliza asked, "How did you arrive at this 'I must have a sweet time' philosophy?"

Shar met her eye, stared into her in the unnerving way she had sometimes, a gaze that demanded *Can I trust you?* then answered itself with equal force *I will trust you!* Eliza felt as though an oath were being extracted from her even when she said nothing. Shar stood up abruptly and tossed herself down in the wing chair by the window. "When I was a teenager, I almost died. *Bonne nuit, c'est fini!* It's not something I like to talk about." By now, Eliza understood not to push when Shar said don't push. "The experience changed me. Fundamentally. For a while I could only think how it divided time into before and after. So it divided me. I found a good therapist. I was already a psychology major, but working with that therapist turned me into a serious student.

"Most of all, what happened swept everything away but life. Life, life, life. Even now, sometimes, I . . ." She looked out the window, searching for the word in the cold bright blue day. "I still can't believe it. I was so close to losing mine. But I didn't. I have this body in this time. We all have these bodies in this time. The usual fucked-up things make us feel separate, the violence we do to each other, to the earth. Our fears. But we are closer than we know." She sat in the same sunlight that turned the pomegranate seeds into a bowl of glittering rubies.

Eliza asked, "Closer to what?"

"To each other. To nature. Closer to whatever we need."

"That sounds pretty New Agey. And too easy."

She huffed a laugh. "It's not easy. And I'm not saying it's like that for all people. I am privileged. I survived. I don't live in any kind of prison. I am lucky. So I try to make a point of not fucking up my freedom. I don't want to waste the sweetness. It is here. In us. It's in the world."

"*Edoni*!" Eliza suddenly remembered the word in ancient Greek. "Of course. It was a whole school of philosophy. Hedonism."

"*Ethical* hedonism. Sweetness for all, without causing pain to others. Have you read Michel Onfray?" Shar jumped up to find one of the hedonist philosopher's books.

That day, and other days, the two women talked. They talked and talked, not touching at all. The restraint was erotic. Talking and not touching was foreplay. But they also talked *while* they were having sex. Sometimes, naked, entwined, one of them said something funny and they ended up laughing so hard that they had to untangle themselves until they had finished, then begin again. Like musicians interrupted by a joke about the conductor, they returned to the score still smiling. One would follow the other to the bathroom, and talk through the slightly open door. Shar talked about Marseilles, where her grandmother still lived. Eliza talked about Fleur, and her clients, and her children. She didn't talk much about Andrew. Shar told stories about the kayaking she'd done on the West Coast, and the trips she'd taken to Italy, where she had an ex-lover-now-dear-friend named Francesca Frangipani. "A tropical flower," Eliza remarked. "Plumeria. Sacred in the Buddhist temple grounds of Southeast Asia."

"In Sicily, it's everywhere. It's Palermo's flower. That's where I met Francesca. In Palermo. She was travelling with Ettore. Her husband."

"Her husband? Did you . . . Was she . . . Wasn't that . . . complicated?"

Shar slid her hand through her hair, twisted a thick lock of it around her index and middle fingers. "Not really. It was . . . convenient. There's nothing like making love all day to a sexy woman then having her husband bring you really good wine at sunset." She clapped her hands, delighted with both the declaration and the memory it evoked. "I highly recommend it." She had been in a relationship with both of them, she explained, though Francesca was the one she wanted. "Ettore was a bonus," she said. "He was a great cook. And he loved to watch."

Sometimes she told Eliza about her studies at the Klippert Institute. Against Institute rules, she recorded and later played her the entire lecture by the great French doctor and scientist Dr. Pierre Foldès, whose study of the internal structure of the clitoris had helped him to restore thousands of women to sexual health after genital mutilation. Eliza gazed down at Dr. Foldès's sonographs: inside a woman's body, connected to the little clitoral nub, an enormous butterfly of tissue spread its wings around and beyond both sides of the vaginal canal. She couldn't believe it. "*All* that stuff is the clitoris?"

"Isn't it beautiful? The erect clit has as much tissue as the erect cock. But it's *inside* the body. So much for penis envy! Until the last decade or so, medical science has ignored the only organ of the human body designed exclusively for sexual pleasure. Because it happens to belong to women, of course. Do you remember all that controversy—in the eighties, maybe?—about the vaginal or clitoral orgasm? It's both. It has always been both."

Shar fed her literally, too. There was always something delicious to eat in her apartment. She presented the food on beautiful ceramic plates, a cloth napkin close by. Eliza was too embarrassed to admit how much she enjoyed this. No one else in her life treated her this way. Even if Eliza brought good food to the apartment, Shar insisted on getting it ready, bringing the offerings into the living room, where they sat and nibbled on Shar's beloved pomegranate seeds, plates of roasted almonds and raw walnuts, homemade hummus with pita, Portuguese tuna in olive oil with dried tomatoes. Even the air was nourishment. The apartment was almost never silent. Music was like air to Shar and they breathed it in: Sri Lankan pop, American jazz and blues, soul and hip hop, old country, a bunch of Finnish rockers who sounded like Johnny Cash, Turkish rock inflected with German cabaret, and a lot of Middle Eastern stuff that reminded Eliza of Greek music, and Lesvos, and Thalia.

Eliza stood at the door, waiting. It was always like this, the thudding heart, her stomach fluttery as she knocked again. The door opened and there she was, the whole long, lean delight of Shar, smiling.

23

Scheherazade

THE HALLWAY WAS FILLED WITH THE SMELL OF CINNAMON and sugar. Eliza followed Shar into the kitchen. A piece of pie was waiting for her on the table. Apple. Still hot. "That smells so good. You never told me you liked baking!"

Shar put the kettle on the old gas stove. "Ah, chief among my secrets. Master baker."

"Really?"

"No. But I like making pies every once in a while."

"You'll make a good wife someday."

"Not! 'Married people' is not a club I want to join."

"Oh, come on!"

"No way. That's what my last girlfriend was all about. Marriage and babies." Shar shuddered. "Marriage is a powerful institution. Powerful institutions give me the creeps."

"This pie is so good. You should open a pie shop."

"That's a big compliment, coming from you."

"Don't you ever feel . . . lonely?"

"Sure. Sometimes. Don't you?"

"I suppose I do." Eliza broke off a ledge of flaky, delicate pastry, popped it in her mouth, considering. "But not the way I did when I was single. Unsalted butter?"

"Of course. Even if we cure cancer and end war, and wife-beating, and child abuse, and hunger, loneliness will still plague humanity. But marriage seems like an extreme solution to an existential problem. Surely people could just . . . take up . . . volleyball. Or roommates."

Eliza laughed. "It could be a generational thing."

"What?"

"Your basic weirdness."

"Thanks a lot. Don't get me wrong. I love *knowing* certain married people. Like Francesca and Ettore. They're a beautiful couple. Their houses in Italy are like the histories of their love for each other, their long time together. And I know that Giselle, my ex, will make a great married lesbian. She'll be a wonderful partner and mother." Shar shivered theatrically again and brought the heavily tarnished silver teapot to the table, then turned away and brought two little glasses down from the cupboard.

Eliza let out a small involuntary gasp.

"What's wrong?"

"I have those *exact* same glasses." Shar set them down; they were decorated in a filigree design of gold and aquamarine paint. "But I've never drunk tea out of them. We use them for sherry, or scotch. I—I—bought them in Istanbul." Actually, Andrew had bought them. For Eliza. They were his first gift to her. It's a sign, she thought. But of what? "Where did you get these?"

"My dad brought them back a few months ago."

"Not from Istanbul?" Eliza asked incredulously.

"Yes. Of course. He was just passing through."

"Passing through? Where was he going?"

Shar didn't answer right away. "He was on his way home. From Iran."

"What an adventurous trip."

"Not really." Shar busied herself at the counter. Eliza almost didn't hear what she said next. "He's Iranian."

The silence scooped out a space between them. Eliza was confused. "I thought he was French."

"No. I told you that we lived in France when I was little." Shar set a silver pitcher of milk on the table, the spoons, the little bowl of sugar cubes. "My *mom* is French."

"But . . . isn't 'Radfour' a French name?"

"Radfour? My last name is *Radfar*. Maybe you turned it into French in your head. Radfar is a common Iranian surname. My father went to study in Paris in the sixties, like a lot of middle- and upper-class Tehrani. He met my mother at a street protest. My parents, the young anarchists! They married first in Paris, then again in Tehran. That's where I was born." She carefully poured the tea; steam rose from the spout, from each of the glasses. The smell of earth and woodsmoke. Lapsang souchong.

Eliza touched the gold edge; it was still too hot to pick up. Her empty hands felt awkward on the table; she put them in her lap. Then lifted them back up and put two sugar cubes in the glass, stirred with a little silver spoon. The clinking seemed to be interrogatory. Why had Shar never told her this? She thought of the painting above the sofa. Those men in the garden, the little channels of water. Script like Arabic. But it must be Farsi.

"You speak Farsi?"

"Of course. I spoke only Farsi and French for the first few years of my life. I still speak Farsi well. But my reading sucks. I used to spend summers in Tehran with my aunt. Auntie Ghazal. She runs a kind of artists' salon in her apartment, and always has people in and out, intellectuals, writers, painters. And incredible musicians. That kept the language going for me."

Eliza sat back in her chair, mouth open.

Shar didn't disguise the annoyance in her voice. "Why are you so surprised? Do you have a thing against Iranians?"

"No. But—I—it just seems like a big part of who you are. I thought you would have told me."

"That my dad is from Iran? Would it have made a difference?" Shar gathered her hair in that familiar gesture of—defiance? or refusal?—and tossed it away from her face. Or was it nervousness?

"No. It's just—I don't know." A light went on. "Your first name is Persian, too."

"Of course." Shar aspirated the r. "Shahrzad. Or Scheherazade, in this English neck of the woods."

"The princess who tells stories to save her life."

"Exactly. But she was also a good lover. Gave good head." She enthusiastically slurped her tea.

"You're so crass!"

"Not at all. A storyteller who is *also* good in bed is worth his or her weight in gold. *The Nights* is crammed with sex. The story beneath the stories is that the king and Shahrzad became passionate lovers. That's why he couldn't kill her. Good sex and fine conversation calmed his violent rage. Saved her ass. That's what my auntie says."

"The one in Tehran?"

"Mm-hmm. Auntie Ghazal says the whole Middle East would calm down if everyone could just have good sex without the looming threat of family shame. Or floggings. Or death!" Shar giggled, her small mouth suddenly big with teeth. She added, in a theatrically deep voice, "Or, especially, marriage."

"Couldn't she get in trouble for saying something like that?"

Shar shook her head indulgently. "God, people think Iran is so backward. The *government* is backward, yeah, but people are pretty sophisticated. My aunt doesn't shout anything from her rooftop. Most people don't, but they live beyond the government in all kinds of ways. They're clever. Cunning, even, like Shahrzad.

"My *mother* gave me that name, by the way. Though my dad likes to tell people that Shar is from Shariati, the famous intellectual he spent time with in Paris. *Shar-i-a-ti*. I love that name, too. I like the idea of having a man's name. Shariati has been dead since the seventies, but he's still famous. There's a street in Tehran named after him. He believed that Islam would evolve into an enlightened force for social justice."

"Wow. An idealist."

"Hard to believe, but in the seventies, people were living through a sort of enlightenment in Iran. It was an amazing time, especially for women. My dad's family is still very progressive. Even now, all my cousins say they're Muslim 'on their passports only.' When my dad was growing up, his main pursuits were pretty girls, poetry and politics, 'in that order,' as he likes to say. In Paris, he planned to find a beautiful blonde French girl, write lyric poetry and overthrow the whole capitalist system in his spare time. And he fulfilled his first two objectives. Shariati was busy translating Frantz Fanon's work into Farsi when my dad first met him. Everyone my mom and dad knew in Paris was a genius, or having sex with a genius. Once they were having coffee with Shariati in a café when Jean-Paul Sartre sat down to chat with them. He and Shariati were friends. Isn't that fabulous? Then we moved to bloody *Ottawa*! What were they thinking?"

"What *were* they thinking?"

"Well, the move was probably the best thing that could have happened. They were very *installé* in Paris—we left Tehran soon after the Ayatollah seized power—but when the Iran–Iraq war began, a lot of their Iranian friends in Paris started going back, either consumed by guilt or full of patriotism. I was just a toddler then, I don't remember any of this. My mom told me that after one of my uncles was killed at the beginning of the war, my dad used to obsess about going home to do his duty. It scared her to death, so she applied for work permits in Canada without telling him. They both got jobs, my father as a highway engineer—his degree was from the Sorbonne—and my mother as a French and science teacher. *Et voilà*. Here I am. Another Canadian mongrel."

"Right. That's the first word that pops to mind when I think of you. Woof-woof." They stirred their tea. "So. Is your dad still an idealist?"

"More a fatalist now. Especially about the Middle East."

"But what about the Arab Spring? Doesn't it show that whole societies can change for the better?"

Shar's eyes narrowed. "What Arab Spring? Nothing but more violence has come from it. Those young protesters, and the old ones, they were all betrayed."

"But regular people forced their dictators to step down."

"Big fucking deal. A hundred more dictators are always waiting in the wings. Egypt is a disaster. Syria is being destroyed as we speak. Libya is a mess. Trust me, there'll never be a shortage of power-obsessed, bloodthirsty Arabs."

"Shar!" Eliza was shocked. "Apple pie and racism are so good together!" She put the last piece in her mouth.

"I'm not being a racist. It's the truth. All they want to do most of the time is kill each other. And anyone else who disagrees with them."

"But . . . aren't Iranians basically . . . Arabs?"

Shar's chair stuttered back across the kitchen floor as she pushed away from the table. "No! Iranians are *not* Arabs. We are *Persians*. Persia was a great kingdom. Persians are *not* an Arab race. It's a different language, a different culture. Persian territories were *colonized*. We still view Arabs as ruthless conquerors."

Eliza shook her head. "Does that include my dry cleaner? He's from . . . Yemen. I think. Or is it Oman? Anyway, how about all those little Palestinian kids in Gaza with rockets blowing up their living rooms? Are they ruthless, too?"

"They will be."

"Getting bombed does nasty things to children."

"Why are we ruining this excellent tea by talking about politics?"

"Why didn't you tell me that you're half-Iranian?"

"Because it's not my defining feature, okay?" She shook her head. "I'm sick of having all that history stuck to me. The *very* first time I got vocal about gay rights was at an International Women's Day rally in my fourth year of university. The speech was filmed, put online and linked to the university website. Over a year later, an old family friend in Tehran saw it when he was checking out universities for his daughter. The man was like an uncle to me. And he immediately phoned my dad." Shar did an excellent Iranian accent in English. "'*Do you kno-ow Shahrzad ees morally seeck? Do you kno-ow you've raised a depraved chile?*' That is how my dad found out that I'm queer. The man said that if I visited Iran again, I risked arrest. My dad took it as a personal threat. This guy had always been envious of him for going to Paris, for marrying a French woman, for coming to Canada. I don't believe anything would happen to me if I went back. Homosexuality is illegal, but there are plenty of gay people there, quietly living their lives. My aunt is one of them. You just have to be careful. But my dad still doesn't want me to go. And Auntie Ghazal agrees with him. So I haven't been back for eleven, no, twelve years."

"Was your father . . . angry?"

"About that asshole? Yes, furious."

"No, I mean . . . about you . . ."

"About me being queer?"

"Yes."

"No. He was just grumpy that I hadn't told him when I told my mother. But I was a kid when I told her, fourteen. I wasn't ready for my *dad* to know. When I started going out with boys, too, my mother thought I had grown out of my 'girlhood crushes.' She said that unless I was *sure* about being gay, there was no need to tell my father."

Seeing the anxious expression creeping over Eliza's face, Shar rolled her eyes. "My dad's not some Middle Eastern patriarch waiting to chop off my head, okay?"

"Sorry. I didn't mean to imply anything. I'm the one who believes that . . . um . . . even bloodthirsty Arabs can be decent humans."

"There you're mistaken. As I've already pointed out."

"So Arab men are vile and Iranian men are civilized? Your dad's friend wasn't very civilized. All people can run that gamut between goodness and evil."

Shar turned away and muttered something under her breath.

"Pardon me?"

"'Another liberal.' That's all I said."

"Oh. I thought I heard you say 'another fucking liberal.' You're in the mood for tossing around the insults today."

"It's a *fact*, not an insult. Canadian liberals *are* naïve. And you fucking *like* being naïve. Believing the best about people, welcoming the world with open arms. Just wait until the Bloor-Yonge subway station blows up."

The two women stared at each other, the smiles gone from their faces.

Though Eliza still didn't understand why Shar was so angry, she recognized the lie: her Iranian heritage *was* one of her defining features. Eliza asked in a mild voice, "Can I have some more tea?" She slid the glass over the table toward Shar, adding archly, "I'm glad I asked where these glasses came from. It's so pleasant to chat about international relations." Maybe they wouldn't have sex today. That would be a first.

Shar reached across the table slowly, past the glass, opening her hand as though to touch Eliza's cheek. Instead she gave a lock of her hair a tug.

"Ow! What did you do that for?"

Shar stood up. "Come to my room and take off your clothes. You deserve a good spanking."

"For what?"

Shar fixed her with a glittering eye. "For getting Persians confused with Arabs! And for being a naïve liberal." She stepped behind her chair, put her hands on Eliza's shoulders and squeezed, too hard.

Eliza flinched. "I wonder what else you haven't told me."

In a low voice, Shar said, "Stand up. Up, up." Eliza obeyed and rose. Shar kneed the chair out of the way and stepped behind her. "Let's go to the bedroom." They went, and undressed. Shar manhandled her in a way that was rough and impersonal but full of unspoken emotion. Eliza knew that the sex was about something else, but she didn't understand what—love? anger? Arabs?—and for the first time, she was afraid to ask.

24

Enigma

LIKE MILLIONS OF COUPLES ACROSS THE CONTINENT, they were lying peacefully in bed. Andrew was stretched out beside his wife in his boxer shorts and white winter limbs. It was too warm on the third floor of the house. Eliza had kicked the quilt off her legs; still she felt stifled. "I should go turn down the heat," she muttered, pushing the quilt further away from her body.

He didn't lift his eyes from his book. "Darling, would you please stop wriggling? It's like being in bed with an eel." He flipped a page.

She glanced up but his face was obscured by *Enigma: The Biography of Alan Turing*. Someone she had never heard of. A scientist, probably. Andrew loved the biographies of big-brained men.

Observe, she thought, wearily closing her eyes, our oasis of peace. Unlike millions of other couples across the continent, Eliza and Andrew were not fighting; they weren't even stewing in silent resentment. They didn't hate each other; she could not imagine that they ever would. They didn't have to: her personal self-loathing would be enough to damage both of them.

Whenever she was quiet, not busy with the events, tasks, messes, calls, distractions and emergencies of any given day, the voice began. *Selfish bitch.* It made her close the bathroom door and cry, silently. *Slut.* That old insult, finally accurate. Sometimes, on her way to work, she wore her sunglasses and wept almost all the way there. When she walked into the studio and bared her face, Kiki would say, "Your eyes are so red from swimming. Aren't you using your goggles anymore?"

But this evening, the voice just annoyed Eliza. *How can you lie beside him, pretending you love him, pretending everything is the same as it was?* It was beginning to sound like her mother at the height of her religious devotion. But Eliza was no longer an impressionable child. And she knew that suffering was not caused by a vengeful God. It was caused by bad luck, poor choices, tragic accidents and unfortunate lapses in wisdom. Such as the one she was currently experiencing.

You take this peace and love for granted every single day. You abuse it. I don't take it for granted. I help to *create* it every single day. I have dedicated my life to it. *How self-righteous! You make family life sound like a religious vocation.* That's the smartest thing you've said in ages. It *is* like a religious vocation. It requires the same level of dedication.

Was it wrong to think of one's conscience as a tiresome nag? That voice was just one more demand on her time and resources. *Do you remember what the Bible says about adulterous women?* Oh, fuck off. Adulterous women in the Bible were stoned to *death.* If I were stoned to death, who would make dinner, clean the lint screen and remember to wash the bedsheets every once in a while? *Don't make jokes about betraying your husband and your family. That's what you are. A traitor. And a liar.*

The last part, she conceded, was true. It was bloody hard work, keeping her lies straight. She recycled the lies she told Andrew and used them with Kiki and Bianca—but she had to make sure she didn't get confused.

The voice went on, *You* want *to get caught. And you will get caught, like every cheater does. Then he'll leave you. He'll abandon you. The children will abandon you. You'll be alone.*

The only way she could drown out the doom was by cleaning something, noisily, scraping out the burned-on remnants in the oven or turning up the water, hard and hot, to scrub the dirt-ring from the boys' bathtub. The house was extremely clean. She'd stopped complaining about doing more than her fair share. Even when Andrew forgot to do some token task, she wordlessly swallowed her resentment.

"Honey," Eliza murmured, "I'm just going to turn down the heat." And clean up the kitchen. Even though they had agreed, after dinner, to leave it messy. Andrew had noticed how much more housecleaning she'd been doing lately. Now he murmured, "Eliza, please stay here and read." He knew exactly what she wanted to do. "We'll clean up in the morning."

"I'm too hot. I want to turn down the heat."

"Why are you so restless?"

The question so surprised her that she had no snappy lie to offer him.

He put his book down on his chest and eyed her over his reading glasses. "You seem very . . . jittery. And you yelled at Jake tonight. What was that all about?"

"When I was reading to the boys, he kept putting his hand on my breast. I told him half a dozen times to stop, but he wouldn't. He knew it was bugging me but he kept doing it. I just lost my temper."

"You're the one who nursed him until he was two."

"What does that have to do with anything? Breastfeeding and touching me inappropriately are not related. Haven't you noticed that he's been a little troublemaker lately?"

"He's more clingy than usual. You've been working so much in the evenings. He misses you. And he's only six. His body remembers the comfort of breastfeeding."

"I can't help having to work, I run a business."

"I know that. I'm not accusing you of anything."

"When *you* get really busy, they barely notice, but with me, it's a different story."

"Come on, that's not true. They miss you, that's all. *I* miss you. And you're tired. You have a shorter fuse than usual."

It grew shorter still. "When the boys are clingy, they cling to *me*, not to you. Why is that? It's suffocating sometimes. I wish *you* would read to them at night."

"Why are you so angry?"

His question walloped her right in the mouth. She couldn't speak. She couldn't tell him the answer. She was angry because she had to be angry. In the midst of her various lies, she wanted one lie to be true: that Andrew had forced her, through depriva- tion, to this division between them. Hadn't he? Hadn't he forced her? She closed her eyes and pressed her fingers to the lids. The tears, burning there, felt acidic, scalding. "I'm . . . I'm not angry." Another lie. Was anything that came out of her mouth the truth anymore? "I'm exhausted." There. True.

"Then stay in bed and relax. The house is clean enough." She felt him rolling over to look at her; his eyes touched her face. His tenderness made her feel sick. He asked, "Do you think it's a disorder?"

For a wild moment, she thought he meant her lying, or her attraction to women, to one woman in particular. But when she opened her eyes, Andrew was smiling at her.

She should just tell him. Be honest. "Is what a disorder?"

"All this cleaning. Maybe it's OCD?"

"I'm not obsessive compulsive, just . . ." Her brain searched dumbly for an acronym, while the rest of her—her body? her spirit?—experienced that nauseating dissonance, of another real- ity, another life unfolding alongside this one. "MWC. Married with children. Even if we clean up together in the morning, who's going to wash the floor? All that rice from dinner. Jake still makes such a mess."

"Dear wife, you are *not* going to wash the floor at ten thirty at night." He reached over and kissed her warm temple. "Do you want to . . . you know." He smiled his flirtatious, come-hither crow's-feet smile.

"Now?" She couldn't imagine anything worse. If they had sex, she would split open. "I don't want to take you away from your book. You were enjoying it until I disturbed you."

He teased her. "You must be *extremely* stressed out if you're turning down sexual advances from your husband."

"Don't make fun of me."

They turned toward each other, kissed, pulled away. "I'm not making fun." He smiled, more handsomely still. "On the contrary, I'm heartbroken."

Eliza shook her head and flipped open her iPad; she would read online trade articles by flower sellers. That would calm her down.

Andrew returned to his book, puzzled but relieved. He only skimmed the math that would eventually culminate in Turing's Enigma machine. He was thinking about the appointment he'd had with his physiotherapist between his third-year class and his master's seminar. The physio had spent forty minutes on him, releasing the facet joints on either side of his spine, studiously going through his new exercises, patiently making sure that he knew how to do them. As she had belted him into the traction machine, he had gazed at her bare athlete's face with childish adoration. She could take away his pain! If she started a religion, he would join without hesitation. His back felt great; it felt *normal.*

That was why he had to be careful. Whenever he was feeling good, he forgot about those two herniated discs. Two summers ago, when he and Eliza went away for a weekend to Niagara-on-the-Lake, they'd had energetic sex the Friday afternoon of their arrival. He'd felt the wobble in his lumbar spine, that indescribable shakiness. But the wine at dinner put him in such a wonderful mood that he went to bed without doing his exercises.

The following morning, when Eliza sauntered out of the bathroom wearing her sexy black outfit, complete with black thigh-high stockings, he forgot about his back. But after their delightful acrobatics, he remembered, acutely, because he could not get out of bed. Muscle relaxants didn't work; he couldn't move without excruciating pain. Eventually, he managed to stand up and take a few hobbling steps, bent over like an old man.

He felt a tapping noise as Eliza touched and re-touched a link on her iPad that refused to open. Her nudges at the screen were small, but passed, pulsing, through the bed. He glanced over just as her article appeared, topped with a photograph of a stainless steel flower fridge. She pulled the blanket up over her body; he did the same, without touching her. It was a relief, really; she was so busy with work that she had stopped complaining about their sex life.

It wasn't even wedding season yet, and she was going to the studio on weekend afternoons. He understood how consuming it was to run the business. But he also worried that she was becoming a workaholic. Though she would never admit it, she liked being overextended because it gave her a powerful sense of being at the centre of things. When she was really focused on work, though, she wasn't at the centre of her own family. These last few weeks, even when she was home, she was scarcely there. Sometimes she didn't hear the boys when they addressed her. She played with them, but he could see how absent she was. And no doubt the boys could feel it.

It will pass, he thought, closing his book. He switched off his bedside lamp and turned on his side. He still felt Eliza's fingertip bumping the screen. He gazed into the shadows blooming on his side of the room: deep grey, purple-grey, tar-black tunnelling into the corners. He loved the darkness. It made him think of the deep interior of his own and Eliza's body. How strange, he thought, that the human heart beats in utter darkness. He closed his eyes, imagining it, the beautiful, unfathomable dark in the heart of the heart.

25

The History of the World

THE NEWS CAME THE NEXT DAY, AS IT ALWAYS DOES.
Three blocks from the Institute, Shar was in a hipster greasy spoon
on Dupont Street, eating a sandwich and skimming the notes
she'd taken that morning in class. A muted TV flickered its images
up on the wall; something made her glance up just as the familiar
face appeared. She quickly read the words scrolling down the side
of the screen and swore out loud, despite the sandwich in her
mouth. Then she took her napkin and spat the food into it.

Eliza heard much later in the day, driving home from Fleur. The
person in the car behind her had to lay on the horn to get her moving.

Andrew found out first, in the morning, moments after he
turned on his computer at the university. His homepage was a
popular newsfeed. Adele Tabrizi, the broadcast journalist with
the great black eyes and pulled-back curly hair, had returned to
Egypt to report on the election. During a street protest, a group of
men in the crowd separated her from her camera crew and han-
dlers. Dozens of men had torn the clothes off her body and sexually assaulted her. A group of old Egyptian women saved her life.
She was recovering in a hospital in Paris.

Shar sits in the wing chair in front of the big front window. The
last of the day's light falls across her left leg, left shoulder. Her diary

is open on her lap. But she writes nothing. She remembers. No one knows what happened in Marseilles. It is the secret that allowed her to reconstruct herself.

But it is also a lie. True, the police never discovered what happened. But she had told her therapist everything, the one in Vancouver who helped her so much. And someone else knows, too. Someone else knew that night.

After returning to her grandmother's house, the elegant old lady had woken up and slipped out of bed, flicked on the light. "*Qu'est-ce qu'il y a?*" she murmured. She stretched out her arms to take Shar in. "*Qu'est-ce qu'il t'a fait?*" What happened? What did he do to you? She knew from the stance of the girl's body, the way she hobbled down the passage, one hand on the wall, her face and her eyes altered. She had seen that face and those eyes in the mirror, decades before. When she was younger than her own granddaughter, a different man had raped her, beaten her unconscious. She, too, had survived.

Shar doesn't turn on a light. Night walks into the room. She writes down one question.

Why is the history of the world
still the present?

Together on the shore of evening, Eliza and Andrew eddied around each other in their bedroom, enacting a ritual not always maintained, the shedding of the day by changing out of their work clothes. Eliza undid the pearl buttons of her grey blouse.

"You heard the news?" Andrew asked, and drew an old sweatshirt over his head.

"On my way home." She slipped the arms of the blouse off each shoulder and stood there in her bra. Below her feet, the boys whooped in their bedroom—laughing?

"I thought you would be screaming about it."

She crushed her shirt into a ball and threw it across the bed, toward the laundry basket, missed. "What good would that do?" She yanked a T-shirt over her head.

"Nothing. I just . . . It feels . . ." But he could not say what it felt like.

A howl and a string of angry words lifted up from below. The boys were not laughing, but fighting. She heard Marcus bark, "Shut the door!" As though acting of its own accord, the door closed with a sharp smack. Eliza and Andrew stood still to listen. Marcus's words were muffled now. Jake began to cry. They could hear him right beneath their feet. "Stop!" Jake cried. "Stop it!"

Marcus did not stop.

That night, they made love. It wasn't their rare, customary rush against and through each other's bodies; it was not fucking. Nor was it plain old friendly sex. It was the authentic, hungry, almost painful making of love, the breaking of a long fast. They had to be careful, as one who has known famine cannot gorge on food but must go slowly, taking in sustenance little by little. The full-ness and tenderness hurt Eliza especially, because she felt guilty. She felt guilty about Shar; she felt guilty for being safe.

Eliza touched Andrew's face; he had his hand on her head, his fingers in her hair as they kissed. The opening and the thrusting were like eating, as though each part they touched was food that had been long denied and suddenly was given over, gift after gift after gift, the bounty of two bodies, the fingers with their precise, nicked gloves of skin, every handful of the aging, night-alive flesh, freely given, taken hungrily, back and forth, back and forth, *Here, take this, eat,* as though the sweetness might sustain a stranger, undo harm, repair the irreparable by extending a miracle so private that no one else could ever know what it was, what had happened here. It was magical thinking, impossible, yet that was the word-less benediction as they touched each other and moved through the well-known stages. As Eliza's orgasm began, Andrew came inside her as deeply as he could, and remained there, held, locked into her body, his eyes closed as she moved against him.

It hurts, she thought, tears rising in her eyes as she swirled down the vortex of her own pleasure. *It hurts.* She was coming. At the centre of that physical intensity was grief. For the suffering in the world, always there, undeniable. But she could not let go and cry. If she cried, her own mundane truth would pour out, too, her confusion, her wrong. "Stay," she whispered to Andrew. "Stay on top of me. I want to feel your weight." She did want that, to feel the physical heft of this body that loved her body. But she also wanted him to hold her down like a lid, to keep the lies inside.

Less than twenty-four hours later, Eliza paused in the landing of Shar's apartment building. She shook her head to her own objections about being here. Walking up the stairs felt different. But why? Nothing in her life had changed. A woman she did not know—like millions of other women she did not know—had been brutally attacked, raped by a gang of men.

She peered up the stairwell, then at the floor, made of terrazzo, concrete flecked with green rocks and glittering quartz. She didn't know what to do. She was afraid that when she got into the apartment, Shar might start screaming about Arab men, or Muslims in general. It wasn't too late to text an excuse; she could still leave. But her feet kept taking the stairs. She paused on the second landing, too, feeling unwell. *Maybe I'm getting sick; I could be contagious.*

On the walls, she saw the familiar scuff marks, scrapes and dents of bookshelves and chairs, dirty fingerprints, marks made by the many lives that had passed this way. The building was old;

hundreds of people had lived and loved here. Many of them were dead now. Dead and forgotten. As she, too, would die and be forgotten, along with her passion and her stupidity: her very own, as particular as those fingerprints. Yet so similar to other people's.

She shook her head at her own jumbled thoughts. Her hand closed on the wooden banister again; up she went. Shar opened the door; Eliza stepped in with her jacket already off (hooked over her arm at first, then dropped to the floor) as they spoke a few words of greeting, hugged. Eliza could smell wine. Shar's chin knocked against her back as she said, "You heard about Adele Tabrizi?"

"Yes."

"Infuriating."

"Yes." Eliza wondered what else was coming.

Shar pulled away. "But how self-righteous Canadians are about it. Already a bunch of articles are online, decrying violence in the Muslim world and the savagery of Islam. It's pure racism."

Eliza said, "But I thought you were—"

Shar pulled away, her eyes flashing. "What? I hate these white fuckers who pretend nothing is wrong *here*. Like Canada hasn't seen its fair share of slaughter and rape! Hello, foundation of the Western world! Fucking white people!"

Eliza tried not to flinch. Adulterous wife. Distracted mother. Now she had to feel guilty about being white. She decided not to say that to Shar. Instead, she said something worse. "But . . . aren't you white, too?"

Shar turned and swept down the hallway, shouting back, "Oh, I can pass, but if I decided to wear a head scarf, I wouldn't be so white anymore, would I?"

Eliza didn't respond. She quietly followed Shar into the sitting room. The bottle was half-empty; Shar poured her a glass and kept drinking her own. She needed to vent, and vent she did, in a voice that Eliza had never heard before, by turns full of rage, then disgust, then sorrow. She didn't cry—Eliza knew that Shar rarely cried—but she made Eliza want to. Despite what she'd said earlier about racism and anti-Muslim sentiment, she railed against the attack, then she talked about Tehran and a place called the Citadel, *and they burned it down with most of the women and the children trapped inside the walls.* Eliza had no idea what she was talking about, but she murmured and nodded and they drank the rest of the wine and opened another bottle. Then Shar went back to her university days in Vancouver, her activism as a student, *so many women there, lost, murdered. And here, too, right here!*

Eliza did her best to follow the convoluted thread of her outrage, and she glanced around, trying to find the ghosts in the room, but her eyes kept coming back to Shar's face.

Eliza pulled the window blinds shut and flicked on the green-shaded lamp. The bedcovers and sheets were blue; it was like standing at the edge of a pool of water. They stripped off each other's clothes and went in together, slowly at first. Shar's hands fanned out over her ribs, tracked up her spine to the base of her skull, jaw, chin. Her fingers were in Eliza's mouth when they started to kiss.

This betrayal is worse, Eliza thought. The worst.

Because it was not fucking. It was lovemaking. Eliza was making love for the second time in twenty-four hours but for the first time with Shar. She didn't want to make love; it meant too much. Yet they had begun, irresistibly, and irresistibly, they continued, with a tenderness that neither of them were accustomed to with each other. It was like speaking another language, though with words they said almost nothing, certainly none of the intimate smut they both liked. Shar's eyes were huge, dark, all pupil, and Eliza met her steady gaze and went into it. They did not say *love*, yet it was there, glowing, rising to the surface like phosphorescence in the ocean at night.

The silence held, roiling with words, histories, secrets, every world contained inside the body, two bodies, two skins and *millions and millions of pores*, Eliza thought, her hand sliding down Shar's long, muscular back. She admired the different flesh tones of their bodies; they both looked so smooth. *But we're made of openings. The world comes in.*

Eliza felt as though she were scattering into the woman who was now hovering above her. It confused her to be so naked with someone who had already exposed her completely. How many layers were there to nakedness? If she was disintegrating, she was also expanding, filled with declarations she couldn't make.

They declared through kissing. They translated directly through the tongue, until Eliza got on top and slid down the bed and licked Shar stem to stern, ass to cleft, over and over, until it was time to narrow her focus and slide her fingers inside. The phrase *flesh of my flesh* kept rising unbidden to her mind. What she did to Shar she felt in her own body. *Flesh of my flesh.* From where, those words?

Shar was just starting to move her hips faster when Eliza remembered: Genesis. Adam's words to Eve, oft-quoted in marriage ceremonies. Had the phrase been part of her own marriage vows? She hoped not. "Flesh of my flesh," she whispered, so quietly that Shar could pretend she didn't hear.

After, Eliza dressed as quickly as possible. It was almost like the first time she'd been here and rushed away, afraid of what she had done, afraid of her own delight. Now she lied, "I have to get to a meeting," and left without a kiss, thoroughly flayed by love, by feeling love, by loving Shar. She rushed up the street, her eyes already filled, blurred enough to make her fumble the keys at the car door. She sat down in the driver's seat, put her hands and head against the steering wheel, and cried.

26

Hiatus

THE NEXT DAY, ELIZA WENT SWIMMING AS USUAL AT ANNIE'S.
Shar did not. She braved the chilly pool in the community
centre across the park from her house. Good, she thought, plung-
ing into the freezing water, this will clear your head. She attended
her classes at the Institute, read her books, saw her two Toronto
clients—she told them both that she was retiring soon—and, to
make some space between Eliza and herself, booked a trip to
Ottawa on the weekend. Benoît had flown in from Paris a few days
before. And he had been diagnosed with dangerously high blood
pressure. She needed to see him.

Flying from Toronto Island, she watched the city recede as the
coastline of Lake Ontario grew wilder, then wild. That, she
thought, was love. As insistent as a forest. Despite their vulnerability, plants were extraordinarily resilient. The moment there was
a little earth and some water, love took root.

She sipped her weak tea and stared glumly out the window,
displeased with the metaphor. She loved trees! But with clients,
she had learned how to yank out the little love seedlings. Eliza
was not a client, but the same principle applied. Shar had learned
how to retract her emotions, rein in her natural tendency for openness and connection. If she and a client were getting too close, she

always stopped eating and drinking with that person. No more lovely dinners or extravagant lunches, no more excellent wine or coffee. With her regular male clients, she had learned how to bring the conversation back to the body. She could say, "This is it, this is sex. Intelligent, good sex." With her differently abled clients, the relationship was more delicate. She often needed to show them a care that was indistinguishable from love. It *was* a kind of love. What did untouched, love-starved people need? They needed to be touched and fed with love. But she never, ever used that word. It was too loaded, and easily misunderstood. Love was a word that wrought irreparable damage. She was always explicit that she could not be a lover in the romantic sense, that she was a sexual body worker.

Even so. People fell. She fell. At least, she stumbled. The hardest thing about her privileged brand of sex work was not the fear of violence but the danger of love. It was not supposed to happen, but it did. She had experienced that terrible lurch into clients' lives only twice before; both, weirdly enough, had been men. One had lived in Vancouver; the other was from Ottawa. She had had to stop seeing them.

It was different with Eliza, true. But. It was not that different. The territory of their affair included affection, camaraderie, delicious sex. Love was on the other side of the border and she felt herself sliding over. But the only way they could venture in that direction was with more openness. Andrew would have to know. A brief affair was one thing, but it was no longer brief and no longer an affair.

Hence her little trip. It would help her gain perspective. And she could find out how Benoît was really doing.

Benoît! He was the meaning of his name: a blessing. After so many years, yes, they loved one another, but they had uttered words of love only a few times, always on the eve of long trans-atlantic trips, as though to ward off plane crashes or other untimely deaths. *Je t'aime* affirmed that the abiding company they kept was more than affection, and so much more than the money they rarely mentioned anymore. Benoît's Internet security company worked with large corporations and governments all over the Americas and Europe; Africa was his new focus. For years, Shar had been on his payroll as a translator of French and Farsi.

Benoît had played many roles in her life, but each one was marked by similar freedom and privacy. They sometimes joked that he was the husband she did not want; hence the marriage was perfect. He was something like Francesca, a constant presence in her life who was usually far away from her. She would know and love those two for as long as she lived. That sounded dramatic, but it wasn't. It was friendship.

Benoît's high blood pressure worried her. He still worked like he had in his thirties and forties, long days, not enough exercise, too much airplane travel. For his sake and for her own, too, she wanted him to live for a long, healthy time. He had two grandchildren already; more would come soon enough. She looked out the window and smiled. Ottawa was underneath her already, spreading out in its deceptively tidy Canadian way. She smiled at the woods and trees, the white and grey snake of the frozen canal. She hadn't told her mom about this quick trip, so her arrival would be a surprise. Her parents loved it when she dropped in unexpectedly. Maybe the three of them would go for their last skate of the season on the canal. Soon enough, the ice would begin to break up.

More than two weeks passed. Shar and Eliza sent texts professing busy-ness; they left messages, relieved that the other didn't pick up the phone. It was not an ending, but a hiatus.

Mrs. Minta agreed, finally, to the fourth design for her daughter's wedding flowers. Someone at school pushed Jake down the stairwell.

Eliza went to the school to fetch him. He had a purple-black eye and a bad headache. On the way home, he threw up. Andrew stayed home with Marcus while Eliza took Jake to the ER. Seven hours later, near midnight, a doctor who looked more like an eighteen-year-old surfer (blue eyes, tousled blonde hair, a slightly stoned grin) shone a light in Jake's eyes and pronounced, "This kid is totally fine, Momsie."

She resisted a strong urge to smack him upside the head. She replied in an even tone, "My name is on that chart." Assholesie.

He flicked a bright glance at Eliza and grinned into Jake's battered face. "I'm going to give you a little medicine to drink for that headache, then your *momsie* is going to take you home."

One unusually warm morning in early March, Shar reappeared in the change room at Annie's in all her long-limbed glory. That was how she liked to carry herself: in glory. It suited her. She did not care that such a style was too much for the community centre. Often enough, it was too much for Toronto, too, but that was Toronto's problem. The city had to get over its dull Presbyterian hangover from the last century and Shar was happy to help.

Still, knowing how polite and well-behaved most Torontonians were, she was amazed that Eliza had jumped her in the change room of a community pool. It was ridiculous. If it had not happened to her personally, she would not believe it. The ladies of St. Anne's swimming pool were as flat and straight as planks. Well, except for the friendly fat lady. She wasn't straight; she was unabashedly, sexily *round*.

It was Thursday, past eight thirty. After undressing as slowly as possible, Shar stood naked by the bench, pretending to untangle the straps of her bathing suit. Maybe Eliza wasn't going to swim today. Shar stepped into her black bathing suit, wriggled it up, slid the straps over her shoulders. *Quel dommage.* If Eliza wasn't coming, at least she would still get her morning swim in pleasantly warm water. She was just leaving the showers when the change room door opened and a familiar voice called out, "Shar! You're here!"

Shar's heart turned her body like a magnet. She had not realized just how much she had wanted to see Eliza until she saw her, standing there in her white winter coat and green woollen hat; her eyes were green, green, green. Shar skipped back over the wet floor and kissed Eliza's cool lips. She whispered, "I've been standing here for ten minutes, waiting for you. Come swim with me."

An hour later, the women walked out of Annie's, amidst a crowd of three-year-olds who were going out for a walk in the sun. They steered around the toddlers and past the playground, walking along the edge of a larger park of trees and open space. Across the street was a row of brick houses. Three cats were out on the sidewalks, two sitting like sentinels while the third, a handsome grey tabby, rolled around on the cement, its white paws in the air.

"All of a sudden," Shar observed, pulling off her cap, "spring arrived."

"Don't hold your breath. It'll get cold again. March is very deceptive in Toronto." Right now, the city was half-melted and half-frozen, rich with the scent of mud and wet leaves. It was also at its resolute ugliest, an archaeological site of newly revealed winter garbage.

They reached a bench under the maples. Squirrels were flying trapeze in the trees above them. The dog-walkers and their dogs were out, too. One of them stood on the far side of the field, tirelessly throwing a ball for his ecstatic golden retriever. Eliza squinted. Only when she was sure she didn't know the man did she sit down on the park bench beside Shar. "So, you don't think it's love?" she said.

"No, I don't. It's amazing sex and excellent timing."

"Really? It's just sex?"

"I didn't say 'just' sex. I would never say 'just' sex. Sex is one of the big engines of life. Technically speaking, it is *the* engine. People might pretend it's unimportant, but I'm in a field that proves otherwise." She turned her beautiful face to Eliza and patted her knee like an older sister. "Of course I love you. As a friend. I care about you. But it's not love-love. You know, the big love. You love Andrew. You're in for the long haul. That's different. Don't go fucking this up by thinking you're in love with me."

Eliza looked hurt. They didn't say anything for a while. They watched the dog run after the ball. Its legs and belly had turned dark mud-grey. Eliza said, "It's a battlefield."

"Love and sex?"

"No—well, yes—but that's not what I meant. This park is a battlefield. Between the dog-walkers and the non-dog-owners, who are mad because the dogs are here all the time, tearing up the sod and turning the place into a mud pit."

"A first-world problem."

"That's the usual kind, around here. Like my own. This one. You. Me being a liar." She sighed. "I can't contain it anymore. My feelings, the divisions in my life."

"Be brave then."

"So you think we should just—break up?"

"Uh, no. That's not what I meant. I think you should tell him about me."

Eliza shook her head. "We've already talked about this. He would be so furious that it might be the end of my marriage. And no matter how hypocritical this sounds, I don't want to dismantle my marriage. I *do* love Andrew."

"It doesn't sound hypocritical."

"It's *totally* hypocritical. It's disgusting. I disgust myself. If I want to become a lesbian, I should leave my husband and go explore lesbianville."

Shar sang out, in a British melodrama voice, "What? You want to become a lesbian?"

Eliza hissed, "Shh!" She sat up straight to scan the park and the streets bordering it. "Fuck! I can't take you anywhere." To one degree or another—school or studio or playdates or chats at the park—she knew most of the people who lived around here. The irony was that because she was having an affair with another woman, they could appear in public. "No, I don't want to become a lesbian. I want to keep you on the side forever and continue to enjoy all the privileges of my heterosexual life and marriage. See what I mean? Sickening hypocrisy."

"Welcome to the human race. You're not the first person to want both, you know. It's called being human. And queer. To be attracted to both, or many. Possibly at the same time. And I'm not just talking about sex. It's not wrong to want different things. It's human nature."

Eliza's unhappy expression did not change.

"Sometimes if the third lover is a woman, the man in a hetero-sexual couple is not so threatened."

"We are *not* Francesca and Ettore."

"You certainly aren't. They're like a portable opera, those two. By the time I came along, her husband knew about her relation-ships with women. But when they were younger, they fought about it a lot. Once he tied her up during a sex game and refused to untie her for hours. But that backfired; she liked it. They had a lot of violent sex and a lot of arguments, early on. But they got through it. Somehow they came to an agreement that it wasn't necessary to abide by the accepted rules of marriage."

"And?"

"I've already told you! They're still married. They're happy. Francesca's in her late fifties now. We had a great visit last summer. I'll always love her."

Eliza shook her head in disbelief. "You actually had sex together, the three of you? Really?"

"Francesca and I had a much closer relationship, but yes, Ettore was involved, too. I was nineteen. He was in his forties. He was thrilled that his wife and I were having an affair."

Eliza blinked at her, not scandalized but confirmed: her lover lived in a different universe. "You've had an interesting life."

"I *still* have an interesting life."

"I meant so far."

"I mean right now."

"That kind of thing has *never* been part of my landscape. Or Andrew's. Not in any real way." Telling a racy story was one thing; living it was something else entirely. Eliza couldn't imagine having Shar and Andrew in the same room, let alone in the same room *naked*. Which room? The organizational aspect alone would be daunting. Even now, it took weeks of planning to hire a babysitter to go out to dinner and a movie for four hours. "Andrew is quite conservative."

"And so are you, right?"

"I am. In certain things."

"You don't strike me as a conservative person." Shar's voice was playful.

Eliza's was not. "I like having sex with one person at a time." She stood up. "And even that feels disastrous to me lately. Come on, let's go." She pulled Shar up; they continued walking across the park. "Don't you have a class at eleven?"

"Are you trying to get rid of me?"

"Yes. Be gone, wench!"

Under her breath, Shar said, "I love it when you talk dirty to me."

"You're relentless," Eliza said.

"Yes, I am. That's how you like me."

They parted at their usual corner. "Goodbye, wild thing," Eliza said, and watched Shar stride away. She was young; that was part of the attraction. But was thirty-four really that young? Part of the *feeling* of Shar's youth came from the fact that she didn't have children. She didn't want to have them, either. When Eliza asked her about it one night, she'd replied, "Totally uninterested. My younger sister has two kids. I'm the jet-setting auntie."

Eliza was attracted to her freedom, too. But what was freedom, in the free world? Shar had responsibilities, like everyone else. She went to school, which involved copious amounts of reading and attending lectures, like any other student. Once she opened her own practice, she would have the work of running a small business. She was attached to Ottawa, where her parents and sister lived, and to her ex Giselle, and to the mysterious Benoît. Eliza preferred him to be mysterious; she never wanted to know too much about him. She knew he was a sometime lover, though Shar had corrected that term. "I think of us as intimate friends," she had explained. Whatever that meant. Shar baffled her. Her openness and transparency were real, yet simultaneously she was one of the most self-contained, private people Eliza had ever met.

It was as though she lived by another clock, figuratively and literally. She was the only woman Eliza knew who did not feel she was tired, exhausted and overworked. She worked out at a gym, went running or swimming at least four times a week, a luxury Eliza could not imagine. Most bizarre of all, Shar regularly had breakfast in bed. By herself. To Eliza, this was more perverse than a strap-on dildo (the delights of which she continued to resist). Shar did not seem to be entangled in life, which struck Eliza as suspicious. How could you *not* be entangled, when life was all about entanglements?

Before she turned onto Bathurst, Shar glanced over her shoulder and winked, swinging her hips wider as she walked, à la Sophia

Loren. A ruff of wool sweater stuck out from beneath her short leather jacket that stopped above her round butt—she was proud of her ass, and it showed. Just as Eliza thought of how much she wanted to bite one of those creamy cheeks, leave a mark on her, Shar disappeared around the corner.

27

The Land of Ray

ON THE WALK OVER TO JANET'S PLACE, ELIZA WORE A light spring coat. It was almost the end of April. In the twilight, she could see the heads of daffodils opened up, with tulips on the way. Spring was arriving this year slowly, in wave after extravagant wave, the plants and trees adding layers of foliage and flowers as humans shed layers of clothes. Soon lilac and cherry blossom would perfume her whole block.

She wanted to stand in the half darkness and inhale the burgeoning green, but she hurried on. Since the word "girlfriend" had taken on a new meaning, Eliza found it difficult to fit in her *regular* girlfriends. She felt guilty about them, too. She had postponed, made excuses or cut short her visits with them repeatedly over the last three months. If only she could *tell* them how much harder she was working now to fit them all in. Except for mornings at the pool, Janet and Eliza hadn't seen each other for a month. Eliza knew her friend felt neglected. She also knew that Janet had something to tell her; Eliza had been summoned.

The ritual of opening the bottle came first. Janet frowned down at the excellent Ripasso between her knees. She gave the corkscrew two more turns; it wasn't working properly. "Oh, crap! It's shredding the cork. Just a second, I'll get the good one." She left the wine on the coffee table and scurried off to the kitchen, talking all the way, though once she went around the corner, Eliza couldn't make out her words.

She glanced around the living room, determined not to grab her bag and check her messages. But her phone was brand new, the latest iPhone. That was her excuse: she *had* to fiddle with it. Various accounts and calendars were not synchronized to the new system. Stop, she commanded herself. *Leave your damn phone alone!* She eyed her leather tote again, but resisted, and looked at her surroundings instead.

Silver vases on the glass table, silver-threaded pillows on the white sofa. A white sofa! In a house where two little boys lived, you couldn't have anything white except toilet paper. She loved the enormous photograph over the fireplace, a snowscape of a vast field. Her eyes lifted, as usual, to the three small figures walking across the snow. They were as inky black as the woods that bound the far edges of the image. It's a picture of time, Eliza thought, of time passing. She eyed her bag again. She did not want to be an obsessed person. She did not want to have her face stuck to that little screen every spare moment.

She scrutinized the wall closest to her, trying to find a grubby fingerprint. She glanced over the arm of her chair; no bubble-gum wrappers, no dust bunnies in the chasm. She remembered how she loved coming over to Janet's place in the evening.

She heard a metallic clatter in the kitchen. Unable to stop herself, she grabbed her bag and pulled out the phone. No new message. She reread the little poem by a famous Persian poet Shar had sent to her that morning.

> Your eyes are two full glasses of wine.
> Your eyebrows are worth all the land of Ray.
> You keep telling me tomorrow, tomorrow.
> I don't know why this tomorrow never comes.

She tapped away with flamenco fingers.

> Tomorrow WILL come. Next
> week. Monday afternoon? I'll eat

Janet came back into the room. Eliza's heart boomeranged into her throat. She speedily finished

> lunch at your place. How
> about 1? Then a coffee.
> And DESSERT.

just as Janet stepped closer and said, "You're not supposed to be doing business at nine o'clock on a Friday night!"

When Janet bent toward her, waving the fancy silver and black corkscrew, Eliza pressed Send and leaned back into the chair, as though her friend would know instinctively what she was up to. Charlie, Janet's ex, had kept different affairs going with two phones, two computers, much fuckery. Eliza tossed her phone in her bag and exclaimed, "Ugh! The wedding clients are the worst! And the phone's new, so I'm still figuring out all the bells and whistles."

Janet said, "Speaking of which, I wonder if I can remember how to use this contraption." She fitted the large sheath over the neck of the wine bottle. "It looks like a gynecological instrument, but I *promise* you it's not. Charlie loved this thing. So I hid it until he left the province. Ha!" She successfully eased the cork out of the bottle and poured the wine. "We're not going to let it breathe. I need to have this glass of wine *right now*." They clinked glasses and gratefully sipped, smiling at each other. They talked about work, the sweet weather, the angry mess of the Middle East. After the first glass was half-empty, Eliza asked, "How are Sophie and Daniel doing?"

"My son is being so . . . nice! It's confusing, I'm used to the anti-social video-game addict in the basement. Yesterday Daniel came upstairs and gave me a *hug*. And chatted. It's like he's become human again."

"And Sophie?"

"Adolescence. That's how she is. She's not getting into *trouble*. But something's going on. I—I don't know what. She's going through something and she doesn't want to talk to me about it. She's so moody. And angry. Usually angry at *me*." Janet sighed, and reached for the silver bowl of olives.

"Is she still going out a lot on the weekends? Those sleepovers?"

"I talked to the parents like you suggested. And she really does go there. It's not like she's partying with a bunch of guys. She stays at Binta's place—that's the girl's name. Or if they go out, they get in at a reasonable hour. I had a talk with the mother, nothing too deep, but it was nice. Her parents are very proud of her. She's on the honour roll. And she's slept over here a couple times, too, so I know her better. She seems extremely . . . responsible."

"That's what I thought, when I met her."

Janet looked momentarily confused, so Eliza continued, "Remember? When Sophie babysat for us that time."

"Yes. Right. Well, I've realized that Binta isn't the problem. Something *else* is going on with Sophie."

"What does Charlie say about it?" As soon as his name was out of her mouth, Eliza regretted it.

"Who the fuck cares what Charlie says?"

Eliza disguised her wince by craning her head away to scratch her neck.

"Something happened out there, in Victoria, last summer. After being around him and his New Age girlfriend, Sophie came back changed. It started there." Janet picked up the bottle of wine and poured Eliza another couple of inches. The bottle hovered over her own glass as she hissed, "Fuck, I'm still so pissed off at him, the liar. I just *hate* liars."

Eliza took this in the gut but managed not to double over. The nausea came on so quickly that for a few seconds she felt a strong urge to vomit. Physical distraction, even the simple motion of lifting a crystal wineglass, was the only way forward. She took a small sip; the tannins in the wine turned to chalk on her tongue.

Luckily, Janet did not linger on her hatred of adulterous liars. She returned to her thoughts about Sophie, her school work, her attachment to an art teacher at school, a good-looking young man. "Could that be it? A crush? Do you think . . . ? Would any teacher these days be stupid enough to get involved with a student? Besides, everyone thinks he's, you know, playing for the wrong team."

Eliza shook her head, grinned. "Janet, the expression is the *other* team. You mean he's gay, right?"

Janet sat back from her friend, distancing herself from the implied criticism. She picked up a pillow and shoved it behind her back. "Right. Gay. Maybe. I don't know for sure. So I didn't want to use that word."

That word. Eliza felt the sting in a surprisingly personal way.

Janet was still talking. "I mean, it might just be hormones, right? She's become so . . . beautiful in the last few months."

Both women thought of *how* Sophie had become beautiful; she had become frankly sexual. Most teenage girls were beautiful in a way that the girls themselves could rarely appreciate, but Sophie was buzzing with her own heat. She's having sex, Eliza realized. Probably lots of it. And she's only fifteen.

Then something else occurred to her: Sophie was in love. For the first time. Mind- and heart- and body-expanding love. Of course. Eliza had been too distracted to notice. But didn't Janet know it? Maybe she did. Maybe that was the problem.

"I think it's possible that boys have been after her and she doesn't know how to deal with it." Her friend clearly wanted to know and to not know about her daughter's sex life. Janet was forty-seven, had left a long, always rocky marriage; she was approaching the end of fertility. She hadn't even thought about meeting other men yet; she was still recovering. And it had been ages—almost three years—since she'd had sex. Last summer when the kids were away in Victoria with their father, she confided to Eliza that despite how angry and hurt she was, she still missed Charlie that way. "He was such a good lover." Remembering that evening, when Janet's losses had been so clear, Eliza leaned toward her with more tenderness. "Have you asked her what's up?"

Janet stared at her. "Of course I've . . . I've asked her why she's so aggressive with me. With Daniel . . ."

"Have you asked her how *she's* feeling?"

In Janet's non-response to this question, Eliza felt as though she had stepped off a curb but the road was farther down than she thought. The silence was a jarring answer, throwing various joints out of alignment. Janet wasn't telling Eliza everything. Or couldn't tell her. When does knowledge become language, anyway? It's possible to know something and be unable to say it. She herself was becoming an expert in that field.

Janet finally said, "I haven't really asked her. I'm afraid that she'll say she hates me. That the divorce is all my fault. Which it is. I ended the marriage. She *says* she's glad I ended it. She knew about Charlie's infidelities before I could face them. But . . . it breaks a girl's heart, I think, to lose the father she loves."

Given Eliza's own history, this romantic declaration made her grit her teeth. "Janet, Charlie's not dead. He just lives in Victoria . . ."

Janet growled, "He's as good as dead! People go to Victoria to get old . . ."

"And to take up kayaking. Don't forget the kayaking." She and Janet both liked kayaking.

Janet rolled her eyes. "Goddamn hippies."

"Don't be mean to the hippies. They gave us tie-dye."

"All the more reason to be mean to them!" They both laughed.

"Seriously," Eliza said. "The relationship is different now between Sophie and her dad, but . . . she hasn't lost him. Didn't you tell me they Skype every weekend? I've run into her a few times in the neighbourhood. She always looks happy."

Janet asked bluntly, "Where do you think she's going, when you see her?"

"Oh, I don't know. Sometimes she's just on her way to school." Or off to see her boyfriend, Eliza thought. "Invite her out for dinner or something. Talk with her. Not to her. Andrew and I are always haranguing our kids. *Do this, do that. Hurry up, stop here, go there, be careful.* We're so bossy. Especially me. My mom wasn't like that. Where did it come from?"

"Remember how, when we were kids, we used to go out on a Saturday and disappear for three or four hours? When I was nine I used to take my little brother and sister to a park half a mile away. No cellphones. We trusted that the world would not implode without an adult around, and it never did. Little kids are *always* with their parents now. No wonder they flee when they become teenagers! And turn off their cellphones. Man, I would *love* to put a tracking device behind Sophie's ear. *In* her ear. Implant it under her skin!"

The friends came together again over the subject of fretting, needlessly, about their children. Promising to be less like Big Brother, they toasted, then sealed their resolution with another inch of Ripasso.

On the brisk, wine-heated walk home, Eliza took stock of her corroding morals. Three months ago, unwilling to deal with the guilt, she wouldn't have lied to Janet about Sophie skipping school. Over the last couple of months, she'd seen her several times in the morning, skipping *away* from her school. But compared to the other deceptions she had embarked upon, that one was easy to rationalize. Even Janet didn't think it was necessary to keep constant tabs on her kids.

Eliza stopped to check her phone. "Shit." No confirmation yet about their Monday date. She wanted to bite something. Shar, for example. The wine had made her horny. Or was it spring? Lust was making a fool out of her, as it had nameless others in pop songs and Hollywood movies. If sexual desperation was such an old joke, why did it seem so new?

At least the word *adultery* still made her feel guilty. Worse: *adulteress.* She shivered in the cool spring air. It was a word from childhood, from those years of Bible studies her mother had forced on them. In a grave voice, Genevieve had explained, "It's a bad thing that only adults can do; that's why it's called *adult*-ery."

"Then what's fornication, Mom?"

In response to this question, her mother had slapped her across the face, shocking Eliza. She ran away and sobbed in her bedroom, confused and betrayed. Only years later did she understand that her mother was in a sexual relationship with Elder Garry; Genevieve had mistakenly thought that her daughter was making fun of her. But Eliza hadn't had a clue. She only wanted to understand the book of Leviticus, that thrilling compendium of sexual crimes and their corresponding punishments. For both adulterers and fornicators, the penalty was death by stoning.

They still did that to people, didn't they? To women, anyway. In certain far-away countries. Didn't they? As she walked up the porch steps, her phone vibrated against her thigh. Shar.

They were on for Monday.

28

To-Do List

Sync work computer and new iPhone—esp lists of things to do
Sync Outlook calendar with new iPhone calendar (WHY
  DIDN'T THIS WORK?)
Also: write stuff in kitchen calendar onto iPhone
Clean blinds
Call Mom (yesterday)
School council meeting on Thursday—bring list of suggestions
(write f-ing list!)
Send in money for Marcus trip to aquarium ($23.75)
Order chequebooks
Frame last year's school photos
Print out skating and Christmas photos? ever?

Buy photo album
Get Crest white strips
Consider Botox
Botox is poison shit that can kill you, do not do it.

Monday 11:00 AM: Jacob dentist appt.
Lunch?
Lunch.
*** WTF am I forgetting????*

On Monday morning, she sat in the waiting room at the dentist's, racking her brain, scanning her text messages for clues. The alpha and omega of things-to-do lists was in her calendar on her work computer. She hadn't managed to synchronize the two of them yet, though she had spent an hour trying, secretly, in the office, hiding from Andrew, who would have been able to do it for her in three to five minutes. But she refused to give him the satisfaction of making fun of her technological failings. Anyway, she had tried and failed without getting angry and throwing something: wasn't that a kind of success? Usually she could remember everything without a device or a calendar; she just needed a couple of minutes of peace and quiet. There was supposed to be a herb you could take to improve your memory, but she couldn't remember what it was called.

Kiki knew she was working at home this morning, then picking up Jake to take him to the dentist's. Maybe it had to do with the Ayeda proposal? Or that frozen food conference? (They were going to make displays not only of flowers, but of vegetables.) She went through her email and her phone messages. Nothing. Maybe she'd already done whatever it was, and forgotten all about it.

A hygienist appeared at the perimeter of the waiting room wearing tight-fitting purple scrubs. "Mrs. Keenan, would you mind coming into the exam room for a moment?" Eliza turned off her phone and dropped it into her bag. As they walked down the short corridor together, the ponytailed, exceptionally smooth-skinned young woman (did she do Botox *already*?) explained, "Jake was *so* good for the first filling, but as soon as Dr. Bobson said that he needed another needle for *another* filling, he started to cry. Did you hear him out here?"

"Uh, no . . . I was . . . I didn't hear anything." She'd been too busy with her phone.

She sat down beside Jake, who was sitting forward, awkwardly, not letting his back touch the chair. He white-knuckled the armrests. "Mommy, I . . ." The tears poured out Eliza wondered why they had brought her in here; a child would act up more with the mother in the room, wouldn't he?

The dentist glanced in once or twice as he rushed back and forth between exam rooms, raking in the cash. He met her eyes with his usual judgmental expression. Of course! That's why he wanted her here: to punish her. She'd forgotten how obnoxious the man was. He'd once lectured her for ten minutes on the perils of Halloween candy and how his own five children had never had *any* cavities, *not a single one*. On the day when Marcus's X-rays had revealed that he had three.

She took Jake's hand and cooed in low tones, commiserating, then praising his bravery at withstanding the first filling. "If you could just be brave for another five minutes, sweetheart, we'd be all done here."

"Buh I dow wan to be bwave anymo," Jake replied, reasonable despite his frozen tongue. It took another two or three minutes for him to realize that he could neither discuss nor cry his way out of the next filling. Doomed, he finally lay back in the chair, tears sliding into his ears.

Dr. Bobson came back in, energetic, snappy, glancing repeatedly at her with his bright blue eyes. He said, "I knew you could do it, Jacob. No need to be a big crybaby when it comes to a little filling. We'll get it done as quick as we can. And *then* you'll start brushing your teeth more regularly, right? Right, Mom? There is no need to have a new cavity or *two* every time you come here." He gave her a tight smile and pulled the white mask over his lower face. When he angled his face down, she aimed her thought at the top of his head like one of his own drills: *You jerk, this is the last time we're coming here. You've just lost ten years of fees for cleanings and fillings.*

❧

Forty-five minutes later, she drove too quickly down Bathurst Street, aching with guilt. How many times had she stood behind Jake in the bathroom, cajoling and instructing him to brush? And flossing between his teeth herself? They brushed and brushed! She put a timer in the bathroom. And still her children got cavities.

In the end, Jake had remained stoic for the second filling. After, he hadn't wanted to go back to school ("My mowt id till froden!") but she had driven him there and stood beside the open passenger door until he slid glumly off his seat. "In an hour or so, your mouth will feel normal again," she said as she took him to the office and signed him in. Up the stairs he went, scowling, toward his classroom. He didn't even turn around to wave goodbye.

The woman who answered the door looked like a model. The cut of dress was almost conservative—long lace sleeves, dark blue pencil skirt—but the inlaid lace collar extended to the top edge of her breasts. She must have been wearing a low-cut bra, so the cups wouldn't show above the bodice, which was made of the same dark blue material. Grey lace cuffs finished the sleeves. And below those cuffs, Shar's nicely manicured nails were painted a pearly blue-grey.

"Wow! You didn't have to dress up for me!" But Eliza knew that she hadn't. She only dressed like this for Benoît. Shar's regular uniform for life was worn-out jeans and a man's shirt.

"I just got in myself," Shar said, smiling (pale pink lipstick). "Morning meeting." Her eyeshadow matched the powder-grey lace in the dress.

"What, with *Cosmo* magazine? Photo shoot? Everything you're wearing matches!"

Eliza followed her into the living room, looking at her from behind with a mixture of querulous jealousy and craven lust. Shar was wearing a pair of grey stilettos with decorative silver zippers down the back of each heel. She tiptoed on them to keep from making too much noise on the wood floor, then spun around on her toe once she was on the carpet in the living room. Eliza walked straight into her arms, and laughed. "This is no fair! I have to look up at you even when you're not wearing heels."

"That's the idea. To lord it over you a little." She put her arms on Eliza's shoulders and kissed the top of her head, then leaned down farther and kissed her neck. "Oops. Sorry. I left lipstick marks. Here, let me wipe that off." She grabbed a tissue from the box on the coffee table; she rubbed Eliza's neck, then blotted off most of her pale lipstick. "Are you hungry? I have two Cornish hens heating up in the oven. I picked them up at Pusateri's. How about a glass of wine first?" A chilled bottle was on the table.

"Oh, I suppose." She put her hands around Shar's waist, feeling the long, hard muscles there. If she pressed a little harder, Shar would jump; she was ticklish. But Shar slid from her hands and poured them each a glass. "So your meeting was in Yorkville?" Eliza asked.

"Breakfast. A little boutique hotel with an excellent restaurant. What should we drink to?" She put her hand on her hip, which accentuated both her curves and her height.

Eliza smiled and raised her glass. "To your career as a model." They clinked glasses, sipped.

"So you had breakfast with Benoît this morning?"

"Yes."

"That's why you're all dressed up."

"Dressing up suits the hotel." The truth was, Benoît loved her to dress up. And Shar missed this part of her work. She had an extensive wardrobe of sexy cocktail dresses that she rarely wore now that she was becoming a civilian. "It was just breakfast. No time for anything else. He's a busy man."

But the reassurance didn't stop Eliza from receiving a clear image of Shar prone on a bed, legs spread, with a man's hard ass pumping between them. She imagined someone as beautiful as Shar herself, some buff entrepreneur full of energy and sperm. Married, probably. Eliza didn't know the details; she had never wanted to know them. The thing was that Shar might have been naked with Benoît an hour or two ago, and now she was here, flirting with Eliza, getting ready to strip again. *Slut.* The word entered her mind, her mouth, hard and sharp. *Slut.*

She put her hand around Shar's waist, pulled her close. They kissed aggressively, biting, biting back, swallowing each other up as the zippers came down and the buttons opened in the living room.

It was a perfect erotic misunderstanding. Shar was lustful because (though she had dressed exquisitely and shaved and perfumed herself) she *hadn't* had sex with Benoît (he had flown in for an unexpected meeting with a potential American client and would fly out again at the end of the day; with the new blood pressure diagnosis and the medication still taking effect, he was not allowed quickies). Eliza was lustful out of Pavlovian habit, and a big hit of jealousy.

She pulled on the zipper at the base of Shar's neck. Shar undid the cuffs of her sleeves, pulled her arms out of the long tubes of lace, and let the dress slide off her hips. She was wearing a lace slip and thigh-high stockings. Eliza didn't know what to touch first. One hand to a breast, the other hand to Shar's lower back. She immediately began pulling the slip up over her buttocks, and down, to expose her breasts. "Where's that strap-on you told me about?"

Shar grinned. "No!"

"Yes. I'm going to put that thing on and fuck you."

"Hold on, I should get to wear it first. It's my strap-on."

"No way. It's in your bedroom, isn't it? Come." Eliza pulled her by the hand.

"I'm going to dress up like this more often. I like the effect it has on you."

Eliza blushed over the buckles and straps; then she stared down at her new appendage. "God! It really looks like a penis!"

As Shar cinched her in a little tighter, she said, "Some of my girlfriends never wanted me to say that word, when it came to sex toys. No *penis*, no *dick*, no *cock*. They didn't want to refer to the male anatomy at all. That's how this thing got a gender-neutral name. Stacey."

Eliza took it in her hand. Shar looked down, and said, "Stacey may have a gender-neutral name, but it's nice to have a big hard cock, isn't it?"

"It's not *too* hard." Eliza gave it a firm squeeze. "Not too soft either."

Shar stepped back and said in a singsong voice, "Goldilocks thought it was juuuust right." She opened her bedside table drawer and pulled out a condom and a bottle of lube. "It's cleanest to use one of these." She tore the top off, held the condom up and raised the pitch of her voice. "Do you want me to put it on you, baby?"

Watching Shar slide the condom down the shaft, Eliza said in a joking tone, "I do feel quite . . . manly." It was not really a joke. It was a power, to have this big thing attached to her body. She didn't want to put her fingers or her tongue inside Shar, not now; she wanted to penetrate her with *this*.

Shar said, "Doggy-style is easiest for beginners. That way you can see what you're doing." They kissed again. Shar turned, her back to Eliza, and slowly pulled her slip up over her ass, then crawled onto the bed. On her hands and knees, she craned around. "I should have asked you if you wanted a blowjob."

But Eliza's face had already taken on that glassy-eyed drunken lustful look that Shar loved. "Maybe later," she said, putting her hand on the small of Shar's back.

Shar spread her knees wide, eager for what was coming. It was always exciting when a lover did something new, unexpected. Eliza pushed into her slowly, staring down at the cock—her cock!—as it disappeared into Shar's pussy. This disappearing act was so sexy that she wanted it to go on forever. Simultaneously, she wanted to move faster, to get *in*, to be inside. How amazing it would be, she thought, to be a man!

She held onto Shar's hips and slowly pulled herself out. And wanted immediately to push back in, to see what it did to Shar. How keen the urge was, to open her up. They moaned at the same time, Eliza from watching and knowing what it was to be so hungry, and Shar with the pleasure of being filled. Eliza grasped Shar's hips harder and thrust her own hips forward, awkwardly, the necessary rhythm eluding her. It was like learning the steps of a dance that she thought she knew, but did not. When she finally found the rhythm, it took root not so much in her pelvis as in her thighs and lower back. Every joint told her why sex was problematic when Andrew's herniated discs were bothering him.

But she didn't want to think of Andrew.

She concentrated on Shar. She loved *seeing* her, the audacious nakedness of her ass, her long muscular back. She loved the feel of the harness around her own hips and cheeks, the material slicking up between her legs. They talked to each other now, but differently, Eliza more Shar-like and Shar someone else altogether. She started rubbing her clit and Eliza kept going, varying the pace, watching her, wanting it to go on and on.

Slowly, another realization unfolded, and she resisted it somehow and thrust harder, but that brought her closer to the admission that her rhythms, her movements, her pauses, were all her husband's. She had learned how to do this—not too fast, not too slow, following the woman's body, too, her desire—from him. Shar turned her head and pressed her face sideways against the sheets, thrust herself backwards for more, for deeper, and Eliza was pulled down again, into the tumbling wave of black hair, the hot skin, her mouth open, both of their mouths open, wanting and taking each other.

Two, almost three hours later, after sex, lunch, wine, a long hot shower, they were sprawled back in bed. Shar was still wearing the strap-on. Eliza whispered, "I really have to go."

Shar could hear how sad she was. It had happened before: the better the sex, the sadder Eliza could be when it was done. Shar thought of good sex as *annihilatingly* good. She enjoyed being annihilated—by pleasure, and temporarily. There was nothing more exhilarating than shattering the ego with joyful intensity. It was a relief to close the separation between the selves, the body and the mind, the other and the lover, the inside and the outside. Then it was over. Shar was equally skilled at drawing back, pulling herself into herself again. It had made her a consummate professional. She unbuckled Stacey and scissored her long legs out of the harness. "Onwards and upwards," she said, a smile in her voice as she leaned over the side of the bed and set the dildo upright on the table. "Let's not be glum."

Eliza was still languid, slow. "Why didn't I let you do that to me before?"

"Power issues."

Eliza didn't respond. She knew exactly why she had never let Shar do that to her before. It was too much like having sex with a man. She still liked to think that she was "just" having sex with a woman; somehow it didn't count. She pushed that lie away and stared at the ceiling. Something else was bothering her. "I was supposed to do something today and I still can't remember what the hell it was. There's always something like that. A task I didn't get to. The list never ends."

Shar stood up, grabbed a T-shirt off the floor. "We all have a to-do list."

"Even you?"

"Even me." She slipped on her shirt, pulled on a pair of old jeans. "I skipped a class to be here this afternoon." She had also skipped a class to see Benoît in the morning. She worried about her own penchant for writing off commitments that she needed to fulfill, like coursework at the Institute. She leaned over Eliza and finger-combed her messy hair. "I hope you're not indulging in guilt. You shouldn't feel guilty."

"Easy for you to say," Eliza retorted, sitting up.

Shar pulled away. "You know, it's *not* easy for me. You leave, yes. But I'm the one who always has to let you go. I'm aware of your responsibilities and your constraints." Her voice was cool. "I know it's temporary." She waved her hand around the bedroom. "This is a closed box for me, too. That's what it's like to live a secret. Thrilling at the beginning but stifling when the oxygen runs out. Relationships are like plants. They need air and light." She walked around the bed and stepped out into the hall. "I never encourage you to see me more than you already do."

Eliza got up and began putting on her clothes. "That's what you *say*. But you always have to bring up how temporary this is, how it cannot last. It's like a threat."

"I talk about that for both of us. We have to be realistic. You don't want to change your relationship with Andrew."

"Why do you keep harping on that? We've said from the beginning, this is contained, we can contain it. But every couple of weeks, you lecture me about open relationships or being truthful or shifting the fucking paradigm. It's like being in a women's studies course with a twenty-two-year-old. If I tell Andrew that I'm having an affair, it will blow a hole open in the middle of my life. It would be a disaster."

"Telling the truth is too much of a risk for you."

"Yes, it is. You don't understand how marriage works because you've never been married. And we're parents. We have two little kids."

"I'm not suggesting that we ever meet at your house. Haven't you ever hired a babysitter?"

"That's not the fucking point! It's just . . . It's not *possible*."

"You don't *want* it to be possible. Fine. I understand your priorities. And I respect them. Just don't think it's all about you and your needs."

"I know it's not just about me. You have your own life, too. You see other people. Benoît, for example. And you've alluded to other *friends*." Their eyes met. Eliza snapped, "You're *always* safe, right? Condoms, those dental things, whoever these people are?"

"Dental dams." Shar knew that Eliza was not worried about safe sex; she was making a point about sexual freedom. "I don't need dental dams. I don't sleep with other women. Not at the moment, anyway. As you know, I *always* use condoms. And it's not like I have fifty male lovers. I told you that. I have . . . a couple . . . friends. It's a preventative."

"A preventative against *what*?" Eliza could not help that *what* from flying out like a blade.

"Don't be so thick! It prevents us from getting too attached. Whether or not I see other people isn't the point. You're the one who occupies my mind and my bed."

"But you have to pass it on as soon as you've had it, don't you?"

"What is that supposed to mean?"

"Benoît penetrates you and you have to penetrate me? Is your dick bigger than his?"

"What are you talking about? *You* wanted to use the strap-on! Is that why? To compete with Benoît? Really?" She laughed, incredulous.

"What's so fucking funny? You feel no jealousy at all, ever? About *any*one?"

Shar took a deep breath. Exhaled. The truth was the most logical thing at this moment. She could trust Eliza with the truth. Couldn't she? She looked into her angry face. "Benoît is a dear friend. I've known him for a long time. Sure, we have sex sometimes. You know that. But we didn't this morning. We had *breakfast*. Which is what I *said*. I told you that."

"How do I know what you do or don't do with him? With anyone? You're free, right? You're completely fucking *free*."

"I never said I was—"

"Instead of running around fourteen hours a day working and housecleaning and taking care of children and a husband, you just swan from one little lunch date to the next, a few fucks here, a few classes there, planning your next trip to France or Italy. Must be nice."

Shar's eyes narrowed. "Fuck you! Why have an honest conversation when it's easier to insult me and feel sorry for yourself?"

That was how Shar, who badly wanted to have an honest conversation, squandered the moment for it.

Eliza did up the last button on her blouse, jerked her head back like a whiplash victim and spat out, "I have to go right now."

Not to be outdone, Shar replied, "Yes, you do. Go."

29

Telepathy

EN ROUTE TO THE STUDIO, ELIZA PASSED A MINIVAN speeding in the opposite direction and shouted, "Oh, shit fire and fuck dogs!" It was an old Alberta cuss.

The vehicle was *not* Fleur's delivery van—unfortunately—but it was similar enough to remind Eliza of the thing missing from her to-do list, now the thing she had not done. "Oh, no," she said, and swore again. One remembered item dislodged another, and the name of the herb also came to her, the one that could improve a sluggish memory. "Ginkgo *fucking* biloba." What she'd had to do was on her work computer calendar. But she hadn't gone to the studio this morning because, of course, she'd taken Jake to the dentist.

Bianca sat behind her desk eating, with her usual neatness, from a small container of yogurt. "I would say . . . yes. She *is* upset. Kind of." Just like Bianca to soften the blow.

"But did she . . . manage?"

Because Eliza had forgotten, Kiki had had to drive alone to Mississauga after lunch to pick up some lighting fixtures for their first spring wedding. Eliza had promised she would drive the van.

"She didn't have a car accident, if that's what you're asking. But she missed two exits off the highway. Ended up going past Mississauga."

"How do you go *past* Mississauga? It's huge! Wasn't she using the GPS?"

"The GPS would have helped. A lot. But it wasn't in the console of the van. Where it's supposed to be." Bianca licked yogurt from the edges of her lips as delicately as a cat. "Do *you* know where the GPS is?"

"Oh, shit. I completely forgot to put it back."

"After you went to pick up those new planter stands." Bianca pursed her lips, nodded. "And the GPS is . . . ?"

"In the bottom drawer of my desk," Eliza responded, her voice dull.

"I looked in your desk," Bianca said mildly. "But the bottom one is usually locked . . ."

"Because the good camera is in there."

"Right."

"And I have the only key to the drawer."

"Mm-hm. You know, she printed out Google map directions. It should have been fine. But she gets flustered. I couldn't go in her place because she wanted to see the lanterns herself. And I couldn't go with her because we were expecting three deliveries this afternoon." Bianca offered up a compensatory smile. "Kiki called you. A number of times." She put the lid on her little container. "I called you, too." She put it in her lunch bag. "But your phone was off. You haven't turned it back on yet, right?"

Eliza did not immediately respond. Then she lied. "I completely forgot to charge it." Actually, she'd turned it off just before she went in to see Jake at the dentist's. That was the beginning of her early lunch, a meal that had lasted for a long time.

Bianca chose not to respond to Eliza's lie, but the way she wiped her plastic spoon with a Kleenex, eyes down, suggested her profound disappointment. "But . . . the thing is," she said, with an uncharacteristic awkwardness. Her eyes were still downcast.

Eliza nodded impatiently. "What is the thing?"

"She called Andrew."

"What?" Her voice cracked; she cleared her throat. "Why did she call Andrew?"

"Because she knows that he's an excellent driver. He talked her back onto the highway. And . . . she was looking for you, I guess." Bianca raised her eyes. "She said she thought that you were with him."

This was also a lie; both of them knew it. Was it telepathy? Eliza was too agitated to figure out how so much private information got into the air, unless, of course, it wasn't private. What *was* private anymore? Emails, texts, recorded conversations: even professional spies were outed on a regular basis, their covers blown or traced. Everything was recorded somewhere, if only on the skin of a person's face, in the sound of her voice.

Eliza didn't have a ready lie. "All right. Well . . . I feel terrible about this." That was the truth. "I'll just do paperwork until she gets in. Unless we have a standing order that needs filling tomorrow. Do we?"

"We did. Two standing orders. Sunfish. And the Tauron Tower. Kiki did them before she left. They're in the fridge. I'll deliver them tomorrow morning."

"All right. I better print out the proposals I worked on over the weekend." That was true, too. She *had* worked on two August wedding proposals, on her laptop at home; she wasn't a complete slacker. First she went and stood in the fridge, staring guiltily at Kiki's expert arrangements. The Tauron Tower management liked spare, architectural flowers. Kiki had used bird of paradise, crimson ginger and some fiery orange orchids to create a tall, elegant sculpture. Eliza stared at the purple and orange bird of paradise, that beaky reptilian bloom, until she had absorbed enough cold-blooded dignity to leave the fridge.

Half an hour later, Bianca said, "I just heard the van. If you don't mind, I'll leave now. I'll take those proposals home with me and do a bit of an edit tonight. Are you happy with the photos?"

"If you can think of better shots from last summer, you can replace the ones I slotted in. The files came through okay, did they?"

"Yup, they're perfect. And the pics are lovely, too, but I'll give it a think tonight." Bianca hastily slipped her laptop into a padded sleeve and thrust it into her bag; she didn't like it when Kiki and Eliza argued. In less than half a minute, she was gone, out the front door.

Eyes on her computer screen, Eliza listened for the booted footsteps, the big set of keys rattling in Kiki's hand; the few muttered swears in Quebecois she couldn't understand. After the keys clattered down, dropped on the floor, Eliza glanced up to see Kiki's precarious grip on a box that was too wide and deep for her arms.

"Can I help you with that?"

"*Non*. It's too late for 'elping me." Then she lost her grip. Luckily, she only dropped the box on the workbench just below her. Inside, the glass lanterns jostled, then cracked together, but nothing broke. There must have been several other boxes in the van.

"Where the fuck were you?"

At least she's direct, Eliza thought. No passive-aggressive beating around the bush. Just straight interrogation. "I don't blame you for being angry. I'm really, *really* sorry."

"You are always sorry. When will you get tired of being sorry?"

"What is *that* supposed to mean?" Eliza shot back, knowing exactly what she meant. The important thing was to avoid mention of Andrew. She was not going to ask Kiki why she had called her husband. To show any interest in that would betray her fear of the answer.

"Do you know what my mom says?"

"Your mother? What does she have to do with this?" Having a

business partner was like being married. Which made Marie-Josie the second mother-in-law that Eliza did not really like.

Kiki's whole family was made up of meddlers; that was why she had left Quebec in the first place. Whenever she mentioned her mother, it meant one of her sisters or brothers or aunts had been working on her to come home. Slaving among *les maudits anglais* was fine at a ski resort in the Rocky Mountains or Whistler when you were twenty, but only traitors moved to *Toronto* and built a life there.

"She says my job is perfect—for *you*. You 'ave *me*, always, to take care of business. *And* you 'ave your family, your 'usband, your . . ." Kiki roughly pulled one of the lanterns out of the cardboard box and banged it down on the workbench.

"Whoa!" Eliza said, forcing herself to be calm. She remained sitting behind her desk. "That's not fair. We both do plenty of weekends and evenings, we both work hard . . ." But she couldn't go on; she feared that her strap-on afternoon was floating in the room like a bubble-tableau of porn. Eliza coughed and tried to blink the images away—the awfully lifelike silicone cock, Shar thrusting behind her, both of them in front of the mirror, gorgeous with lust—but the flush was already rising up Eliza's neck. She forced her eyes down, to see clearly what was in front of her this second: the lantern on the workbench. It was beautifully treated glass, rustic but expensive-looking, too. Just what a cottage wedding couple would like. The first wedding of the season.

"My mother says I should come back to Montreal. I could modernize my own family's business. And I could get *married*." In her most colourful Quebecois, she uttered several insults about the "American" men of Toronto. "You know, I begin to tink she's right."

"Your mother would swear she had the perfect man sitting in her kitchen eating poutine in order to get your ass back there. Doesn't she *always* want you to come home?"

"Why shouldn't I go? I see 'ow convenient it is for you. I do all dis work and—"

"And I don't? All this is not my work as well as yours?" Eliza spread out her arms.

"Lately you are not . . . you are not 'ere in da same way. I don't know what is going on. You also forgot dat client meeting last week. And we were supposed to go to Mississauga *together*. You *know* I can't stand driving 'ere. It terrifies me. You tink it's funny, how upset I get, but what if I 'ad an accident? I couldn't breathe. 'Ow could you forget today?"

"I do *not* think it's funny. I'm sorry that happened. My new phone and my computer calendar aren't hooked up, and I was racking my brains all morning, knowing I'd forgotten—or was going to forget—something. Then Jake had an awful appointment at the dentist. And I'd *just* dropped him off at school when my phone died."

"You see? You take care of your kids, you take care of your life. But me, I just work all da time and date perverted idiots and almost die on da road to Mississauga."

"I should have called. From the restaurant. I had an emergency lunch with a dear old friend who's . . . thinking she might . . . she might . . . divorce her husband. I . . . I just had to let her talk." Eliza shook her head at this blatant lie. Yet—maybe it wasn't a lie. She might be foretelling her own future. "She's in a mess." She certainly was.

Kiki's face changed as Eliza watched; an invisible force sucked the anger out of her and pumped her full of sadness. "She shouldn't get divorced. She will become like your other divorced friend. Janet. Alone in da world and getting fat."

"Janet isn't fat! She's voluptuous. She's in great shape. And her ex-husband was an asshole."

"But it's still sad for 'er kids. Dat's what my mom says. One ting for parents to separate, impossible for children." She sighed, and pulled a second lantern out of the box. This time she put it down gently. "Anglophones don't think about it the same way."

"Good grief, stop being so romantic. Don't people in Quebec get divorced, too?" She allowed a hint of a smile to soften her words. "Going back to Montreal doesn't make sense demographically. There are more single men in Toronto. It's a bigger city." She didn't need to mention that Kiki's departure would be a disaster for Fleur; Kiki knew this as well as she did.

"But all my sisters are married. Even the youngest one already has two kids. She has a *life*."

"Violette got pregnant by accident and dropped out of university. You said she still regrets it."

"Yes, but she has a *family*."

"And a husband whose name I can't remember because you always refer to him as 'the loser.' Come on, Kiki. None of your sisters have struck out on their own the way you have. You've become a successful businesswoman in what is essentially a different country. You're the part-owner of the company that we've built together. We're doing better every year."

Kiki kept her mouth tightly shut. She removed four more lanterns from the box. "The lights fit in right there, the centre well. They're all rechargeable." She held the lantern up for Eliza to look at. "See how the glass is textured? *C'est très beau!* The light"—she flicked it on, and held up the glowing chamber—"looks like a candle." She switched it off, and turned to put the lantern on the shelf behind her. "I am sick of making udder people's weddings so beautiful."

"You want to get *married*." Eliza meant to sound fond, and nostalgic.

Kiki spun around, red hair swinging. "Stupid, isn't it, when I know so many people who *are* married but don't appreciate it."

She dismantled the empty box, tearing the flaps open one by one, then wrestling the cardboard until it was flattened. She raised it, shield-like, in her hands. "There are three more boxes in the van. It would be nice if you could 'elp me *now*." She turned away and disappeared out the back door.

30

I Forgot About This

THE HEAVY TRAFFIC WAS A BLESSING; IT KEPT HER from reaching home. What did Kiki *know*? The light changed from red to green but still only a few cars got through the intersection. Eliza sat behind her windshield like everyone else, each man or woman wrapped in his or her own suffering, tribulations, various ruins. And amusements. One sat picking his nose, no apology. Another one talked agitatedly to herself or, rather, into a cellphone mike that dangled from her ear on a little wire.

But surely some of these people were happy. She surreptitiously examined the man in the Saab beside her: his lips turned down grimly and his cheekbones jutted out. His hair was just beginning to grey at the temples. An angry-looking man. But maybe he was sick. Maybe he was between chemotherapy treatments.

You never knew what people were going through; it was a mistake to presume. She herself, for example—what was wrong with *her*? She had been happy just a few months ago. Undersexed, yes, but happy. Now what was she? A lying, hungering, craven idiot. She had been sleeping the dreamless, calm sleep of the 24/7 married-with-kids life. Now she was wide awake, a hounded insomniac. A hound, howling at the moon, saliva running down her chin. How could sex *still* be a problem?

Yet it was also the most fundamental pleasure. Wasn't it? What else did she have for herself alone but the pleasure of her own body?

The light changed to green. She burst into tears. The momentary blur made her think of getting into a car accident. Death or maiming, the Old Testament all over again, punishment for the whore! She would do the same thing to her kids that her damn father had done to her: she would die in a car accident! She fumbled with the stick shift, still crying; she ground the gears once, then sped through the intersection as the light turned yellow. A driver on the other side of the intersection, trying to make a left on that yellow light, honked long and loud.

"Oh, shut up!" she yelled, talking to herself. "You stupid slut!" After a few more ragged sobs, she roughly wiped the tears off her face. She didn't like crying about her predicament—tears dripped emotional hypocrisy on top of dishonesty—though sometimes a good sob was necessary to keep her head from exploding. As she turned onto Bloor Street, she deflected her own guilt with the thought that adulterous men probably didn't feel so guilty. Men had more practice at destruction; it was an ancient masculine activity. Weapons: Glocks and semi-automatics, submachine guns, rocket launchers, drones in the sky. (Her own children were already obsessed with fighter jets, tanks, guns of all sorts.) Global deforestation. The big money men on Wall Street were not wringing their hands about the five million Americans who'd lost their homes in the economic crash.

Beside the greater crimes, what was a little adultery?

The voice addressed her out loud, calling her on the rationalization: "Eliza," it said, "you are disgusting."

"I know," she replied, not resisting this time, her eyes once more filling with tears.

The kitchen was dark. She flicked on the light. "Marcus! Jaa-aake!"

Where were they? It was Monday, wasn't it? Yes, still Monday, the dentist appointment, the drive she didn't do with Kiki. Monday, the day Andrew picked the boys up early from Annie's. They were usually home by 4:30 or 5:00. She glanced at the clock on the stove: it was 6:00. "Andrew?"

Where were they? What *had* Kiki told him?

It was like being hit by a wave from behind, knocked over, dragged under. Andrew had taken the boys. She stood there beside the island. The house was silent. This is how it would be, the unravelling, the separation. The wreckage.

She grabbed her bag, dug into one side pocket, the other, scrabbling for her phone. When he answered, after two rings, she yelled, "Andrew!"

"Eliza?"

"I . . . I . . . What's happened?"

"What do you mean?"

"Where are you?"

"At Annie's. The boys started their swim lessons today."

"Oh, my god!" She was so relieved that she folded down onto the floor and gulped back a sob of sheer relief. "I completely forgot!"

"Yeah, I know," he said, cautiously. "Me, too . . . Are you okay?"

"Yeah, I—I was just—" How to explain her panic? "—expecting you all to be home."

"We're getting old. The swim class was up on the kitchen calendar and everything. We just missed it. The boys didn't have their swim stuff, of course, so I rushed home to pick it up. Hey, why don't you come to Annie's? They're just getting into the water now."

⁓

She ran, heedless of puddles on the sidewalk. She ran as if she were a runner, toward the three of them, two boys, one man. She could hardly wait to see them.

She slipped off her shoes and socks and pushed through the public access doors, rushed into the humid chlorinated air and up the bleachers, stumbled, found her footing. Out of breath, she excused herself around one dad's knees, then a mother's, her eyes already on Andrew's face; he was smiling directly into the pool. The fact of him shoved her into gratitude. He was right here; he still loved her. She had to restrain herself from running toward him along the narrow length of benches.

She followed the arrow of his gaze; the boys smiled back at him, skinny and bare-chested in the pool, showing him the tensed muscles of their biceps, wrists curled over, fists clenched, miniature muscle men at the beach. In rapid chorus they counted (their swim instructor's stern call flattened by their high echoing voices), "One-two-three!" and jumped straight up only to fall backwards—*splash!*—into the water. Spluttering and laughing, they came up again to more scolding from the instructor. Slick and beaming with delight, they waved at Andrew and flopped back to the side of the pool, still shaking with laughter.

In the next breath, Andrew became aware of someone coming toward him, too quickly for a stranger. He turned, saw Eliza, and rose to meet her unexpected embrace. It unbalanced him in the narrow space between bleachers; he hugged her tighter, regaining his balance, then pulled away, the watching-the-boys smile still on his face. "Did you see that? They're such comedians!"

She could only smile, she was breathing too hard to respond. She looked—frightened. They sat; he squeezed her hand. "It's good you came. And so fast!"

"I ran."

"Are you all right?"

"I—I—was so sad when I got home, expecting everyone to be there, and no one was. I forgot—I forgot—about this." He heard the fear that had brought her here, running. He watched her as she waved toward the boys.

"And you forgot about Kiki today, too. What's up?"

"Early Alzheimer's. And emotional . . . exhaustion. I was having lunch with an old foodie friend. She's . . . going through a nasty divorce."

Andrew frowned; what friend? He would ask her later. "So *that's* why you were upset when we weren't home. You wanted to come home to your adoring family."

"Exactly," she said. They turned to watch the kids, who had started diving into the deep end. Jake glanced at Andrew nervously, preparing to take his turn. *Are you watching me?* His hands met in a point. He bent his knees, curved his back, then pushed off into a shallow dive. A mere three or four seconds later, he burst out of the water, head smooth and dark as an otter's. He glanced at them again. *Did you see me? Yes,* Andrew thought, *I saw you. I always see you.* That was part of the job. He had to see his children. He and Eliza were the first witnesses to the boys' lives.

Eliza asked, "Was Kiki all right? When she called, I mean."

"She was extremely upset."

"I don't know why she called you."

He turned to her. "You're kidding me, right? You don't know why she called?"

Eliza's eyes grew round again; her head gave a wobbly shake. "I just know she was lost."

"She was scared shitless, Eliza. She was in tears. Do you know why she called me?"

"Because she couldn't get hold of me."

"Obviously, but beyond that." He saw the flash of fear in Eliza's eyes. What was wrong? "She called me because I'm her English-Canadian father. And you're her English-Canadian mother. Well, maybe you're more like a big sister who speaks crappy French. When she couldn't get help from you, she called me."

"Oh, come on! Kiki *has* parents. And she's a part-owner of Fleur, not some helpless girl."

"I didn't say she was helpless. Or a girl. But today she needed help. I felt like her dad. She was having a panic attack of some sort. She didn't even understand how the highway signs work. She kept thinking she was on the 401, but then when she'd see a new sign naming an exit, she would think that the highway itself had changed names. She was in Brampton by the time she called me, parked and crying, so I talked her back to Mississauga. Once she got the lanterns, she called me again and I got her back downtown."

"What a disaster. The GPS wasn't in the van either, so she was really on her own."

"I doubt a GPS would have made a difference. The highways just unsettle her. She never drove much in Quebec."

"Thank you so much, honey, for rescuing her."

The children lined up to do more dives, but he kept watch over Eliza's face. "From now on, leave your phone on during the day, okay? We have to be able to find you. All of us."

From the pool's edge, the boys plunged into the water.

"What foodie friend? Who's getting a divorce?"

31

Just a Phase

FOR THE REST OF THE WEEK, SHE DIDN'T CALL SHAR.
Though, once, she sent a text.

> I'm sorry. Stressed out. Guilty. Jealous
> of your freedom. & you are. Free.

Enough, she thought. That's *enough*. It's time to take a break. She
worked hard, took Kiki out for lunch. But she was already imagining the next week, or the week after, how and when she would see
Shar again.

She figured out how to sync her calendars. As she ticked items
off her to-do list, one by one, she added more items. She did not
miss any appointments. Flowers arrived in boxes and left in elegant
or soft or tightly sculpted displays. At home, she lifted the filets of
salmon out of the marinade sauce, grilled them perfectly and listened attentively to Andrew. She cajoled and humoured Marcus and
Jake through their homework; they printed; they added and sub-
tracted. She policed Jake into brushing his teeth more diligently. In
the mornings, her shower was quick. She did not go swimming.

On Saturday night after putting the boys to bed, she cleaned
the whole house from top to bottom, thinking, as she washed the
kitchen floor on her hands and knees, that it could be like this

again, as it was before. She could do it. She would stop seeing Shar.

When she finished washing the floor, she was hot, sweaty, and so tired that she lay down where she'd started, which was already dry, and began to remember her lover. It was a form of saying goodbye. She played out the details of one encounter after another, conversation, laughter, that spontaneously written private language of in-jokes, tenderness, moment after moment, hip bones, breasts pushed together, nipple against nipple against clit—the extreme particularity of sex with a woman, the intelligent specificity of the tongue and fingers searching, pushing, insisting, opening. Stacey! If men knew about strap-ons, they would want them banned. She'd been right to resist that instrument of sexual delirium, a threat to heterosexual marriages everywhere. Or maybe a gift?

In the dark, on her clean kitchen tiles, she pulled off her sweat-pants, spread her legs and came as quickly as her fingers could get her there. She lay shuddering in her whole skin, every pore, millions and millions of them, each one open like a mouth.

Eliza held the door for Janet, then followed her in. The café was packed with the Sunday morning crowd. She looked around gratefully. She loved being in a place where the code held firm: people paying for good food and drink, people making money from that service. They read the chalkboard menu and ordered. Besides the coffee and egg sandwiches, it was baked goods and tattooed hipsters and the old painted trays on the walls, rectangles and circles of teal and sienna, worn-out ochre and robin's egg blue. The food wasn't fancy but it was delicious, made in the cramped kitchen at the back. The young woman behind the counter had dreadlocks; her tattooed hands put two Americanos down on the wood counter. "I'll call you when the sandwiches are ready," she said with a smile.

Janet forged ahead and found a table at the window. They poured cream and stirred; Janet kept looking around. "It's a cute spot. I can't believe I've never been in here."

"I've been here a few times now." Three times, with Shar. After swimming. "You said Sophie likes it."

"She swears by the coffee." Janet took a sip. "And she's right. It's really good."

"So, what's up? You were being very mysterious on the phone."

Janet stared at her for a solemn length of time, then said, "I'm only telling you. Don't tell anyone else, okay?"

"Our secret." Eliza tore open a packet of sugar and stirred it in.

"All right. It's about Sophie . . ."

"I thought it might be." Sophie was pregnant. She would get an abortion, wouldn't she? Eliza took a sip of her coffee and saw Janet's fearful expression. Oh, god, Sophie wasn't sick, was she? "Janet, what's wrong?"

"Sophie is . . ." Her voice dropped so low that Eliza saw the shape of the word before she heard it. "Gay."

It was like stepping on the old garden rake, so obvious there in the grass, so stunning when it knocks you in the head. "Gay?" She matched Janet's whisper.

"That black friend of hers is. That *Binta*."

"Binta?"

"I told you how Sophie was always going to her house. Sleeping over!" Janet shook her head.

"Oh. Binta is Sophie's—girlfriend?" Eliza sat there open-mouthed, her mind snapping back to that night when Sophie babysat, the house so quiet when she opened the door. The two girls coming down the stairs like sleepwalkers. She nodded slowly, feeling stupid. In the midst of her own secret attraction, the obvious had not even occurred to her. "Sophie's a . . . a lesbian?"

"No! It's just a phase. You know, she's experimenting. It doesn't mean anything. Didn't you ever fall in love with a girlfriend when you were in high school?"

Eliza blinked, then expelled a laugh. "Ha! No. I mean, yes. I know what you mean. But . . . what did Sophie *say*?"

"She said she's gay and she's in love with Binta. And Binta's parents know. They've *always* known. It's unbelievable that they would let the girls be . . . doing . . . whatever it is they do. Can you believe that? Like, is that something black people do? Just . . . let their kids . . . The parents didn't even tell me! I can't believe how angry I am. I am *so* furious at her. At them, too. I already talked to a lawyer, but he said there was nothing—"

"A lawyer?" Janet was homophobic *and* racist? "Janet, what do you mean, something that black people do? Have gay children?"

"No! I mean, why didn't they tell me? It's so irresponsible! When . . . when . . . Who knows what the girls have been doing?"

"I have a pretty good idea. And maybe Binta's parents think their daughter has a right to privacy."

Janet stared into her face, shocked. "But they're just . . ." Her mouth opened, closed.

"In love?"

Janet exploded, "How does she know she's in love? How can she *know* that?" Several people at nearby tables glanced their way, and Janet dropped her voice. "She's fifteen fucking years old! How can she know she's in love if she's still a *virgin*?"

The words knocked the breath out of Eliza's chest. She wanted to stop the conversation, or at least slow it down, so she could prevent her friend from doing more damage. She sat back and spoke as calmly as she could. "Sophie's not a virgin if she's having sex with another young woman."

Janet's forehead cinched up. "But what if they're just . . . just . . . fooling around? It's not the same thing. It's not . . ."

Eliza shook her head, speechless for a few seconds. Then she leaned forward and whispered, "It's sex."

Janet leaned toward her. "I know that what I'm saying seems offensive. And I'm sorry. But it's just . . . I find it so . . . not exactly disgusting, but . . ." Just as she made a visor of her hands over her eyes, which were tearing up, the dreadlocked barista called out, "Two breakfast sandwiches."

Eliza went to get the food. Food was good. Food calmed the body. And chewing would make Janet shut up. Eliza carried the plates to the table and put them down. "Let's eat. And drink this excellent coffee. Let's think about how much we love Sophie. She's bright, she's . . . engaged with the world. She's your girl." Those words turned the spigot; the tears spilled freely down Janet's face. Eliza handed her a handful of napkins. "Blow your nose and eat your breakfast. Then we can talk."

They did precisely that, chewing slowly. When Eliza commented on the food and the coziness of the café, Janet looked forlorn. She said, "Sophie comes here a lot with Binta. This is their café."

"We could have gone somewhere else."

"No. I wanted to come here." Janet pulled her napkin across her lips. "I don't know why I'm so upset about it. I think because she lied to me. She's been lying to me all this time. She somehow knew that my reaction would be—would be—"

"You'd be surprised and upset."

Janet leaned toward her over the table. "But, Eliza, I'm not just upset. I'm . . . *horrified*. And it's not because Binta's black." She closed her eyes. Opened them. "Really. Though somehow that made it more . . . I don't know! But really it's Sophie wanting to be, *saying*, that she's a lesbian. I've never thought about it before, except in a distant way. You know, Pride Day, the rainbow flag they all have, whatever. It's fine. For them. Gay people can marry each other, have kids. It has—it had nothing to do with me.

"There's that couple across from Annie's with all their kids, you know, the dads. Anybody can see they're great parents. And I have a gay co-worker, Amelia. I have no problem with gay people. Really. But. Why Sophie?" She turned her head to the window, shielded her face with her hand, and wept.

Eliza's sympathy for her friend was nearly drowned by her anger. *Why Sophie?* As if it were a disease. Yet she knew that Janet was afraid of the difference. To have a child who was the anomaly, the one among many. Eliza knew because she was afraid of being that, too. She wasn't one of *them*, she was just *flexible*, as Shar always said, with a laugh. They laughed about it, she and her lover, gay, bi, queer. Liar, adulteress. Fucking slut. She was a married woman with two little kids. She loved her husband. Yet she was passionately involved with another woman. Despite her week of quiet restraint, that was the fact of the matter. She could not imagine her body existing in the world without Shar. What was that, but love? She felt strangled, her throat thick with confusion. With shame. Not shame at the substance of her secret but shame that it *was* a secret. So Eliza folded her outrage up and put it away, because at this moment she had to speak well. For Sophie. Who had the courage to be honest. Which was remarkable. She coughed, to warm herself up. "I think . . ."

Janet met her eyes, her own full of yearning. "What? What do you think?"

Eliza picked up her coffee cup. "It's understandable that you're shocked. When you told me that Sophie was having a lot of sleepovers, I thought it was probably to cover for a boyfriend." It sounded so lame now. So plainly dumb.

"Exactly! That's why I started digging around. I snooped in her phone. I watched her key in the password a week ago. Then, two days ago, while she was in the shower, I looked at her photos."

"Oh, Janet."

Her face crumpled with guilt. "That's not all."

Eliza felt her anger roil up again. "What else did you do?"

"I deleted them. All the pictures of her and Binta. And they weren't even bad. They weren't bad pictures. She's not a bad girl. They were hugging and kissing. But . . . I didn't want anyone else to see them. That's how it all came out. We had a huge fight."

"Did you apologize?"

"About the pictures? I did. Yes. But she's furious. Said she's been invaded. She called me a racist, homophobic asshole. She's gone to Binta's house and she says she never wants to come home."

"She'll come home. After she . . . forgives you."

"I keep thinking I must have done something wrong, you know, when I was pregnant with her. Isn't there a study, about stress on the fetus? How that can turn babies into homosexuals? We moved into this neighbourhood when I was pregnant with her. It was so stressful! Charlie's work was all over the place. We didn't know if we really had the money for the mortgage payments. I was already beginning to think that he was having an affair. Way back then. Maybe the stress did something to her brain . . ."

"Janet, moving while you were pregnant did not make your child gay. Do *not* feel guilty about that. You don't need to. Sophie is a wonderful young woman. Just think, she's in love for the first time. She must feel so alive. Remember what that was like? To feel that way?"

In the contours of Janet's face Eliza could see Sophie's face, too. It was like seeing another woman underwater. Eliza's anger softened. Sometimes the depth of life with children felt unbearable. "There's only one question here."

"What's that?"

"Do you love her any less?"

"No. I love her more. Having her leave the house—it was awful. I just feel . . . destroyed. I can't lose anyone else in my family. How could I not love her?"

"Just tell her that. That's all she wants. Your love, no matter what. The rest you will figure out one day at a time." Thank god clichés were so dependable. She took Janet's hand on the table, kneaded the strong, muscular root of her thumb. "You know what girls are like with their phones. I bet Binta has most of those photos anyway. Or the best ones."

"She told me that herself. Screamed at me. *Mom, forget it, you can never delete who I am!*"

Eliza said, "So your next move is simple. You call her up and you tell her that you would never want to delete who she is."

32

Thalia

ANDREW FLICKED OFF THE TV IN DISGUST—THE NEWS had not been good—and said, "Why don't we go to bed early tonight? Lie in bed and . . . read." He peered down his legs at Eliza, wedged in at the end of the sofa, sewing a button on one of his shirts. "What a good woman."

"Does it turn you on to see me doing wifely tasks?"

"Sewing on a button is good. But nothing gets me going like you washing the floor."

She raised a single eyebrow. "Were you spying on me, the last time I washed the floor?"

"You wish. Why, what were you doing?"

"I really needed an orgasm."

"Eliza! I hope this didn't happen during daylight hours."

"The other night. I was discreetly tucked in the corner. Even the kids, coming down the stairs, wouldn't have been able to see me."

"Hallelujah." He stood, winked at her. "I like your hair like that. It's long enough for you to put up again."

"More traditional romanticism." She snipped the knotted thread. "My hair's a mess. I just haven't had time to get it cut."

"A sexy mess."

She balled up his shirt and tossed it at him. "Your shirt, husband."

"Thank you, wife."

Their eyes met. She held his gaze, her expression slowly becoming more suggestive.

"You've lost weight. All that swimming. You look great. Have I told you that lately?"

"The chlorine is turning my hair into straw," she said, putting the lid on the cookie-tin sewing basket. "I don't know what I would do without that pool. Swimming keeps me sane."

"You're my mermaid."

She closed her eyes, trying to remember the word. "*Sirena*, in Greek. Come, let's go up to bed. I already turned off the lights in the kitchen."

On the stairs behind her, Andrew said, "I thought the sirens were the bad ones, who lured innocent fishermen and brave warriors into the water with their beautiful songs."

"They drowned happy."

"How long has it been, since you were young and in Greece?"

"Twenty years."

"You're keeping track, I see. Normally it takes you five minutes to figure out how many years ago anything happened." They were in their bedroom now, undressing. "Martin's there right now."

"Where?"

"In Athens. Some conference."

"Hmm. It's an interesting time to be there. A heartbreaking time, I think. Poor Greece. I often think about the paradise it was then and the disaster it's turned into now. Lesvos especially. Did you see that article in the weekend newspaper about all the refugees? More and more of them are landing on the island."

"I wonder how that woman is doing."

"Which woman?" Though she knew precisely who he meant.

"Your hot lesbian affair. On Lesvos! Didn't it ever occur to you what a cliché that was?"

"It's not like I planned it. The taxi driver dropped me off at the wrong ferry. I thought I was going to Crete."

"Yeah, sure."

He followed her into the bathroom as she continued, "I was exhausted from that bloody train journey through Italy. And I had no idea how to get my backpack; it had disappeared into some oily hold. The ship's purser was so sweet to me. He said that his ferry company would honour the ticket even though I'd gotten on the wrong boat. So I went to Lesvos."

Andrew was already brushing his teeth, but she understood his response. "And duh rest is pushy-licking hishtory."

"Andrew! What's up with you! Have you been watching porn?"

He grinned through the mouthful of toothpaste. They finished up their nighttime ablutions, though Eliza always took longer in the bathroom. Female maintenance was a chore she liked to do privately. She leaned toward the mirror, searching for errant hairs—eyebrow, chin, nose. Pluck pluck pluck. Then there were the creams for this spot or that spot, and the regular moisturizer, and that brightening Vitamin C–based elixir that was supposed to make her glow like a twenty-year-old. She had been sucked into that around Christmas, by a persuasive, expertly Botoxed lady at the Bay cosmetic counter. She had since discovered that the only thing that made her glow like a twenty-year-old were multiple orgasms, a luxury not for sale at any department store. As she finished putting the cream on her face, she chanted, "Love the crow's feet. Love them!"

Andrew called, "What are you doing in there?"

"Praying."

"What was her name again?"

Why was he asking about all that? Maybe because Martin was in Greece. She walked into the bedroom. "Thalia."

"Do you think about her sometimes?"

"I think about her every time I open the newspaper and read about Greeks picking through the garbage for food. Or chopping down all the trees in their neighbourhoods to heat their apartments. I remember how much she hated the idea of Greece joining Europe. The country was still trying to get into the union, but Thalia thought it would be better to wait another century, to see how the Eurozone would pan out. It's weird, how right she was. She used to say that only the shitty history repeats itself. She'd go through the list: the Romans, the Venetians, the Ottoman Empire, the English, the Germans, the Americans, all the foreign powers that had occupied or manipulated Greece. 'And now Europe will fuck us, too.' That was her position on joining the EU."

"You never told me that she was some great political oracle."

"Oh, a lot of the Greeks had the same idea. The old shepherds in the countryside, they all felt the same way. They disliked big foreign powers and they loved to talk about it. But Greeks love to talk about everything. Loudly. When we'd go out for dinner, I'd hear all these people yelling at each other and I'd think, okay, tonight someone will throw a punch. But Thalia always told me not to worry, they were just arguing about politics, or someone's sheep getting into someone's field. Or who should have won the soccer game."

"Maybe we should go there. For a holiday."

"To Greece?" Eliza lifted her head off the pillow.

"Sure. It's time we went on a family holiday abroad. There's a mathematics conference in Athens in June. Not this summer, next. That would give us time to save."

"June weddings."

"Kiki could survive without you for two or three weeks."

"Two, tops."

"Come on, three. We haven't taken a real holiday in years. We both need a break. And the boys are old enough now. It doesn't have to be a Cuban all-inclusive anymore."

And it couldn't be his parents' cottage now they had sold it. She felt a rush of impatience. "You know, we would be able to take more holidays if your brother helped foot your parents' bills. They lost *their* retirement money, but that doesn't mean we can afford to lose ours."

He didn't respond. This argument between them was already ancient history.

"How can she spend two thousand dollars every month on non-essential items? Bed, Bath and Beyond? The Linen Closet? Does she really need new bath towels and sheets? I saw the most recent Visa bill."

"It wasn't two thousand."

"Eighteen hundred. Same difference."

"I will talk to them."

"No. Talk to *her*. And to Martin. You always talk to your dad, but he isn't the one who's spending the money."

Andrew sighed heavily and reached over to his bedside table to pick up his book.

She instantly regretted being so aggressive; he'd made a lovely suggestion and she had responded bitchily. She was doing that more often than usual. Snapping. Being rude to him. Allowing small arguments to become bad blood between them, when before, pre-Shar, they would have been moments of passing discord. She was ashamed of trying to make Andrew into some kind of enemy when he remained her dearest, most reliable friend. This little spat was her fault: she had changed the subject because talking about Thalia felt too dangerous.

But he'd recognized the feint in the conversation, because he looked up from his book and asked, "Was she beautiful?"

"Why are you so curious about this now?"

"I don't know," he said, honestly. "It's in the air, I guess."

He *does* know, she thought. Somehow, he knows. Jake got his telepathic tendencies from his father, not from her. Eliza tried to be light. "Of course she was beautiful. Auburn hair. Green eyes. Not what you have in mind, really, when you think *Greek*."

"Green eyes," he said, admiringly. "What kind of auburn?"

Eliza laughed. "I can dig out a photo if you want. Actually, you've seen the album. I've shown you pictures of that summer."

"Really? I don't remember. What colour is auburn?"

"Light brown. And reddish." She tried to remember herself. Did she really know, anymore, what Thalia had looked like? What she remembered, more than her hair, was her skin, sun-dark and smooth, almost hairless. "And coppery blonde, from the sun and the sea. Long hair, but she usually wore it in a ponytail. She was taller than me. And bigger. Broad-shouldered. The first time I saw her I thought she was a man."

"What was she doing?"

"Riding a white horse on a road above the sea."

"Get out of here!"

"Honey, I've told you this whole story, I'm sure of it."

"Riding a white horse? I don't think you told me that. How could I have forgotten?"

"The sun was behind her. I couldn't see her face. I just saw this big, handsome man riding toward me. Like something out of a cowboy movie. You don't see many women riding horses on Lesvos."

"And what, she just scooped you up and took you to her hideout in the hills and ravished you?"

Eliza laughed. "Is that how your fantasy goes? I didn't even talk to her, that first time. Though I fell in love with her right there." She cocked her head to the side, reconsidering. "Not love. Lust."

"Thinking she was a man."

"Just—presuming she was. She looked like a man. Later I saw her again, with the same horse, but she was on the roadside near the beach, where tourists used to walk. She had two other horses, too, a little bay and an island horse, dappled grey. And a couple of donkeys. She used to take people on rides in the countryside. She was saddling the horses that second time. And I thought, Ah, it's him. Closer up, I saw that 'he' was a woman. I was flummoxed. And . . . well, thrilled. I had to meet her." Eliza sighed nostalgically. "I wasn't the only one. She slept with a lot of straight women. She kind of liked that, the seduction of the dumb heterosexual. She said as long as they would go down on her by the third date, she'd give them the full treatment."

"The full treatment?"

"Lots of fucking and free horseback riding."

Andrew laughed. "You said you worked so hard in the restaurant that summer, learning how to cook! Sure. Now I know why you stayed there so long!" Eliza swatted him. He laughed more. "How were her breasts?"

"You *have* been watching porn!"

"Mmm. It's been too long since we've . . . you know. Like six weeks?" He put down his book again.

"Darling! You've been counting." She was flattered and disturbed; he usually had no idea when they'd last had sex. "Maybe we should remedy that situation."

Andrew pulled the blankets away from his body as he turned toward her. His voice fell to a whisper. "Tell me a story about Thalia. What did she used to do to you?"

Eliza crawled on top of him. "Oh, my!" she said; under his boxers, he had a fully committed hard-on. She began to whisper to him about the beautiful Greek woman in her little stone house in the hills. Inevitably, though, Thalia morphed into Shar, in her big bed in the apartment off Queen Street.

"At first she was sitting back on her knees, massaging her breasts. A little smaller than mine. She used to wrap them for riding, that's partly why she looked like a guy."

Eliza pulled off his shorts; his cock sprang to attention. She slid her hand up and down. Andrew murmured dreamily, "An Amazon."

Eliza's gut lurched. "Well, once she unwrapped herself, she had lovely breasts. Two small handfuls." Still on top of him, holding herself up on her knees, she slowly pulled off her T-shirt. "One day, she sat at the end of my bed, massaging them, making her nipples hard." Eliza took her nipples in her fingers, and moved back to the tops of Andrew's thighs, so she could touch him easily. She licked the palm of her hand and stroked him. "She had a gorgeous muscular body. Beautiful skin. She took her breast in her hand and bent over me and started to rub her nipple on my clit. It was one of the most erotic things I've ever experienced in my life. I'd never put those two body parts together. She switched sides, sliding back and forth until her whole chest was wet from my pussy. She rubbed me like this." Eliza took her right breast in her hand, leaned over Andrew, and rubbed her nipple over and around the head of his cock. She rose up on her knees as she slowly squeezed out the silky, clear fluid, nature's thoughtful lubricant; it came in two glistening dewdrops, one after the other. She licked it up, swirled her tongue around the head. They both watched his penis in her hand, shining from her licks. She got on top of him, squatted, rubbed him against her clitoris. "She reached up to my breasts and started massaging them, squeezing the nipples while still pushing her breast against my cunt." Andrew took the cue and reached up to massage Eliza's breasts; she stopped talking.

"Keep talking," he said. A sharp groan escaped him because Eliza suddenly sat on his cock, swallowed him down, then rose up again and returned to rubbing the head with her clitoris. They watched his penis slide into her. He put his thumb against her clitoris; she moved against it, then repositioned his hand to get the spot just right, and kept going. "Keep talking," he said, until she couldn't.

A while later, he whispered, "I want you to come." As much as
he could feel the orgasm increasing the strength of her thrusts, he
saw it rising in her face, almost like pain; he loved how her face
changed. Seeing that alteration released the knot of his own lust.
He had to hold back, which was difficult when she was on top and
so horny. He felt his cock get harder and gripped his stomach
muscles, trying to resist the intensity of the pleasure, its inevitable
end. If he waited, her orgasm pulled him into his own. That was
the wonderful Moebius strip of their best sex, of any good sex, he
supposed, like Eliza feeling in her own breasts what Thalia felt;
his body spiralled into her body, turned back into his own body,
spiralled into hers, leapt through him extravagantly, literally, ecstat-
ically out of him. They turned and turned in the air, on the bed,
the rest of the room gone, the world disappeared. She was still
coming when he came with a yell, so unexpected and unlike him
that the noise startled them both. Aftershocks surged through
their bodies, that shuddering, aching pleasure. The curtains beyond
the bed reappeared; the walls re-formed around them.

Then Eliza started to cry.

33

Not Henry

STILL ON TOP OF HIM, SHE THRUST HER FACE INTO THE pillow so she could make some noise. Her crying pushed his penis out of her body. He quelled the instinctive desire to leap up and go wash himself off. It should be, he knew, a universal rule for men to never leave a woman who is having a post-coital cry. She was not typically an after-sex weeper, yet she was sobbing now, so hard that he felt not only confused but worried. He couldn't figure out where she had gone.

And then he did. She moved off him, curled over on her side, away from him, and continued crying. He lay beside her, the length of his hot body pressed against the cooler side of hers, his hand on her jutting hip. He couldn't help himself from admiring the dip of her waist, the muscles tightening and releasing in her back, over her rib cage, following the jagged loop of her breath. They were similar, he thought, distractedly, distracting himself from his own realization, distancing himself with the interesting idea of the similarity between orgasm and crying. First there must be tension, physical and emotional, then the contractions rise, culminate, release. The throat, the vaginal canal: they looked extraordinarily similar when viewed through a scope. Where had he seen the scans compared? A biology class? An article in a science magazine? He kept his hand on her back, agitated by this burst of grief, or whatever it was, but showing nothing. He wanted to be calm for her.

She cried and cried. He waited until she was done. She released her head from its hiding place in the pillow, but turned her face away from him, which confirmed his suspicion. "You still long for her, don't you?"

"Can you give me a Kleenex, please?"

He whisked one out of the box on the bedside table and handed it to her. She blew her nose, noisily. She rolled over on her back, eyes shut. He knew his dogged patience was a gift here. Waiting was part of mathematics, attending the problem silently, approaching the work repeatedly, from different angles. A mathematician had to be interested in the problem. He had to *love* the problem. "Is that it? You're still thinking of Thalia. Right?"

"I'm remembering . . . what happened after."

"So what happened?"

"When the horse threw me. The way we were attacked by those stupid village guys."

"What? You told me that some kids on motorcycles scared the horses."

"I never told you the whole story. They followed us on their motorcycles. Three of them. In a little valley close to an old monastery. Thalia and I were going there for a picnic. That seemed to make them angry. They wouldn't pass us, so we turned up a little donkey track, off the main road. They followed us into a field. They were yelling at Thalia, taunting her. They started driving in a circle around us, getting closer and closer, laughing. I couldn't understand everything they said, but it was nasty. It was . . . We backed ourselves up against a fence, trying to slow the horses down, and to see the road, if anyone was coming. But the whole place was deserted. When my horse started rearing up, they yelled harder. They loved it."

"And then?"

"I went flying. Landed on the stone fence, started screaming. Lucky I fell on my shoulder, not my head. Or my back. I was screaming because it was excruciating but also because I was scared to death." She covered her hands with her face, rubbed her wet eyes. "I was afraid of what they would do to her. To us."

"But they left."

"Thalia told them she was going to report them to the police and they would be charged with assaulting a tourist. They roared off, laughing."

"And you rode back to the village."

"There was no other way to get there."

"Then you left the island."

"Soon after, yes. I left the island. And I left Thalia."

"Are you . . . regretting that? All these years later?" Both of them could hear the genuine puzzlement in his voice, and something else, too: hurt or fear.

"I—no. No. But she was so wrecked. She loved me. But I couldn't do it."

"I've never heard you talk about it like this. Has the whole thing with Sophie reminded you? You were *so* upset about Janet's reaction." She was silent. Andrew felt the insistent pressure of unspoken words in the air. "Is there something else?"

Eliza stared up at the ceiling for another full inhalation. Exhalation. She said, "I'm very attracted to that woman from the pool."

"Oh. The tall one. Who shaved her legs that time."

"Yes."

To clarify how well he remembered, he added, "The one who bent over." He thought, *Do I want to know the details?* Aloud: "I don't want to know the details."

But he did. He shared with Eliza a meaningful attention to detail. It was a predilection that united them. They both examined and figured out the puzzle: Eliza with her business, Andrew with mathematics. It was a physical experience for him, as though he could feel the electric charges in his cerebral cortex, those microscopic synapses snapping together, making a map of sense. He followed the line of Eliza's crazed busy-ness into the boys' regressive behaviours—more bickering and crying, essentially—straight into his own gut, the discomfort he felt at the distance between them, as though, when they spoke to one another, it was muffled, underwater.

The path was made suddenly clear, not through the numbers he loved for their deceptive absolutism but through words, which defined humans as humans. And—he carried on resolutely with the formulation—enabled us to lie. Humans were the only species capable of lying, right? All her extra time *at work.*

I'm very attracted to that woman from the pool. It made perfect sense.

Farther north—at night the sound came clearly through the open window—a freight train went by, beating steadily over steel ties, rattling its low, industrial music down the warm streets. Both of them thought of Jake, who loved the toy trains and wooden tracks that Marcus hadn't been interested in.

"I wonder if obsession is genetic," Eliza said.

"Are you obsessed by her?"

She heard the anger in his voice.

"I was thinking of Jake's little trains. And that railway crossing that he loves us to drive through. You know, just off Dupont Street. I hope he doesn't grow up to be a trainspotter." She had not planned her confession. But somehow the sex, conjuring up Thalia, Janet finding out about Sophie: it was all right here. An invisible woman lived with her. With all of them. It was not Shar. Eliza was the invisible woman. That is what lying does, she realized. It erases you.

She turned toward him and put her hand on his side, which he allowed. She felt the span of ribs there, beneath his cooling skin; the guilt squeezed, viselike, on her throat.

Andrew said, "It makes sense, these past few months. That afternoon, when Kiki called me. I knew she was upset about something else, too. After she hung up, I stood there with the phone in my hand, wondering what was going on. Does she know?"

"No. I haven't told anyone. Maybe she suspects."

He glared at the ceiling.

"Andrew, I'm sorry. I—yes. We've . . ."

"You've slept with her. You should be able to say it. Just say it."

"Yeah, I've slept with her."

"How many times?"

It was past the point of keeping track. "Many times. I'm sorry."

Sorry. What a joke, he thought. He was conscious of wanting to feel furious at her, and *sorry* almost opened the gates. The dangerous flood was somewhere on the other side of that useless word. She had lied to him. Months of deception. Time stolen from him, from the boys. From her own work. "When did it start?"

"Mid-January. No, February."

"Four months of lying. Impressive." He swore quietly. "Do you want to separate?"

"No." It was too small, the sound. She raised her voice. "No. That has never even crossed my mind. I love you. But . . . But I . . . I was feeling desperate for more physical contact. The first time I met her, there was an immediate attraction. I woke up. I haven't felt this way for so long."

He clenched his jaw. Unclenched. He would not swear. He was not going to swear. "How can you be so fucking selfish? I can't believe this. Do you think you're still a single thirty-year-old fucking boys at the restaurant? Life is more than sex."

"This is not the same as *that*. And there's no need to bring up the past. I was single then and I had lovers. So what? Life does *involve* sex. But you're not that interested anymore."

"Fuck off!" He yanked the sheet over himself and sat up. "As if I never touch you! Was what we just did so awful? We've had this conversation a thousand times. We have two small kids. I have a back injury. What am I supposed to do?"

"Why don't you just admit it? Sex is not as important to you as it is to me."

"It's not as important as raising a family, having a life together, building something that lasts. It's not as important as love."

"So sex is *not* that important to you. Which means that for the last few years, I've mostly done without it."

Fucking slut, he thought. He wasn't entirely sure who he meant—his wife or the other woman? They were both fucking sluts! Which made him think, What can that fucking slut do for you that I can't do? He stared furiously at Eliza, thinking exactly those words. Fuck her. He didn't want to know what she could do that he could not. Besides, she was a woman. She didn't have a cock.

"We do have good sex. When we have it."

That turned the key; anger opened in him as he stared at her lying naked on top of the sheets. He leaned close to yell in her face, "How can we have good sex when you're off fucking someone else?" Then he reared back, straight up, and lowered his voice. "This is not even *about* sex. It's about you lying to me. For months. Listen to you telling me what *I've* done wrong. How I've failed. It's unbelievable. I've done *nothing* wrong."

"I'm not saying that you have."

"Think about what we just did together. Wasn't that good enough? I cannot believe that I'm in our *bed* discussing this."

The pause that followed was excruciating; she knew what he was thinking. *Have you ever been with her here?*

She whispered, "She's never been inside the house." She put a hand on his thigh.

"Don't. Do not touch me." He caught her eye. "I hope you don't think I should be thankful you kept it out of the house."

"No. I just wanted you to know."

For a long time, neither of them said a word. Then Andrew spoke again. "It's not the sex. It's not even that you lied to me. I don't want to think about how many times. Attraction is human. Lying is also human."

She heard him breathing. It was the first time she had noticed him breathing in a long time. How could she have stopped hearing that?

"It's . . . It's . . ." The breath hooked in his throat and became another sound. He began to cry, which shamed her. She had seen him cry only twice, each time she had pushed their babies into the world. When he saw them unfold, covered in that white waxy stuff, and watched the arms, with fisted hands, shoot out like sprouts from their curled bodies, when he heard their shocked cries at the light and the cold air, Andrew had wept, his face transformed.

He coughed. He cleared his throat, wilfully drying up. Part of her wanted to cry again, pathetically this time, angling for sympathy.

She waited for him to jump out of bed and leave her. He didn't. They maintained their positions, her lying naked, him sitting up, his long elegant feet sticking out from under the sheets. She closed her eyes again, saw dark purple lights on the insides of her eyelids. She was coming apart again, unforming. She didn't know what she was doing.

She had destroyed her marriage, just like that. By being truthful. Too late. Was it wrong to tell the truth? She opened her eyes; he looked different, too, partly because he was so angry. She scrutinized his face, thinking she might not ever be here this way again, naked in bed with her husband. Yet he was the only man she had ever loved fully, completely.

He swore under his breath.

"What did you say?"

He put up a hand, as though to silence her.

"No, please, go ahead. Let's get it out in the open."

He met and coldly held her eye. "I said, 'You fucking slut.'"

The curse floated lightly in the air between them. Which was peculiar, for two words with such hard consonants. "I have to agree with you. I think I've been brave, mostly. In my life, I mean. And honest. But with this, I didn't know what to do. I didn't want to break up our marriage over, as you say, just sex." She was still being untruthful, in her heart. But "just sex" was the simplest, most acceptable thing to call her passion for Shar.

"What are you going to do?"

"Shouldn't I be asking you that question?"

Andrew looked away. With the side of her head pressed against the pillow, what she heard most insistently was the surge of her blood, its swooshing pulse inside her head. She closed her eyes again; the noise became more intense.

"Eliza. Open your eyes. What do you want to do?"

She opened her eyes. "I want her to come to dinner."

As though stung by a wasp, Andrew leapt out of bed, yelling, "Is that supposed to be funny? Don't fucking joke about this."

She was completely still, staring up at him, pinned to the bed by her own audacity. And stupidity. It was possible, she realized, to take a hammer to what you most loved in the world and bring the hammer down and shatter it. What had she been thinking? Andrew did not move to cover his nakedness; his soft cock hung there, not so far from her face. He said something else now, but his words didn't penetrate as much as the sight of his penis did. She saw how recklessly far she had gone; she did not know what he would do now. But after he got to the end of his rant, she said, "I'm not joking. I want you to meet her."

"You're out of your fucking mind. Do you hear me?"

"You're yelling. The boys are going to wake up."

"Why the fuck would I want to meet your *lover*?"

"From the beginning, she told me to tell you. That it was wrong to keep it a secret. That it didn't have to be a secret."

"Jesus Christ. What planet does *she* live on?"

He put one leg after the other in his boxers, carefully, not wanting to be further humiliated by losing his balance. He pulled a holey T-shirt over his head. "Good god, Eliza! You may think you're Anaïs fucking Nin, but I am *not* Henry Miller. I don't want to share you. That was not the agreement when we got married."

Eliza sat up and pulled the sheet over her belly and breasts, buying time. She tucked the bedsheet under her arms like a woman in a movie. "Did we ever talk explicitly about monogamy? How *boring* it can get?"

"Yes, we did. And we agreed that some boredom was the price to pay for stability. That we would be creative and enjoy ourselves no matter what and that we wouldn't have sex with other people. That was the agreement."

Eliza didn't remember that conversation. As she opened her mouth to say so, Andrew whipped around. "Don't you dare tell me that you don't remember we agreed to be monogamous. Maybe it wasn't explicitly stated in our vows, but obviously we were monogamous. And that's not even the point here. If you wanted to start having sex with someone else, you should have told me."

"So it's only me. As if you've never been attracted to anyone else."

He looked at her with disgust. "I've never been seriously attracted to anyone else. *Never* in a way to betray you. It has never once entered my mind."

"What about your brilliant student, the one you often talk about? What about Kajali?"

"One of my students and one of my colleagues. My oldest, most trusted, happily married colleague? Can't you do better than that? You won't find any dirt on me because I've never cheated on you . . ." His voice began to rise. "And I've never lied to you, I've never *abused your trust* in any way. Don't try to bring me down to your level."

"My level? My *level?*" It was impossible to answer her indignant, rhetorical question, because Andrew was right. She had fallen into someone else's arms, body, life. And she had lied. Andrew did not lie about important things. His body aligned rightly to his moral compass. His true north was reason modulated by common decency. She said, "It's hard to be married to someone who is basically perfect."

He turned away and opened the slats on the blinds. On one side of their back garden was the well-lit laneway, on the other side, their neighbour's messy backyard. "Don't try to make *me* feel guilty."

"I'm not. I know I'm in the wrong. I haven't stopped feeling guilty for a second."

Still staring grimly out the window, he said, "I'm sure guilt was the farthest thing from your mind much of the time."

It was almost two in the morning. One of them would have to get up in four or five hours. He closed the blinds and sat down. "I'm not sleeping in the spare bed."

Eliza rolled away, pulling the sheet behind her. "I'll go."

"No."

She remained, wrapped up, on the edge of the bed.

He said, coldly, "You don't want to leave me?"

"Andrew, no, I don't. I never—"

"Don't say anything else." When she moved to touch him, he said, "No. I am really angry. And hurt. You've lied to me over and over again." He felt wrecked by it. "But I'm willing to see if I can still sleep in this bed with you."

She nodded. They said nothing else. They each went to the bathroom, separately, closing the door behind them. They came back to bed and lay down without touching, each of them altered, confused. They were also tired, spent by the emotions of this night. Side by side, they slept the deep sleep of exhaustion.

He woke before she did, into sweet forgetfulness. Then the wall rose up as though in a nightmare, but he was fully awake, remembering. Her lies threw him against that wall, and threw him, and threw him. Their life, as they had once known it, was over. The dislocation was physical; the pain retracted and re-entered him like a blade not once but repeatedly. After a few stabs, he was livid. He was furious with himself that he had let her sleep in the bed with him.

He was turned on his side, as usual, facing away from her. He could hear her breathing and hated the sound of it. Lying, fucking bitch.

It was past six. The light was pushing through the blinds. He would get up and dress and leave the house. He could not hear the boys stirring downstairs. She could get them ready on her own, take them to school alone. Let her see what life without him would be like. He listened for a few breaths more, getting ready to slide out of bed and go. He was done. The marriage was over. He was leaving.

But, instead, he carefully turned over to watch Eliza's sleeping face.

34

Endless

IT WAS A PERIOD OF IMMEASURABLE TIME, TIME WITHOUT end, yet apocalyptic, in the ancient Greek sense of the word— *apo*, from; *calypso*, to uncover. Their lives were laid bare. Eliza and Andrew experienced time as the most unfortunate European polar explorers experienced it: trudging through the heart of a frozen immensity, the compass lost or broken, the supplies gone. It was a place they did not understand. Would they perish? Or would they survive?

Eliza lay beside her tall, golden husband and wept, some of the tears catching in her ears but most of them sliding into her hair. Once, returning from Annie's, Marcus had given her an uncharacteristically gentle, long hug, touched her hair, pulled his hand away. "Why's your hair so wet, Mom? Have you been swimming?"

Because they had never suffered greatly as a couple, they were unprepared for this long, horrible travail. Andrew's bitterness and anger astonished them both. One Saturday afternoon while the boys were at simultaneous playdates—two different friends' houses at the same time constituted a minor miracle—after a conversation that turned into a loud argument that lasted for two hours, Andrew fell back, spent, and said, "This is worse than all the renovations we've lived through."

Which made them laugh. Then they stopped laughing.

Most often they talked in their bedroom, sometimes lying on their bed, or sitting in the rattan chairs by the window. The children had to be sleeping, or outside playing, or at Annie's. Andrew and Eliza lay on their backs, not holding hands, or holding hands tentatively, and talking, or not talking, though surely there was some other verb for the anxiety of pulling words out of silence, or holding down that silence like a rabid animal, frightened of it. They discussed their lives together, their children, Eliza's attachment to this shadow woman named Shar. Eliza used the word "attachment." Andrew said "love."

Eliza had just dumped the clean laundry out on the long storage bench at the foot of their bed. Andrew was sitting against the headboard, his legs stretched toward her. As she folded one of his undershirts, he said, "But if you're in love with her—"

"I told you, I have *never* used that word."

"Avoiding the word doesn't erase the feeling. I feel it when you talk about her."

When Eliza answered this only by trying to unknot a bunch of thong panties—underwear she would never have worn, pre-Shar—Andrew asked, "How can you love many people at one time? Love requires enormous amounts of energy."

"Love is elastic, isn't it?" The word came to her directly from the stretchy material in her hands. She quickly stuffed the tangled ball of panties into the bottom of the pile and pulled out a clump of boy T-shirts and jeans. "If we had five children, would we love each of them less?"

"Shar is not our child. She's outside our family."

"I know that." Two shirts, folded. Three. A pair of pants. "You say 'our family' a lot lately, have you noticed that?"

"I think you need reminding that you have one."

Eliza nodded, then changed her mind. "That's not fair. I still do everything I did before. More. I never stopped putting them to bed, getting their teeth brushed, doing their homework with them. I never stopped fulfilling all my motherly duties, and there are *many* of them!"

"I wasn't talking about the kids." The hurt was plain on his face. "I was talking about *me*. Aren't I part of this family?"

"Yes! And—I haven't stopped being present for you, either. I'm *here*."

"But not always. And you don't always want to be here. You want to be with her."

"Not only. I don't only want to be with her."

He stared at her, incredulous.

"You know, she'd be open to sleeping with both of us."

"Are you *out* of your fucking mind? The sex therapist who does *threesomes*? Don't these people have any oversight? Isn't there some sort of code of conduct from the sex therapists' association?"

"I'm not her client."

"Thank Christ!"

"Anyway, I've never brought that up before because it's too much. I've always told her that you weren't into—"

"You mean you've discussed this with *her*? Eliza!"

"No, I *haven't* discussed it with her. I said that we were conservative. But I'm telling you about it so that you can understand what she's like. Sexually she lives in a different universe. She's extremely . . . adventurous. And independent. And she knows that I don't want to leave you. That I love you."

"I don't understand how you can be so naïve. Don't you see that if you continue this relationship with her, whatever it is, it changes things between *us*? Between you and me? That it already has changed things? Your emotions for her might become stronger than . . . this." His hand swirled around, gesturing toward the whole house. "Bringing a third person into a marriage is dangerous.

That's why people choose monogamy, despite the boredom. Don't you see that?"

"It doesn't have to be that way. Who is truly monogamous?"

"Most people, I think. Most of the time. Some unhappily, maybe, but a little unhappiness is worth it. You think you can just decide to end your relationship with Shar. What if you *can't*? For all I know, during these past few weeks, you've still been sleeping with her."

"I have not. I told you I wouldn't see her and I haven't. We've spoken on the phone. A few times. And I told you about that, too."

"But I never asked what you said."

Eliza did not answer the implied question.

"So, what *did* you say? That you're working as hard as you can to get your husband onside? Or into bed with her? Jesus Christ."

"No. I've told her that you know the truth, finally. That we're talking about it. You and I. That I've been honest. Finally."

"But what if I decide, Fuck it, I can't share you? What if *I* want to end the marriage? Is that fair to Marcus and Jake? No. I don't want our kids to live through all that crap just because of *sex*. Ugh! Suddenly our ground as a whole family has shifted."

"I shifted it," she said guiltily.

"What's new? You *like* change. The reason I married you is because you were willing to change. You let go of Thalassa and started a new career from scratch. You upended your life and you liked doing it. But it's different now, because of the boys. My life, Marcus's life, Jake's life, they're so intertwined with yours. I'm trying to understand how to keep you and let you go at the same time." He shook his head. They stared at each other.

Andrew saw the way the familiar curve of her cheek looped around to her mouth, her chin. Eliza's face! He knew it would be easier to hate her if he didn't like her so much. Most of the time. But that was not what he chose to say. Instead, he emphasized his own magnanimity. "I am an idiot. But the fact of the matter is, I want you to be happy." He swung his long legs over the side of the bed. "We can try. I *am* trying. But no more secrets. And your relationship with her cannot interfere with our family life. I don't want to feel like I'm babysitting our kids while you're out with your lover. We'll either figure it out or . . . we'll separate."

"No, we won't. I'll end it with her."

He expelled a short, loud roar. "You don't *get* it! Separating isn't only your decision." He stood up, and walked around her. She was almost finished folding; the thongs were still there, the last of the pile. He glanced at them briefly as he picked up the boys' stacks of clothes. "It would break my heart if our marriage ends. It would be the biggest mistake of my life. And of yours. But I don't know how I'll feel about anything in a month's time. What hurts me is that you are willing to take that risk." He shook his head, at a loss for words. With the boys' clean clothes in his arms, he left their bedroom.

Eliza stared down at the ball of lace and elastic that she still had to untangle.

35

The Change Room

THE TALL GUY WITH THE GOATEE STARTED IT. *VAS-Y,*
Shar thought, smiling underwater as he began to match her, stroke
for stroke. *Go for it, buddy.* He was in the lane right next to hers
and worked hard to pull in front. He was a big splasher; she pulled
to the far side of her lane to avoid his turbulence.

She let him go but stayed right there at his feet. Goatee was one
of the tall fit guys. True: they could swim faster than her. In the
short run. She took in a deep gulp of air and pushed forward, so
he could feel her there and see her when he flip-turned in the deep
end of the pool.

They swam like that for three lengths, then four, her forward
stroke hand sometimes in line with his feet, sometimes reaching
up to his waist. He thought she was trying to catch up with him.
She wasn't. She was just tiring him out. The tall ones were fast
swimmers but they didn't have her endurance. She knew she would
pass him at the next flip-turn, and she did. *Au revoir!* She pushed
away from the pool wall and glanced under her arm before breach-
ing the surface. The tall guy had stopped in the deep end, osten-
sibly stretching his legs underwater, but Shar knew better. She had
beaten him at his own race.

It wasn't the first time.

She kept swimming fast lengths now, her shoulders and lungs

burning. It was strange to think of how afraid she'd been of water for a while. The year right after Marseilles had been the worst, back in Vancouver. More than water, she was terrified of boats. She couldn't approach a dock or marina without having a panic attack or a crying jag. So she had started to practise, often in the company of Emma, a lesbian friend from the queer support group on campus. She told Emma that as a child she'd been stuck in the hold of a sailboat during a bad storm; it had left her with a phobia she was determined to resolve. Every week they went down to the False Creek Marina, and slowly moved a little closer, until Shar could walk down the dock and step onto Emma's family boat. It took another six months before she could drink a cup of tea in the galley. More than a year later, Shar boarded a twenty-four-foot sailboat to accompany Benoît on a day trip up the Georgia Strait.

She finished her last length and, not even glancing at the guy with the goatee, pulled herself out of the water and walked into the change room.

When she came away from the showers, the fat goddess lady was putting on her makeup. Janet was still there, too, rubbing her long wet hair with a towel. Because Janet was friends with Eliza, Shar was always careful to keep conversation with her to a minimum. If Janet and Eliza were both in the change room, Shar might engage in some polite chit-chat, but that was all.

Coming up behind the goddess lady, Shar met her eyes in the mirror and recognized the complicity in her little smile. At least she hoped that's what it was. Shar smiled back, grabbed her towel and briskly rubbed herself down. The woman said, "Good swim? You're still breathing hard!"

"Yes. I was racing that tall guy."

"Did you beat him?" Her voice was full of innuendo.

"Not exactly. But I outlasted him."

"Honey, I am sure you did!" She brayed loudly. "You are *such* a good swimmer. Have you seen this woman swim, Janet?"

Janet pulled up her light cotton pants and murmured, "I have." She did not sound impressed.

The goddess lady went on. "Eliza told me that you used to swim competitively?"

Shar nodded. "When I was a kid. I quit when I was about fourteen." She was putting on her bra. "Didn't like the bossy coaches. Still love swimming though." She put one leg then the other into her jeans and yanked them up. The sooner she got out of the change room, the better.

In a sugary, knowing voice, the woman went on, "Where *is* Eliza these days? She hasn't come swimming *forever*."

Hoping Janet would respond, Shar pulled her T-shirt over her head. But Janet said nothing. Shar tucked in her shirt, fastened the button on her jeans and glanced up again. Both women appeared to be waiting for *her* to answer.

Shar blinked at them, all innocence. "Maybe she's not feeling well?"

Without missing a beat, the goddess lady said, "I bet she has spring fever, ha-ha-ha!"

Janet didn't laugh; Shar bent down to pull on her socks, her boots. When she stood back up, Janet was walking out of the change room. She did not say goodbye.

A few minutes later, Shar, too, walked out into the warm May air. *Spring fever. Why did the woman have to be so obvious?* She strode across the newly green park toward Dupont Street; she had a lecture at the Institute at ten and had to hurry. Eliza definitely did *not* have spring fever. She had the diametrical opposite, the chill of the chastised spouse.

Shar was glad that Eliza had told Andrew. *Of course* she was. But Eliza had done it in the worst possible way, without any forethought or planning. Shar shook her head and muttered aloud, "Right after sex, too. *Mon Dieu*. Civilians." Yet she realized that the only way Eliza could have told her husband the truth was exactly the way she had done it: accidentally.

"*Yes. Yes!*" Shar muttered. "I'm glad she told him." And she was. But she was also grumpy. She hadn't seen Eliza for six weeks. They had spoken several times on the phone; Eliza had emailed her a few times, explaining that she and Andrew were talking about their relationship, what the affair meant to their marriage, et cetera, et cetera, all the right and necessary conversations. Shar emailed back messages of support and affection. She knew that these heart-to-hearts would probably lead to the end: not of the marriage, but of her relationship with Eliza.

She stopped for a red light; the cars began rushing past and she stepped back from the curb. It wasn't so difficult to retreat to her usual position of non-attachment. She wasn't in love. She was not. But she loved having sex with her. They were an excellent fit. Eliza wanted sex to turn her inside out; turning a lover inside out was Shar's specialty. And Eliza could flip the energy around and take control.

The light turned green; she hurried across the street, thinking of something Benoît had said on the phone the night before. Shar had been trying to explain why she was so attracted to Eliza. Benoît asked how much the attraction arose from the fact that Eliza was *married* to a man.

"Why would that make her more attractive?"

"She is more forbidden to you."

"Come on, I'm used to the forbidden. A married woman hardly strikes me as a forbidden lover. I've been a queer sex-worker for most of my adult life, remember?"

"But you're anxious about becoming a therapist. You've been worried about it for years. Maybe Eliza is some kind of substitute for the clients you've already said goodbye to?"

"What an astute question. *You* should be the psychologist."

"I'm learning at the feet of a master," he said. "Er, mistress. It's just a thought. Do you still have your Toronto clients?"

"Just one. And he is very occasional. Every six weeks. Then one in Ottawa."

"You mean, besides me?"

"Okay, two in Ottawa as well. Sorry, I don't count you as a client anymore." She had already asked him this, but wanted to hear him say it again. "And you will refuse my resignation, isn't that so?"

"Indeed I will. Please do not resign from the company. We need French-English translators more than ever now." He was joking; though he paid her every month, she had never worked as a translator.

They were quiet for a moment, thinking about their long unorthodox relationship. Shar said, "It's strange, isn't it?"

"No. It's perfect."

"You've become sentimental."

"Of course. I'm a grandfather, it's natural. So . . . what will you do about Eliza?"

"Meet her husband. I hope, anyway. I suggested she invite me to dinner."

Benoît laughed. "Shar! You are too much."

"That's the most civilized way to manage an affair, isn't it? Meet the husband."

"*Aïe aïe aïe*! I'm glad you never told me that you wanted to meet my wife." Benoît was still married to his first and only wife.

"That's because you and I never had an affair."

"Ah, I see. That's the beauty of a professional relationship. Everything is so clear."

"Exactly," she agreed.

She arrived at the Klippert Institute for Sexual Therapy and Research and stood on the sidewalk, staring up at the four-storey brick building. Since the last year of her undergrad degree, she had known that she would come to study here. Now she was almost finished her one-year postgrad program. At the beginning of June, she would begin a full-time counselling practicum at a queer-focused sexual health clinic downtown. She had already visited the clinic, met the counsellors, the nurses, the consulting doctors. Because of her master's work—on sex workers and client intimacy—and her queer orientation, the Institute director had recommended her specifically for the summer practicum. The pay would be low, but if they offered her a full-time position and salary in the fall, she would accept it. And she would tell her last two clients that she was retiring.

Her stomach clutched at the thought. Don't be afraid, she said to herself. It's just a new life. She pulled open the glass door and walked inside.

36

The Good News

ELIZA SAT ON THE FLOOR BESIDE THE SOFA, PLUCKED the remote off Andrew's chest and killed the TV.

He rubbed his face with his hands and groaned. "Couldn't it be *brunch*?"

"No."

"Not enough time has passed."

"We've been talking about it for two months."

"Is that all? It feels like an eternity." He shook his head. "I don't know, Eliza. I think I'm too old for this." He addressed the ceiling first, incredulously. "What has my life become?" And then stared down his supine body at his wife: "She *wants* to meet me?"

"Of course. We've talked about it. Several times."

"Can we do it another weekend?"

"You know how my weekends are from now on. Even for the weddings that Kiki manages, I still have to be available in case of unforeseen disaster. Too many people are getting married."

"Fucking idiots."

"Andrew!"

"Brave souls, I meant. Just a slip of the tongue." He shook his head. "If Shar *really* cares about our relationship, why doesn't *she* babysit the boys while you and I go out for dinner?" They both laughed.

When the laughter petered out, he added, "I'm kidding."

"I know."

The boys sat in the back seat, uncharacteristically silent and well-behaved. Andrew glanced at them in the rear-view mirror. At least Jake was no longer sniffling; he'd cried when they left Eliza behind at the house. Marcus, whom he could see in the mirror, slumped on the back seat and stared out the window like a sad orphan.

Andrew didn't blame them for being out of sorts; though he and Eliza had never once argued in front of them about the affair, he knew the boys could feel the ground shifting beneath their small feet. Both of them had become clingy, especially Jake. He didn't want to let Eliza out of his sight. This trip away from her, on a Saturday morning, was especially unwelcome.

"Boys! Come on! Grandma and Grandpa are excited that you're coming to spend the night. They've got a new movie and everything."

Marcus said, "We've probably already seen it."

"No, it's still out in the theatre. Someone gave them a special copy. And . . ." He had raised his voice too high, so the manufactured excitement sounded fake even to him. "Grandma's made her fudge and ice-cream cake!"

Jake immediately rejoined, "But Mom's been working on her special cake *forever*! And you guys are going to eat it all without us!" Marcus merely shrugged, and turned his head to the window again.

Andrew deepened his voice to announce, "I solemnly promise to save my sons a piece of that cake. Okay? I bet your mom planned to do that anyway. She loves it when you guys eat her special treats."

Jake was not going to let it go. "Then why are you sending us away?"

"Jacob, it's just this afternoon and one night. I'm coming to get you again tomorrow."

Marcus caught his eye in the rear-view mirror. "But what if you *don't* come to get us?"

"Of course I'll come, why wouldn't I?"

"Maybe something will happen. Maybe you'll . . . die. Like Mom's dad. The grandpa we never met."

Andrew gripped the steering wheel more tightly, trying not to let any anger seep into his voice. This was *her* fault. She'd caused all this fear and anxiety. He took a deep breath. "That's *very* unlikely. Your other grandpa died in a car accident because the roads were really bad. Covered in ice. But look at this beautiful day! The sky is blue, summer is almost here. Plus, I'm an excellent driver."

Marcus said, "But what if you're so mad at Mom that you get divorced?"

Andrew burst out laughing, from the shock of the words or the unexpected relief of hearing them spoken. When had the boys heard him sounding angry? For the last two months? At the moment, he didn't feel angry at all, just knocked open, winded by his love for his children. "I've told you guys, and Mom has told you, that we've been going through a hard time. That doesn't mean we're going to get divorced. We still love each other and we love both of you. Don't be afraid of losing us when we get mad at each other."

Jake said, "But Mom's not mad. *You're* mad."

Andrew gave a thoughtful half nod. "The good news is, I'm not mad anymore." He smiled. "That's why we're having a little dinner together."

Jake asked, "So you're going to make up and be friends again?"

"We've already made up." He glanced into the mirror. "Did you hear that, Marcus?"

"Yeah. Does that mean we can come home with you after visiting Grandma and Grandpa?"

Before Andrew could answer, his phone began to ring on the seat beside him. He popped the microphone bud in his ear, swiped the screen with his fingertip and said, "Hello! What are you doing here?"

While smearing mustard paste onto the meat, Eliza realized that herb-encrusted rack of lamb was the wrong dish. How could she have forgotten? They'd eaten the same thing the night that Marcus had almost been hit by a car.

She inhaled the heady aroma of Dijon and rosemary, not sure whether to keep going or to wash her hands and think up another meal. Besides a brown-rice pilaf, the side dishes were dandelion greens and a beet salad with feta and roasted pine nuts. Some warmed olives and roasted cherry tomatoes with basil on the table as a starter. It was a simple, delicious menu, nothing fussy.

But the tidy criss-cross of bones beneath her hands seemed like a bad omen. What else could she make? Pasta? Eliza had never cooked for her lover before. Cod? Wild salmon? She didn't want to run out at four o'clock and battle the weekend hordes at the market. And she couldn't. She didn't have time now to go shopping, clean up the kitchen, take a shower and fulfill her promise to Andrew: that they would have a preparatory drink together, just the two of them. Husband and wife would sit in the living room before their guest arrived at seven. It will be civilized and enjoyable, she thought, as something eel-like twisted in her stomach, then began to slowly snake up her throat.

She thought of popping a Gravol for her nausea. But that might make her sleepy. Did a fine French red mix with Gravol? She'd researched the wine, read all the reviews and written down the name of it for Andrew; he would stop at the liquor store on his way home. Another reason why it was too late to switch to fish. She crushed more rosemary between her fingers, releasing its brisk, medicinal scent. "It will be fine," she said to the meat under her fingers, and sprinkled on the extra rosemary. Every bone seemed to point at her. She flipped the rack over and continued sprinkling. "You will be delicious," she intoned in a fortune teller's voice. "We'll be happy to eat you. Thank you for joining us." The lamb they'd eaten with Bruce and Corinne had come out of the freezer, but this one was fresh. She picked it up yesterday on her way home from work.

An hour later, just as she was beginning to get anxious about where he was, Andrew came in humming, loose-limbed, as though he'd spent the afternoon in the sun instead of in the car. Eliza said, "What? You brought me *flowers*?" He was carrying a bouquet of not-bad corner-store gerberas and a full tote bag from the liquor store.

"I would bring you flowers every day if you didn't work in a flower shop. So, the boys were grumpy on the way out there, but we had a good talk. And my parents have been preparing for days. My mom likes to keep up that Miss Manners thing around us, but Marcus and Jake have her number. She'd do anything for them. You should have seen the baking!" He put the flowers down on the island. "She's going to take them on a little horseback ride tomorrow at the crack of dawn. They barely waved goodbye to me." He turned away to put the bottles down and hang the tote in the broom closet. "And I got your fancy wine, wife."

"Thank you," she said, noticing that he had not once met her eye. "I *know* your parents love the boys, honey. We should go see them more often." She gestured to the rack of lamb, the greens, the beets, peeled and draining on the counter. "Everything's ready to go. The cake turned out beautifully." He slipped past her, fleet-footed. From that faint air of escape about him, she knew that something had to be up with his family. Maybe Corinne had asked for more money. "Andrew . . . why are you being weird? What's going on?"

He had already made it to the living room. "This is a surprise, I know. And I'm sorry. But it can't be helped."

Her voice was flat. "What?"

"At least we have plenty of food. And last time, I said that when he was in town again, he would come—"

"No!"

"—to dinner and see the boys and—"

"Martin is *not* invited to this dinner. No! He's not coming."

Andrew was at the end of the hallway, about to round the corner and disappear upstairs. Instead, he lifted his hands in that faux-helpless gesture: *What else could I do?* "He called me from Ottawa."

"I don't care where he called you from."

"Eliza, I promised you that the next time he was in Canada, I would make sure he came to see us and to see the boys."

"I can't believe this."

"And I can't tell him to go stay in a hotel. He only has a couple days. He'll come for dinner, then we'll go out to Mom and Dad's tomorrow. They'll be thrilled to see him."

She turned her head to the ceiling, as though beseeching a higher power, and saw a little grey moth instead. "Damn!" she muttered. "I thought I'd killed them all during the winter!" Andrew was coming back toward her now. She realized that getting angry would ruin everything. But how like Martin to show up when she least wanted to see him.

Andrew tore away the paper around the flowers. She'd already made and brought home an elegant table arrangement from Fleur. These ones could go on the little table in the entranceway.

"Where do you keep the vases again?"

"You could have asked me first. For form's sake. Obviously you want him to be here so we won't be able to discuss anything openly."

"Maybe I don't *want* to discuss anything openly." Projecting fake officialese, he said, "All right, Shar, you can fuck my wife on Monday mornings, Wednesday afternoons and Friday evenings, but her children need her the rest of the time."

"Darling, I'm going to take that as a joke. That's not how we would talk. About anything. The children are not—have never once been—neglected. So you'd *never* say anything like that." She smiled. "Fine. I can hardly wait to see your lovely brother. The vases are in the sideboard. The green ceramic one will work with those."

He wheeled around and went to the sideboard. After poking around inside, he said, "I don't see any green ceramic thing in here."

"In the back. Behind the glass ones. You'll have to take a few out to get to it."

He brought the green vase to the counter. "I told you that I wanted you to be happy, remember?" He let the generosity of the declaration stand. "Seeing Martin will make *me* happy, no matter who our dinner guest is."

"Did you put him up to it?"

"Eliza, please. He had a meeting in Ottawa and was supposed to go straight to New York, but he had a spur-of-the-moment desire to see us."

Eliza pursed her lips. Andrew's only serious fault was that he loved an obnoxious man. But if Andrew had not loved his brother, she never would have met him. Martin was not heinous. He did important work—for an egomaniac. And he was a good story-teller, at least at the beginning of a dinner party, when there was still a lot of space.

As Andrew began arranging the flowers, she said, "Dear, let me do it." She took the scissors, removed the flowers from the water and began trimming the waterlogged ends.

Andrew stood beside her, watching. "Oh, you're so good at that."

"Piss off."

"I love the way you handle those flowers. They certainly know who's boss." He stepped behind her, put his arms around her waist and bit her neck.

She shrieked. "Be careful. I have scissors in my hands. And I just sharpened them."

"She sharpens her own scissors. What a woman! Let's go to bed right now."

"I was hoping to do exactly that, after dinner . . ."

He lifted his hands to her breasts. "Don't tell me that you thought the three of us might leap into bed *tonight*? Eliza. Please."

She pushed his hands away. "I meant you and me."

"You did not."

"I did. See? *You* are the one having fantasies."

"No! I'm just trying to do the impossible and keep a step ahead of you. I can't believe what my life has become."

"It's not that bad, is it?" She snipped away. "Our lovely children are not in the house. *Anything* could have happened. But now Martin is coming to dinner. So nothing will happen. Except a lecture, or three, by the famous anthropologist."

Andrew leaned against the granite island beside her.

"I'm glad we didn't have a fight just now," she said.

"Me, too."

"Just try to keep Martin from taking over the whole evening, would you? And not a word to Martin about . . . this."

"What?"

"Shar is just a friend of mine."

"With so many benefits."

"Andrew."

"Don't worry. Sex is one thing I never discuss with him. Too private. And I'm the boring math brother, remember?" He laughed.

With a little too much delight, she thought, drying her hands.

37

What a Coincidence

ELIZA HEARD THE DOORBELL FROM THE THIRD FLOOR. She was standing in front of the mirror with one eye closed as she applied dark blue eyeliner. Martin's voice boomed into the house. She pictured the brothers giving each other a serious hug, more Russian than North American.

She blinked into the mirror, the made-up right eye markedly bigger than the left. Smiled. "Martin!" she said in a low voice, practising. "What a wonderful surprise!" She stuck her tongue out at her reflection. She did her other eye, then applied her lipstick and rubbed her pale pink lips together. Smiled and tried once more, with feeling. "You bastard. How did you manage to show up *tonight*? Why couldn't you have come next weekend?" There. Perfect sincerity.

Her husband's laughter carried up from the first floor. Or was that Martin? Their voices were like echoes. No, it was Andrew. Her mouth felt dry; she was so nervous. She exhaled a long slow breath. Shar and Andrew were going to meet tonight.

It didn't matter that Martin was here.

By the time Andrew poured them a glass of wine, Martin was in full grand-man mode, talking and gesticulating. Eliza was sitting across from him but to his left, to be out of the direct line of fire.

He was regaling them with details from his latest adventure. She listened more carefully than usual, because he'd been in Greece.

"But the day before, some anarchist—they actually have self-proclaimed *anarchists*—had thrown a bomb at one of the government buildings, and there was a huge protest downtown. I couldn't get it out of the cab driver, though: Was the protest related to the bomber, or was it against something the government had done? Total chaos, basically, like the economy. Because of the protests, the roads were jam-packed. I almost missed my plane." He laughed heartily. In the end, he did not miss his plane, and leaving behind a mess never seemed to bother Martin. He always described his experiences in the fucked-up world with jocular excitement.

Eliza, she scolded, do not be a bitch. Appreciate the fact that Martin the Great is being more restrained than usual.

He went on talking. "I guess that's what happens when you accept honorary degrees in disintegrating countries. But I'd never been to Athens before, weirdly enough, so I wanted to see it. You know, before the total collapse. And one of the conference organizers has a house on an island. Gorgeous place! Oh, I almost forgot!" He rose, went back to his luggage in the entrance hall. From the depths of the bag, he produced a rectangular tin can and returned to the room, proffering the gift to Eliza. "This is the most incredible olive oil I've ever tasted. For you. It reminded me of Thalassa. And you learned to cook in Greece, right?"

"You have a good memory, Martin," she said, accepting the gift. "Thank you. We'll have this on the dandelion greens tonight. And the salad." As she read the label on the tin, her heart started to beat double-time. Lesvos. Martin had been on Lesvos.

Without noticing the expression on Eliza's face, Andrew asked, "Do you really think Greece is disintegrating?"

Martin sat down. "It's pretty fucked up. They took all that money for joining the EU and used it to line their own pockets. That's what my Greek university friends talked about throughout the conference. There was so much thievery that nobody could keep track of it. The country is a mess. And now they're being besieged by Syrians, Afghans, Libyans, thousands of illegal migrants."

"Uh, *refugees*," Eliza said.

"Yes, they *are* refugees, but Europe hates the responsibility that term carries. And it's just going to get worse now that Syria is exploding."

Eliza held up the can of oil. "And for those who want to get to Europe, Lesvos will be among their first points of entry."

"Exactly. I couldn't believe how close it is to Turkey."

"That's the island you visited, right?"

"Yeah." His eyes brightened. "Hey! Didn't you live on Lesvos?"

"Mm. On the west side of the island."

"In Eresos?"

"Yes, in Eresos." Eliza nodded.

"The birthplace of the poetess Sappho! What a coincidence! That's where my colleague's family is from. He has the most gorgeous house there, in the countryside. An extraordinary view of the valley and the Aegean." He grinned at Andrew. "Man, you are lucky she ever came back to Canada. I think it's one of the most beautiful places in the world." He raised his glass. "To Lesvos!"

Eliza smiled, shakily, and drank the toast. Martin knew so much about a place that had shaped her life. She had *lived* there. Why had she never been back? She knew the answer immediately, and hated it: she had been afraid. A memory came: Thalia walking across the field, hauling a bucket of water for one of the horses. Eliza had just told her that she was returning to Canada. Thalia set the water down for the horse and kept walking.

Martin had hit his stride. "It's too bad about Greece as a whole. We should start vacationing there, to help the wrecked economy."

Andrew said, "We were just talking about going there next summer." He was giving Eliza an out, to talk about something lighter, but she didn't take it.

Instead, she asked, "Isn't the real failure the Eurozone? Greece didn't used to be a failed state. It was just small. And poor."

"Everyone I talked with there said that the country has always been corrupt. There just hasn't been enough political will to change the culture, despite all the financial opportunities. It's tragic. The modern Greek tragedy. Not everyone knows what to do with the responsibility of money."

Eliza shook her head, frustrated. She glanced at Andrew. He wanted her to change the subject, did he? All right. She would. "You know," she said, slowly, "Andrew and I have been talking about exactly that, only when it comes to families." Martin smiled at her blankly, eyebrows lifted. "Sorry to change tack so abruptly. But all this talk of economics had reminded me of . . ." Her voice trailed off. She could feel Andrew looking at her now but she ignored him. "It's not easy to talk about this on the phone." She and Martin never spoke on the phone for more than thirty seconds. "We're really worried about your parents." Andrew was staring so hard at the side of her face that she could feel the pressure of his eyes on her jaw.

"My parents?" Martin said, sitting up straighter, the smile dropping away from his face. He turned to Andrew. "What about our parents?"

Andrew turned to his wife and said, "Eliza. Let's not talk about this now." He pulled his hand down over his mouth and cheeks, rubbing the day-old growth there. "This is not the time."

"Yes, Andrew is right. Let's not talk about it now. But in the near future, we do need to discuss the financial disaster closer to home." She knew that if she didn't state the facts clearly, Andrew might never do so. "We just can't keep covering so many of their expenses. It's too much for us. As a *family*, we need to figure out what the plan of action will be if one of them gets ill. Those assisted-living homes are expensive."

Martin's voice rose in alarm. "What's going on?" He kept looking at his brother, who was staring at the olive oil tin in the middle of the low table. "Is one of them sick? Is Mom ill?"

Eliza's tone became softer. "They're both fine. For now. I just don't think much money is left, except for your father's pension."

She finally looked at Andrew, expecting him to growl at her. But his head was angled down. He ran a hand through his hair, scratched. Martin asked him again, "What the hell is Eliza talking about?"

Oh, she thought. The astonishment hit her hard, but slowly, like a drill going down. Martin did not know that his parents had lost their retirement savings. He did not know that she and Andrew were supporting them.

Andrew said, "They didn't want you to know. Especially Mom." He explained the situation to Martin carefully, without revealing to Eliza why it had been a secret from his brother all this time. Nor did he give away any clue about why that secret had been secret from her. While he spoke, he slowly drank her entire glass of wine. Martin shared the last of the bottle between the three glasses. "I'll get another bottle," she said.

Then the doorbell rang.

They all froze. Shar.

Andrew put his hand on Martin's arm. "We can talk about this tomorrow, on the drive to Uxbridge. Eliza, I'll get another bottle of wine. You answer the door." He jumped up and rushed off to the kitchen. She wondered if Martin might be angry, but he only looked baffled. And weary.

The front door was visible from the living room. They both stared through it to the hazy figure on the other side of the frosted glass. Eliza rose to open the door and Shar stepped into the house, her hands so laden with tulips and wine that the two women could not embrace. They kissed each other's cheeks instead, and talked at the same time, then laughed. "Should I take off my shoes?"

"No, no, come in. What a beautiful dress! Is it really that warm out?" Shar was wearing a vivid blue linen dress, sleeveless, which Eliza had never seen, and open-toed purple sandals with heels. She looked summery but formal, and taller than usual in the shoes. She had straightened her hair, which fell in two shining black folds around her face. Glittery pink lipstick.

It's amazing, Eliza thought, as a cascade of lust fell through her, how quickly the mind and body can change gears. She sought Shar's eyes but Shar was gazing into the living room. In fact, she was looking at Martin. Eliza could see that she recognized him. She must have read his books, or seen one of his documentaries.

She put the flowers and wine on the bench by the door. It was only a few steps across the carpet that marked the boundary between the living room and the entrance; Shar followed her in. Martin was watching her, too. Eliza hoped that he wouldn't flirt with her all night. She smiled. "Do you recognize him from his books?"

Shar looked shocked. "I—I—didn't know your husband was a writer."

"What? No! This isn't my husband, this is my brother-in-law, Martin! Didn't you get my text?"

"I've been out for the last couple of hours, I haven't even checked my phone."

"I texted you. This is *Martin* Taylor, Andrew's brother, our unexpected dinner guest from Geneva. Author of numerous books about linguistics and disappearing languages. Maybe you've seen his documentaries?"

Shar said, "Yes! You look so familiar." When she smiled at him, Eliza wanted to step between them. She introduced Shar, working hard to smooth down unexpected spikes of jealousy. Shar asked Martin, "Have you literally just arrived?"

"I was in Ottawa yesterday for a meeting. But I barely slept last night, so I'm feeling pretty wiped out." He gestured to the table. "That hasn't stopped us from downing a bottle of wine."

Eliza said, "Shar, please have a seat. Andrew just went to get more wine. I'll go see what's keeping him."

38

Tell Me

SHAR SAT DOWN ACROSS FROM MARTIN IN AN UPRIGHT wingback chair and crossed her legs as unsexily as possible. "Hello," she said again, with a warm smile. No threat, no threat; she'd let him decide what to do. There was no need to say anything, if he didn't want to. She'd had these brushes with fate before. Once, she'd found herself in a Gap store, standing one rack away from a former client and his wife; Shar saw him before he saw her. She did an about-face, straight out of the shop, out of the mall. Another time, walking in downtown Ottawa, she'd passed a politician who'd just become a cabinet minister—she had seen his craggy face in the media for a week—and their eyes had locked for two or three seconds, long enough for Shar to see that he feared her. That sobering moment had made her glad that she was in the master's program. She didn't want to depend on the vicissitudes of sex work for much longer. The politician had been set to become a regular—they'd had a few languid, post-coital talks of a chateau hideaway in the Gatineaus—but she never heard from him again.

Martin said quietly, "It's weird to meet you here. Now." His jaw muscles rippled.

Her response betrayed no nervousness. "I have to say the same of you."

They heard the voices of Andrew and Eliza in the kitchen, suddenly raised; it was impossible for her to tell if they were arguing or attending to some minor kitchen mishap. Martin downed his last mouthful of wine. He leaned forward to put his glass on the table and whispered, "What . . . what are you *doing* here?"

Shar smiled. "Like you, I've been invited to dinner."

He didn't smile back. "I mean, are you . . . do you live here now?"

"I left Ottawa last year. Career change. I'm now a Master of Psychology. After I finish my specialization at an institute here, I'll start practising as a therapist."

"Oh," he said, abruptly sitting back. She could see how badly he wanted to fold his arms. "I . . . Well! That's great. Good for you." He folded his arms.

Her voice was a quick, low murmur: "It was, what? Three years ago?"

"Uh. Hmm. Maybe." He looked away. "I think it was longer." He turned to stare out the window.

But she knew it was three years, because she'd just begun her master's at the University of Ottawa. It was, in fact, in early October. Martin had been a one-time client. After a delicious dinner, they'd gone to her work condo for the big dessert. She'd been genuinely attracted to him; it was going to be an easy date. But after ten minutes of excellent foreplay, he still didn't have an erection. When she asked him about it, he got angry, stood up, said he was leaving. He had already paid her, according to her rules. And though she had nothing to apologize for, she apologized, and soothed; she didn't mind. She was concerned about him, in that complexly braided professional-personal way she cultivated with most of her clients. "It's all right. We had so much fun at dinner," she said. "Let's just have a drink and keep chatting." After he let go of his embarrassed bluster, he began to talk. Because she kept asking him the right questions, he couldn't *stop* talking.

He told her what few people knew about him: when he was a boy, he had fallen in love with one of his teachers. That's what he called it. Love. Shar was surprised to discover that he'd only been eleven when the sexual play began. He was thirteen when he and Marlene, his former Grade 6 teacher, started to have intercourse. When he was fifteen, in high school, his mother found out and went to the school board and the police. Rather than incriminate Marlene, Martin accused his mother of concocting crazy sex stories. The cost of protecting his "beloved" was not only his relationship with her—she moved away and ceased all communication—but also his relationship with his mother. He also disconnected as much as possible from his father. He left for university as soon as he could, then moved farther and farther out into the world. "I'm a world-famous linguist, speaker of many languages, but I can't talk to my mother for more than two minutes without feeling . . . Goddamn it! Everything comes up again. It's like some part of me is still a teenager. And absolutely furious. And now *this* has started to happen. My body—my dick!—is failing me."

"I'm not so sure your body is failing you. It seems to be talking to you in a way that has your full attention."

"But what the hell is it saying?"

"You can figure that out. A good therapist could help. That's what I'll do eventually, by the way. You know how my website says I'm a student? I'm doing a graduate degree in psychology."

"Oh, no! Psychologists are all nutcases."

Shar nodded. "Thank you! I love it when people say that."

"Why?"

"Because I'm going to break the mould and save this whole insane science of the soul. Hurrah for me!" She winked at him. "I'm one of the sanest people I know. Come on, Martin. We're in the twenty-first century. You've just had a session of talk therapy." He wrinkled his nose. She smiled. "After talking, don't you feel lighter?"

He tilted his head back and forth, taking stock. "I suppose so. Maybe. Why is that?"

"Because there is no pain as heavy as secret pain. The body gets tired of carrying it alone."

"How can such a young woman be so wise." It wasn't a question.

"I hear the sarcasm in your voice, but it doesn't bother me."

"Why not?"

"Duh! Because I'm wise, of course. You're the one who has to deal with your sarcasm, not me."

They laughed, and finished their scotches. He said he was ready to go, and stood up. "That was one expensive therapy session," he said sheepishly.

"Look on the bright side. Good therapy is cheaper than a high-class call girl. This was an unlikely beginning. I hope you find some-one to talk to. A professional. Who's not wearing a garter belt."

Saying goodbye, they didn't touch each other; they didn't even shake hands. Yet she knew from the expression on his face that he felt close to her. He felt shaken and grateful and—she was certain of it—lighter than he had in years.

Here, in Eliza and Andrew's living room, his silence worried her. But with each passing moment, his face and his body softened; he, too, was remembering their evening together. She hoped that he was healthy enough not to feel angry about the vulnerability he had shown then. He met her eye, then glanced anxiously toward the wide corridor that led to the kitchen. It was safe, she thought. He was safe. He wasn't going to out her and expose himself in the process.

From her chair, Shar couldn't see or hear if anyone was coming. Another upsurge in Andrew and Eliza's voices was followed by the sound of running water. She quietly asked, "Have you seen anyone since then? Someone qualified?"

The expression of distaste on Martin's face was answer enough. "You know, that *was* quite a while ago. I was really stressed out with work and—" He stopped abruptly and cleared his throat, as though readying himself for a big statement. Instead, he whispered, "Can you do me a big favour, so that we can get through this evening with a minimum of discomfort?"

Shar inclined her head in what she thought of as the courtesan's nod. "Confidentiality is a necessary thing. I don't know you. That goes without saying."

A moment later, they heard Andrew's heavy tread in the hallway, then his voice, buoyant with good humour. "It also goes without saying that my absence as host has been inexcusable!" Into the room he came with two long strides, and stopped, a tall, slightly flushed man, light eyes flashing. He was wearing jeans and an old button-down shirt of faded turquoise, the sleeves rolled up. (So much depends upon a man's forearms, Shar thought.) Andrew brandished another bottle of wine. "But *please* forgive me. Eliza needed me to sear the meat. Rack of lamb. She's just putting it in the oven now."

Shar had to laugh then, for the sheer relief of it. "That sounds both delicious and dangerous," she said, releasing her wolf-grin. "I love lamb."

Andrew swung his whole body in her direction and came forward with his right hand out. "Shar," he said. "I've heard so much about you." She almost burst out laughing again, from nervous tension and because the words seemed flirtatious—was he being flirtatious? She rose gracefully. They shook hands, smiling at each other as though they had just cut a deal, and his hot grip made her think they had. *Doucement*, she thought. Easy, girl. She had not expected Andrew to be so attractive. Eliza had told her that he was. But in Shar's experience, women usually exaggerated their husbands' qualities, while men tended to underrate their wives'.

Certainly, he was handsome. But regular good looks were nothing when a man beamed into a room like a lighthouse.

As Shar sat again, Andrew said, "Let me open this bottle. Have you been standing in for me, Martin, entertaining our newest guest?" Martin's chuckle could have been a cough, but their host didn't seem to notice. He sat down beside his brother and set to peeling the metallic seal off the bottle. "I'll have you know that my wife has been very wine snobbish for this meal. She sent me out today with a very specific list, all Nuits-Saint-Georges this and Burrowing Owl that. If I don't decant this properly, I'll be fired." He glanced back toward the kitchen. "Don't remind Eliza that I didn't rinse out this decanter. She told me to, but hopefully she's forgotten that by now." He poured the wine into the circular glass vessel, then caught Shar's eye. "Would you prefer something else? I could mix you a drink if you'd like."

"Oh, no, thank you, the wine is fine. I mean, excellent." She flourished her hand in the air above her head like a flamenco dancer. "Superlative. Brilliant!"

The men grinned at her. Shar was surprised by how similar the brothers looked and how profoundly unlike they were. Andrew was quick on his feet, despite his height, and he carried himself with ease. A naturally graceful man, at home in his flesh. A perfect fit inside one's own skin was a quality as rare in men as it was in women. Martin was not heavier than his brother, but he seemed to be.

Andrew smiled. "Eliza told me that when you first came in, you thought that my brother was me. Ha! Impossible! Though flattering. I'm the dull math professor and Martin here is the world-travelling linguistic genius. Just so you have us straight." He raised his glass. "To brothers dropping in unexpectedly." And turned to Shar. "And to" —a heartbeat here—"swimming partners."

They drank the toast. Holding the large globe of glass made Shar aware of her sweating palms. She took a deep breath and settled more comfortably into her chair. She used the wine to calm herself down, fanning it open with her tongue, not swallowing it right away but letting it pool, plummy and rich, in the bottom of her mouth. She sat back in the chair. "This is delicious," she said.

Martin said, "Swimming partners?"

Shar said, "Eliza and I met a few months ago at the local pool. We've become good friends."

Andrew added, "We're all so busy that this is the first time we've been able to organize our schedules for a proper dinner." Andrew and Shar held each other's gaze. Then they simultaneously turned to Martin, not wanting to leave him out, or reveal anything. It was all right, she thought; Martin is more worried about his own secrets than he is interested in trying to figure out anyone else's.

It was not work, no. But she was an expert at charming men; with some mild exertion, she could enchant them. "Andrew, this wine *is* excellent," she said, lightly swishing it around in her mouth. As she swallowed, she looked at one brother, then rapidly took a second small sip and looked at the other. "What is it, what *are* we drinking?" What she meant was, Talk to me. Tell me. I will listen to whatever you say.

39

Flowers Instead

AT THE STOVE IN A WHITE APRON, ELIZA CALLED OUT, "My past and present professions come together in this dish!" With a spatula, she lifted the stuffed yellow zucchini blossoms one by one, "Let them eat flowers! Ha!" and slid them into the oil-snapping skillet. Andrew was adding water tumblers and a carafe of water to the table. Shar asked, "Can I help?"

"Why don't you pour the last of this bottle?"

Then they took their refilled glasses to the island and watched the chef poke and turn the blossoms, now an even brighter yellow from the oil. Martin said, "I was just eating those in Greece."

"Lucky you. I made hundreds of these at Aphrodite's that summer. I think I remember the Greek. *Kolo . . . kitho . . . loulouda*!" Eliza said. "Yes," she nodded to Martin, "Greeks love these. Flowers stuffed with feta and dill."

Shar said, "The Italians eat them, too. But isn't it early for zucchini blossoms?"

"By three weeks. These are from an organic greenhouse in Pickering."

Andrew, passing by with cloth napkins in hand, said with mock formality, "Eliza maintains many contacts from her former profession."

"Even the lamb is from my old supplier."

He added, "The same guys who did the kid goat for our wedding."

"A goat was at your wedding!" Shar grinned.

Eliza clarified. "Yes, a goat attended the ceremony, and for his pains, we ate him. *Very* tender. Crispy skin. Goat is less fatty than lamb. But rack of lamb is special."

Shar drank more. Ah, wine in her mouth, the smell of food, and this beautiful woman, all in the same room. The poet was right; it was heaven. And her husband the lighthouse, shining. Even her nervousness about Martin had calmed: he was friendly enough, though not too involved. He'd moved away from the stove and was standing near the island, beside a small dark-green forest of wine bottles. He tried to read the labels, but had to take his glasses out of his breast pocket. She remembered, from that night in Ottawa, at the restaurant, he had been man-of-the-world, wanting her to know that he was cosmopolitan, lived in Geneva, in New York. She was used to the way men liked to display their power in public; he had done that mostly with his brain, she recalled now. He glanced up, caught her looking, smiled.

She smiled back, aware of the extra glitter and juice of her youth. In September she would be thirty-five: a strong number. In her twenties, she would have enjoyed having sex with every person in the room, together. They were drinking wine, after all. That was Greek, too, Dionysus, the god of the vine, getting together with his ecstatic friends. The occasional orgy was a wonderful thing, as long as the sex was safe and each participant was in a good, well-lubed mood. These days, though, she had no desire to participate in such shenanigans, though the thought still made her giddy. It was something she had often discussed with her clients, especially the ones who had experienced a lot of dysfunction or pain, either physical or mental: sex as play for adults; delightful, zany, surprising. Sex as pure, unadulterated *joy*. It saddened her to know that so many people in the world, men and women, had so little of it.

Eliza lifted her eyes away from her sizzling flowers and grinned over her shoulder at Shar, who stuck out her tongue and shimmied it back and forth the way she did when Eliza was close to coming. They both felt a shared tentacle of delight shoot down and flick up *snap!* right *there*. Eliza, embarrassed, canted her head back down to her zucchini flowers. Shar started giggling. If only she could jump over the island and tear off the chef's apron, and the little mauve dress.

Alas. She would eat flowers instead. She put her hand under her hair and rubbed the back of her neck, then stretched her arms above her head. From their opposite sides of the room, the brothers were staring at her. "It smells *goo-oood*, doesn't it?" she asked. "Makes me so *hungry!*" She had to quell an impudent howl of laughter. Yes, quell, quell. She did not jump over the island to grab Eliza; she merely grasped the edge of the granite countertop. Cool hewn stone would cool her down. (A vision came to her: the granite swept clean, an altar, with the chef lying naked and moaning on top of it.)

Eliza said, "It's getting hot in here," and turned on the fan.

Shar asked, "Who wants a glass of water?" She went to the dining table and began to pour. She mustn't be too obvious; Martin should not know about her and Eliza. Just as Eliza and Andrew must not know about him. She inhaled: hot olive oil, the freshness of dill, meat in the oven. No problem. She was good at keeping secrets. People liked to give them to her. She had not misplaced a single one.

"Andrew, darling, *please* put on some music!" Eliza cried above the whir of the fan, and began fishing the next round of flowers out of the oil. She slid each tooth-picked blossom onto paper towel. Shar watched Eliza's hands, deftly moving, the rare ring she wore sometimes on her tough but long fingers, its small single diamond glinting under the stove light. Her wedding ring.

Eliza turned the already-hot water to boil again. "For the greens," she said, bending to open the oven door and check the lamb. "Two minutes more. Then we'll let it rest. But we can start to eat before that, if we're hungry." She turned to the men, Martin among the bottles, Andrew at the CDs. "Are we hungry?"

Andrew grinned. "Famished."

Eliza pulled the tray of roasted tomatoes out of the oven and set it next to the olives. "Here we go. Some *mezedes*. To start."

Martin said, "Should I open another bottle of wine?"

Shar licked her lips. "Is that wise?"

Martin met her eye. "You tell us. Is it?"

Shar's eyes glittered. "*In vino, veritas.*"

"But the truth is not the same as wisdom."

Andrew interrupted. "Open the damn bottle, Martin. Nobody's driving anywhere."

Eliza announced, "Done! The last of the zucchini flowers. We can add these to the olives and tomatoes." The cork popped out of another bottle of wine. Martin came forward and began refilling glasses.

Shar raised her hands and announced, "Ah, I feel a quatrain coming on . . . The great Persian poet Omar Khayyam. Wait! Eliza, can you turn that thing off? Omar hates competing with kitchen fans."

Eliza flicked the switch. No one realized how loud the whir had been until the relief of silence filled the room. Shar looked from face to face, blinking, took a deep breath, and began to recite the rhyming lines in Farsi. It was unexpectedly mesmerizing to hear another woman enter the room through Shar's mouth. Then she repeated the lines in English:

They say there's a heaven with beautiful women in it
Rivers of wine flowing through, sunlit
What if I find myself a woman and wine right here
It's the same heaven, however you reach it.

Eliza and Martin clapped. Andrew said, "Ah, poets! That's exactly why I need to tend to the music."

"Oh!" Shar spun a half turn. "I brought my iPod. Would you like to use it? I have a bunch of different playlists."

"Sure," he said. "That would be great." Shar dug in her bag, then went to stand next to the lighthouse, who leaned over the stereo. After a moment, he said, "I think that plugs in right here. Sorry, it's too dark at this end of the room. We need a lamp over the stereo."

"No problem." Andrew stepped away as she kept fiddling. No need to stand so close. She was close enough. She was in his god-damn house! Who was she? And had she ever met Martin? He was almost sure that he'd heard her say, *I don't know you. That goes without saying.*

She was taller, heftier, than he had expected. He thought she would be slight, a needy woman, starved somehow. But the word that came most readily to his mind was the opposite. Was it an insult or a compliment to call her *queenly*? The black hair slipped like liquid, falling forward as she bent over the stereo. She was not Hollywood beautiful; she had enormous, dark eyes and an almost Roman nose, yet the lower part of her face was delicately narrow. Very full lips above a small chin. Altogether, physically, she was . . . what was the right word? He did not know what he felt, this close to her bare, muscular shoulder. This body, he thought, looking down at her narrow waist, knew Eliza's body intimately. Anger shot through his head like a bullet, and was gone, leaving in its wake the right word to describe her: stunning.

He blinked as she pulled the cord out of his fingers. Too slowly. Time itself had slowed in inverse proportion to the speed with which night had fallen. It was not the disaster he feared.

Night was home, too, shining through the windows. "Oh, *merde*! This doesn't work either!" Shar said, shaking her head. She put her hand—blue polish on her nails—on his forearm. He started at the touch; her head swivelled toward him slightly. The electricity went through him again. He mumbled, "Ridiculous."

"I know! It usually works without a problem."

He just had to focus on the technology—that would calm him down. Eliza, seated at the table, sang out, "What's happening with the music over there?"

Darkness and stark streetlight butted every window. No one had shut the blinds. The kitchen walls were green-blue; they floated inside an aquarium. Andrew took a step away, muttering, "I need my glasses to do this."

"No," Shar said, "I've figured it out." He stepped close again, behind her now; it was like a dance. I am drunk, she thought, and pulled the pin out of one of the outlets in the stereo and stuck it into another. Still no music. Was her iPod too old for the sleek little stereo? "Maybe my device is outdated."

"I think your device is just fine. You have to keep looking for the right . . . spot."

"Uh-huh." Suddenly the speaker blared music, surprising her; she jumped away, into Andrew; he did not step away. Lightly, they pressed together, front to back. "Ah, there we go!" he said. She felt his hands lift her from her elbows; he launched her. "Oh!" she said, stepping forward, almost losing her grip on the iPod.

She scrolled through a list of singers and countries, travelling decades and continents . . . Tinariwen, Emilie-Claire Barlow, John Grant, Mes souliers sont rouges, Lhasa, Silvio Rodríguez, TamilBeat, Snow Patrol—*Just Say Yes!*—Ahmad Zahir, Sogand,

Sarah Dugas, Caetano Veloso. Of all the old men she loved, she loved three Iranians the best: Banan, Shajarian and Nazeri. She loved Yölintu, too, those old rocker Finns, but vodka baritones weren't right for this evening. "Bear with me!" she called out. "The DJ is picky about the playlist." She slid past a hundred songs in a dozen languages. The Iranian pop star Googoosh must sing tonight, but her entrance could only come at the end of the evening. She decided on the next couple of hours. Pink Martini, Laura Mvula, the Moondoggies, and Zaz, to keep the mood light, and light-filled; the song "Je veux" had recently made the young French singer famous.

This very moment, though, she touched the screen until an unmistakably Greek arpeggio climbed the air and Eleftheria Arvanitaki stepped singing into the room.

Eliza shrieked, knowing neither the words to "Defteri zoe then exei" nor their meaning, but recognizing the nostalgia of the song. "Oh, my god!" she exhaled, pulling the lamb out of the oven. "How beautiful!" No one was sure what she was talking about: the meat, the music, or the other woman in the room.

40

Who Eats Her Cake

AFTER THE FIRST FEW CUTS INTO THE LAMB, ELIZA held up a delicate rib in her fingers. "It is *wrong* to leave a scrap of meat on these bones! Eat with your hands!"

Martin and Andrew raised a toast to Eliza: "Still the most beautiful chef in the world." Shar was happy to listen to stories about Thalassa, how delicious the food had been. They talked, often with their mouths full, about food and wine. With unabashed enthusiasm, Shar told them about amazing meals she had eaten, in Palermo, in Venice, in her grandmother's Marseillaise kitchen, in Tehran. Her listeners watched her face and her hands, which moved as though she were signing her language as well as speaking it. "Some say that the Iranians are the great artists of the Middle East, both in food and in music. I promise to play you my favourite Persian singers before the night is out." She described the artists' salon that her aunt held every month, continuing the tradition of her grandfather, who had been a well-known musician. "He was considered one of his generation's best *ney* players, the Persian flute. He also loved to sing."

"You never told me that," Eliza said, in a tone that sounded too proprietorial. She added, "I mean, you know, when we were talking about family history stuff."

Martin said, "Shar's a woman of secrets."

Shar glanced at him with a cool eye. "No," she said, lightly, plucking another olive from the dish. "I just wanted to save a few stories for this dinner."

Eliza said, "So tell us about these salons at your aunt's place. What were they like?"

She turned in Eliza's direction. "I was a wide-eyed teenager amongst the gods. I used to perch on the edge of a crammed sofa or, more often, on the staircase that went up to the roof, discreetly waving cigarette smoke out of my face and leaning forward to hear the poets recite their work, and the famous singers sing, and the daring political dissidents argue about the government. I was too young and shy to participate, but I chatted around the edges, I asked questions. Sometimes one of my aunt's friends would draw me out and ask my opinion about things, or tease me. It was so much fun, to be alive in that language. My mother is from France, yet we agree that only people who don't know Farsi can *possibly* say that French is the language of love. I miss it!"

Martin asked, "But don't you go to Iran anymore?"

"I haven't been for a while. Too busy with school. I have to admit, though, since moving here, I've been speaking a lot of Farsi. This is Tehranto, you know. It's *full* of Iranians."

Martin and Shar began to compare languages. She spoke five to his seven. After the initial listing—where they'd learned or studied their languages, and how—the conversation opened up again. Eliza was mystified. Was it really possible that they would get through an entire evening without Martin being brilliant in Borneo, magnetic in Mongolia? It was almost worrisome.

Eliza glanced around the table, listening, not listening. Shar's straightened hair fell away from her face. Cleopatra, Eliza thought. Sarah Bernhardt with finer bones. Or Sophie Marceau with thick black eyebrows. *This or that great beauty does not compare. I could look at her all day, all night long. I want to know her for the rest of my life.* Then she met Andrew's inquiring gaze.

He lifted his glass ever so slightly off the table; she did the same, smiling. After their private, wordless toast, they each took a quick sip. Eliza felt a pain under her heart, or in her stomach, along her shoulders, a pain so pervasive there was no way to locate it. Love skinned you alive. It was the quick beneath the outer layer, the house and the work, the edifice of success, those new pipes in the basement (so dependable!), the boxes of glasswork at the studio, hundreds of carefully bred flowers, shipped across the province or the continent or the world, each of them already decaying, not nearly so time-worthy as the cutlery in the drawers behind her, the expensive coffee maker, the acacia-wood napkin holder, the accent lamps, the matching towels, this endless accumulation of objects and layers and belongings—so many dumb belongings!—most of which could not be abandoned until they were cast off, finally, once and for all, in a future she could not fathom.

Correction: *she* would be cast off, cast out of life, out of time. But the damn cutlery would go on shining! Death lay in wait inside her, but she could not imagine it, not now, not yet, when she felt so alive. As she grasped it, the reason and heart of her own life, right here, in the house, Shar, Andrew and Martin burst out laughing at a joke Eliza had missed. She didn't mind. Uncomprehending, she began to smile, too, and thought, This is true. It's real. And mine.

Martin waved his hand over the table. "I hate to tell you this, my friends, but we've eaten everything."

Shar put her hands to her cheeks. "*Mon Dieu*, we'll starve to death!"

Andrew added, "Or get fat!"

"Here," said Eliza, holding out a plate, "a few more flowers. And two pieces of bread. We shall survive."

"Give me a slice," said Shar, putting out her hand. "Does anyone want to eat the last of this oil? It would be wrong to waste olive oil from the island of Lesvos!" She dunked the bread in the last of the greens, and took a big bite. "I've been waiting all evening for this!"

Eliza stood up. "And I have a *very* special dessert—also from Lesvos. And we have coffee. Or tea. Who wants what?"

Martin asked for tea and Eliza went to fill the kettle with water and get out the dessert plates. Surreptitiously, she watched Shar talking to Martin and Andrew; she watched the men respond to her natural charisma. Tonight her charm and irreverence seemed even sexier. Sexier in a . . . straight woman's way! Eliza frowned.

Andrew, coming over to help with the tea things, caught the expression. "What is it, dear?"

"Oh, it's . . ." She looked past him, around the dining room, down the hallway to the living room. "The blinds are still open," she said. "I forgot all about them. Will you make the tea? Six teaspoons, okay? No one likes watery tea!" She went from room to room, pulling down fabric rolls, closing slats and letting curtains drop.

Andrew explained, "We usually leave them open until after the kids go to bed. Jake's afraid of the dark and the house is actually *darker* with the blinds closed. He likes the streetlights to shine in."

Martin asked, "Is he still having those nightmares?"

"It's not so bad anymore, thank heavens." Andrew addressed Shar. "Sometimes he wakes up screaming. It used to scare the hell out of us."

"When I was little, I also had bad nightmares! Always about death, in one way or another. But the summer I turned six, my mom and I spent a few weeks with my grandmother in Marseilles. One afternoon I fell asleep in her garden on a little daybed. I woke up hours later, in the dark. Somehow, I thought I had died. It was dark, my mother was gone. But all the night flowers were open

around me. Jasmine, angel's trumpet—those big white blooms—
and little fuchsia ones that are even sweeter than jasmine. The
moon was up and the flowers were glowing. Really, they were
glowing! And I thought, I am dead, yes, but this is *heaven*. I'm in
heaven! Then I heard my mother calling my name. And my childhood nightmares ended."

Andrew said, "But maybe you *did* have them again, later. After
you returned to Canada. And you just don't remember."

A smile touched Shar's mouth and eyes. "A child often has a
keen memory of fear or distress. And so she—or he—remembers
when the fear ends . . . Don't you think so, Martin?" It was the
first time during the evening that she had said his name. Andrew
looked from Shar to his brother, curious.

Martin replied, "I've always thought amnesia was the saving
grace of childhood."

Eliza brought the teapot to the table. "It's definitely the saving
grace of parenthood. I've kind of forgotten how horrible Jake's
nightmares used to be."

Andrew said, "How could you forget? You're the one who used
to get up to comfort him. And he's still so afraid of the dark."

Eliza loaded up a tray and brought the rest of the tea and dessert
things to the table. Martin lifted the lid of the ceramic teapot. "It
might not be steeped enough, but that's better for me. I'm beat.
I'm sorry, everyone, but I have *got* to go to bed." He reached over
to take a small turquoise and gold–painted tea glass off the tray.
"That trip to Turkey, right?"

"Yes, and here is the cake!" She brought it to the table, set it down
to *ooh*s and *aah*s, and deftly cut into the dark heart of it. "You
cannot be too tired to eat this cake, Martin. It's too good to miss."

She set the velvet brown dessert in front of him. "Chocolate?"
he asked.

"No! Guess what the taste is."

He was the most snobbish eater among them, diner at fine restaurants all over the world; she had always enjoyed impressing him with her cooking. She handed out two more small plates to Andrew and Shar, then sat down with her own.

They began to eat. Martin raised his eyebrows, chewing, moving the crumbly but smooth sweet around in his mouth. He nodded, impressed. "*Ridiculously* good. Did you make it yourself?"

"Of course I made it myself. I can't have a dinner party with a store-bought cake."

He took another bite. "I have no idea what it is. Not chocolate. Almost spicy. Buttery. And very sweet but not a hard sugary note anywhere. What is this?"

Andrew said, "She's obsessive. Why can't we have a store-bought cake once in a while? Don't encourage her, Martin, by giving her compliments."

"I *will* give her compliments. This is incredible," he mumbled through another mouthful. "Did you ever make it at Thalassa?"

"Do you want another piece?"

"Just a sliver. A big sliver."

She set down her fork and cut him another slice. "I made it maybe once a month. It's extremely labour intensive. Shar, do *you* know what it is?"

Shar opened and closed her mouth, puckering up and smacking her full lips. "This is harder than wine tasting. Mmm . . . Raspberry? A touch of overripe peach?" She laughed. "Burnt leather?"

"You have no idea?"

"There must be butter, it's so creamy. Almond?"

Eliza ducked her head slightly and looked coy. "Neither. Any more guesses?"

"No," Martin said, "but I'm all ears. What is it?"

"On Lesvos, it's a cookie called *koulouromou-hrovrasto*—no, wait, that's too many syllables, but something like that. At Thalassa,

I developed a recipe to turn it into a cake. It's *fig*. And a whole litre of extremely good olive oil."

Andrew complained, "She boils and boils and boils figs until the whole first floor feels like a jar of hot jam. Fig-jam sauna cake is the translation of *koulourrooboohoo* or whatever it is in Greek."

Shar whistled. "Aren't we lucky to eat it, then? *Bella fica*! *Brava*!" She considered telling her dinner companions that *bella fica* in Italian also meant "beautiful pussy." But instead she smiled politely, put more cake into her mouth, and chewed as slowly as possible.

41

An Almost Perfect Life

FROM THE SECOND FLOOR, ANDREW CALLED DOWN THE staircase, "Where are the sheets for the guest bed?"

Eliza responded, "In the damn linen closet! Above the sticker that says 'twin beds.'"

He brought the crisply folded sheets into the office. "Sorry that we didn't have time to do this earlier."

"Don't worry about it. I could even sleep in one of the boys' beds."

"Your feet would hang off the end. So will theirs, soon enough. They're growing like weeds. Wait until you see them tomorrow." Andrew snapped a white sheet over the narrow bed. "At least I managed to clear my research books and student papers off."

"Andrew, I can do it. Go back to your dinner party. Sorry I couldn't keep up."

"She's quite a live wire, isn't she?" Andrew turned slightly, to gauge his brother's reaction.

Martin felt his brother's old familiar watchfulness. "Both of them are. A lot of electricity down there." He didn't want to talk to Andrew right now; he just wanted to lie down. Music floated up from the dining room; something Middle Eastern and melo-dramatic, it sounded like, synthesized. A few peals of feminine laughter rose through the music. Martin's small suitcase was rest-ing, open, on a low bench. He turned his back to Andrew and unzipped his toiletries bag, retrieved his toothbrush, his tooth-paste, biding his time until his brother left.

Andrew finished the bed-making. "So can I ask you something?"

"No." Martin turned around. "I really need to sleep. We'll have time to talk tomorrow, on the drive out to Mom and Dad's. It seems we have *a lot* to talk about."

"The only reason I didn't tell you is because Mom didn't want me to."

"I understand. It's okay." He thought, *Still reporting to her. Doing what she says. Sad, really.*

"You're not angry at me?"

"No. You had your reasons." Martin rolled his lips over the edges of his teeth, and bit down on them to keep from rising to the bait.

"What's that supposed to mean?"

But—see?—he rose to the bait. "It means that you, like every-one else on the planet, had particular reasons for pursuing a par-ticular course of action. In this case, not letting your only brother in on a significant family development. Which is *fine*." He expelled air out of his nose like a bull. "I thought they had sold their shares in that Florida development."

"They *swore* to Eliza that they were selling. Then they didn't do it."

"How many times did I tell them just to buy a decent rental unit on Palmerston Boulevard and you can't go wrong. Or three crack houses in Parkdale!"

"They didn't want to have the headache of taking care of prop-erty in Toronto."

Martin laughed savagely. "Florida was so much better than a regulated banking system and a rising market. Jesus Christ. No wonder Eliza's pissed off. This was Mom, wasn't it? Her dreams of being richer than her rich Uxbridge friends."

"Don't blame it all on her. Dad's responsible, too."

"Come on. You know exactly what she's like. Delicate and lady-like and a goddamn bulldozer, running people over whenever she feels like it."

"Martin." Andrew's voice dropped a notch. "She's an old lady now. You can't be angry at her forever." He stepped past his brother and closed the door.

Martin looked at the light cotton pyjamas he had just tossed on the bed. He wanted to take them in his hands again and rip them apart. Why was this shit all right here at the surface? Because of Shar. She had reminded him so keenly of his past because she actually knew something about it. "Have you ever thought that if I weren't so angry at *Mom*, I might hate *you*? You were the one who told her."

"Jesus! I was only twelve. But even I knew you shouldn't have been having sex with a teacher! It was abuse. She was abusive."

"Maybe she was. Of course she was. I know that now. But she cared about me, too."

Unlike—the thought slid like a red-hot poker into his mouth, but he held it there, clamping his jaw down, burning his teeth—unlike their name-calling, narrow-minded mother. *What's wrong with you? Aren't you ashamed of yourself? With one of your old elementary school teachers! Martin, what you've done with her is disgusting. Shameful!*

She never found out how long it had gone on—Martin couldn't possibly tell her. He thought she would be as repulsed by that as she was by the relationship. As if he didn't always feel bad about it, responsible somehow, in a way he couldn't name; he had been a child. Yet the guilt stifled him for years. He always felt that he hadn't resisted *enough* when he was little. He had been Marlene's special friend. Then it began to feel so good. The terrible, wrong act was pleasurable. Every orgasm with her was a sin. When he was a teenager, he could only turn it into a love story, to understand it, with himself as the gangly, passionate, brilliant hero who could never let his beautiful lady get into trouble, and lose her job, and go to jail. He had saved her, and lost some essential part of himself. His childhood, his adolescence.

The mistake of not telling still haunted him. Had she continued abusing students? After he finished his degree at Harvard, he'd tried to track her down, but she seemed to have disappeared. Maybe she'd married, changed her name. Maybe she left the country. Maybe she died. Everyone does. He sat down on the bed, thick hands on his knees. "I'm so tired of it." Yet the thought was sharp in his mind: *I have to tell Mom. And Dad, too. I want them to know what really happened. How young I was. How they failed me.* But could he do it? Was it possible to tell the truth?

Andrew was standing at the closed door, but still he couldn't leave. "It's so strange the way this has all come up again." Martin had closed his eyes, waiting for Andrew to go. Yet there he stood, wanting more from his older brother. As usual. "It leads me back to the place where this conversation started."

Martin rubbed his face and opened his bleary eyes. "Uh, what place was that?"

"I said, 'Can I ask you a question?'"

"And I said 'no.' Remember? Jesus, Andy, you're like a dog with a goddamn bone."

Andrew stepped away from the door, lowered his voice, unable to help himself. "Have you seen Shar as a therapist? I have the feeling that you two have met before."

Martin started laughing. He laughed for a solid twenty seconds, during which time Andrew's eyebrows slowly knitted together in embarrassment.

Then Martin stopped laughing. "Did you hover in your own hallway listening to our conversation? Still spying on me, forty-five years later. I just do not get it. You've *always* been jealous of the way I am with women. It's so fucking weird. Especially considering who you married."

"What's that supposed to mean?"

"You married a beautiful, fun, smart woman. You have two lovely kids, a lovely house, a job you enjoy. A perfect life. Okay, I know you have to do a shitload of marking. So, an almost perfect life. Why would you care what I say to a dinner guest over a glass of wine?"

"You're dodging the question. And I wasn't eavesdropping. I was just coming into the living room, and I heard her saying something about confidentiality. About how she doesn't know you. Meaning the opposite."

"All right, fine. I met her a few years ago. In Ottawa."

"As a therapist?"

"More or less."

"What does that mean?"

"We talked. It was talk therapy. I guess."

Andrew frowned. "You guess?"

"Would you *please* let me go to bed?"

"Did you have sex with her?"

"Why? Are you weirded out by the idea that your wife clearly likes to flirt with a woman I've already had sex with?"

Andrew tilted his head thoughtfully, moved his lips as though chewing this idea. Nodded once. "Possibly. It would be weird."

"Don't worry then. I didn't sleep with her."

"Really?"

"Cross my heart. If you want—and only if you want—you can tell me about Eliza and Shar tomorrow. I didn't need to snoop around to see that they're into each other. Big deal, it's just a phase." He stifled a yawn. "You can tell me tomorrow. Right now, *you* will go back to the beautiful women, and *I* will go to sleep." He closed his eyes, lifted his legs off the floor and lay down on the bed. "Have fun!"

But Andrew did not budge. He was still the brat, still rooting around for more. He loved the problem.

As though reading his brother's mind, Andrew pressed on. "But—*how* did you meet her?"

Martin gave a great, internal shrug. Fine. If his brother loved the problem, he could have it. "Shar used to be a call girl. *That's* how I met her. High end, very classy. But we never slept together." He heard the bedroom door open. "She was kinda doing therapy even then. On her clients." The door slammed. Martin smiled to hear footsteps rushing down the stairs.

He fell asleep to three human voices rising, louder, higher, the words unintelligible but passionate, like Greek, he thought, descending into sleep, or birdsong, a dream already coalescing— blue sea, island—in his mind.

Eliza thought, He sounds just like the boys, crashing down here like that. Out of habit, she almost yelled, *Stop running!* She and Shar turned to see Andrew stride into the dining room, his face alight, eyes flashing from Eliza to Shar, who was sitting across the table. Their smiles left them. He was a man involved in an emergency. "What's happened?" Eliza began rising out of her chair; rose; stepped close to him. "Is Martin all right?" She put her hand on his forearm.

She did not let go. He stared at her, searched her face. "Andrew, you're scaring me, what is it?"

Shar whispered something in French or Farsi. It was hard to tell through the silky crooning of Googoosh, the famous Iranian pop star. But Eliza saw the knowingness on her lover's face. She saw regret. Or was it resignation? "Shar?"

Andrew spoke loudly. "You don't know."

"Know what?"

"What she does."

Shar immediately said, "Did. And I am not ashamed of it either."

Andrew roared across the table, "Then why did you keep it a secret? Who *are* you?"

Shar stood up so abruptly that Eliza thought she was leaving. But she just crossed over to the stereo and turned off the music. The sudden silence in the room silenced them, too.

Various triangles of eyes formed, changed, and formed again. Shar was close now, a step away. Eliza thought, I could touch her so easily. But she didn't. She looked at Andrew. Then she turned to Shar, and shook her head. "What secret?"

"Let me," Shar said, and faltered. She walked back around the table and sat down. "Let me tell you a story."

Acknowledgements

August 22, 2016, 7:58 AM
Toronto, my messy office/bedroom
surrounded by paper, undone taxes, camping gear
(at this rate, we'll make it out of the city by midnight)

Dear Reader,

Thank you. Your book clubs, your discussion groups, our email exchanges—in Canada, the U.S. and other places around the planet—have nourished and challenged me as a writer, thinker, and citizen. By responding to my written lives, you have often shared and illuminated the rich complications of your own. You inspired me to write a book about Everywoman, and Eliza Keenan was born.

Dear Todd Kjargaard, gifted creative director at Jackie O Floral Affairs and Event Design in Toronto, my gratitude to you (and the flowers) for letting me hang around your studio and pester you and designer Jen. Your insights about creativity, freedom and *les fleurs* are priceless. *Of course* you are located on Liberty Street. Dear Carlyle Jansen and company, of the fabulous sex shop Good For Her, thank you for introducing me to strap-ons and explaining all the ins and outs. With patience and professionalism, you put more joy, acceptance and sweetness into sex of all kinds.

Dear HVs of Tallinn: I am indebted to you all for the vodka and the advice about *The Change Room*'s ending. And to the marvellous Head Read Festival in Tallinn for making it all possible. To Kätlin Kaldmaa, fellow writer and preeminent translator, bless you for your passion in a cold country, and for giving me an example not to follow, re. the Typical Estonian Sex Scene: *They went into the room and closed the door.*

Dear Anne Collins, my editor and publisher at Random House Canada, and intrepid Jackie Kaiser, dedicated agent, I appreciate how you scarcely blinked an eye when I told you I'd cancelled *The Depressing Novel* and instead handed over fifty pages of orgasmic sex, flowers, and housecleaning (in order of importance). I thank you both and everyone at Penguin Random House Canada for making this book and sending it out into the world. Waiter, a bottle of champagne to Jennifer Griffiths for the perfect cover image!

Dear friends on Lesvos, whose lives and work I have adapted shamelessly and genderbendingly to my own novelistic ends: *filia kai kouragio*. Mireille, Panagos, Yiorgos, Eleni, Maria, Andoni, Patricia, your children: part of me remains with you. May the suffering on the island and beyond it end soon. To Anne and Soren, *euxaristo* for our fascinating discussions about marriage, sometimes quoted here almost word for word, including Soren's assertion, some forty years after the wedding: "The secret to my happiness is my acceptance that I do not understand her."

To Robert Chang, my husband, who could say the same thing every morning, I adore you for asserting the opposite (at least once in a while): that you *do* understand me. I am blessed that you and Timo Chang, our wonderful son, make a home with me, love me, let me go and call me back to a house full of light. Thanks for all the fights, too, pillow and otherwise.

Shar wouldn't exist without the real women and men who inspired her creation: Amelia Perkins, for the harrowing tale of a woman who left Marseilles; poet, lawyer, and lover of rivers, Tessa Manuello; my Iranian friends, especially Ghazal M; the late, great Iranian photographer Kaveh Golestan, for his pictorial tribute to the women of Shahr-E No; fellow writer Zagros Chiya, who introduced me to Googoosh and other musicians in Iraqi Kurdistan, and who translated Shar's quotations of Baba Taher and Omar Khayyam; my beautiful sister-niece Jennifer Kochis, who shared her stories and reminded me to be careful with my words.

Shar is the fictional sister to those brave, fiercely intelligent people at the forefront of the battle to decriminalize and humanize sex work. I salute you for declaring the irrefutable truth, and lending it to a recent Amnesty International campaign: **sex workers' rights are human rights.** I am grateful for interviews in person, on the phone, by email, for our exchanges on Facebook and Twitter, for your generous websites and blogs (safersexwork.ca, POWER.ca, Maggiestoronto.ca, Kitty Stryker, TitsandSass, Nathalie-Lefebvre.com, Maggie McNeill's WordPress blog The Honest Courtesan, postwhoreamerica.com and many more). Your courage, honesty, and sense of humour are a constant inspiration. I am also indebted to the fearless scholar and advocate Caroline Newcastle, for sharing her research on sex workers' lives and relationships.

Just as I was finishing this novel, tragedy struck, as it sometimes does, for no good reason. Many generous, kind people donated the blood and money that saved my brother David's life and allowed my sister Mara and me to bring him back to Canada. We will always be grateful for your help. Life is, indeed, a gauntlet of momentous change. And love is the only way through it.

And you! My close ones, dear and distant friends, family born and chosen and found again after long silence: you know who you are. You help me to live this precious life. I love you so much. Where have you been? Come for dinner. Let's go for a walk. Let's go swimming! Soon, while we still have time.

xok

KAREN CONNELLY is the author of eleven books of bestselling nonfiction, fiction and poetry, the most recent being *Come Cold River*, a family memoir in poetry. She has won the Pat Lowther Award for her poetry, the Governor General's Award for her nonfiction, and Britain's Orange Broadband Prize for New Fiction for her first novel, *The Lizard Cage*. Published in 2005, *The Lizard Cage* was compared in the *New York Times Book Review* to the works of Orwell, Solzhenitsyn and Mandela, and hailed in the *Globe and Mail* as "one of the best modern Canadian novels." *Burmese Lessons*, a memoir about her experiences in Burma and on the Thai-Burmese border, was nominated for a Governor General's Award for Nonfiction and the British Columbia National Award for Canadian Nonfiction in 2009. Married with a young child, she divides her time between a home in rural Greece and a home in Toronto.

A NOTE ABOUT THE TYPE

The body of *The Change Room* has been set in Adobe Garamond. Designed for the Adobe Corporation by Robert Slimbach, the fonts are based on types first cut by Claude Garamond (c.1480–1561). Garamond was a pupil of Geoffrey Tory and is believed to have followed classic Venetian type models, although he did introduce a number of important differences, and it is to him that we owe the letterforms we now know as "old style." Garamond gave his characters a sense of movement and elegance that ultimately won him an international reputation and the patronage of Frances I of France.